Doctor of the Heart

Men of Mercy Series

A Novel

by:
Grace Maxwell

Copyright 2022 Blind Date Publishing

All rights reserved. No part of this publication may be reproduced, distributed or transmitted in any form or by any means, including photocopying, recording or other electronic or mechanical methods, without the prior written permission of the author, except in the case of brief quotations embodied in critical reviews and certain other noncommercial uses permitted by copyright law.

This is a work of fiction. Names, characters, places and incidents are a production of the author's imagination. Locations and public names are sometimes used for atmospheric purposes. Any resemblance to actual people, living or dead, or to businesses, companies, events, institutions or locations is completely coincidental.

Men of Mercy: Doctor of the Heart/Grace Maxwell — 1st edition

Dedication and Thank You

Thank you Dr. Angie for being a fantastic doctor and an incredible resource. I'm grateful to you for giving me your time and your advice.

Thank you to my family for all of your support. I do this for you.

Thank you to my editors Jessica Royer Ocken and Diana Loifton. You took my story and made it everything I ever hoped.

Readers, thank you for taking a chance on me. I hope you love Davis and Paisley as much as I do. And hopefully Arabella doesn't steal the story too much.

Chapter 1

Paisley

One…two…three… I count in my head, trying to maintain some level of patience while I navigate the world's most annoying phone call here at my office. It's Friday morning, and I'm ready for the weekend.

I paint a smile on my face, even though the customer can't see me while we're on the phone. "Mr. Chapman, let's see if we can figure this out for you."

He heaves a deep sigh. "You're the third person I've spoken to about this erroneous charge on my credit card from the Strong Night Games website. You need to reverse the charges."

"Just one moment, please." I scan through our records and find the charge. "Hmm. It looks like the charge originated with an account named MarcNinja007, and it's for a subscription to Navy SEALS."

Now, he groans. "That's my son. He's only twelve years old. Can the charges be reversed?" Mr. Chapman seems much calmer.

I click through multiple buttons, cancel the subscription, and stop the monthly charges. "It's all done. I've reversed the most recent charge, but as you probably know, this isn't the first time this has happened. It looks like your son re-orders his subscription each time we stop it."

The line is silent for a moment. "I see. Well, he won't have his iPad for the next year or two, so that won't be happening again." Mr. Chapman clears his throat. "Thank you."

"I'm happy to help. Is there anything else I can do for you?"

"No. It seems I need to have a long talk with my son. Thank you."

"Goodbye, sir." I disconnect the call and turn to Anna Jones, a new worker I'm training. She was listening to the call.

She nods approvingly. "Wow. He was very upset, and you got him happy. But I thought you weren't supposed to offer refunds like that."

"We're not, really. But he was honest and admitted his son had most likely approved the charge. If he went to the credit card company, they'd reverse the charges, anyway. I don't blame him for being upset. But you can see it's not difficult to research the account information and tell him why the charges kept coming back."

"Brilliant." Anna nods.

She puts her headset back on, and we work another hour of phone calls. Answering phones for a gaming company's customer service isn't my life goal, but it pays the bills. Maybe one day I'll be able to go back to my first love and work as a sculptor.

In between work calls, my cell phone rings in my purse. Caller ID says it's my sister's school. *Crap!*

"Hello?"

"Ms. Brooks? Arabella isn't feeling well, and she has a fever. Can you please come pick her up?"

My stomach drops. This will be the third week in a row I've missed work to take care of my sister. Mother Nature can't decide if it's winter or spring in Vancouver, and Arabella is constantly sick.

I stand up in my cubicle like a gopher peeking out of its hole and look around. I don't see my boss. Anna has someone else to train with this afternoon, so I scribble a message to my boss, explaining that Arabella is being sent home with a fever, and I head out to pick her up.

I take the bus across town to the school. The ride is over an hour, but that way I can afford a rideshare home for both of us. As soon as I arrive, Arabella runs out and throws her arms around me, nearly knocking me over. "Bells, what's going on?"

Tears shine in her eyes. "Can we just go home?"

I feel her head, and she seems clammy but not feverish. The school nurse looks down her nose at me. "You've been warned before, Ms. Brooks. Arabella isn't to come to school with a fever."

"She didn't have a fever this morning," I try to explain, knowing I sound defensive.

Fevers are bad news for Arabella. I look down at her again. Her lips are slightly blue, and she's struggling to breathe. This is part of what happens when her heart is working too hard. It has a hole in it — an atrial septal defect or ASD — that was diagnosed when she was a baby. That means it has to work harder to beat, which creates other issues, including fluid in her lungs.

I'm becoming more convinced it's going to take a surgery to fix it, but it's hard to get a straight answer from her doctor these days. I feel her forehead again. I'm still not sure she has a fever. But maybe she did earlier. Either way, they're not going to let her stay at school.

"Come on, Bells. Let's get a milkshake from White Spot and go home and rest. How does that sound?"

Arabella nods.

The rideshare is waiting for us when we exit the school, and Arabella curls up in the backseat, resting her head on my lap. Despite being ten years old, she's the size of maybe a small first grader. I stroke her hair as I watch the traffic, grateful that we're in a car rather than on the bus. "Did something happen today?"

She shrugs. "Mrs. Gagnon wasn't happy that I kind of took over the class when she started talking about chain reactions. I suggested we make a Rube Goldberg machine."

"Oh, I bet that would have been fun."

She nods, keeping her eyes closed. "After I explained what it was, everyone started looking at YouTube videos on our tablets, and she was upset. But we figured out how we could build something to feed the class hamster, starting with just a few dominos."

My heart breaks. Arabella is so smart. It kills me we can't get her a scholarship to a better school—a smaller one that could challenge her academically. The one I like best would be a haul from where we live near the Vancouver airport. And they don't give full-ride scholarships anyway. I barely make enough for us to live on with her in public schools. "She won't even remember by Monday," I promise.

The rideshare drops us off a few blocks from home, and by the time we have our milkshakes, my happy-go-lucky little sister is back. If only keeping our lives on track was actually that easy.

"Okay, my mom has officially taken over Arabella duty," announces Lucy Yang as she enters my bedroom the following evening. She's been my best friend forever, and she's just pawned my sister off on her sweet mother, who has agreed to be the babysitter tonight. Despite my worries about Arabella after she came home from school yesterday, she seemed fine today, and Lucy is convinced I need a night off, no matter what I say.

"They have plans to make cookies, play games, and

watch movies tonight," she continues. "*You* are going to do something other than take care of your sister and work. We're going to meet men tonight. Lots of men!"

I laugh. It's been far too long since I had a night out, and as for sex... Well, it's been even longer. I probably have cobwebs inside my vagina at this point. Or maybe a sign that reads, *Closed. Do not enter.* There's just not been a lot of room for *me* in my life these past few years.

Lucy is stunning in a tube dress that hugs every single one of her curves. She's definitely ready to go out, and I have to say, I am too. I think I've reached a breaking point with stress, and I just need to turn my brain off for once. "You've convinced me," I tell her. "I'm going. And I'm wearing the vintage Chanel we bought at Kits Resale Shop when we were in high school."

She nods, and I dash off to the bathroom. I love this dress. Once I have it on, I twirl in the mirror. It's black, and the halter top has silver stars. The A-line mini is silk chiffon. After dusting them off — did I mention I haven't been out in a while? — I put on my favorite silver Jimmy Choo sandals, also resale. I hope I can make it through the evening in these sky-high heels.

Lucy sighs when I return. "That was the best find ever. If you hadn't bought it, I would have. That lady at the store was so mad that you got it and she didn't."

"That's one of the best memories of my life." I adjust the halter top to be sure the girls are in place and lotion up my pasty-white legs one more time. I've got a lot of leg showing, and I don't want them dry and scaly. How they manage to be dry, I'm still not sure. We have rain nine months a year around here, so it's plenty moist. There's also not much sun, so at least I know why they're white. No one tans here anyway — unless it's sprayed on in a booth. Or from a vacation, which I can't afford.

I apply deep red lipstick and check my makeup — and teeth — again. "Where are we going?"

"There's a new club north of Hastings in an old warehouse," Lucy says. "It's called The Lion's Den, and tonight women get in free. So, our goal is to make sure men buy our drinks all night."

I smile, but I can't remember the last time a guy bought me anything. At five-foot-ten, I'm very Amazonian for Vancouver. It seems like most men here come up to my boobs. That's never very fun. Height difference matters even when you're lying down.

When we're ready, we walk out to the front room, and my younger sister gives me a cat call. "You look beautiful."

"You're just saying that." I wink at her. "Lucy's dress is going to bring us the men."

"No, Arabella is right. You look beautiful," Lucy insists. "You're going to have the men eating out of your hand tonight."

"Maybe we'll be lucky and get invited into the VIP Lounge." I wiggle my eyebrows.

Lucy nods. "That would be so cool. We should definitely try."

Our rideshare pings its arrival. I wave goodbye to my sister and Mrs. Yang. "Thank you again for hanging out with Arabella," I tell her. I kiss my little sister on the forehead. "If she has any problems, it's better to be safe than sorry. Call the ambulance first, and then call me. I'll meet you at the hospital."

Mrs. Yang waves my concerns away. "We'll be fine. I needed an excuse to make chocolate chip cookies, and she'll eat most of them anyway."

Arabella smiles eagerly. We don't eat a lot of sweets — not because I withhold them, but because we can't always afford them. If I have to choose between a bag of cookies and a gallon of milk, I will always choose milk. My baby sister has lots of growing to do.

With a final wave, I close the door behind me, leaving all those thoughts at home for a while. Lucy and I settle into the back of the rideshare, and for our ride over, we gossip. I can feel the strain of managing everything slipping away.

"My new boss is hot, hot, hot, but he totally knows it, so he's a total dick," Lucy reports. "He even made me break up with his latest girlfriend for him because he didn't have the balls to do it himself."

I shake my head. "That's awful! You're never going to change a player, so don't waste your time."

My last boyfriend was a player. We broke up after I found him in bed with another woman. His complaint was that I required a condom. He always told me he wasn't *condom trained*. Whatever that means.

"Where is your mom these days?" Lucy asks, shifting the conversation in a new direction.

"The last I heard, she and her boyfriend were spending the winter in the South Pacific, but they'll head toward Europe for the summer."

"Maybe she'll send you tickets to meet her in Paris."

I snort. "Not likely. It's not clear the boyfriend knows we exist."

Lucy puts her arm around me. "You know that's all her and has nothing to do with you or Arabella."

"I know, but it's hard. I've only been working for Hardnight Games a little over three months, and I've already missed six days of work. My boss is not particularly understanding about my situation. I don't want to lose yet another job. I have to pay the bills."

"You're such a talented artist. It would be great if you could just work doing that."

I nod. "Maybe after Arabella is doing better. At her last checkup, the doctor said she was moving closer to the surgery again."

"How long has it been since she was supposed to have it?"

"Almost five years."

"That doesn't make any sense. It shouldn't take so long.

My mom couldn't do her gallbladder surgery on the Chinese New Year, so they rescheduled it right away. What's the hang-up here?"

"I honestly have no idea. The surgery scheduler doesn't return my calls, and the doctor tells me something a little different every time I ask." I sigh. "I've left dozens of messages. But meanwhile, Arabella is getting worse. She gets tired easily, and she's so tiny. All this is too much for someone who's only ten years old."

The rideshare comes to a stop in front of The Lion's Den. It's early to be clubbing, but the line is already long, probably because this place was written up in the *Vancouver Free Press* this week as the new "it" club. We get in the back of the line, and I try again to shake off my worries. Honestly, I don't care if we get in at all. I'm more interested in hanging out with my friend. We don't do that nearly enough these days.

Lucy cranes her neck to see the front of the line. "I thought we'd be early enough to avoid this mess." She looks down at my shoes. "We can go out for sushi when your feet start to hurt."

"I'll be fine for now. We've got this." I know she's excited, and I'm not about to complain.

It's early April, so I'm grateful it's not raining, but with the high humidity, I can already feel my hair going from glamorously straight to weird frizzy waves—not cute. I hate that. Still, I try to locate and then channel my inner diva, so I'm in the right frame of mind when we get inside. I'm not going to be my usual cautious self this evening. I'm going to be fun and flirty and carefree.

A group of men get out of an expensive car with a driver, and Lucy elbows me so hard in the ribs I almost tumble over. "Look at those guys!"

Four stunning men, dressed in expensive clothes and an air of confidence, move toward the doors of the club as if they don't even see the line.

"They do put the yum in yummy," I murmur. "But they may be a little *too* good looking, at least for straight men."

The one with chocolate brown hair and piercing dark eyes suddenly looks over at me, and his mouth turns up at the corner. *Yeah, he knows he's hot.* But I force myself to hold his gaze, smiling back at him with more confidence than I truly feel.

He whispers something to the bouncer, and then the crowd swallows him up.

"How are things going for Arabella at her school?" Lucy asks, turning back to me.

Girl, you gotta stop asking me this stuff, I lament internally. But I know Lucy means well, and we hardly ever have a chance to talk. "It's okay, I guess. I hate the school nurse. I think she'd be happiest if Bells was homeschooled."

The bouncer walks down the line and stops next to us, saving me from having to say more. "You ladies have ID, right?" he asks as he opens the rope.

I manage to nod and also ignore the catty looks we get from some of the other women we're leaving behind in line. We follow the bouncer to the door and hand him our IDs. He gives us each a red bracelet.

"This will get you into the VIP section," he explains. "I highly encourage you to check it out." He winks at Lucy, and she giggles.

"You don't have to ask us twice," she declares.

"What just happened to us?" I ask her as we step inside the club, which is a red brick warehouse on the waterfront, and find a wall of windows showcasing the view of the water.

"I have no idea, but just go with it," she says, giving me a squeeze.

The music pulses, the lights are dim, and despite the relatively early hour, it's packed. The high ceiling with exposed duct work gives the room an industrial feel. There's a large bar to our left with at least a half dozen bartenders working like a well-oiled machine, and on the other side, the dance floor is already a bobbing, throbbing mass of bodies.

I take a deep breath and remind myself of my mantra. I'm going to relax and have fun tonight. I am going to enjoy myself and let loose. I can sleep tomorrow. "This place is great," I exclaim. "I'm glad I've used my first night out in a zillion years for something worthwhile."

Lucy smiles and then practically jumps up and down as she spots the stairs that lead up above the dance floor to the VIP section. I follow her over, and as we climb the stairs, I can already tell it's busy up here. At the top, we flash our wristbands, and the VIP-room bouncer waves us through. We receive looks of pure disdain from several of the women milling around.

"I don't want to hang out up here for too long," I tell Lucy.

She nods. "I know. I fear for my life. Given the opportunity, someone's gonna claw my eyes out with her fake nails."

I giggle. "I guess they're not happy to see more competition up here."

She shakes her head. "Forget this. Let's go dance."

I nod. "Sounds perfect."

We walk right back down the stairs to the dance floor. We push our way to the middle and get lost in the movement of the crowd. I tease Lucy with my Elaine from Seinfeld impression while she does the sprinkler. We're laughing too hard to keep track of the beat when a tall man with his hair slicked back sidles up to us. He's wearing a tight T-shirt and jeans, which I'm sure he's packed with a sock. He gives me the universal head-bob greeting. I turn to Lucy, looking for help, and it seems she has her own weirdo.

I catch her eye and jerk my head to the side. Without a word, we turn and leave the two guys dancing without us.

"That guy tried to dirty dance with me," Lucy says once we've reached the sidelines.

"Ewww," I say.

"Jeez," she gripes. "You'd think before he gets up close and personal, he'd at least ask my name."

She gives a full-body shudder, and then we're laughing all over again. When I wipe my eyes, I realize the hot guy who most likely pointed us out to the bouncer outside and one of his friends have come up to us.

"Hey." He grins, and my panties melt.

"Hello." I smile demurely at him.

"Why didn't you come upstairs to the VIP section?" He looks me up and down as if I'm an ice cream cone in the middle of the desert.

I shake my head. "Didn't feel that welcoming. Too many women ready to scratch our eyes out."

He grins, and his eyes warm. They appear almost black, but up close they have specks of gold in them. "Well, it looks like you need a drink. Can I buy you one?"

I nod. "My friend needs one, too."

He tilts his head. "I think she's covered. What would you like?"

I look over at Lucy, and this guy's friend is snuggled up close. I guess he must've asked her name. Turning back to my new friend, I note his form-fitting designer T-shirt, pants that outline his powerful thighs, and sharp jaw with the perfect amount of scruff. I don't want to order something too fru-fru. "How about a Manhattan?"

He laces his fingers with mine, and we walk over to the bar. "David, great to see you," the bartender says as we approach. "What can I get you?"

"A Manhattan and a Blue Label with one ice cube."

The bartender nods and steps away to get our drinks.

David turns to me. "What's your name?"

"Paisley?"

"My name is Davis."

"Did the bartender call you David or Davis?"

"You caught that, did you?" He smiles, and I see a hint

of two dimples in his cheeks.

I nod.

"It's loud in here. Many people make that mistake. Were your parents hippies?"

I shake my head. "No, my dad liked it, so my mom went with it."

Our drinks arrive, and we step away from the bar and then toast. "To new friends," Davis says as we take a sip of our drinks. He watches me closely, and even though I'm rusty, there is no mistaking what he wants. It's me. "You're positively beautiful."

"Do you say that to all the women you meet?" He's backed me against the wall.

"Only the ones who are beautiful."

"You're handsome and a charmer." I pluck the cherry garnish from my drink and pop it in my mouth.

"You think I'm handsome?"

My mouth quirks. "Are you fishing for compliments?"

"Not in the least." He dips his little finger in my drink and runs it over my lips. Bending down, he licks the drink away, and I open my mouth to him as our tongues tangle. Heat and desire pool in my belly. *Wow, I've never felt that before.*

Davis tucks us farther into a dark corner, and he turns to set our partially finished drinks on a nearby table. When he turns back, his body shields mine. "I hope you don't mind. I wanted some alone time with you."

I smirk. He's a player. I know a line when I hear one.

"You're safe here," he assures me. "Are you okay?"

I nod. "Yes."

He runs a gentle finger over my collarbone and then between my breasts. "Your skin is so soft and pretty."

He's only touched exposed skin, but still I let out a little shudder. My center is pulsing. Holding me in place with one big hand, he cups the back of my head and bends to whisper over my mouth. "How about another kiss?"

Suddenly, nothing else exists. The loud, pulsing music is silent. He has such nice, full lips, and he knows what to do with them, too. I stand on my tiptoes and gently press my lips to his. He encircles me in his big, strong arms and cups my ass in one hand, massaging my bottom. He rubs his hardness at the apex of my thighs.

Wide-eyed, I stare into his face as he pulls back. He presses tender open-mouth kisses up my neck and beneath my ear. I sigh. It's been so long since anyone has touched me. I'm amazed that I remember how to respond. OKAY, SO THIS LETTING-GO THING MIGHT BE BETTER THAN I T

HOUGHT. I never do this sort of thing, but for some reason, just like he said, I do feel safe here.

His fingers slide up the outside of my thigh beneath my skirt, all the way to the waist of my panties. He raises an eyebrow slightly, but I don't stop him as he draws them down over my legs, our eyes locked. I can't believe I'm doing this in a public place. Anyone walking by could see us, and I quiver with anticipation.

His hungry gaze roams my body as he slides a hand over my heaving chest and tugs the halter aside to free my breasts. He drops his head and feasts first on one and then the other, pulling each swollen, pink nipple deep into the heat of his mouth until they both stand achingly erect and glistening. He grins against my flesh. He's aware of how he has me panting and writhing.

Parting my thighs, he runs his fingers over the dampness of my pussy, testing to see if I'm ready. I'm incredibly slick and wet. He circles my bud, and my breath hitches. One finger slides in and then another. He pivots in and out roughly.

"Tell me how that feels," he demands.

"So good," I breathe.

When he finds my G-spot, he works it deep inside me, his thumb twirling around my clit. It's practically throbbing, which sends my hands tangling desperately into his hair.

Trembling, my entire body begins cresting on a wave so big I worry I might pass out from the force of it. "Oh, God, yes..." I gasp as he keeps up what must be a personal quest to see me come harder than anyone has ever come before.

Finally, I'm unable to hold back. I let out a gut-wrenching groan, chest heaving, head thrashing wildly. But when my vision clears, the club is so loud that no one seems to have noticed. I struggle to let go of his hair, since it seems to be the only thing preventing me from floating away.

He reaches into his pocket and pulls out a small packet, tearing into it with his teeth while he watches me. With a feral grin, he murmurs, "And now I'm going to fuck you until they can hear you over the music. How does that sound to you?"

My eyes fly open, pretty sure he means it, since he's already had me hollering like a maniac. I'm not usually a screamer, but this is something I've never experienced. "Yes, please."

My heart is in my throat as he lifts my leg over his arm and rubs his cock through my folds. He gazes into my eyes and pauses. "What color are your eyes? It's hard to tell in this light. All I can make out is that they're pretty."

"They're blue," I say, holding his gaze. "Why? What color are yours?"

"Brown," he says with a smile, dropping a surprisingly tender kiss on the end of my nose.

Spreading me even wider with the head of his cock, he thrusts his hips and pushes into me, inch by incredibly long inch, until I shift my hips, wincing as I try to take every last bit of him. Biting my lip, I fight not to groan at the exquisite feel of him claiming my body, stretching me so delectably tight.

Finally, he's buried balls deep. "Fuck, you feel good," he says. "You're so nice and tight. And your pussy seems to like this, too. It's sucking me in."

Wrapping my arms around him, I lift my feet off the floor and circle my other leg around his hips, allowing him to drive even deeper with his next thrust. "Hmm..." I moan against the thick column of his neck. No one has ever talked dirty to me before, and I have to admit, it's pretty hot. I never thought I'd be into something so shockingly lewd.

He adjusts so he can see my face. "You like this too, don't you?"

There's no point in being coy, so I nod and murmur, "Yeah, you feel good."

Closing his eyes, he thrusts his hips again. "Are you ready?"

Chapter 2

Davis

Her pussy is like a vice. It feels incredible as I push in and out. In no time her soft moans send me over the edge, and I fill the condom. *Damn.* I guess I should try something like this more often, although I almost feel like it wasn't my choice. Something called my eyes to her in that line outside, and after that, I couldn't look away. I still can't.

I don't have to work tomorrow and spending the rest of the weekend with her—seeing how flexible she is—suddenly sounds like a lot of fun. I lean down and lave her nipple before I bite it and pinch her clit. With that she screams, and her wetness floods my hand. "Fuck, that was good," I tell her after she's had a moment to collect herself.

"It was pretty nice," she says, lowering her feet to the ground. I stand in front of her, blocking the view as she puts herself together and I button up my fly.

I snort. "I'd say so." I love it when a woman can let go. I don't know quite what I'm feeling right now, but I know there's more to come for her and me. But first I need liquid refreshment. "Stay here. I'll get you a drink," I tell her.

"Another Manhattan?"

Her eyes dart around. "Oh, um…how about a glass of ice water?"

"That's it?"

She smiles, and my pants grow tighter. *What is it about this woman?* "I'll be right back," I tell her. "Don't move."

I step ten feet over to the bar and catch the bartender's eye. "What can I get for you?" he asks.

"I'd like a Johnny Walker Blue with one ice and a bottle of water—lid on."

In minutes, I have both drinks and return to where I left the beauty. But she's gone. I look around and don't see her anywhere. Panic knots my gut. But why? *What is wrong with you, Davis? You don't even know this woman.*

I wander back up the stairs, scanning the room, and then look out over the dance floor from the VIP area. I don't see her anywhere. It's like she vanished. If my dick wasn't so eager, I'd have to wonder if I made the whole thing up.

I go back over and sit at the table with my friends. Steve has two women all over him. I drink my scotch and watch the dance floor. After a moment he realizes I'm back—and alone. "Where's the woman you went chasing after?" he asks.

I shrug. "I don't know. We were doing fine. Then I went to the bar and ordered her another drink, and she disappeared."

Steve's eyes go wide. "Did she ditch you?"

My lips curl. "I suppose so."

"That's a first."

I don't know that it's the *first* time a woman has done this, but I don't usually pursue women in clubs like that either. He's right, though, that when it comes to dating, I'm the one who walks away. Not many women can hold my attention for long, mostly because theirs isn't truly on me. It's on my family name or my bank account. Now I'm feeling even more irritable. "Where is Jack?" I ask. He was with her friend.

Steve shakes his head and returns his attention to the women on his lap.

I look down on the dance floor again. Paisley shouldn't be hard to miss—stunning, tall, blonde, and legs that go on forever. But she's not anywhere.

I'm nursing my drink when my cell phone vibrates in my pocket.

Griffin: Hey. Where are you? I'm at your place.

Me: I'm at The Lion's Den. I can be home in fifteen.

Griffin: I'll be raiding your fridge and watching your television.

Me: Stay out of my booze. I'm on my way.

I let Steve know Griffin needs me, and he hardly nods. He's got a hand under the dress of one woman and his tongue down the throat of the other.

I send my driver a quick text, and he'll be outside waiting for me.

"Dr. Martin," Candy mewls as I approach.

She's the VIP concierge and a little too eager to please, if you ask me.

"Goodnight, Candy. Tell my brother, Phillip, that tonight was a lot of fun."

She smiles. "Let me know if I can get anything—or anyone—for you."

I shake my head and walk through the dance floor on my way out, still looking for Paisley through the dense crowd like a lost puppy. Even I know I'm being ridiculous, but as I step out the door, I take one last look. Nothing.

On the short ride home, I look through social media for the name Paisley. It's surprising how many are listed, but none of them is her. Who doesn't have social media?

When I get back to my building, I take the elevator to the penthouse. My brother has a pizza open in front of him from our favorite place, Luigi's, and he's watching sports highlights.

"What's up?"

He shrugs. "It was a tough day in the emergency room."

I grab a slice and sit with him. Griffin and I are the two of our four brothers who broke rank and went to medical school rather than joining the family business. He's an ER doc at Mercy Hospital, where I also work. He loves the fast pace and adrenaline rush that come with emergency medicine.

"We had an ugly case with a homeless family," he says after a moment. "They had a child with them, a little boy. He was begging for money and was pushed into the street in front of an oncoming bus."

My heart stops. "I'm sorry."

"This kid was a fighter, man," Griffin chokes out. "He came back to life three times, but just couldn't hang on."

I sigh. "I'm really sorry. That's a crappy day."

"The mother lost it, and we had to admit her for a mental health evaluation."

"I can't imagine that's easy."

"What about you?" he asks. "Where were you?"

"I went to Phillip's new club with Steve and the guys." My three closest friends, Steve, Jack, and Michael, also work with us at Mercy Hospital in downtown Vancouver.

"Oh yeah? How was The Lion's Den?" He sits back and props his feet on my coffee table.

"I had some fun. You'll enjoy this. I met a woman there, and she ditched me."

My brother shoots me a look, his eyes wide. "You? You're a chick magnet."

"Do they call it that anymore?" I snicker.

"Stop evading. She obviously didn't know who you were."

I shrug. "That was part of the appeal. She just thought I was some guy."

"Did you get her name?" he asks.

"Just a first name, and I've already checked. She's not on any socials, at least not that I can find."

"Damn." He takes a sip of his bourbon. "We'd better mark this day and time. Davis Martin found a woman who didn't worship him."

"I didn't say she didn't worship me," I clarify. "She just moved on faster than I would have liked."

Griffin laughs. "Where the hell did you find a private place in that mess of people?"

"Dude, there are several. Maybe if you got away from sourpuss Teresa, you'd have some fun." Teresa Snow has been Griffin's girlfriend for years now, but no one in the family is a fan, not even my parents. She doesn't seem to enjoy much of anything or have any particular interests of her own, but she must be able to suck a golf ball through a garden hose, because despite her being clearly in this game for the Martin name and not much else, my brother is still dating her.

Griffin rolls his eyes.

"Where is she tonight, anyway?"

"She had plans with her sister. I didn't want to bother her. Plus, she doesn't always understand."

I nod. People not in medicine don't always realize how hard death is, not only on the patient and their loved ones, but on the doctors too.

Chapter 3

Paisley

"Okay, what else happened at school today?" I ask Arabella, trying to gauge how she feels. We had a good run in there, and it had been almost two weeks since she needed to come home from school early. But today I got the call again and had to scoot out of work, hoping no one will notice. I haven't worked at Hardnight long enough to have vacation, and I've used all my sick and personal time.

She shrugs. "We did math."

"I was doing great with math until the alphabet started showing up," I tell her, trying to get a smile. "I mean, really? Who thinks one times A should equal anything?"

She looks up at me with a grin. "Don't worry, I'll help you when you need complicated math."

I smile back. *There's my girl.* "Perfect. Artists don't need to do much math beyond the basics."

We hop off the bus and walk past several people, all hustling toward one thing or another as we move toward our apartment. At least it isn't raining. Then she'd really be unhappy. Sometimes, Arabella's mood makes her feel worse, and I needed to unpack what's going on in her class.

"What else did you do today?" I prod.

"Nothing."

I roll my eyes. "Really? You just stood there and looked at the walls all day?"

"No," she replies, as if I'm being silly. "We did school stuff."

"When I was in school a long time ago, we sat in circles on the floor and read books. My favorite was always *The Babysitter's Club,* and my favorite time was gym class."

"Only you like gym. That's for boys."

"I don't remember when I started liking boys," I muse.

"Oh God, the girls all talk about getting married. As if that's all fun and games."

"I know. After your fourth wedding, it must be hard to feel excited," I mock.

Arabella looks up at me with a giant eye roll.

"Who are you hanging out with?"

"I was hanging out with Natalie, but she doesn't want to be my friend anymore."

I stop on the sidewalk outside our apartment building. "Why not?"

"Brady told Natalie not to be my friend."

"It's her loss, but why would he say that?" I secretly hope it's something I can fix. There's already so much in Arabella's life I can't fix.

"Because I'm dying."

I close my eyes for a moment, and a pang of hurt curls in my stomach. Arabella is too young to be dealing with this crap. "Of laughter?" I ask, hopeful.

She gives me a dramatic groan. "No."

"You're not dying. Well, everyone is dying, but that doesn't mean you're dying today."

Arabella coughs, and instantly I'm on alert. I need to make sure there isn't blood in her hand without being too obvious. She's on to me, though, and tucks her arm close to her side so I can't be sure. But I'll be on the lookout. If I spot blood, it's a return trip to Mercy Hospital's children's emergency room. We should have reserve seating and express checkout there.

Once I get Arabella upstairs in our apartment and she's tucked into bed, we run through all the required health checks for her: fever—low grade, so we'll keep an eye on that. She's congested, but that could be just allergies. We have a lot of mold around. Her lips and beneath her nails aren't blue, but everything feels cold. She's still talking and sharing, though. That's a good sign.

According to the usual drill, I'm supposed to check this every hour until we've gone at least twenty-four hours without a fever. Arabella's temperature and coloring aren't bad enough that they'll want to see her in the emergency room right now, so I sit down at our piece-of-crap home computer and bring up my bank balance. This month is going to be tight if I lose my job, but I don't have a choice. I'm long out of time off, and until my sister gets her surgery, I won't have much hope of making it to work on a regular basis.

I look at the time and do the math in my head. It's after two a.m. in the South Pacific. And that's at least where I think she is. I dial, and after a few rings, Mom groggily answers the phone.

"Hello?"

"Hey, Mom, it's me."

"It's in the middle of the night," she groans. "Could this have waited?"

"Arabella is sick again. I think I'm going to lose my job because I've had to take too much time off."

She sighs in frustration. "I can't keep asking Thomas for money. What do you need?"

I didn't know she'd asked Thomas for any money. "Nothing. The silver lining here could be that Arabella may finally get her surgery. She's sick. I thought as her mother you might want to be here for her."

"I don't know…" Her voice is hard and crisp. "That hole is supposed to close on its own. Follow Dr. Bartlett's advice. She's the expert. Don't do anything reckless. I don't want to leave Thomas behind, and I doubt he'd want to come with me for a visit, especially if I'm going to be stuck in a hospital all day."

I stifle a sigh. I want to believe my mother isn't a bad person. She's just self-absorbed, and she's never been a nurturing parent. That was my dad. He took care of all of us until he died.

"I'll keep you posted," is all I can say.

My father died shortly after Arabella turned five. Mom had a very hard time getting over it, but eventually, she met Thomas Ashurst. He's a travel writer, so she goes with him wherever he goes, but she doesn't work. She gave us about ten thousand dollars when she left three years ago, but that was gone in a little less than a year. Rents aren't cheap in Vancouver, and neither is food.

Arabella misses our mom, but I don't. I don't think she's capable of caring about anyone's needs except her own. I only wish there was something I could do to help Arabella. They thought I was joking when I offered to give her my heart. But I wasn't. I'd do anything for my sister. She's my ray of sunshine, and I love her more than my silver Jimmy Choo sandals that I found at a secondhand store, and that's saying something.

I've mostly moved from angry to indifferent about our mother. She'd only be another mouth to feed if she was here. She has no actual skills or inclination for working. She's best at dressing nice and making polite chitchat at a party or wearing a bathing suit poolside.

A wet, heavy cough fills our one-bedroom apartment, and that ratchets up my anxiety. I go into the bedroom to check on Arabella and find her struggling to breathe. Her forehead is hot, and she's lying in a pool of perspiration. I scoop her up and call a rideshare to the emergency room at

Mercy Hospital. If they refuse to admit her this time, I'll go apeshit on them. She can't continue to live like this.

Chapter 4

Davis

"Where are you going?" Amanda Miles, one of my residents, sidles up next to me as I move briskly down the hospital corridor.

I have my tuxedo over my shoulder, which makes me stand out. I promised my mother I'd stop by her party. "I'm on call now that my surgery is over. I have my phone. I need to step out for a bit. If anything happens here, I'll be right back."

Amanda gives me a look. "Looks like you're headed somewhere fancy. You're not sneaking away to get married, are you?"

I scoff. "Never."

"I mean, why would you?" she teases. "You have your pick of nurses, interns, residents, and every straight female within a fifty-mile radius. Why ruin a good thing?"

I know she's teasing me, but I can't muster a smile. I don't want to go to my mother's event. I wave my hand without looking back, push through the doors, and jump into the waiting car. My last surgery went long, and I should be dressed already, but I didn't want it to be obvious I was heading out. So much for that with eagle-eye Amanda. I try very hard to keep my personal life private. And I consider my sexual habits to be personal, not that I plan on having sex tonight.

A little while later, the car drops me at the Fairmont Hotel Pacific Rim, which overlooks Coal Harbor. I'm hoping to skirt into the men's room before I'm seen.

"Davis!" my mother says as I'm halfway across the lobby.

No such luck. "You weren't supposed to see me like this," I tell her. "My surgery went long, and rather than answer a thousand questions about what I was up to, I just ran out the door. I thought I'd change here."

She reaches for my arm. "I hope it was a successful surgery."

I relax. "Yes. The little boy is going to be fine."

"Okay, change and meet me in the ballroom. Buffy Flanders' niece is in town from Los Angeles, and we want to introduce you."

I close my eyes and breathe through my nose. My mother is dying to be a grandmother, so she works on fixing my three brothers and me up every chance she gets. Even when Teresa's on Griffin's arm, she's been known to introduce him to eligible bachelorettes. "I'll be right in."

After I change, my first stop *should* be the bar for a strong drink. I could use a good scotch, but I'm on call. So instead, I walk up and order a sparkling water.

It's not the same.

Turning, I take in the elaborate room. Out the window in the distance, I can see cars crossing the bridge on Highway One. To the side of that, a giant family photo taken last year at our place up in Whistler is projected on a large screen on the stage—my parents surrounded by their four sons.

My father, Henry Martin, Jr.—or Chip to the world—may have built a multibillion-dollar empire, but my mom,

Julia Martin, is the true powerhouse in our family. She sits on many nonprofit boards and is involved in everything from the arts to the environment to indigenous people to medical research.

My grandfather was an enterprising immigrant to Canada from Ireland and saw the future of radio. He and his assistant tinkered until they'd created radio receptors that could be powered by ordinary household electricity, making them an instant consumer hit. Unfortunately, he died before he turned forty, leaving my grandmother a widow with a single child — my father.

She had to sell the business to my grandfather's less-than-scrupulous assistant. But when my father was old enough, he raised the capital to buy it back. He then went on to purchase several radio and television stations, and today we have an extensive portfolio of media assets in Canada and around the world, as well as wireless, television distribution, and telephone services.

In my peripheral vision, I spot my two older brothers as they approach me. The oldest, Henry, works for the family business, and Phillip also has an office and does something there, but he's more focused on his investments, including The Lion's Den.

That thought prompts me to look around the room for Paisley. Ever since we were together — nearly two months ago now — I find myself scanning crowds to look for her. Something in me says it's not over between us.

"Where's your drink?" my brother Henry asks in greeting.

I hold up my sparkling water. "I'm on call."

He nods. "You may want to hide from Buffy Flanders."

"Why? What's wrong with her niece?"

Henry takes a deep pull on his drink. "She's beautiful, but you won't like her."

"What would make you say that?"

"She's a miner."

"Ahhh..." I nod. I should have guessed. That's our code for someone who's only interested in our bank accounts and name, not actually us. "Good to know. I can steer clear."

"I thought it was because she's too much like him," Philip says.

"What does that mean?" I ask.

My brother Griffin has appeared from somewhere and now puts his hand on my chest. "What our brother is not saying very well is that she's an actress. She thinks because she has a small, reoccurring role in a television show, we should be grateful she's spending time with us."

"And that makes her like me because..." I'm truly confused.

"You think you're God's gift to pediatric cardiothoracic surgery." Griffin takes a sip of amber liquid without looking at me.

I snort. "I am. I work on children's hearts. I'm not an ER pud like someone. And the statistics about my success don't lie. I'm very good at my job."

I may boast, but I really am one of the best pediatric cardiologists in North America, and I'm not about to take this crap from my brothers. People travel from all over for me to fix their children's hearts. I take a drink of my carbonated water, still wishing it was scotch.

"Did Griffin hurt your feelings?" Henry teases.

I shake my head. "Nope. I'm just wishing I had something stronger for this bullshit tonight."

"It won't be that bad," Phillip says.

I survey the scene and realize a gaggle of women standing across the room is watching us. I recognize most of them. "I see Renee Walsh and her friends."

"Yeah, I'm avoiding them," Henry says. "They're a nightmare."

"Talk about miners," Phillip quips.

Renee and Henry went to school together, and they were an item when they were younger. Henry has moved on, but lately she seems interested in rekindling their romance.

"What's the plan for this weekend?" Henry asks.

"The Lion's Den was pretty fun last weekend," I offer. I've gone back quite a few times since my encounter with Paisley to see if she ever returns. So far no luck.

Phillip preens. "It's a fun place. And I'm working on building a back room for more private activities, since my brother was caught on camera having sex."

I close my eyes. Really? He's going to bring that up again now?

"How much did they catch?" Henry asks, rubbing his hands together.

"His body blocked most of it, but that shit could get me closed down."

"No," I scoff. "Your VIP concierge who offers anything or anyone to your VIPs will get you closed down."

Phillip rolls his eyes. "I need to fire her. She's just supposed to be upselling the liquor where we get a better return."

Henry shakes his head, his eyes gleeful. "Teresa must hate the place," he tells Griffin.

Phillip laughs as we see Teresa glued to our mother on her way across the room. I'm sure my mom would like to ditch her, but she'd never go so far as to admit that. Our mother is entirely too nice.

My cell phone vibrates, and I pull it from my pocket as my mother approaches. I read the text.

Mercy Hospital: 10 YO female, with ASD complications.

Me: I'm on my way.

I look up at my mom. "There's a ten-year-old girl with an atrial septal defect at the hospital. I need to go."

"In English, please?" she asks with a sad smile.

"She has a hole in her heart, which is probably making her breathing difficult, so she has low energy, among other things."

Mom waves me off. "Go make that little girl better so her parents can dance at her wedding."

"Congratulations on your award, Mom. You make us all very proud."

She leans in and kisses me. "You've made me proud every day since you were born."

I'm a little sad not to see my mom get her award, but I'm grateful not to have to stomach another rubber chicken dinner. I text my driver to be ready for me and head back out toward the entrance.

Renee, now separated from her posse of miners, is waiting at the hotel entrance as I exit. She steps in for a hug. "Davis, you always look so good in a tux. Where are you headed?"

"I'm on call, and there's an emergency, so I need to get back to the hospital. Enjoy your evening."

She touches the perfectly coiffed knot at the base of her neck. "I hope when you return, you'll save me a dance."

After watching what happened with her and Henry, there is no chance I'd ever open myself up to that quagmire, nor do I plan on being able to return before this event wraps up. I'm just hoping to be home before sunrise. Much depends on the overall health of the little girl.

I give Renee a forced smile. "Enjoy your night."

I walk out to the car, and as I open the door, I realize I've left my scrubs behind. Oh well. The hospital always has more.

Chapter 5

Davis

Typical Friday night in the emergency room—it's stuffed full of people who've made poor decisions. I can spot most of the issues at a quick glance.

A man is holding his hand with a bloody wrap on it. *Knife incident.*

A baby is curled up in its mother's lap but can't be calmed. *Ear infection.*

Swollen ankle. Possibly a break but more likely a sprain.

I'm still dressed in my tuxedo when I approach the main desk. After just a moment, the head nurse for pediatric cardio surgery appears. "Anita, what do we have?"

"A ten-year-old girl with ASD," she reports. "High fever and heavy coughing." I look through the chart. *Ugh.* They've done nothing to fix this. Why? In Canada, the healthcare is free. It's supposed to help alleviate these sorts of situations. This is a mess.

Rather than take the time to change into scrubs, I head right to her curtain. As I approach, I hear a melodic voice reading a familiar book—*Harry Potter and the Goblet of Fire.*

I pull back the curtain and walk in, still reviewing the information on the intake form. "Hello, Arabella. I'm Dr. Martin. Sounds like you're not feeling well—"

When I look up, my heart nearly stops. After weeks of looking for her, I realize part of me had decided she might not even be real. But now, here she is. Sitting with my patient is the woman I met at The Lion's Den. Paisley.

Recognition flares in her eyes, and her face reddens.

My dick wakes up. Seems it has forgotten that this is one-hundred percent *not* the time. I take a deep breath and look down again at the notes in Arabella's electronic medical chart on the laptop in my hand.

She has a fever that's too high and a wet cough. They've given her Tylenol, and it seems to be bringing the fever down. This is good news. I pull my stethoscope out and look at her mother. "How long has she been feeling like this?"

"They called and said she wasn't feeling well at school, and I brought her home just after lunch."

"Fevers are so dangerous with her condition. Why didn't you bring her in immediately?"

"She didn't have a fever until later in the day. We came as soon as her condition worsened. Forgive me if I'm a little gun shy, but the last time we came in, I was reprimanded by the doctor on call for being too cautious. I was told you had too many emergencies to deal with a hypochondriac."

I shake my head. Doctors should stick to their own specialties. "Your daughter has ASD. There's no such thing as being a hypochondriac."

Her ears turn pink, and she's opened her mouth to speak again when her cell phone rings. "Excuse me." She puts her phone to her ear. "Hello, Jean."

I busy myself with the patient, but I also eavesdrop on her conversation as I press my stethoscope to the girl's chest. It doesn't take a genius to figure out Paisley's being fired for taking care of her daughter. I wonder where her husband is. Glancing at her left hand, I see she's not wearing a ring. She didn't have one on at the club either. Thank goodness for small miracles. I don't get involved with married women. Ever.

"I understand," she says quietly into her phone. "I'll be by next week to pick up my things." When she turns around, I see disappointment on her face for half a second, and then it shifts to resolve. She walks over to my side. "What's the plan?"

"Did you just lose your job again?" Arabella asks, her voice small.

"Don't worry about it," Paisley assures her. "I'll always find another one."

I like her spunk. She's obviously a strong person. I turn back toward her, prepared to discuss medicine, but instead, I just look for a moment. She was beautiful that night in her fancy dress, but tonight, even in the bright light of the hospital, she's gorgeous. Her golden hair is tied in a knot on top of her head, and her legs look delicious in yoga pants. A big fisherman's sweater hides her perfect, pert breasts that even now make my mouth water, and she's wearing Hunter knock-off rain boots—the uniform for the rainy season in Vancouver.

I force myself to focus on the matter at hand. That's certainly what everyone in this room deserves. "Why hasn't your daughter had surgery to close the hole in her heart or at least a stent placed to open the flow of blood?"

"She's not my mother. She's my sister." Arabella corrects me and giggles. It's an infectious laugh.

"Ah, okay," I tell her with a wink. Then I turn back to Paisley. "I'm sorry, but my question still stands." I'm frustrated that Arabella is suffering needlessly.

"They had scheduled her for the surgery years ago, but when it was time, our father had just died and our mother couldn't manage it."

My frustration morphs into a different kind of anger. This woman has had more thrown at her than most people twice her age. I nod. "Where is your mother now? I need consent for surgery."

"Our mother is out of the country. I'm Arabella's legal guardian, and I have the medical power of attorney. We've been hoping for another opening for surgery, but it's been five years, and we've not been able to schedule."

I don't like what I'm hearing. "It should have just been rescheduled. People can't make their surgeries all the time. We're not that strict."

She holds up her hand. "Well, my mom also heard that shunts create risks and problems like atrial fibrillation and pulmonary hypertension, so then she started to reconsider. And we were told that the hole could close on its own—"

"Not a hole of this size," I argue.

"Okay, but after a while, our mother wasn't sure. And then once I took over, I couldn't get anyone to call me back."

It's difficult to hold my tongue. *Who does that to their child?* Then I look at who's listed as Arabella's cardiac physician, and I'm not overly surprised she's in this situation. "Well, we're very late making the repair, and it could be difficult, but it's the right thing to do. I'll schedule the surgery for tonight. This is an emergency."

"Wait." She holds up her hand. "Have you been drinking? I don't want you near my sister's heart if you've had *anything* to drink."

"I had just arrived at the event when I was paged. All I did was change, drink a carbonated water, and come here."

She looks down at her dark green rain boots. "I'm sorry we interrupted your night."

I shake my head. "I should be thanking you. My mother had a line of women for me to meet." My attempt at lightening the mood falls flat.

I can't help but wish I could comfort her, give her a break from what is obviously a very stressful life. I'd love to know if that night we were together was a bit of a respite for her. But again, *not* the time.

"Okay, Arabella, we're going to try to fix your heart and help you feel better. The nurses will be in to get you prepped in just a moment. I need a few things done prior to performing surgery."

She nods, and I turn back to Paisley.

"What is your full name?" I don't really need it, but I want it. I can't stop myself from asking.

"Paisley Brooks."

"And your mobile number?" I can't stop myself from asking that either, and fortunately, she rattles it off without question. I'm sure she's in shock. "Fantastic. Once Arabella goes in, you can go get a bite to eat or whatever."

She shakes her head. "I'll be here waiting. Please take good care of her."

I nod, honoring her commitment to her sister. "I promise to take excellent care of her." I turn to Arabella. "You're going to radiology for a couple of pictures that will give me more information about your heart. They'll also do a blood draw—"

"I can donate if you'd like. We're the same blood type," Paisley interrupts.

I nod, impressed. "Thank you. Most people don't think about that. The nurses can let you know if it's necessary." I turn back to Arabella. "After that, we'll go into surgery. You'll be asleep the whole time, and when you wake up, you should be able to breathe easier. You'll also be sore for a little while."

Arabella gives me a feeble smile. "I know. I'm ready." Her hands shake, and Paisley quickly reaches for her and holds them tight.

"Are you planning on performing surgery in your tux?" Paisley asks.

I tuck my pen in my pocket. "No, thank you. I'll change. These shoes would be murder to stand in for that long."

She smiles, and my heart skips a beat. "I feel the same way about dress shoes."

I say goodbye to Arabella for now and ask Paisley to join me in the hallway, forcing myself to stay focused on the present. "Listen, I have to be honest, and I don't want to pretend this is going to be easy. This surgery should have been done five years ago."

Her eyes sparkle with tears.

"I'm going to do everything I can to take care of your sister," I assure her, all the while praying that I'm right about what needs to be done. This could change to a much more complex surgery.

"Thank you," she whispers.

"I know this isn't easy, but please take some time for yourself while she's with us. I have your cell number, and I'll call if I have any questions."

"I'll be in the waiting room," she tells me.

Rather than argue further, I just nod. "Okay, I'll see you after surgery."

I head to my locker to trade this monkey suit in for a set of scrubs. I've just pulled the door open when I hear a voice.

"Hi, Davis." Melanie Brown, a surgical nurse, leans against the wall, her cleavage in her scrubs top on full display and her scrub pants painted on. Melanie has a habit of meeting doctors in the on-call room for a quick romp, but that's not why I'm here. "You're looking very fine in that tuxedo, but I'd bet you look better out of it." She gives me a seductive smile.

"I have to prepare for an ASD repair."

"You could do that in your sleep." She leans in. "In fact, I had a dream where I was hiding under the surgical table and took care of you while you did surgery."

I stop and look at her. She's delusional. "Melanie, your comment is completely inappropriate. Please don't ever speak to me like that again."

"You weren't saying that as I was making you come last month," she replies.

"Go away, Melanie. I have a delicate surgery to do on a

ten-year-old girl. I need to concentrate."

"You know where to find me," she says over her shoulder as she saunters away.

I shake my head. She was such a mistake. I was too amped to sleep one night, and we used each other to take the edge off. As soon as we finished, I knew it had been a lapse in judgment. If she doesn't back off soon, I'll have to make it clear that I don't do repeats.

I roll my head from side to side, hoping to release the tension. I've done this surgery a million times, but I can't screw this up. I want to help Arabella, and I want to help her older sister too. My heart swells for a moment at the thought that after all this time *I've found her*, but I bury that thought before it can bloom into any kind of fantasy.

Once I've changed, I coordinate with Anita and the surgical ward to get space for Arabella while she's in radiology.

I've just finished checking in on my patient from this afternoon when Arabella's echocardiogram and ICG arrive. As I study them, I realize the hole is bigger than I thought. I won't be able to do a percutaneous closure. This is going to require open-heart surgery. My stomach turns, but the surgeon in me is excited.

I walk back out to the waiting area and spot Paisley with a tablet in her hand, though she's looking off into space.

"Paisley?"

She jumps up. "That was really fast."

I shake my head. "I haven't started. After looking at the radiology reports, I can see that the hole is too big to go in through the vein in her leg. It's going to require open-heart surgery, so we're looking at five hours or so."

A cloud of fear crosses her beautiful azure eyes, but she nods.

"I promise she's in expert hands," I tell her. "If you want to lie down, I can get you a room with a bed?"

"No, that's okay. I want to be here when she comes

out."

I nod. "I'm going to have a nurse come and sit with you. You can ask her all your questions, and she'll have privileges in the surgical ward in case you want to know what's going on."

"What is the possibility that something could go wrong?" Paisley's eyes search mine.

I don't want to even try to answer that question. "I know this is scary, but I've done this many times before."

Paisley chews on her thumbnail. "Thank you."

"I'll call you as soon as I'm done."

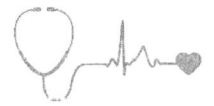

Five and a half hours later, I remove my surgical gown and throw it and my gloves into the hazardous waste bin. I sigh as I lean against the wall for a moment. That was a rough surgery. Arabella was not in good shape. Her heart required three stents, and the hole had signs of a tear, but I rebuilt the area, and we'll watch it closely.

It's after three in the morning, and I'm a dead man walking, but I still have work to do.

I walk out to the waiting room and find Paisley sitting forward on the edge of her seat. When she sees me, she stands.

"A nurse told me she was being moved into recovery."

I slide my hands into the pockets of my lab coat and nod. "Arabella did fantastic. The hole in her heart had gotten bigger, so I'm glad you brought her in."

Paisley nods.

"You can plan on Arabella being here for about two weeks. We'll have her in intensive care for a good part of that, but you can visit with her as often as you want or need."

"Can I sleep here?"

I shake my head. "I don't think they'll let you do that.

Where do you live?"

"We're in Richmond, by the airport, so a ways away."

"That's a good hour without traffic. Do you have someone close by you can couch surf with?"

Paisley is quiet a moment. "No. Not really."

"I may have a lead on a place where you can stay," I tell her. "Can you wait here a minute?" *What the hell am I doing?* I can't believe I said that.

She nods. "Of course."

I walk back to my office. I need to think about this. The two-bedroom nanny/housekeeper quarters in my condo is sitting empty. It's a separate apartment with its own entry, and no one ever uses it. I can move one of my cars to my parents', and she can have a space in the garage. It's close to the hospital, and she could be here for her sister. It's only two weeks.

Is this the smart thing to do? I don't even know this woman, and I'm inviting her to move into my condominium. But I can't seem to stop myself. It just feels like the right thing to do. I remove the key from my key ring, and on the back of my business card, I write my home address and the code to the door.

I walk out and offer her the card. "Here you go. The address is on the back of my card, and the code on the bottom is for the door. If you give your car keys to the doorman, he'll show you how to park in the garage. The building has an elevator. The apartment has two bedrooms, so when your sister is released, you can both stay there while you work through all the follow-up doctor appointments." Her eyes widen, but she doesn't say anything. I decide to fill the quiet. "You can stay as long as you need to. It sits empty most of the year." *What am I thinking?*

"How much is the rent?" she finally asks. "I, uh, don't really have a job right now. With everything going on, I missed too many days of work, and they let me go."

I shake my head. "I've worked it out with the owner.

It's a nanny apartment within their condo. They don't use it, and instead, it's often used as a place for people who need to be close to the hospital."

"I feel silly. Are you sure?"

I nod. "Yes, it will be fine." She sways slightly on her feet, and I know she's exhausted. "You can leave your car here, and I can run you over. Your sister won't be able to have visitors until much later this morning. And even then, she'll probably still be asleep. You should rest."

"I actually don't have a car. I use public transportation or rideshares."

"Great. Then I'll drive you to where you're staying. Let me get a quick shower and change. How about I meet you on the main floor by the green elevators in twenty minutes?"

She looks down at the elevators, seeming unsure. "You don't have to do that. I can take the bus."

"In the middle of the night?" I want so much to reach out and take her in my arms, assure her that her sister has a long road, but we'll get through it together. Honestly, I don't even know where all this is coming from. Instead, I clear my throat. "I can do this for you. It's no trouble at all."

Finally, she nods. "Okay. I'll meet you downstairs."

I've never showered so quickly. I'm out the door in less than twenty minutes, only to find Paisley sleeping in a chair in the sitting area beyond the elevators.

I gently jostle her shoulder. "Paisley?"

She jumps. "I'm sorry. I didn't mean to fall asleep. If I'm holding you up, I can get a cab or something."

"Will you stop? You don't have to do this all on your own."

She snorts. "Yes, I do."

"Really, you don't. I've got you."

She rubs her eyes and stands, and I motion for her to follow me. She moves like a zombie as we walk out to my Tesla Model X in my assigned parking space.

By the time we make it to my place, she's asleep again,

so I leave her in the car as I unlock the apartment and turn some lights on. The last time I had anyone staying here beyond a quick overnight was when my roommate from university came to work here a half-dozen years ago. He works for the company that provides all of British Columbia with electricity, so now he can afford his own place. Other than that, it's just been a crash pad for friends when needed.

I return to the car and scoop Paisley into my arms. I carry her upstairs on the elevator and put her on the bed in the main bedroom of the apartment.

She immediately rolls over and murmurs, "Thank you."

I feel ten feet tall.

Before I head over into my place, I cover her with a blanket. A minute later, I return with a pair of sweatpants, a T-shirt, and a hoodie that will be entirely too big for her, but at least they're clean.

Then I close the door between her apartment and my condominium and lock it behind me. I'm not ready for her to know she'll be staying in an apartment I own, attached to the place where I live. Given our history, that might be more than she can sort through right now, and I don't want her to get the wrong idea before I've even had a chance. I still don't know why she disappeared that night at The Lion's Den. But I'm most certainly going to find out.

Eventually. That's likely going to be way down the list. Tomorrow will be another long day, and I'll want to get in early to see how Arabella is doing.

Chapter 6

Paisley

A noise I don't recognize startles me from a deep sleep. *Where am I?*

Then I remember. I'm not sure how I got here, but I must be in the apartment Dr. Martin set up so I could be close to the hospital.

When my heart finally stops pounding, I sit up in bed, then tentatively begin to explore. The apartment is amazing. It's decorated with high-end furnishings in mostly white, beige, and coffee colors. I finally spot a clock and find it's after seven. The sky is gray, and of course, it's raining. Welcome to spring in Vancouver.

I'm still exhausted, but I need to get back to Arabella right away. She's all alone in a hospital, with no one there to comfort her as she comes out of recovery. On a couch I find a note on top of some sweatpants and a Harvard Medical School T-shirt, along with Dr. Martin's cell phone number.

He's offered to drive me to the hospital, but after looking at the map on my phone, I can see it's walkable. It'll be a good, healthy walk, and I could use the exercise.

Then I remember the rain. Change of plans.

In the next fifteen minutes, I quickly shower, put on the T-shirt and sweatpants, and call a rideshare to take me to the hospital. A passing glance in the mirror shows I look terrible, but right now, I don't care.

I gather my things, step out of the apartment, and take the elevator down to the main floor. When the doors open, I'm shocked. This apartment building overlooks Coal Harbor and Stanley Park. Holy crap, the view is spectacular. As I watch, a float plane comes in and lands on the water, and the tips of the spires on Lion's Gate Bridge are visible above the tree line of Stanley Park. I've heard about this building, and I think it's the one considered the most expensive in Vancouver — each unit has at least two floors and something like seven thousand livable feet. This is way beyond my budget, and I'm grateful all over again that the owner of the unit I stayed in is kind enough to share it with people who can't afford a hotel close to the hospital.

I watch as another float plane lands on the water. I've always wanted to see the islands from the air.

I need to let Lucy know what's going on — with Arabella, I mean. Not with this crazy apartment. I'll save that for later when my brain isn't so scrambled. I send her a quick text.

Me: Arabella had emergency surgery last night. They've finally fixed the hole. She's in the Pediatric Cardiac ICU at Mercy Hospital, and I'm headed over now to see if she's awake yet. You'll never guess who her doctor is. Call me.

When I arrive at the hospital, I check in and am escorted to Arabella's bed in the intensive care unit. She's shielded behind a curtain and hooked up to a thousand different monitors. She has a breathing tube. Her eyes are still closed, but I reach for her hand and hold it tight.

Tears pool in my eyes. I hate seeing her this way, but I hope with all my heart that this is a step in the right direction, the change she's been needing since they discovered the hole when she was just a few months old.

There's a tap on my shoulder. "Ms. Brooks?"

I wipe my eyes. "I'm sorry."

The nurse gives me a warm smile. "This is very stressful. But thankfully your sister is doing fantastic."

"That's great news."

"I need to change her dressings. You can stay, but I need to get closer to her."

"Of course. I need the bathroom anyway."

"You can use the staff bathroom," she says. "It's just down the hallway on your left."

I stretch as I stand, feeling the tension in my shoulders.

As I walk to the restroom, I spot Dr. Martin, and he seems to be in deep discussion with Arabella's cardiologist, Jeannine Bartlett. Mom has loved Dr. Bartlett from the beginning, but she certainly hasn't impressed me much these last few years. We were always told she's one of the best pediatric cardiologists, though, so I told myself it didn't matter that she has a holier-than-thou personality.

I step into the bathroom and almost fall asleep sitting on the toilet. That would have been embarrassing. I stretch again to try to clear my head.

As I wash my hands, a nurse comes to stand next to me, primping and re-coating her blood-red lips with more lipstick. "Nice shirt. Did you go to Harvard Medical School?"

I shake my head and chuckle. "Hardly. I didn't finish my first year at Emily Carr." That's a nearby university of art and design. I had to drop out to take care of my sister, but that's not any of her business. "This isn't my shirt."

"Do you know Dr. Martin?" she asks, putting my radar on high alert.

"He did my sister's heart surgery yesterday."

"But you didn't know him before then?"

"No," I lie, becoming more and more curious about her questions. "Why?"

She turns to me with her hands on her hips. "He's my boyfriend, and that's where he went to medical school."

Oh boy. Seems I need to talk her away from the edge of the cliff. "You're so lucky." I give her a smile. "Dr. Martin is a very talented surgeon and quite handsome."

She nods smugly. "Yes, he is. Women are constantly throwing themselves at him, but he's not available." She looks ready to go to fisticuffs right here in the bathroom.

Given my experience with Davis, they can't have been together long, and unstable and jealous doesn't seem like his type. But that's between them. I don't need this crap.

I smile again. "Right now, my priority is my sister and her recovery." Then I scuttle out of the bathroom as quickly as I can. At least I'm more awake now.

I return to find Dr. Bartlett in the room with Arabella. Our long-elusive medical provider doesn't even acknowledge me as I enter. She types away on her computer and fiddles with a few of the machines.

"I'm sorry you were pressured into the surgery," she finally says, but she doesn't look up from her computer.

I'm able to stop myself from laughing out loud. "We've been waiting for over five years," I tell her. "We weren't pressured."

"Your mother told me she didn't want to take the risk."

Why is she saying this now? She's never mentioned it before. "My mother gave up that responsibility when she sailed off with her boyfriend. And I'm certain I've mentioned how anxious we were to get it done at each of our appointments."

She shakes her head. "Dr. Martin should never have performed the surgery without consulting me. Your sister is too frail. It was extremely risky."

Now, I'm too stunned to say anything. I'd like to tell her off, but I don't want to jeopardize Arabella's care. She'll only be in the hospital for so long, and then we'll need a pediatric cardiologist again. If Dr. Bartlett's as good as they say, we need to stay welcome at her practice.

She turns and leaves without saying goodbye, and I'm left worrying whether the surgery was a sound decision. I've been so convinced it was what Arabella needed, but now, I don't know what to think.

Dr. Martin steps into the room and brings me back to reality. "Hey there. Did you get any sleep last night?"

I nod. "I got some. Thank you. And I'm sorry I fell asleep in your car. I don't remember arriving at the apartment."

He smiles. "I carried you up. You were light as a feather."

No one has ever referred to me as light. I'm too tall for that. But I appreciate his kindness. "Thank you. Your girlfriend introduced herself to me in the bathroom. I'll get your shirt back to you as soon as I can. My plan is to get a suitcase of clothes together this afternoon."

A funny look crosses Dr. Martin's face. "I don't have a girlfriend. Who told you she was my girlfriend?"

"She actually didn't give me her name. She just recognized this as your shirt."

He tilts his head to the side. "What did she look like?"

"Blonde, red lipstick, lots of cleavage..." I don't know how to say in a polite way that she looked like a hooker in scrubs.

After a moment, he nods. "I think I know who you could be talking about. I'll speak with her. Please keep the shirt as long as you need it. Anyway, I don't have any surgeries today. I have a few things to get caught up on, but would you like a ride to your apartment?"

I shake my head. "You've already done so much. I don't want to put you out. I can take the bus."

"I need to finish my rounds and do some paperwork, but I can drive you to your place after lunch," he assures me.

"You said you were south of the airport in Richmond?"

I nod.

"No problem. We'll miss the traffic leaving downtown, and you'll be back before your sister wakes."

"That's too much. I can manage." I show him my bus pass. "I'm good."

He crosses his arms in front of him. "Why won't you let me help you?"

"You don't even know me. Why would you want to help so much?" Aside from being above and beyond, this will not make that nurse in the bathroom happy at all.

He smiles and shakes his head. "By helping you, I help Arabella," he explains. "She needs a stress-free environment, and if you're worried about a roof over your head or spending two hours on a bus with all those germs, that isn't satisfactory."

I sigh. He's willing to drive an hour each way in traffic to my apartment. I don't know why I'm fighting him.

Okay, I do know why. I remember what happened the first time we met. I wasn't myself, and I have no regrets. It'd been so long since a man even looked at me twice, let alone paid that kind of attention to me, but I never thought I'd see him again. Now I don't know what to do.

I look at his eager face. He's not flirty, so maybe he doesn't want anything more than to be helpful. From the very beginning, he's seemed too good to be true. I sigh. "Fine, but only because you're insisting."

He nods. "I'll text you a little later, and you can meet me the same place we met last night."

"Okay."

He turns toward Arabella and examines the machines she's hooked up to.

After a moment, I remember what Dr. Bartlett said. "Was Arabella too frail to have the surgery? I mean—"

He turns back to look at me. "She was frail, but her condition was never going to improve without the surgery.

We didn't have much choice. It would have been easier if she'd had the surgery when she was younger, but she's doing fine. She's going to come out of this much stronger."

"She's going to be okay?" I ask, more hopeful than I've ever been.

He smiles. "Right now, we have her heavily sedated in what is often called a medically induced coma so her body can concentrate on healing. The machines are doing everything else for her. I know it looks intimidating, but this is all good news. If she continues to do well, we'll bring her out of the sedation soon."

Relief flows through me. I don't know why I trust Dr. Martin more than I trust Dr. Bartlett, but I do. Deep down, I know he's the person who saved Arabella's life.

After a few minutes, he moves on to his next patient, and I settle in next to Arabella's bed. I know she won't be awake for a while, but still, it's hard to leave her lying in a hospital all by herself.

My phone rings. It's Lucy calling, as I instructed her.

"Hey, you," I answer.

"Hey yourself. How is Bells doing? What happened?"

I give her the rundown on the day yesterday, which finally culminated in the surgery we've been after for so long. "It was stressful, but she's doing great," I conclude. "They have her in a medically induced coma so she can build her strength. The hole had torn."

Lucy gasps. "Was there any permanent damage?"

"No. Or at least they haven't said anything about that. But she'll be here in the hospital for at least two weeks."

"I will be by to visit."

"Well, thank you. Right now, she can't have visitors who aren't family, but I'd love to see you eventually."

"Yes! We have a lot to catch up on. Oh — and who's her doctor?"

"You won't believe this, but it's the guy I hooked up with at The Lion's Den."

Lucy screeches. "No fucking way!"

"I know. I can't even believe it. Never in my life did I think I'd see him again, particularly not like this. And you should have seen him in his tuxedo. That man puts the sizzle in hot."

"Wait, what? In a tuxedo? I thought he was doing surgery. Did he recognize you?"

Her questions come at me like a hail of bullets. "He came from a party to do the surgery, and I talked to him before he changed. Yes, he did seem to recognize me, but I don't think it matters. My boss called while he was in consulting with Arabella, so he got to hear me lose my job. That was great advertising for what a dumpster fire I am."

"What?" she gasps.

"It was so embarrassing." I sigh. "But it may have helped us in the end, because he's hooked me up with a temporary place to stay near the hospital. It's too far to schlep all the way back and forth to Richmond. Anyway, it's beautiful and super nice, and you'll have to come see it soon." If I told her any more about where it was, she'd be over tonight and she might never leave. As much as I'd love to see her, until I can thank the owner and make sure visitors are okay, I'm not going to do anything that could get me kicked out.

I hear a muffled voice in the background on her end. "I've got to go," she says. "But I want to see you soon."

"No problem. I'm looking forward to it. You know where I'll be."

Chapter 7

Davis

My knuckles are white from gripping the steering wheel as we inch across town in heavy traffic. It's Saturday, so all bets are off, I suppose. I'd forgotten how big Richmond was, but Paisley and her sister appear to live in the shittiest part of it, right beneath the flight pattern of the airport.

"You can park here." Paisley points just ahead and looks around as if she's expecting to see someone. "I won't be long."

I parallel park and turn the car off. "I'll go with you."

"Are you sure you want to leave your car? There's a chance it won't be here when you get back." She pauses a moment. "I mean, no one would hurt me, but selling this car could make for a nice steak dinner."

I chuckle. This is a hundred-and-fifty-thousand-dollar car. "It should fetch more than a steak dinner, but it'll be fine. It's one of the hardest cars to boost. Plus, if anyone tries to touch it, I'll get an alert on my phone."

She shakes her head. "Your choice."

I follow her into a two-story building featuring cracked

paint and mold in the shadier spots of the exterior. She winds her way upstairs to her apartment and digs for her keys. The door is not a fire safety door, and with one easy kick, someone could break into her place. *I don't like this at all.*

Inside, the apartment is small, neat, and clean, but I spot mold on the ceiling and can smell the musty, dank odor that comes from it. This can be common in Vancouver where we get nine months of gray and rain each year, but there are ways to treat the mold, and a good landlord would be on top of that. *I'm so glad I'm getting them out of here. This is not a safe place to live.*

"I'll just get a few days' worth of things." Paisley looks around frantically. She's nervous that I'm here. *I like that. It means she still likes me.*

Suddenly, a hum begins and grows steadily louder.

"What's that noise?" I ask in horror. *How loud is it going to get?*

Paisley gestures toward one wall. "The laundry room is next door. It does that when the machine is in a spin cycle."

The dishes in the kitchen rattle. *What the hell?*

"Don't worry. It only goes on for a few minutes—three times in a twenty-minute span." She shrugs as if this is acceptable.

It's not. "Only during daytime hours?"

She chuckles. "No. It happens whenever someone has to do laundry."

I groan. "How much of what's in here is yours?"

She looks around. "All of it."

I nod. "I'll have a mover come and put it in storage for you."

"Why? The other apartment is only temporary while Arabella is in the hospital. I'll need to come back."

"The other apartment is yours for at least six months. It's going to be that long or longer before you don't need to be at the hospital at least once a week. Why pay rent when you're not living here?" *Plus, the mold here is not healthy. I should call someone and have this place condemned. It's a shithole.*

Paisley blanches, even though I didn't say that last bit out loud.

"I may not be able to put the deposit down on the apartment again," she whispers. "If I'm here, we'll have a place to stay, even if I'm late with the rent."

"Don't worry, you'll be fine." I wave that off. I'll give her the money if she needs it, but after seeing this place, I can't let her live here.

She gives me a fiery look. "You don't know that, and neither do I. I don't even have a job right now. Finding an apartment without proof of income is nearly impossible."

"I *do* know, and you can live in the apartment for as long as you want or need to. Rent free. You'll have at least six months to get a new job, help Arabella get healthy and on her feet, and figure out the next place you want to live."

She shakes her head, still not seeming convinced. "How can you say that? Do you know the owners? They might care if I stay for six months and don't contribute anything."

"I do know the owner. You'll be fine." Something in me feels so protective of her. It's even stronger than my dick's interest in her at this point, and that's saying something. "I promise, I've got you covered."

"I don't need your pity," she says through clenched teeth.

"Trust me," I tell her. "This isn't pity."

She looks away, her shoulders tense.

Then my cell phone sounds a deep, loud foghorn. We both jump.

"Someone has touched the car," I announce.

Paisley's eyes go wide.

"I've got this," I assure her.

I call up the app, and I can see them on my phone. Right now, they're just looking inside. They probably don't see many Teslas around here. But then one of them slides a slim-jim from his pocket and positions it between the window and the seal to get to the unlocking mechanism. I push the button that alerts the police, and then I get into action. "Hey, guys. You see that bubble thing on the dashboard? That's a camera. It's now taken your picture. If you wish to continue, the police are on their way."

"Man, that's just a recording," one of the would-be thieves says to the other.

"No, man, this is me talking through my phone to you," I explain. "I wouldn't break into the car. You can't drive away with it, anyway. You can actually see me if you look upstairs. I'm standing in the window in an apartment on the second floor."

They scan the windows quickly, but they must miss me. "Man, this car is going to be fun to drive," the bolder one says. "It has falcon doors."

"Yeah, those falcon doors were one of the reasons I bought the car," I tell them. They look again up at the window where I'm standing, and this time they spot me. I wave. "You realize there's a kill switch, right?"

The police come driving up the street with lights and sirens, and the guys take off.

"You got them to move on without being arrested."

I turn to her and smile. I need to go talk to the cops, but we're not changing the subject. "Do you have the money for next month's rent without working?"

She sighs. "I've saved enough to pay one month. After that, I'm going to have to figure something out. I hear I could sell a kidney."

I shake my head. "Promise me you'll never do that. Selling organs is an ugly business, and often the person who harvests isn't a fantastic surgeon. You'd be putting your health at risk."

She turns a delightful shade of pink. "I was just kidding. I draw the line at selling my body or my soul."

I nod, relieved. "Good. I'm sure that won't be necessary."

If I were talking to anyone else I can think of about living indefinitely in my condo, I'd be sprinting for the hills. But with Paisley, I'm not, Though that would certainly be more convenient. Paisley is the sister of a patient. And she was a one-night stand. Those things should remain separate, shouldn't they? But I'm insanely attracted to her, so I can't think clearly. Perhaps if we were to revisit our fun, I could get her out of my system and move on to bigger and better things.

"Why don't you just bring as much as you can now?" I suggest. "We'll figure out your living situation later. And be sure to get Arabella's things, too. I think you'll want to have some clothes she'll feel more comfortable wearing, eventually."

With a sigh, she finally nods. "Okay. I think I have a box we can put some things in."

"I'll be right back. Pack up as much as you can while I go check in with the police."

I take the stairs two at a time and jog out to see the cops parked near my vehicle. After introducing myself, I open up the car to show them my license and registration. They ooh and aah over the falcon doors as I explain that the would-be thieves ran off.

"I only notified you when they brought out the slim-jim," I tell them. "Then they heard you coming and ran."

"Are you moving in around here?" one of them asks, handing me back the paperwork.

I shake my head. "Just helping out a friend."

Since there's nothing to be done, they move on to their next call, and I return to Paisley's apartment. Paisley has emptied most of her closet and dressers into a rag-tag suitcase and some large garbage bags, and we're ready to get back to my car.

"I can't believe the police didn't stick around," Paisley says as we walk out to an empty street.

"Not a big deal. The guys moved on."

We stow her things in the trunk and begin the ugly trek

back downtown. It takes two or three tries to get through each light. It's frustrating, but in another hour, I know it would take twice the time.

"Have you received any updates on Arabella?" Paisley asks.

I shake my head. "Let's find out together." Using the in-car system, I call the nurses' station in the cardiac unit of the ICU.

"Cardiac. This is Gina Roberts," a nurse answers.

"Good afternoon, Gina. This is Davis. I'm checking in on Arabella Brooks. How is she doing?"

She clicks on a computer keyboard. "She has some arrhythmia, and some pulmonary hypertension, normal at this point post-op, but not what you'd consider a fantastic start."

Nurses sometimes get bitched at for offering their opinion, but I've worked with Gina long enough that she knows what I'm looking for. "Agreed," I tell her. "I'm on my way in. Prepare IV meds to increase the ketorolac to point-five micrograms every six hours for the next forty-eight."

"With a morphine chaser?"

"Yes, please."

"It'll be ready when you arrive."

After I disconnect the call, Paisley looks pale. I reach over and take her hand. "You heard Gina. These are normal reactions, and we need to give her body time to get better. I'm going to keep her sedated, so she won't be waking up today. Maybe tomorrow morning."

Paisley nods, and I feel terrible. This is not what I wanted to share with her. But the surgery on Arabella should have been done years ago, and we have no choice but to deal with the aftermath. I blame her cardiologist, Jeannine Bartlett. I need to look at the records, but I seem to recall that she lost her surgical privileges after a few too many mix-ups in the operating room about the time Arabella fell off the list for surgery. It seems a little too convenient that Dr. Bartlett blames Arabella's mother. Jeannine is a conniving bitch who evidently would rather let someone die than have them seen by someone else. But we've had quite enough of that. I'll be referring Arabella to another physician for her follow-up, and I hope Paisley will take my advice.

But now is not the time to put all that on her. She likely needs to think about something else for the time being. "Have you always lived in Vancouver?" I ask instead.

"Pretty much. My parents were from Regina, and like so many others, they came here for the weather. What about you?"

I nod. "It's hard for me to believe it sometimes, but the weather is a draw. While I was in med school in Boston, I realized that at least you don't have to shovel the rain."

Paisley chuckles, and my heart stirs. "I don't drive often, but I agree, getting around in rain is better than the snow."

"Where did you go to school then?" I switch lanes and glance at her.

"A public high school in Surrey, and then I was working full time for a law firm while I went to Emily Carr for a degree in sculpture. But I didn't get very far, because a couple years after my dad passed, my mother met someone and made me Arabella's legal guardian."

My eyes widen a moment, but I quickly school my features. Paisley doesn't need my judgment of the situation. *But who meets a man and walks away from their sick child?* Maybe this is how her mom is processing her grief. "That must have been really tough."

Paisley shrugs. "I didn't mind. Arabella's amazing and so smart. She's struggling at her school, though not academically. There she's far ahead, but socially, she's behind. They find her absences disruptive. And her best friend just told her she was going to stop being her friend because she was dying."

"Are you kidding me? Why don't the teachers get

involved?" My anger is closer to the surface than I would like.

She shakes her head. "She's smarter than most of her teachers, so that's often a challenge as well." She tells me several funny stories about Arabella taking over the class or stumping the teacher with her questions. I can tell she adores her.

"Do you have any siblings?" she asks.

I nod. "I have three brothers. One is an emergency room doctor at Mercy, and two work for our family business."

"What kind of work does your family do?"

It's so refreshing to talk to someone who knows nothing about me and hasn't researched me and planned our future.

"They have a communications company."

"Very nice. I guess it's something to fall back on if this medicine thing doesn't work out."

We both laugh. If she only knew.

"What do you do for yourself?" I ask.

"I don't have a lot of time, but I read when I can, and I try to run. It doesn't cost anything, and it helps me clear my head."

We're nearly back to my building now, and suddenly, I feel a bit anxious about that. "Let's drop your things off, and we'll go see Arabella. She won't be awake, but you'll feel better, and maybe a little later we can grab some dinner."

Her smile falters. "I shouldn't."

"Why not?"

"You've been so incredible—arranging a place for me to stay, driving me to my apartment, getting information on my sister, not to mention being her *doctor*. I can't take a meal from you, too."

"I wouldn't have offered if I didn't want to spend the time with you."

"I shouldn't," she says.

It feels like we're at an impasse. I worry she's going to disappear again. "Why did you leave that night?"

I'm not sure it's an appropriate question right now, but I have to get it out in the open.

She shrugs. "That girl was not me. My best friend, Lucy, had encouraged me to go out and let loose to take a break. I definitely did, but..." She shakes her head. "Plus, I wasn't sure you were going to come back."

I shoot her a look. "I gave you every indication that I was coming back, and in fact, I did. But I couldn't find you anywhere."

She shakes her head. "I hit the restroom to clean up and then danced until one."

I nod. Now I feel like a crazy person. Asking Paisley to join me for dinner was too much. I should have known better. I pushed too hard. When women do it to me, I feel the same way. She's dealing with a ton right now. She's not looking for a date.

When we arrive at my place, I park and help her over to the back elevator with all of her things. I push the button to call the car, and she turns to me.

"I'll see you around the hospital. Thanks again for driving today and for everything you've done for Arabella and me."

"What do you mean?" I ask. "After we take this stuff upstairs, I'm still driving you back to the hospital."

"Are you going there?"

I nod. "I'm going to adjust Arabella's medication to see if that will speed up her recovery."

"Oh, okay then." The elevator arrives, and we step inside, but she doesn't look at me.

I need to change the subject, so she doesn't dwell on this any further. "I understand your fridge was stocked today. Do you want to take a sandwich or anything with you?"

"They stocked the fridge?"

When the elevator opens, she goes into the apartment and immediately to the fridge. It's stuffed full of fresh vegetables, meats, cheeses, and beautiful fruit. "I can't afford this."

"I don't think they're looking for you to pay for the groceries. Consider it a welcome. They know you're staying here because someone you love is in the hospital. Just don't let it go to waste, you know?"

Her eyes are as big as saucers.

"Go ahead and get yourself something. I'll take these bags to your bedroom."

I head down the hallway while she makes herself a giant turkey sandwich with all the fixings, a container of berries, and a small green salad. As she finishes up, I email my best friend, Michael, to see if he can join me for drinks at our favorite place. I can't be hanging around here tonight, knowing she's so close. I'm not ready to let her know I'm her benefactor. I don't want her to feel obligated to me in any way.

Me: Hey. Joe's tonight for drinks and oysters?

Michael: Perfect. How about 7?

Me: See you then.

"Okay, I'm ready," Paisley calls. "They even got my favorite sparkling water."

I smile. I love that simple things make her happy. "All right then. Let's get out of here."

We return to the hospital and park in my assigned spot before we go up to the cardiology unit of the ICU. As we arrive, I send her on to her sister's room and stop at the nurses' station.

"This is a surprise," Anita, the head nurse for the pediatric cardiac unit, says as I walk up. "What brings you in? I didn't see you on the schedule."

"I spoke with Gina a bit ago about Arabella Brooks. I'm here to oversee adjusting her meds."

"Ah. That makes sense. Gina's on her dinner break, but she left some things behind here." She points to an IV bag. "Arabella sure is a fighter."

I nod. "I agree. We're going to get her healthy, no matter what it takes." I smile and gather the medications. "Thanks, Tammy."

She nods as I head off to Arabella's curtain.

When I arrive, I stand outside a moment and listen as Paisley tells Arabella all about the apartment and our drive out to get their stuff. She even tells her about the guys who tried to steal my car.

Pulling the green curtain back, I smile at Paisley and the giant meal she has laid out in front of her. "You look like you're going to have an excellent dinner."

She smiles big. "So good!"

I trade out the IV bag and add the medication I ordered. "She's doing much better than she was before. We just need her to be a little stronger before we wake her. Do you want me to stay with you?"

Where did that come from? I'm not usually the guy who offers to do anything for patients' families. That's way outside my job description.

She shakes her head. "No. You have a life outside of me. Will you be by about this time tomorrow?"

"I'll be by in the morning. I don't want you to stay too late, okay? You need to get a good night's sleep."

She nods, not looking at me.

"I'm going to have a rideshare meet you downstairs at the main entrance at eight thirty. It's not good for you or for Arabella for you to be here all night, and the nurses will probably kick you out at that time when visiting hours are over."

She nods. "I can walk back. The fresh air will do me good."

"No, it'll be dark, and it's not at all a safe neighborhood at night. Let's be careful. Your sister needs you."

She rolls her eyes.

"Did you just roll your eyes at a doctor's orders?"

She blushes. "I'll never tell."

"Don't make the rideshare wait. Downstairs at eight thirty."

She nods. "I'll see you here in the morning, then."

I'm not sure if she's placating me or not, as she's disregarded my requests before. I can't stop thinking about that damn night at the club. But at least, this time, I'll know if she blows off the rideshare.

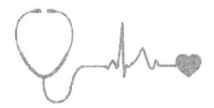

Joe Fortes is a fantastic steak and chophouse with a great bar on Robson Street. It's the best place for oysters on the half shell and top-shelf drinks, and my buddy Michael Khalili and I are frequent fliers there, so it rarely requires a reservation when we sneak in.

When I arrive right at seven p.m., I look around, but I don't think he's here yet. I find a table in the back of the bar, and the bartender smiles. Before the server can greet me, she has a glass of amber liquid headed my way.

"Nancy says you would like two fingers of the Johnnie Walker Blue and to tell you a dozen of the PEI oysters on the half shell are on their way," my server announces when she arrives. She sets the glass in front of me.

I should be embarrassed that the bartender knows my order, but I've come here at least once a week for over a decade, and if I had to bet, Nancy has worked here since Joe opened this place in 1985. I nod. "Nancy is right. Thank you. Let her know Michael is coming shortly."

She nods. "Anything else I can get you?"

"A tall glass of ice water would be great."

A few minutes later, I'm swirling the liquid in the glass

when Michael slides into the chair across from me. "Hey, man, how's it goin'?"

"Not too bad." I look up, and the server is placing a Shirley Temple in front of Michael. I snort a laugh.

"Get too drunk one time in the late nineties, and you never live it down." He shakes his head as he takes the drink and empties it in three gulps. He looks back to the server. "I'll have what he's having."

She nods and walks away.

"What's going on with you?" he asks. "I'm seeing this oh-so-hot nurse from pediatrics tonight for a quick round of hokey-pokey."

I look at him skeptically. "You should know better than to pee where you eat." Michael is an OB/GYN, also at Mercy.

He gives me an impish grin. "She just graduated from nursing school and needs some additional instruction."

"You're terrible. Mark my words, you're making a mistake. If she's young, she'll be a hanger-on, and since she works with you, you'll see her for years."

He shakes his head. "I deliver the babies, not take care of them. My goal is the mother, not the spawn." His drink arrives, and we raise our glasses in silent toast.

Michael and I grew up together. His family immigrated to Canada from Iran when he was three. His father owns several oil and gas companies around the world, and his mother wants him to marry a nice Iranian, preferably Persian, woman who will give her beautiful grandbabies to further the Khalili name. Michael likes his women blonde and only interested in his dick, not his bank account. And as soon as they seem to want anything more, he moves on to the next one.

"Anyway, what's new with you?"

"Not much." I'm not ready to tell him about finding Paisley, though I did tell him about that crazy night at Phillip's club. He'll never understand — hell, I don't even understand — and I don't want the ribbing.

The server returns with two more glasses of amber liquid. "These are from the women at the end of the bar." She sets the glasses in front of us.

Michael lights up and waves the women over.

"Hi! I'm Scarlett," a busty redhead says as she joins us at our table. "And this is my best friend, Toni." Toni has dark brown hair and eyes. She seems shy but has a friendly smile.

We chat for a minute, and both women are nice enough, but I find I'm more interested in the blonde who's now living in my extra apartment.

"What do you do for a living?" Scarlett asks, looking between Michael and me.

"I work for Martin Communications," I offer. It's not totally off the mark. I do sit on their board.

"You mean the cell phone stores?" she asks.

I internally chuckle. "Exactly."

They look over at Michael. "I do a little of this and that," he says with a shrug. "What do you do?"

"I'm an account manager at the Ford dealership, and Toni works for me." Scarlett leans in. "If you ever need a deal on a Ford truck, let us know. We can get you employee pricing."

"Really? That's awesome," Michael says.

I chuckle because Michael only drives very fast foreign sports cars. I usually rib him about compensating for his pencil dick.

My cell phone pings, and the receipt for the rideshare fare pops up. I rest a little easier knowing Paisley has made it home. Michael seems to be enjoying himself with these ladies, so I hang on a little while longer, but when the clock strikes nine, I stand. "Well, I have an early morning at the cell phone store."

"Which one do you work at?" Scarlett asks. "Maybe I can stop by and have you show me how to work my cell phone." Her eyes twinkle as she looks at me.

"I'm at the one in Mercy Hospital."

She gives me a flirty look and arches her back, making sure her breasts are well showcased. "See you soon, handsome."

I get my car and drive back to my condo, thinking about Paisley. I need to keep it professional. Her sister is my patient. And she doesn't seem all that interested anyway, though part of me is still convinced there's something worth exploring there. Maybe it's not the right time. Or maybe I just don't like rejection.

When I get inside, I drop my keys on the counter and turn to see Paisley standing in the doorway between our units. She wears a look of surprise that I'm sure mirrors my own.

Chapter 8

Paisley

In my exploration of this apartment, I realized there's a door in the kitchen that seems to connect it to another unit. The owners', I'm guessing. So I've been listening carefully for noise in the main condo. Since I'm their guest, I wanted to introduce myself and thank them for being so kind to allow me to stay and for filling the fridge with so much food.

When I discovered the door between the units was unlocked, I fought the urge to snoop. That was a colossal task. Instead, I just left the door ajar so I could hear them come home.

When I heard the elevator ping and the light turned on, I came to the doorway, looked into the kitchen of the other condo, and was floored to see Dr. Martin standing there.

"Are you the owner of the apartment where I'm staying?"

He looks like a deer in the headlights. "Umm, yes. I am."

"Why didn't you tell me?" *Does he do this all the time?*

He sighs. "I didn't think you'd say yes if you knew it was my place."

My shoulders fall. A part of me is furious that he didn't tell me, but he's probably right. I never would have allowed myself to stay in *his* condo. But after I said yes, he could have told me.

"Do you host people in your extra apartment all the time?"

He shakes his head. "I've had a few friends stay, but I've never done this before. Not once."

My blood runs cold. Just what does he expect from me? Is this because of our night at The Lion's Den? "Why would you be so nice to us?"

"Like I told you before, I want you stress free to take care of your sister."

"Yes, but this…" He stands expectantly, waiting for me to finish, but I don't know why I'm arguing. I have no better option right now. "Okay," I say instead. I turn to head back to my apartment. "Thank you. I'll stay out of your way."

He rushes over. "Wait. That's not what I want. Actually, quite the opposite. But that can wait until your sister gets better. Really. You're not a bother at all. In fact, I think I like you being here when I get home." His words tumble out quickly, and then his eyes search mine.

I see a need there, but I can't identify it. Is it sexual? I told him that wasn't really me that night at The Lion's Den, but maybe he doesn't understand—or doesn't care. He's seen the reality of my life now. Does he think I owe him? This man with his chiseled jaw, dark curly hair, and killer brown eyes can't want someone like me—an unemployed high school graduate who's barely keeping it together. But I'm not a whore, so I need to give him what he wants some other way. "Do you want a housekeeper? I'm a decent cook, and I know how to clean."

His eyes widen. "No, no. I don't want you to do those things. You have plenty on your plate already. This arrangement is supposed to make your life simpler, so you can focus on Arabella."

"But how will I ever pay you back?"

"I don't expect you to pay me back. Look around, Paisley. I need nothing. I'm happy to have this opportunity to share with you."

I drop my shoulders. This is too good to be true. Not real. I'll have to keep my guard up, but I force a smile. "Okay. Thank you again."

He nods and seems nervous again. That's certainly different than the way he was at The Lion's Den.

"You mentioned you like to run," he says. "How about tomorrow morning we go for a run along the sea wall? Depending on how far you like to go, we can do a three- or five-mile loop down toward Canada Place. It's good people-watching as the cruise passengers wander with their cameras."

I have to chuckle at that. "They do have a look about them that's pretty funny, like a neon sign that glows *tourist*."

"Or if you prefer, we can run toward Stanley Park. We'd turn back at the aquarium or go all the way to Lions Gate Bridge. You tell me."

"I don't think I can do all that. But what if we run along the sea wall to the point and back? That's maybe a mile and a half each way."

"That works. I'll want to do rounds at the hospital around eight. We can leave about six. Would that work for you?"

I nod.

"Good."

"Okay, well, I guess I'll see you in the morning." I wave and turn back to my apartment, closing the door behind me. I have no idea how to explain this. I should call and discuss it with Lucy, but I really need to give my mother the update on Arabella. It's late morning, if she's still in the South Pacific, so I call her cell phone.

"Hello?" she singsongs in greeting.

"Hello, Mom."

"Darling, it's so wonderful to hear from you."

Since when? I'm guessing this means she's not alone. So I'll cut right to the chase. "As you know, Arabella got sick a couple nights ago, and the emergency doctor decided to do the surgery to repair her heart."

"Oh, that's nice," she says.

Now I know she's not alone. "They had to crack her chest open because you turned down the surgery five years ago. The hole was over ten millimeters, and the repair required three shunts."

"I'm so glad she's doing well."

"Well? Who said she's doing well? She came through the surgery, but she's still in a medically induced coma. She has a lot of healing to do. And Dr. Bartlett was really weird about the whole thing. She's more interested in herself than Arabella."

"That's fantastic."

What on earth is going on with her? "Is it? I don't think you've processed a word I've told you. Is this a joke to you?"

"Great news. Continue to keep me posted, okay?"

Then it hits me. Arabella and I don't fit the narrative she's created for herself. She doesn't want to be part of what's happening with us, so why am I trying to include her? She's not contributing anything at this point.

"No, this is my last call," I tell her. "We needed you, but instead, you're where *you* want to be, with us out of sight and out of mind. I can see now you've made your choice, so I'm done trying. You can be as self-centered as you want. Arabella and I don't want to do this anymore."

I hang up.

Tears sting my eyes. She doesn't even call back and pretend like we were disconnected. Nothing is crueler than finding out your only remaining parent doesn't love you.

My tears continue to fall as I crawl into bed. I don't know I'll ever explain our mother's choices to Arabella — if she makes it through this. That's what I really needed to talk to my mother about. I'm scared. Arabella's not strong, and I don't know what's going to happen.

Again, I consider calling Lucy. She would have been a better choice than my mother, it seems. But it's late, and I can't let myself dwell on what life would be like without my sister. She's only ten, but she's the light of my world. I can't imagine not seeing her every day, hearing her laugh again. Everything feels so surreal right now. I look around this beautiful bedroom, and my mind drifts to Davis and why he's being so generous. Though he seems kind, I'm still waiting for the other shoe to drop. I've likely gotten myself into yet another messy situation.

I lie down and try to sleep, but my mind bounces between my sister, my narcissistic mother, and Dr. Martin. I feel like I'm never going to get any rest, but then my alarm wakes me at ten minutes to six.

I groan. Why did I agree to run this morning?

I drag myself to the bathroom to wash my face and pull my hair into a high ponytail. Then I put on a pair of leggings, a sports bra, and a long sleeve T-shirt. At six o'clock, I open the door between our units, and Dr. Martin is standing in the kitchen, dressed and ready to run.

He looks down at my feet. "Those runners look like they have about two hundred too many miles on them."

They do look pretty sad. I shrug. "I'll get a new pair eventually. These are nice and broken in."

"Don't let my buddy Steve hear you say that. He's an orthopedist and would tell you otherwise."

I roll my eyes. "Well, when you're a rich doctor, you can afford new shoes several times a year. I'm neither a rich nor a doctor, so I do the best I can."

He raises his hands in surrender and has the decency to look a little embarrassed. "Fair enough," he says. "Let's get out there before it gets too busy."

We take the elevator down, and I feel a little nervous. What have I gotten myself into? "Do you mind if we stretch before we go?"

He nods. "I insist on it, and you can set the pace. I don't want to push you too hard."

My shoulders relax. "If I'm too slow, you can go on

ahead. I can find my way back, and I have my key."

"Let's just see how this goes." The elevator doors open, and Dr. Martin stops at the front desk to introduce me to the security guard. "She has full access to my apartment through the front or back."

The guard nods, and we continue out to the front of the building. I'm impressed as I watch him stretch his hamstrings. After a few minutes, I feel more ready for this run.

"Ready?" he asks.

I nod.

Dr. Martin opens his arms. "After you."

"Thank you, Dr. Martin." I trot off, and he runs alongside me, guiding us down through the streets that lead to the sea wall. I have to admit, it does feel great to run again. It's been a few weeks.

"You don't have to call me Dr. Martin when we're not at the hospital," he says after a few minutes. "In fact, you don't need to call me that there either. Please call me Davis."

I look down and nod. Again, I don't know what that means. "Okay."

"You have a sprinting pace," he adds after another block.

"I feel like I'm slow."

He shakes his head. "This is faster than I typically run."

"Oh, I'm sorry. You can set the pace then."

He smiles. "I like the competition. You keep going."

"I may slow down as we hit the two-mile mark. I haven't gone running in a few weeks, and I didn't sleep well."

"Why not?" he asks. "Was the bed too firm?"

"No! Not at all. I just have a lot on my mind." He nods, and I hope that comment is self-explanatory, but after a moment, he looks over at me again.

"Anything I can help with? I know you're concerned about your sister, but we're doing everything we can."

"I know," I assure him. "I'm trying to be patient about that. I called my mom last night to give her the news about

Arabella. She was with someone, and she couldn't or wouldn't step away, so we didn't even have a real conversation. I finally told her I wasn't going to call anymore."

"I'm sorry to hear that."

"I think it's probably for the best. I don't want to burden you with my drama, but let's just say it's been Arabella and me for the last three years, and it will continue to be that way. And we'll get along just fine."

"I can tell Arabella adores you," he says. "She worries about you."

"You think so? I hope not. She's too young to deal with so much."

"What about your friend you were out with at The Lion's Den?"

I smile. "That's my best friend, Lucy. She's been my strength since my sister was born with her heart defect. Like I told you, she had to talk me into going out that night. It had been a long time since I'd done anything for me."

"I'm glad she did."

I glance at Davis and find perspiration is making his shirt stick to his skin, showing his very defined chest. But I try to block that from my thoughts. "Would you mind if she came over to the apartment and had dinner with me? I promise we won't laugh too loud."

"Knock yourself out. It's your place. You can do what you want."

"Thanks. I'll organize a kegger then."

He chuckles. "If you want."

"I don't know enough people to invite to something like that, so I'll keep it to a bottle of wine with Lucy."

We run down the seawall and around the small marina, coming out the other side of Stanley Park. It's full of walkers, other runners, bike riders, and the occasional rollerblader. I'm glad to be out this morning. It rained last night, and the air is crisp.

"Tell me about your parents," I say to Davis.

He sighs, breathing hard. "My father was very much about his work when I was growing up. I have three brothers. I'm a middle child, which is great because I never wanted to work in the family business. My oldest brother is going to take over when my father finally retires."

"That must be a relief."

He nods. "Yes. My mother is the glue that keeps us all together. She is incredible. She worked hard to make sure we had a normal life and pushed us so we didn't become too complacent. She didn't have a paying job, but she's a professional volunteer. She gets asked to sit on all kinds of nonprofit boards and run fundraisers. The night you and Arabella came into the ER, she was being honored as a volunteer of the year."

I envy their support for one another. "It's nice that she's recognized for all her hard work."

He nods again. "What do you do besides run and take care of your sister?"

"These days I seem to be great at looking for new jobs and fighting with the school."

He laughs. "I can help you find a better school that will be more willing to help manage her illness, and hopefully, it will become less of an issue for her over time."

I don't know what to say to that, so I just smile.

"What would you do if you could do anything?" he asks next.

I do have an answer for that one. "If money wasn't an object, I'd sculpt."

"Like with clay or marble?"

"I enjoy mixed materials. I once did a whole series using natural wood and metal. That was probably my most successful project. I even sold one of those pieces at a gallery."

"Why aren't you doing more? Does the gallery not want more?"

"Well, it takes money, and I don't have enough to even

buy the supplies."

He stops and puts his hands on his knees a moment. "You have a talent, and you're short on funds. Does the gallery know this? I'm sure they'd front you the cash."

"How do you know I have talent? For all we know, the buyer bought it to melt the silver down. But the gallery never said anything to me. It was a student show and just a fluke that my piece sold."

We hit our midway point and turned around to go back. Now, it feels like we're salmon swimming upstream, and we dodge the oncoming walkers, runners, and bikers to get back to the path that will take us to Davis' building.

When we arrive at the building, I walk in circles with my hands on my hips to cool down. I take big gulps of air as my heart slowly finds its regular beat and my lungs burn less.

"Tomorrow morning, it should be a little easier for you."

I laugh. "Maybe for you too. We can go toward Canada Place."

He laughs. "It's a date."

He says that with so much confidence that I almost fall over. Is that actually what he meant? Before I can decide if I want to ask, he speaks again.

"Come on. We need to get to the hospital. I want to check on your sister before the two surgeries I have scheduled today."

I follow him inside. "Don't let me slow you down. If you need to get to the hospital, just go. I can walk or get a rideshare."

"My rounds aren't until eight, so we have time." The elevator arrives, and we ride up. "Let's meet in an hour," he says when the doors open on our floor. "Would that work?"

"I'll be ready."

As I head toward my apartment, he calls, "Leave your shoes here so you don't mark up the floor."

I jump. "Of course."

I should have thought of that. I quickly toe out of my shoes and race inside to the bathroom. I have an hour, but I want to blow dry my hair this morning. Otherwise, with the humidity, it will stay damp all day.

Chapter 9

Paisley

Fifty-five minutes later, I'm showered and dressed, and I've packed a lunch, snacks, and dinner, along with my computer and tablet so I'll have plenty to keep me busy while sitting at Arabella's side. I'm not leaving until they make me. And if we're lucky, she'll be stronger today and they can ease the medications so she can wake up. I miss her so much.

When I step into the hallway, Davis is standing at his door, ready to go. I stuff the last of my things in my bag. "Are you sure you don't mind driving me? I'm really okay with figuring this out on my own."

The corners of his mouth turn upward. "We're going to the same place."

"Do you work a lot of Sundays?" I ask as we move toward the elevator.

"I'm on call six days a month. Otherwise, I work when I have surgeries and patients in the hospital, so it can change from week to week."

"Do you ever have patients to see in an office?"

"I'm a hospitalist, so I mostly see patients during

rounds. Most of my patients come to me in an emergency, but when it's determined that a child needs heart surgery, we schedule it, and I meet them in my office in the annex next door to the hospital. Once Arabella's released from the hospital, you'll go back to seeing your cardiologist."

We step into the elevator, and he looks over at me. He opens and shuts his mouth, then furrows his brow.

"What is it?"

"I'd like to recommend a different doctor for Arabella. Dr. Bartlett is good for certain pediatric cases, but I'd like to have you see someone who specializes in post-surgery care of ASD."

I nod. He's the expert, and I could certainly use some guidance. "Okay. We can do that. Do I need to tell Dr. Bartlett when she comes in today?"

"No. I'll have you meet with Dr. Cavanaugh, and you can make sure she's a good fit for you first."

"Thank you. Again, I owe you." I hate owing anyone, especially someone I don't have the foggiest idea how I can pay back. Arabella and I like to make cookies. Maybe we'll make him some of our favorites. I don't know.

He shakes his head as we exit the elevator in the parking garage. "You don't owe me anything, really."

We climb into his car, and I'm stunned when he drives onto a platform and barriers drop before we rise into the air.

"Is this a car elevator?"

He grins like a little schoolboy. "Don't tell anyone. I know the view is spectacular, but the car elevator is why I bought in this building."

I throw my head back and laugh. "That's hilarious."

He smiles. "You really should laugh more."

I blush. "I haven't had a lot to laugh about recently. Thank you."

Traffic is mercifully light on our ride over to the hospital, and when we arrive, he parks in his spot and we walk in together. He splits off to go to his office, and I walk directly up to see Arabella in the intensive care unit.

The nurse greets me with a smile.

"How did she do last night?" I ask.

"She continues to improve," the nurse reports.

I feel tension I didn't realize I was holding rush out of my shoulders. "Do you think Dr. Martin will wake her up today?"

She smiles again. "If not today, certainly soon."

That doesn't tell me much of anything, but maybe I'll get a more direct answer from Dr. Martin—Davis, I guess—when he comes by. I get comfortable in the chair next to Arabella's bed and tell her what I've done since leaving her yesterday.

"Bells, I know it sucks that Mom is in love and sailing around the South Pacific, but maybe she'll show up when typhoon season hits." I tell her about my run this morning and the encouraging words from Dr. Martin about my art and how that's got me thinking about creating something again.

Then I get to the minutia. "Let's see... I got a free pass for Netflix, so we can watch all kinds of things while you recover. That should be fun once you're awake. And I have some—"

"Good morning." Dr. Martin waves hello to me and introduces the two residents he has with him. Then he turns his attention back to them. "What can you tell me about Arabella Brooks?"

The woman stands tall. "Arabella Brooks, ten-year-old female presenting with ASD. Following an intracardiac echocardiography, transcatheter closure was not an option given the change in size over time of the hole between her left and right atrium. Instead, a Gore Cardioform Septal Occluder was placed, along with three left-to-right shunts." She goes on to rattle off the medications and the reason for the prolonged medically induced coma.

Dr. Martin nods.

The male resident looks at me with a compassionate

smile. "She's a loved sister, and she's fighting hard to get better," he says. "We're watching for pericardial effusion, device embolization, and cardiac thrombus. At this time, there are no indications of any of those issues. However, her blood pressure is on the low side of normal, and we're seeing some continued indications of atrial arrhythmia. She'll need to be removed from the coma within the next forty-eight hours if she's going to sustain the repair in her heart."

I look at Dr. Martin, my eyes big. That was a lot of medical jargon, but it didn't sound great.

"That's correct," he says. "But her body is stronger today. Arabella is a fighter." Dr. Martin checks his computer and then examines Arabella's breathing tube and takes her vitals. He turns to me. "She's doing great. Her vitals have improved significantly, and the atrial arrhythmia is normal as the heart adjusts to its new rhythm."

The residents walk out of Arabella's curtain, and Dr. Martin turns to me before he follows. "I'm not kidding, Paisley. She's doing great. Students were more clinical than they should be, but they just lack experience. Soon, we'll bring her out. I know she can do it. Oh, and Dr. Cavanaugh will be by shortly. I think you'll like her."

I nod. "Thank you," I choke out as he disappears.

I feel numb. Here I was thinking about my art and talking about the fun I'm having with Davis. But this isn't the time for any of that. I need to focus on Arabella. She needs my undivided attention.

I also need to look for a job. I open my computer and start sifting through the various listing sites. The positions I'm qualified for that actually pay well are all out of reach, for one reason or another: I can't take work on a cargo ship and be gone for months at a time. This is where Annabelle's doctors are, so I can't leave Vancouver. I can't work jobs that have extended hours, because there's no one to be with Arabella. I can't work on the oil sands in Alberta and be away for three weeks and then back for one. Working for McDonalds isn't enough to pay our bills, and they don't offer a flexible schedule anyway.

I sigh in frustration. I'd have so many more options if only I had help.

I look up when a petite woman with long, dark braids enters our curtain in the ICU. She's wearing dark pants and a lab coat over a bright, floral-print blouse. She smiles and extends her hand. "Hello, you must be Paisley Brooks. I'm Dr. Sydney Cavanaugh."

Her voice has a Caribbean lilt to it, and her friendly demeanor puts me immediately at ease.

"Hello. Yes, I'm Paisley, and this is my sister, Arabella."

She opens her computer. "Dr. Martin has walked me through the surgery and what led you to have the ASD repair done later than normal."

I sigh. "I think my mom really thought it would repair itself."

She nods. "Arabella is doing fantastic. She's not showing any signs of rejection, and late complications are unusual. My philosophy is going to be close monitoring of her heart with echocardiograms and watching her diet—lots of iron. We also need to get her into some therapy—possibly in the pool—and activities to not only strengthen her heart but also work her lungs."

I nod. "Did Dr. Martin tell you when he was going to wake her up?"

"We've been talking about it, but I'll leave that to him. He has my opinion."

"Okay, what do I need to do about Dr. Bartlett?"

"If you're okay with the change, we'll put the paperwork through," she says. "You shouldn't have to worry about it."

I'm relieved, but I manage to nod politely, instead of hugging her like I suddenly want to. "Thank you."

I go back to looking for work, and after I eat lunch, I

continue reading the Harry Potter series to Arabella. We've read them before, but she really enjoys them. I only leave her side to use the restroom a time or two.

As the sun starts to go down, I prepare to have the nursing staff move me along. Instead, the next time the curtain parts, Dr. Martin steps in. "How did she do today?"

I stuff my e-reader in my bag. "She's been sleeping peacefully."

He checks his computer. "Her vitals have improved, and we haven't seen any atrial arrhythmia today. I'm going to give her tonight and tomorrow morning to continue resting, and then we'll bring her around. How does that sound?"

A wave of joy passes over me. "That sounds wonderful. And you think she's strong enough?"

He nods. "She'll need to stay longer in the hospital, but yes, her heart continues to beat well and her lungs are progressing, so we should be good. I'll have Dr. Cavanaugh here with us as we reduce her medication so we can all work together. But she's doing great. We have to have faith."

I once again stifle the urge to hug the doctor in the room, and I do a little happy dance. But I stay in my seat, so hopefully, it's not too crazy. "Thank you so much. I'm looking forward to having her back with me. Can I stay with her tonight?"

He shakes his head. "How about we go find some dinner and get you a good night's sleep? We can talk about what you can expect over the next few weeks and months of her recovery."

I look around the room, unsure about leaving. "I have a sandwich I made for dinner."

"You can save that for tomorrow." He crosses his arms. "You have ten minutes to get your things together, or I'll be carrying you out over my shoulder." My eyes widen, and he leans in. "I'm not kidding."

I sigh. I guess I'm going. "Where do you want me to meet you? At the base of the elevators again?"

"I can meet you back here, and we'll walk out together." He stands straight. "Maybe if you're with me, I'll get out of here without being harassed too much."

I nod. "Ten minutes. I can do it."

He turns and leaves, and I quickly organize and pack up my things. I don't want to leave anything behind. "Bells, I'll be back in the morning. I can't wait to hear your beautiful voice tomorrow. I'll be here as early as they'll let me and plan to stay all day. I'm so excited to hug you."

I give her a kiss on the forehead and hear Dr. Martin behind me. "Are you ready?"

I squeeze Arabella's hand and pick up my bag. "As ready as I'll ever be."

We walk out, and Dr. Martin begins explaining the process of how they'll remove Arabella's ventilator, reduce her medication, and watch her vital signs. "It could take several hours or even a day or two for her to be fully awake," he says. "We're not going to rush it."

He nods to a few people along the way, but as he predicted, being deep in conversation as we travel through the hospital keeps him from being waylaid. When we get to his car, he loads my bag into the storage area and opens the door for me. I've never known such a gentleman. It's a little shocking.

"What would you like for dinner?" he asks once he's in the car next to me.

"I don't have a ton of cash, so something easy and cheap."

He frowns and purses his lips. "I invited you to dinner. I'll pay. What are you in the mood for? Steak and lobster? Oysters? Indian? Sushi?"

I haven't had sushi for so long. "Sushi would be great."

"I know just the place." Davis exits the hospital, weaves his way through downtown, and not very far from his condo, he pulls up at a valet stand. "I've locked your bag in a compartment where it will be safe," he assures me.

I don't know what to say or do. The valet opens the door, so I get out. Davis quickly rounds the car and extends his hand to me, and for some reason, it feels perfectly natural to take it, even though that means we're holding hands and walking into a high-end Japanese restaurant looking like a couple.

He squeezes my hand and whispers, "I've got this. Enjoy, and let me spoil you."

Again, I'm not sure what to do, so I just smile and follow his lead. When we walk in, the sushi chefs all yell, "Irasshaimase!"

That puts a wide smile on my face.

The hostess seats us in a back corner, and I'm surprised when Davis puts his back to the restaurant and sits across from me.

Immediately, our server arrives with green tea. "Welcome back, Dr. Martin."

"Thank you, Jade. This is my friend Paisley."

She bows slightly. "Welcome. Would you like to see the menu?"

Davis looks at me. "What won't you eat?"

I think for a moment. "I'm not crazy about sea urchin or raw squid, but they may make it in a way I'll enjoy." I shrug. "I'll eat anything you put in front of me."

Davis' eyes turn darker for a moment, and I realize what I've said. I look down at my lap and try not to turn forty shades of purple.

Davis clears his throat. "We'll take the Miku aburi dinner."

"Outstanding. I'll let the chefs know." She disappears.

"What did you order?" I ask.

"Aburi-style sushi are pieces of fish seared with a butane torch. My favorite here is the surf and turf—grilled lobster wrapped in seared beef. It's outstanding. But tonight, the chefs will make what they want for us. Jade will tell them our preferences, and we are in for a treat.

"Okay." I nod approvingly. "I don't think I've had aburi-style sushi before. I usually visit the restaurants that have little conveyor belts or cups floating in the water and you pick up the sushi as it passes by."

"Those are good too." He adjusts the napkin on his lap. "How was your day?"

"I applied for a few jobs, but we'll see if any of them call me back. It will not be easy finding something flexible enough that I can take Arabella to appointments. I think I may end up doing temp work."

He nods. "You're going to need a nurse that lives with you in the apartment for the first few weeks."

Fear grips me. "I can't afford that."

He shakes his head. "It's all covered by our provincial health coverage. I'll write it up, and I spoke with someone today who's available. It will be great for you to have someone with medical expertise there around the clock. Arabella has had a pretty extensive surgery. She'll need more care than you can provide."

I breathe out a rush of air. "This is so much. I'm grateful you're here to hold my hand through this."

"Literally." He gives me a wink, and I smile in return, though that starts up the little voice in my head that wonders what he's ultimately going to want from me in exchange for all this.

Our first course arrives, distracting me from my wayward thoughts, and we enjoy a toasted piece of salmon with a sliver of a jalapeno on top. I follow Davis' lead with soy and wasabi, and we both eat with our fingers. It tastes so good.

"I could eat this every night," I exclaim.

"This is only the first of seven courses. Wait until you see what else is coming."

My eyes are wide. "Seven courses? I don't know if I can eat that much."

Davis leans back in his chair and pats his stomach. "I've

got you covered."

The voice in my head stays mostly quiet, and we have fun over dinner. I eat much more than I expected. I'm surprised at how comfortable I am with Davis. He lives in a different world than I do, but we seem to find plenty to talk about. And I know our chemistry is explosive—or at least it was for one night.

But I need to keep my mind focused on Arabella and her recovery, not anything else. And I need to keep my guard up in this crazy situation anyway.

As we're finishing the fourth or fifth course—I've lost count at this point—a woman approaches the table. "Davis?"

He looks up at her, seeming surprised. "Renee. It's nice to see you."

"I was just telling Bunny Stevens we didn't get to spend any time with you at your mother's celebr—"

"Please meet my date, Paisley Brooks," Davis interrupts her.

She takes a moment to look me up and down, then dismisses me. "I can't believe you didn't even see your mother get her award, and I thought I was going to get that dance you promised."

Davis doesn't respond to that, so she fills the silence by prattling on about people who must be in their circle of friends. She's dressed casually, but she has the look of refined money, not something my big sweater and jeans convey.

"I'm assuming you'll be at your mother's Toast for the Coast benefit for the Vancouver Aquarium later this month?" Renee asks. "She's talked me into a table, and I can save you a spot if you'd like."

"I think my mother would be upset if I wasn't at her table," he replies smoothly. "Maybe I'll see you there."

She looks over at me. "Sure."

Davis says nothing else, and I give her a small smile.

Then the server arrives and begins to explain the next course while Renee continues to stand next to the table. It's awkward.

Finally, she seems to decide it's time to move on. "Call me and let's grab some lunch," she says to Davis.

She sashays away, and my brows are in my hairline. "She has an actual set of balls on her, doesn't she?" Davis laughs, and I realize I've said that aloud. "I'm sorry. Sometimes, my inner voice becomes more vocal than it should."

He shakes his head, chuckling again. "Don't apologize. She feels more important than she actually is. Our mothers are friends. She used to date my older brother, and she's fishing for a husband, but it will never be me."

"No? You would look good together."

He tilts his head to the side. "I don't need a social-climbing bitch who only wants to spend my money."

"Okay." I'm a taken aback by his obvious resentment.

"I'm sorry. She's what my brothers and my friends and I call a *miner*."

I snort. "Ah, yes. She's looking for a rich husband. I love it."

I manage to stuff in at least a taste of the remaining two courses, and when we stand to leave, I feel a bit like a sausage. Every woman in the restaurant tracks Davis as he walks out. It reminds me of the night at The Lion's Den, and all over again, I wonder why he's choosing to hang out with me.

When we settle in his car, I turn to him. "When we walked out, I think a couple of women actually took your picture."

He shakes his head. "All I saw were the men staring at you."

I laugh. "Maybe to figure out why you'd be out with someone like me."

Davis' brow furrows. "You don't think you're beautiful?"

"I clean up okay, I guess, but I think I'm average. And I *like* being average."

He eyes me for a moment but seems to decide against saying anything. We make the short drive back to his building in silence. We pull into the garage, and the elevator takes us to his parking spot. We're walking toward his apartment before he speaks again.

"Paisley, once Arabella is released and transitions over to Dr. Cavanaugh, I was wondering if you'd be open to dating me." He turns to look at me in the elevator.

I turn toward him. "Dating? Why would you want to date me?" I can't believe I said that aloud. "I mean, I'm a hot mess. I have my sister to take care of, and if I'm lucky, I'll find a job."

"I like you. And you're not a hot mess, You're beauty under fire. I admire your dedication and everything you're doing for your sister, and despite what you think, you're far from average. You are exquisite. My feelings about that aspect of you should have been clear since the night we met."

He pauses until I meet his eyes. I've probably blushed fuchsia at this point. "If you're open to dating, we can go at whatever speed you'd like—and only after your sister's care has transitioned over to Dr. Cavanaugh. I certainly don't want to make anything awkward or do anything that might compromise her recovery."

I look down for a moment and take a deep breath. My mind is whirling. I need to buy some time. "Okay, well, thank you. You've certainly given me a lot to think about." I don't want him to think I'm not interested, though. I most certainly am—I think. My *body* is, but I need to be sure this is a smart choice. I need to be focused on what Arabella needs. "Does that mean we shouldn't go running in the morning?"

The elevator doors open, and he steps out. "I definitely want to go running. In fact, wait just one second..." He opens the door to his apartment and steps inside. He returns holding a box and hands it to me. "I got these for you. My buddy says this is the best brand for running."

My eyes narrow. "Is this why you wanted me to take

my shoes off and leave them by the door?"

"I'll never tell." He grins, and I can only shake my head.

"You're pretty crafty."

"I need you in good shape to take care of your sister." He shrugs. "Tomorrow morning, I'll meet you at six right here."

I nod. "Okay. I'll be wearing my new shoes."

He winks and walks away, and when the door closes behind him, I kind of wish he'd kissed me. As it is, this hardly seems real. But I also know my brain is scrambled enough, and kissing him wouldn't have helped that. It's good that we can't jump into anything right away. That way I can figure out for sure what this is, so I don't end up looking like a fool.

I pull my cell phone from my bag and find I've missed a call from my mom. No, thanks.

Chapter 10

Davis

I had to take a shower and rub one out before going to bed last night. Otherwise, I never would have slept. I can't tell exactly what Paisley is thinking about my dating proposal, but I know I can win her over. I know we could be great together, if I can just get her to see our potential and to see herself the way I see her. She's gorgeous, and so real and funny, and the poor woman just needs a break. She's worked so hard for so long that she doesn't even realize it. She's focused on giving, rather than getting, which is a refreshing change from so many of the people I know. It makes me want to do everything I can for her.

I had a voicemail on my phone last evening that was an earful from Jeannie Bartlett because she rightly guessed that I'd had something to do with transferring her patient over to Dr. Cavanaugh. I have no regrets, though. What she did with Arabella is unconscionable. I'm pretty sure the reason Arabella hadn't had the surgery is that Dr. Bartlett was trying to hold off until she has her surgical privileges back at the hospital. She wanted to do the surgery herself. That feels like malpractice to me, and if she pushes, I'll have to report it. But I need to talk to the head of pediatric cardiology and get his take on the situation first. Fortunately, having Dr. Cavanaugh involved now gives me hope that Arabella is going to live a long and fruitful life, regardless of how the beginning of her treatment was bungled.

I pull on my running clothes and lace up my shoes. When I step out into the hallway, Paisley is already bouncing on the balls of her feet. "These are fantastic."

I smile. "Don't leave me in the dust."

"I may make you chase me."

"I'm already doing that, but at least when we run, I'm guaranteed to enjoy the view."

She blushes.

We have another great run, and I enjoy the view several times, but mostly we run next to each other, keeping a steady pace. After we return to the condo, we agree to meet in an hour to drive in to the hospital together.

I find myself a little giddy as I shower. It's as if the prospect of dating her has opened up a place in my heart I didn't know existed. And when Paisley walks out to meet me in the hallway, she takes my breath away. Without a stich of makeup, her skin is flawless, and I want to run my hands all over her. Her black jeans hug every curve, and the red blouse she's wearing offers a hint of cleavage, a tantalizing reminder of what I know lies beneath that fabric. I've never been like this with a patient's guardian before, but there is nothing at all usual about this situation. Everything with her has happened out of order, but I wouldn't trade any of it. I just have to bide my time for now.

When we arrive at the hospital, she heads directly in to see Arabella, and I go to my office. As I enter the suite, the head of pediatric cardiology, Eric Silver, approaches. I can tell he's been waiting for me, and I'm pretty sure I know why.

"I understand you suggested the Brooks family change doctors for Arabella's continuing care."

Just as I expected. Dr. Bartlett is nothing if not predictable. "Yes, I did. Jeannie has been their physician since Arabella was six months old. She's now ten, and nothing had been attempted for repair. Dr. Bartlett seems to have initially convinced the girl's mother that the ASD would repair itself. I understand waiting until she was two years old, but beyond that doesn't make sense. The hole was very clearly not closing on its own. It has actually reached ten millimeters and had torn, preventing a percutaneous closure. When I operated, Arabella was close to complete heart failure. In my opinion, Dr. Bartlett's continued delay of the surgery was malpractice, and I will swear to that in any deposition the family brings. You can look at the film from the surgery. We recorded it."

He rubs his temple. "I see. Have the film sent to me and try not to siphon any more of her patients away."

I shake my head. "I'll do it again if I see something like this. Eric, it's important that the hospital is prepared. She's a real danger to her patients. She doesn't even have the surgical privileges to help them right now."

"You know we can't go through her charts unless we have a court order."

"I do, so my recommendation is that we put together a discovery letter for the College of Physicians and Surgeons of BC. They serve the public by licensing all of us. She shouldn't be practicing medicine in this hospital or anywhere else."

"You know we can't do that. The liability alone would kill us."

My anger flares, but I don't say any of the things I'd like to. "Look at the film and decide about going to the CPS of BC," I suggest calmly. "This was malpractice."

"She said the family didn't want the surgery." He doesn't look at me, likely because he knows this excuse won't hold water.

I snort. "Did she also tell you they had it scheduled once, when Arabella was five, and then her father passed away? They had to postpone, but Arabella's sister says she called repeatedly to try to reschedule and brought it up at every visit."

"Okay. I'll look into it." He turns and walks down the hallway, and I sit behind my desk. In a few strokes, I send the video of Arabella's surgery over to him, and then I review her chart. She continues to be stable, so I think that means we're ready to bring her out of the coma. I'm lost in thought when my residents knock on my door, ready for rounds.

I stand. "Let's get Arabella Brooks back with us."

We walk and talk. They give me her vitals and report how she did overnight—things I already know, but they're required to know. "They removed the intubation, and she's breathing on her own," says Dr. Miller, one of my residents. "Dr. Cavanaugh is with the pulmonologist, and they're happy."

When we reach Arabella's curtain, Paisley is sitting close to her sister, but out of the way while Dr. Cavanaugh and Dr. Reed, the pulmonologist, conference. She has her arms wrapped around herself and is chewing on a fingernail. The residents step into the room first, and Paisley immediately turns to them.

"What does that indicate?" She points to a machine that is beeping.

"That will monitor Arabella's breathing as the medication keeping her sedated is reduced," Dr. Miller says. "A machine has been breathing for her, so we're going to carefully watch her progress for a few days."

"That's correct." I give Paisley a nod as I step into the room as well. "Let's see how she's doing this morning." I step around to Arabella's bed and read through the notes.

"As Dr. Miller mentioned, we're ready to bring Arabella out of her sedation, so we're decreasing the meds." I turn to Paisley. "She'll slowly regain consciousness. It could take twenty minutes or twenty hours, and chances are she'll open her eyes and go back to sleep almost immediately. There's nothing to worry about."

Paisley nods, but I can tell she's nervous.

We reduce the medication, and nothing happens. The machines monitoring Arabella's heart rate continue to beep. Dr. Reed and Dr. Cavanaugh excuse themselves to attend to other patients.

"That's anticlimactic," Paisley sighs.

I chuckle. "I suppose you're right. It may take some time. We're going to finish our rounds, and then I have surgery all afternoon. But I'll be checking in, and the nurses will monitor the situation. Just keep doing what you did with her yesterday—talk to her, read to her. That will help."

"Okay."

I'd love to sit with Paisley for a few minutes and help her feel more comfortable about this. I wish she didn't have to be alone all the time. But I have a schedule to keep and a pack of residents following me around, not to mention professional boundaries to keep in place right now, so there's nothing I can do.

My patients are doing well, but I still feel unsettled when I've finished rounding with the residents, so I head back to my office and call the one person who can help me.

"Hey, Dad," I say when he answers.

"Davis! We missed you for dinner again last night. What has you calling on a beautiful Monday? Shouldn't you be in surgery or on a golf course?"

"I have a feeling you're on a golf course."

"I just finished thirty-six holes," he tells me. "Your mother beat me both rounds."

I laugh. If anyone else were to beat him, he'd be irate, but he loves that my mom can beat him at golf.

"I have a surgery in a little over an hour, but listen, I need a background on someone."

"Is it a love interest?" my mother asks over the speakerphone.

"Possibly. She's someone who's interesting. Her name is Paisley Brooks."

Men of Mercy: Doctor of the Heart

I give them the information I have. I have the address from the apartment we visited to get her clothes, and I used Arabella's records I check spelling of their parents' names. I've been burned before, and if I'm going to potentially be involved with Paisley, I need to make sure this isn't the same thing.

"You should have the initial by this afternoon, and Felix will have the rest of it to you in three days," Dad confirms.

"I'm looking for details on her parents, her debt, and general information to compare to what she's said to me."

"Sounds good."

"Davis, what did you say her name was?" Mom asks.

"Paisley Brooks."

"Could there be more than one Paisley Brooks in Vancouver?" she muses.

"I don't think so. There aren't any Paisleys on social media."

"Do you remember Isla Farrow, my art buyer?"

The hair on the back of my neck stands on end. "She's the one who found you the driftwood-dipped-in-silver sculpture."

"Davis, how did you remember that?"

"Paisley has mentioned she was a sculptor and talked about that series."

"Do you think she targeted you?" my father asks.

I think about it for a moment. In my heart of hearts, I don't believe this background check is going to turn up anything other than what Paisley has told me is the truth. But I also can't stop myself from making sure. "No, Dad. I don't. I just didn't put the two things together until now."

"I'd love to meet her," Mom not-so-subtly hints.

"Maybe for a Sunday night dinner sometime. We'll see. Right now, her younger sister is my patient."

"I know Isla would like to meet her, too."

"I'll keep that in mind." That woman is relentless.

"Thanks for your help, Dad. You two enjoy your day."

I head off to prepare for my surgery, stopping by the nurses' station to check on Arabella on the way. Her vitals continue to strengthen, which is a good sign.

Then I change into my surgical gear, scrub, and start the day's work.

My first patient is a sixteen-year-old with congenital heart disease, and once the procedure is underway, I realize he needs a triple bypass. This is more complicated than what we'd initially planned, so my second surgery gets transferred to another surgeon.

It is eight o'clock by the time I've finished and made sure the patient is stable. I am dead on my feet, not to mention starving, but all I can think about is checking on Arabella.

When I walk into the ICU, I can hear the faint murmur of Paisley's voice. She's reading again. I check the charts. Arabella was awake for about twenty minutes earlier this afternoon and then again for almost an hour this evening. This is fantastic news.

I pull the curtain back, and Paisley's lying on the bed, reading to Arabella. Arabella's eyes are closed, but her head rests on Paisley's shoulder.

Paisley lights up as soon as she sees me. "She woke up! She was awake for a short time at first, but she talked to me and held my hand for a few minutes. Then she slept for a while and was awake again for almost an entire hour. Her throat is super sore. It makes talking hard."

I nod. "That happens after a tube is removed. That's very normal."

"She had a headache, but she said she felt strong."

"That all sounds normal. Have the nurses said anything about you being in bed with her?"

Paisley shakes her head. "Is that not allowed?"

I shrug. "We rarely like it because if we need to get to the patient, having someone in bed with them makes that hard. But maybe they thought the pros outweighed the cons in this case." I smile at her. "She probably won't wake again until tomorrow morning. Let's head back to the condo, and you can get some rest."

Disappointment clouds her eyes, and I understand, but she'll be better off sleeping in a room of her own. I go through the rest of my checks on Arabella as Paisley picks up her things. "I'll meet you downstairs in twenty minutes," I tell her when I've finished.

Paisley nods. "Okay."

I circle back for a final check on today's surgical patient and talk to his family for a moment before heading back to my office. I scrub my hand over my face as I start down the hallway, and when I arrive, I'm surprised to find Felix Pérez, head of security for Martin Communications, standing at the window in my office, waiting for me.

"What brings you here?" I ask as I close the door behind me.

"Your father said you wanted this." He hands me an envelope, and I pull out the paperwork. At first glance, it seems pretty standard.

"What has you concerned?" I ask.

He picks at a thread on his shirtsleeve. "You rarely ask this of women you're spending time with."

That's because I don't often spend much time with any one woman. I don't know how to explain things to Felix without violating even more of Paisley's privacy. "I moved her into the suite in my condo while her sister is in the hospital."

He nods. "She has a lot of debt and struggles to remain employed."

I nod. "Her father died a few years ago, and she had to drop out of school to take care of a sick younger sister. Her mother is no help, isn't even around."

Felix puts both his hands in his pockets and rocks from his heels to the balls of his feet.

"What aren't you telling me?" I ask.

"Her mother has been living down in Seattle for the last three years."

I look up, surprised. That's not what Paisley thinks or at least not what she's said. "What does that mean?"

"She's going to be trouble for you."

That means he feels like she's going to be interested in my money. "Does it seem like they have a relationship?" As far as I knew, they weren't speaking much, but maybe that's not the case.

"I don't think so. I'll have a bit more in a few days."

"Okay. Thank you." I stuff the report in my bag until I have time to go through it later.

Felix and I chat a little further as we walk to the elevator, and when we get to the main floor, I see Paisley staring out the window, watching the traffic on Burrard Street. Felix walks away as if we're strangers who happened to share the elevator.

She turns to me and smiles. "There you are. Thank you. Thank you for taking such good care of my sister. Even though she's still in the hospital, she's looking better than she has in a long time. I hope all your patients are doing so well."

I nod. "You're very welcome. Helping Arabella is my pleasure, and I believe I helped someone else with a troubled heart today too. Time will tell. For now, come on," I tell her. "Let's order takeout, and we can stream a movie or something."

She hardly stops talking as we work our way across town. She tells me all about her afternoon with her sister. Her enthusiasm and compassion wake something inside me that has been dead for a very long time. This reminds me of the real-life implications of the work I do. I've been lost in the technical details for a while, I think.

When we get back to my condo, she puts her things away and then comes through the door into the kitchen. We look through the takeout menus and decide on pizza from Luigi's—one with everything and one margherita.

"It's been so long since I've had good pizza." She rubs her hands together. "The frozen pizzas from the grocery store just aren't the same."

I smile and resist the urge to take her in my arms. "We can order pizza anytime you want."

As if she's read my mind, she leans over and squeezes me in a hug. "That's for taking such good care of me and Arabella."

I keep her close and softly brush my lips over hers. She stills but doesn't push me away. I kiss her again, and her mouth opens. She presses against me, and every ounce of blood in my body pools in one place.

I break away. "I don't want you to think that because I've helped your sister, you need to do this with me. I've thought about you since the first night we met, and the more I get to know you, the more wonderful you become."

"I… Thank you," she says. "Thank you for saying that. I really want to believe it's true." She shakes her head. "Even if it isn't, right now, I want this. Dammit, today has been incredible, and I want to celebrate a little." She gives me a look that short-circuits my brain.

I scoop her up and walk her back to my bedroom. I've never had a woman here, and I should be freaking out, but with Paisley, I'm not. I just want to enjoy my time with her for as long as she allows. I set her gently on her feet and fiddle with the buttons on her shirt, but my surgeon's hands are failing me. It isn't coming off. Paisley saves me by lifting it over her head, revealing a utilitarian bra. She drops it to the floor and crosses her arms over her breasts.

"You're beautiful. Don't hide from me." I kiss her belly and then nibble my way to her breasts. I couldn't really see them so well in the dark club, but now, I know they're perfect. A generous handful with small areolas and nipples, hard and wanting.

I need her out of her jeans yesterday. She unbuttons them and pushes them over her hips, hopping around until she's left in plain cotton panties with a little bow at the front.

The smell of her arousal encircles me, and I just stop and look at her for a moment.

"Am I the only one getting naked?" She crosses her arms over her middle.

I kiss her fiercely while pulling my pants off. I break away only long enough to pull my shirt over my head, and then I take her in my arms and walk her backwards toward the bed.

Chapter 11

Paisley

I have to admit, I feel like that girl at The Lion's Den again. And I didn't even need Lucy to get me there this time. I saw what Arabella's life could be—what *my* life could be—today. She's stronger already, and she just woke up. There's joy inside me that just needs to come out, and damn, if Davis doesn't look fucking incredible. I could never have imagined the brains and heart inside that beautiful package. This may all be too good to be true, but in this moment, I'm going for it.

I slide his underwear to the floor and look his manhood in the eye. The one-eyed monster is weeping, and I lean in to lick it off.

He even tastes delicious. I take him deep into my mouth, but he pulls back. Goose bumps prickle across my skin as his hands glide over me. He slides my panties down and leans me back.

His mouth finds my nipple while his fingers part my thighs and slide between the folds. "You're so wet."

"Is that a bad thing?"

"Never."

His finger circles my clit, and my back arches off the bed. I feel his mouth between my legs, his fingers still playing with my nipples. "I'm going to fuck you with my mouth."

His dirty talk sparks something in me, and with him French kissing my center and his hands roaming all over me, in no time, my orgasm explodes. When my vision clears, he's smiling down at me.

"That was a nice appetizer," he says. "Now, I'm ready for the meal."

He dives in again, and I grab the sheets to hold on as he pulls another climax from me. I'm ready to collapse when he leans over to his pants on the floor and pulls a condom from his wallet. "I have an entire box in the bathroom, but I think I'll need to restock." He smiles. "Are you good with this?"

I can feel myself blushing. "It may have seemed like I have a lot of experience when we met at the club, but I really don't."

He nods, positioning himself on his elbows as he nudges the head of his cock inside me. "I'll go slow."

He kisses me, and I can taste myself on his lips. I push my hips up to impale myself on his manhood. It pinches because he's so big.

"You're so tight," he growls.

Once he's fully inside me, he looks down at where our bodies connect. "That is pure beauty. One day, I'll take a picture of us like this."

I laugh. "Not likely."

He rocks in and out of me. He's so deep that I can feel the ridge of his cock hitting that special spot, and when his finger strums my clit, my orgasm hits me hard. I see black, then fireworks, then white light.

"Davis!" I yell. They can probably hear me in Seattle.

When I open my eyes, he's once again wearing a very satisfied smile.

"You're spoiling me," I gasp. "I don't think I've ever had this many orgasms in one night."

His chest puffs out with pride.

"I'm not selfish," I assure him. "What can I do for you?"

"No one would ever call you selfish," he agrees. "But get on your hands and knees and show me that ass."

I get on all fours and look back at him as he strokes his length and caresses my ass. Lining himself up, he pushes in, and the new position gives him a different feel. Holding on to my hips, he pivots in and out.

"You feel so good inside me," I breathe.

For a few minutes, the only sound is our flesh slapping together until he hisses my name and collapses on top of me, gasping for air. "Damn, aren't you a sexy minx?"

I suppress a snort. Somehow, he makes me feel that way, it seems. "I don't think any of my past boyfriends would tell you that."

"Give me their names, and I'll let them know how wrong they are."

I shake my head, and my stomach growls.

"We haven't ordered our pizza yet." He reaches for his phone on the side table. "I'm going to need sustenance before our next round."

I look at him, and instinctively, my legs close. "Again?"

"Can you handle more?"

I give him half a smile. "I think there's a good chance you can talk me into it."

He settles in next to me, and I rest my head on his chest while he types in our order on the web.

"This has just been the most amazing day," I murmur. "Thank you so much for helping my sister. I know she's going to get better, and the two of us are going to have a life we couldn't have imagined a month ago."

"I'm so glad you're feeling optimistic," he says, giving me a squeeze as he finishes up. "Can you tell me a little more about how it came to be just the two of you? What happened to your dad?"

I sigh. "He got colon cancer. He waited too long to see the doctor, and then it was too late. We knew for less than a month that he was sick."

"What did your mom do then?"

I snort. "She froze. He was our caretaker. She was lost for a very long time. I dropped out of Emily Carr and started taking care of Arabella because Mom just couldn't function. Then, one day, she announced she'd met someone who was a travel writer and wanted to sail around the world. Then she was gone. For a while, we talked to her every now and again, but it's not even worth that effort anymore. Being without her is harder on Arabella than it is me."

"You don't seem angry."

I shrug. "Being angry is a waste of time. But there are days when it's really hard, and I wish *someone* was here to help."

He kisses the top of my head. "You are truly amazing."

"Before you go thinking that, you should know I can't sing. I dance like Elaine from Seinfeld. And my cooking skills are nothing gourmet."

He laughs, and I love the deep, rich sound.

"What about your parents?" I ask. "Are they still together?"

Davis smiles. "Yes. They met when they were at university. My mom tells the story that she and her roommate were out together and met Dad at the same time. My dad took a liking to my mom, but she wasn't so sure. Then her roommate made it clear that if my mom didn't want him, she did. And that sealed the deal for her."

I giggle. "That's great. Sometimes it just takes the right motivation, I guess."

He nods. "They didn't have two pennies to rub together when they first married and started having kids. And my dad will tell you she's the real powerhouse behind his company."

"You mentioned they were in communications. What

kind of communications?"

"He's the Chairman and CEO of Martin Communications."

I get up on one elbow and look at him. "You mean like the telephone and cable company?"

He nods slowly.

"What? What about—why? Does everyone at the hospital know this?"

He shrugs. "Some have put it together because I end up in the society pages, but no one has asked me for a free phone or anything."

I roll onto my back and try to wrap my brain around this. "People ask you for phones?"

"When I was growing up, they did all the time. These days I have a tightknit group of friends, and we're always protecting each other from people looking to take advantage."

"Like I've done."

He looks at me sternly. "No. You haven't taken advantage. You reluctantly took me up on what I've offered you freely."

"I don't want your money, Davis Martin."

"I know that. Remember when Renee dropped by our table last night at dinner? She's what we watch out for."

"Really? She was raised to be a CEO's wife and host all the galas and parties."

He kisses the tip of my nose. "Maybe, but that's not what I'm interested in. And that's not who my mother is. Behind the scenes, she's the one running the show."

I lie back and look up at the ceiling. I wouldn't mind never having to worry about paying rent or being free to order pizza every night of the week. But I think about how closed off Davis is. He doesn't trust anyone. How could you not feel burned by that?

A phone rings. Without answering, Davis announces, "The doorman is bringing the pizza up."

"How do you know? That could be your mom on the

phone."

He grins. "They don't allow delivery people upstairs, and that was the house phone. Stay here and stay naked."

I wrap myself in the sheet and watch Davis pull on his jeans, salivating again over his chest.

In a moment, he returns with the boxes of pizza and a handful of napkins. "Beer, wine, or what would you want to drink?"

"Beer with pizza. Definitely."

He retrieves two bottles, and we relax into the bed and watch television while we eat.

After we've finished, I realize it's getting late, and that's why my eyelids are so heavy. I want to be at the hospital tomorrow morning first thing, so I slide the covers back and start to pick up my clothes.

"Where are you going?" he asks.

I look over at him. "Back to my room. I need to get some sleep."

"Why? Can you stay with me tonight?"

My eyes are wide. This is not what we talked about.

"I want you to stay," he pleads.

I look at him closely. "You're still Arabella's doctor. I don't think that's a good idea. *This* wasn't a good idea."

He scrubs his hands over his face. "I know." His eyes search mine. "I just feel like I've finally found you, and I want to be with you as much as I can. She'll be released in a few weeks."

I can't imagine why he feels this way about me, but I have too much on my plate to even entertain his flattery. Leaning down, I press my lips to his. "Davis Martin, you have a way about you that makes it easy for women to lose their wits."

"What are you trying to say?"

I slip on my panties and bra. "I need to go back to my room. I need to focus on my sister and on figuring out what's next for us. I need to find a job. Tonight was incredible, and an indulgence it seems I needed, but I can't get involved right now…if that's even what you truly want. I'm your patient's sister and caregiver."

"I want to help you with all of that. And I've told you, you can stay in the apartment as long as you need to." He sighs loudly and looks away. "Why do I feel like we're fighting?"

I pull my shirt on and lean over him. "I'm not fighting with you. I'm grateful for everything you've done for me and for my sister. I feel hope and joy today that I never have before. I just need some distance. I'm not that crazy girl who was with you in the bar. I can't stay the night."

"Well, what if…"

I kiss him and fight the urge to stay. I can do this. I will resist the urge to indulge Davis Martin and whatever he thinks he wants from me. I can't let my guard down any more.

I didn't sleep well last night, and my run with Davis this morning was awful. He ran behind me and hardly spoke a word. He doesn't have to be at the hospital this morning, but he offered to drive me in. I refused. I can't depend on him forever, and it's clearly a mistake to get any more entangled than I already am.

Sure, it feels great to escape my life every once in a while, and yesterday did merit a celebration. But I can't lose focus on what's important. If I want the life Arabella and I deserve, I have to keep working for it. Right now, I'm an unemployed big sister who has nothing to her name. Also, Davis can be a bit of an arrogant ass, with the ego the size of a tanker ship gliding into the port here in Vancouver. I can't be a doormat.

I pack a salad for lunch and a sandwich for dinner, plus

some beautiful strawberries and blueberries for snacks. I guess this is one indulgence I'll continue to allow myself.

When I arrive at the pediatric cardiac ICU at Mercy Hospital, I hear a sound that raises all my defenses. I listen again, and I know that voice belongs to my mom even before I see her. After all this time, I can't believe now is when she's decided to reappear. Pulling the curtain back, I find her in an expensive ivory pantsuit and soft green blouse. She looks refreshed and carefree, the opposite of me in every way.

"What are you doing here?"

"You told me my baby was having surgery, so I came as quick as I could."

Arabella is beaming from her bed, and I feel a pang of jealousy. I've been here for her day in and out, and she's never been that happy to see me.

"How did you know where we were?"

Mom shrugs. "This is the only hospital in Vancouver that has a pediatric cardiac unit. The cab dropped me off and pointed me here." She turns her back to me and fusses over Arabella.

I hold my tongue and drop my bag by the bed.

After a moment, she turns back around. "You look terrible." She looks me up and down but doesn't reach for me. "Why are you wearing that ugly sweater?"

I look at her, dumbstruck. "Because I can't afford anything else."

"I left you with ten thousand dollars. What did you spend all that money on?"

I really don't want to get into it here, but she seems to be searching for a fight. "Let's see, you left that money three years ago. Rent each month was fifteen hundred dollars, and then there's the cost of food."

"But you have a job. That was only to supplement. Why aren't you working?"

I take a deep breath. Forget the fact that I should be an art student. "Because Arabella needed me to take her to her doctors' appointments, and employers aren't very understanding when she gets sick."

"That's ridiculous. You're just lazy and can't hold down a job."

My mouth drops open just as Dr. Cavanaugh walks in. She extends her hand to my mom, but Mom doesn't take it.

Somehow, I manage to speak. "Dr. Cavanaugh, this is our mother, Vanessa Brooks."

"What happened to Dr. Bartlett?" Mom asks.

"Dr. Cavanaugh specializes in post-surgery pediatric ASD repair, so she's the best expert for Arabella's care right now."

Dr. Cavanaugh smiles, and my mother gives her a haughty look.

I need some air, so I step outside while the doctor talks to my mom and does her evaluation of Arabella. Where's that euphoria I felt yesterday?

After a few minutes, Dr. Cavanaugh exits. When she sees me, she smiles. "You look tired."

"I'll be fine."

"I was just telling your mom that I think we'll be able to move Arabella out of ICU and downstairs to the pediatric cardiac unit in a few days."

"That sounds great. And then how long do you expect her to be there?"

"Probably two weeks."

I nod. "Okay, I'm looking for a job that will give me the flexibility to manage Arabella's appointments. And I need to reach out to her school and let them know when she might be back."

Dr. Cavanaugh props her laptop on her hip. "It would probably be better to get her a tutor to finish out the last month of school and make sure she's ready for fall. Her appointments are going to be fierce for a while, and I'm not crazy about her returning to an active school environment right away."

My stomach drops. How many things am I going to have to handle? "Okay. I'll see what I can do. I may have to be the tutor."

She smiles. "I'm sure you'll be great." She looks at the clock. "Gotta get moving to my office. I'll see you tomorrow."

"Thank you."

She winks at me. "Thank Dr. Martin."

I cringe inside. I already did that last night. I wave to her as she goes and then collect myself for a moment before I walk back into Arabella's curtain.

"Where did you go?" My mother looks at the Rolex on her wrist.

"It gets a little crowded in here sometimes."

"I'm not sure I like Dr. Cavanaugh." She smooths Arabella's blankets.

"Why not?" I ask, my heart sinking.

"I just think Dr. Bartlett is better suited for Arabella."

"Mom, you appointed me to be Arabella's guardian, and I have her medical power of attorney. I think Dr. Cavanaugh is the right person, and she was suggested by the surgeon."

Mom shakes her head. "This surgery was a mistake. Arabella is going to fall behind in school, and her body would have eventually repaired itself."

Clearly, we're not going to be having a rational discussion. I suppose I should just try to speak to her while she's available. "Arabella is going to need a tutor. I suspect it will be about five hundred dollars a week. Can you direct deposit that into my account?"

"You don't need money for that. School is free."

Before I can formulate a response, the curtain pulls back, and Dr. Martin is standing there.

"Dr. Martin, this is my mother, Vanessa Brooks," I tell him. I turn to my mother. "Mom, this is Dr. Martin. He did the heart surgery for Arabella."

"The unnecessary surgery," she admonishes in a

flirtatious way. "I'm disappointed that you took advantage of my girls. Arabella will have a huge scar she has to explain to men her entire life."

Davis is silent a moment, probably trying to process that onslaught. He gives her a tight smile, and the flex in his jaw muscles tells me how he feels about my mother. "Mrs. Brooks, it's nice to meet you. I know Dr. Bartlett must have told you the hole in Arabella's heart could close, but if that was going to happen, it would have done so by the time she was five. That's why she was scheduled for surgery some years ago. I understand that procedure had to be delayed, but in the interim, the hole grew larger. Arabella is lucky Paisley brought her in when she did. The hole had torn and could have caused irreparable damage."

Mom stands straight. That doesn't seem to have been the response she wanted. "You're being too dramatic." She bristles.

Before things get ugly, I step in. "Mom, why are you here?"

"When Thomas heard you telling me about Arabella's surgery, he insisted I come."

"I thought it was Travis Bailey you were staying with in Seattle," Davis says.

"I'm sorry?" My mother turns toward him, her eyes wide. But she fidgets and then turns away.

Fuck. Me. She was in Seattle? And with someone else entirely? I can't imagine how Davis had that information, but right now, shock and anger crowd out everything else. "Mom, have you been in Seattle this whole time?"

"No. I just got to Seattle a few months ago."

Months? "Why didn't you call or come visit?" I search her face, trying to understand. "Why didn't you come home?"

She dismisses me with a wave. "You don't need me."

Arabella has tears in her eyes. "I need you."

Our mother scowls. "Travis didn't want to come to Vancouver, so I was working on him."

I would love to know why my mother is choosing a selfish asshole—or actually it seems like a series of selfish assholes—over her daughters, but rather than scream at her in the ICU, I walk out of the curtain.

After a moment, Davis follows. "Are you okay?"

I nod, and he leads me down the hallway, stopping just outside the ICU. "I can't even believe she's here, and I can't believe her attitude," I tell him. "Just when I thought there was no way the situation could get worse." I rub my hands over my face and remember the other issue currently at hand. "How did you know she was in Seattle?" I ask, looking Davis in the eye.

He holds my shoulders and looks steadily back at me. "I don't want you to be upset, but I ran a background check on you. I invited you into my home, and I realized I needed to make sure you hadn't been to jail for killing an ex-boyfriend or something."

I roll my eyes. I know he's teasing, but I suppose that makes sense. He's opened his life to me, and I'm a stranger. Still feels a little violating, though. It's not like I was hiding things from him. "And that gave you information about my mom?"

He nods. "She's been living in Seattle with a man named Travis Bailey for the last few years. He hit it big by creating a mapping application that was bought by Microsoft. He gives her a ten-thousand-dollar-a-month allowance for clothes and whatever she wants."

I close my eyes to hold off tears of anger and frustration—at her, at Davis, at everything. "That sounds like a lot of details about her, not me. I've never hidden anything about myself from you. Why did you really run a background check? And why didn't you tell me you were doing it?"

He fiddles with a pen in his hand. "I'm sorry. I just needed to be sure you hadn't set up an elaborate ruse to meet me and get into my life."

My eyes grow wide. "I don't even know how to

respond to that."

I turn to go, but Davis reaches for my arm. "Wait. Think about it from my perspective. I invited you to stay at the apartment, and you figured out it was me right away."

I shake my head. "The door was left open, and I wanted to thank you for your generosity. I've never asked you for anything, and I don't want a single thing from you. I thought I'd been clear about that. But you know what? I can move out of the apartment today."

He shakes his head. "No, you can't."

"Says who?" I put my hands on my hips. I can't even believe this.

"I moved your furniture into storage and told the landlord you wouldn't be back."

"He's going to keep my security deposit," I screech. That's three thousand dollars, and now I don't even have a job. How will I ever find us a place to live?

Davis shakes his head. "No, he won't. I'm pretty sure it was deposited back in your account yesterday."

I'm so furious I can barely process that. But it doesn't change anything. This whole situation feels wrong now. I can't believe I had sex with someone who ran a secret background check and snooped in my life. And my mother has been lying to me for probably three years? "I can't believe you did this—any of it. And all the stories I told you were true, weren't they? How does that make you feel?"

He shifts uncomfortably. "You need to understand, I've been burned before. I needed to protect myself."

I cross my arms across my chest. "You could have told me."

"Look, I'm sorry I wasn't honest sooner. I checked you out, and I can't tell you how relieved I am that you're exactly who you said you were. I knew in my heart that would be the case, but I just have to be smart, for my family, as well as myself."

It still feels humiliating. "I'm not looking for any

handouts."

He steps in close. "I know. You're strong and brave, and you deserve the world."

I step back. This is not where my attention needs to be right now, and I don't even know what to think. "I can't do this." I walk back into the ICU and into Arabella's curtain to find her crying and my mom staring at her phone.

She looks up at me, her face angry. "Great. Travis has told me not to come back. Look what you did."

"What did I do *exactly*, Mother?"

"You called too much, and he thinks I'm neglecting my kids."

My eyes pop wide. "I called you after her surgery, and before that it had been weeks. I told you I was done because you *are* neglecting your kids. Your ten-year-old daughter is being cared for by your twenty-three-year-old daughter, who dropped out of school to be a full-time parent. Meanwhile, you're off living an entirely separate life and not contributing a cent."

"It's not my fault you can't keep a job."

"Just go back to Seattle. We don't need you here."

She glares at me and storms out. *Good riddance.* Arabella wails, and I sit with her on the bed and rub her back. "I'll never leave you, Bells. I've got you. We're a team."

"It's all my fault," she cries into my neck.

"What do you mean?" How could she think this?

"If I hadn't been sick, Papa would have taken better care of himself."

"We don't know that. Your heart has nothing to do with Papa's illness."

"Then Mom left." She grasps my shirt desperately.

I pull back and lean forward so we're eye to eye. "Arabella, Mom's choices have nothing to do with us. I don't know why, but she's only thinking about herself. I love you, and we're a team. You're going to continue getting better, and we're going to figure everything out and have a fantastic life."

She nods, though she continues crying, but eventually she settles down and falls asleep in my arms.

A little while later Davis returns. He opens the curtain tentatively. "Everything okay? How's our girl? Where's your mother?"

"My mother is gone. I don't know where she went, and it doesn't matter. She doesn't matter. Her being here only made Arabella upset all over again." I sigh. I cannot believe any of this. "I'm sorry for getting so angry."

He shakes his head. "I understand. I'm sorry I didn't handle that better. You'd given me no reason not to trust you, and I should have been honest. I'm also sorry if I've made you uncomfortable. I told you we wouldn't start anything until after your sister wasn't my patient." He takes a deep breath. "Last night, I couldn't help myself. But I should have. I promise to do better going forward. Please don't leave. I want Arabella to have the support from you that she needs, and I hope that means you'll let me support you."

Chapter 12

Paisley

Arabella has spent the last two weeks in the hospital getting stronger and stronger. She meets with the physical therapist every day, and she's able to walk laps around the ward. She's made lots of friends on her trips to other parts of the hospital. She's quite the chatterbox. The repair on her heart is working, and she's been weaned off the big IV rejection medications. The cardiac team has continued to monitor her heart, and today, provided her final therapy session goes well and nothing changes on her tests, she should get to go home. She's so excited she can hardly stand it, but I'm trying to stay calm. I'll believe it when we're exiting out the door.

Dr. Cavanaugh has told us that after being released, Arabella will need to increase her iron intake and continue to build her endurance. Her body used to work so hard just to breathe that now she needs overall strength.

Since we've been out of the ICU and able to have more visitors, Lucy has come by almost every day. She works for a law firm as a paralegal, and they're in between big cases, so the timing couldn't be better. She's brought plenty of things to keep Arabella entertained while we gossip about Davis and her love life, and of course, she had to come by today, hopefully, for the last visit here.

"Look at this!" Arabella shows us the coloring she's doing from her hospital bed. Today, Lucy brought an adult coloring book, and we've all taken a page. Arabella is using colored pencils to fill in the face of a lion. She's done all neon colors, but I still like it.

"What did the guy say when you met him?" I ask Lucy again, sure I misheard her.

"He thought I was too old."

"Too old?"

She nods. "He saw I'd opened my dating profile over a year ago and figured the picture didn't look like me anymore because I seem so old now by comparison."

"You've not aged at all since you were sixteen," I say incredulously. "What was his deal?"

"I think he was looking for someone younger."

"You're twenty-three. Was he looking for eighteen?"

She shakes her head and colors a turtle. "Tell me about Davis."

"There's not much to tell." I stare at her and then at Arabella, silently trying to remind her that some things aren't for my baby sister's ears.

Lucy clears her throat. "Have you *bumped into* him again like you did the first time you met?"

I give her my you've-got-to-be-joking look. "Yes, but it was a mistake."

Lucy shrugs, and fortunately, the physical therapist arrives to take Arabella for her afternoon stroll.

"We're going down to the orthopedics unit, and you can strut your stuff for all the kids wearing casts," she tells her.

Arabella's eyes light up. "Do you think they'll let me sign them?"

"Let's go find out!"

Once they've gone, Lucy pounces. "Very soon you'll no longer be Dr. Martin's patient's sister. Does that mean you'll be together?" Her eyes twinkle, and her smile is all teeth.

"Not likely. Every time I think about trying to date on top of everything else, I get overwhelmed. I'm not sure I have the capacity to take anything else on, practically or emotionally. And once Arabella's out of the hospital, finding time to do anything for myself will be nearly impossible. I still have to find a job!"

"Okay, breathe," Lucy encourages. "You definitely have a lot on your plate, but that's all the more reason you need something for yourself. You need to let someone in. He clearly wants to take care of you a little. What's wrong with that?"

I roll my eyes. "I just don't see how it could go anywhere long term, so that makes it a distraction from what I need to stay focused on."

Lucy crosses her arms over her chest. "Why couldn't it go anywhere? That man picked you out of a giant line of women at The Lion's Den. He's clearly smitten."

"Come on, Lucy. I need to protect my heart. The man is kind, beautiful, and has the world at his feet."

"And you're the female version of that."

I snort. "Hardly. My life is in shambles."

Lucy tilts her head to the side. "You've been given a raw deal, but that doesn't seem to faze him, nor should it. You're dealing with a tough situation, but you're doing it with grace and courage, and you're staying true to yourself and your sister. He recognizes that and really likes you. Why wouldn't he?" she asks, waving her arms. "You can lie to yourself all you want, but I think you like him, too."

I throw my arms up too. "Of course, I like him. He's not a hard man to fall for. But how would we even do this? I can't hit the town every night in a ball gown for a fancy party. That's his life."

"You're being too hard on yourself. You deserve to be happy too. There are not a lot of people who would have taken up the slack when their mother deserted them."

"You would have done the same thing for your little brother."

"No way. I would have stuck him in our front yard with a sign on his neck that said, *Free to a good home*. And then I would have crossed out *good*."

She's so ridiculous that I have to laugh. "I adore you. Thank you for being the president of my fan club."

"I adore you, too. I've gotta run, but think about what I said."

I sigh. "I will."

"I know you're going home today," she assures me. "Text me later with the good news when you're officially free."

I hug Lucy goodbye.

"I'll see you ladies at your place later this week," she promises.

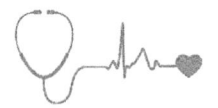

A little while later, the therapist returns Arabella to her room. She says Arabella is making great progress and can continue to do a lot of the same exercises with her home therapist after we're discharged. I thank her for her help, and Arabella gives her a hug goodbye.

Almost before the door has closed behind her, Arabella focuses in on me. "When can we go?" she whines.

I shake my head, though I know how she feels. After two weeks in the ICU and two more in this room, it seems like we might never get out. "We need Dr. Cavanaugh to give us the green light to go home."

Dr. Martin has officially transitioned us to her care. As

far as I know everything has checked out for Arabella today, so we should be all set. We just need to be discharged. We're ready.

Whatever my feelings about Davis personally, Dr. Martin has been a godsend. He's used his connections and expertise to find a nurse to help Arabella with her rehab. Kathrine Hall, or Nurse Kate, will also double as Arabella's tutor for the summer to make sure she's caught up, and she'll go to all of her appointments so she can keep up with what the doctors want. As Arabella gets stronger, Nurse Kate will transition to other patients by the end of the summer. But for now, because she'll be spending so much time with Arabella, I'll have the flexibility to get a job. I just hope I can actually find one.

A few times Davis has mentioned taking me out once the time is right, but he's been absent a lot the last two weeks. We run together each morning, but we don't really talk, and each night he's made a point of dropping me back at the apartment. I'm still not sure there's a way it could work for us to date, but I'll always be grateful that he's given me a way to be close to the hospital and a cushion so Arabella and I can get on our feet.

"All right!" Dr. Cavanaugh finally comes in. She smiles at Arabella. "I'll see you tomorrow in my office. I'm across the street, so it shouldn't be too hard to find."

"Finally!" Arabella cheers.

Dr. Cavanaugh and I both laugh.

"Have a good night in your own bed," she says.

We're finally free. As he requested, I text Davis to let him know we're being discharged.

We gather our things, and I look around the room one last time as an orderly arrives with a wheelchair for Arabella.

"Are you ready for this?" I ask as he pushes her down the hall.

She smiles in return, but she's seeming more anxious now.

A little part of me is disappointed, but none of me is surprised that my mother isn't here. She left after that one day she visited, and she hasn't reached out since. I meant what I said about not needing her, and I know not having to fight her on everything makes this process easier, but it kills me that Arabella is taking it so hard.

"Does Mom know where to find us?" she asks again.

"Of course," I tell her. "She always has my phone number." Who knows if she'll ever use it, but now that we know she's only two hours south of us, maybe we can go visit. Maybe. I return my focus to Arabella. "What are you looking forward to doing this summer?"

Arabella needs to take things easy, but with that in mind, there aren't a ton of limits on where we can go. We'll have a nurse with us, Arabella will have physical therapy three times a week to rebuild her strength, and we'll have echoes and HCGs weekly for the next six weeks. I want to be sure we do some fun stuff too.

"I want to go to the aquarium in Stanley Park."

I nod. "I think that would be awesome. They have so many cool things there."

"Do you think the otters will be my favorite again?"

"They're pretty cool, so they might be."

"I also liked the penguins, but they smell terrible."

I laugh. "Yes, they do. A little too fishy if you ask me."

We walk out the front door of the hospital just as Dr. Martin arrives to pick us up in a Range Rover Sport. This morning, he insisted on being our ride back to the condo. I think he thought we'd try to walk, but I would have just gotten a rideshare.

Arabella looks out the window as we drive. "Are we not going to our apartment?" she asks after a moment.

I take a deep breath. This is all about to get so much more complicated. "Well, you know I've been staying in an apartment close by while you're in the hospital. Dr. Martin actually owns it, and he's going to let us live there while you're still having lots of appointments at the hospital. Nurse Kate is going to stay with us too."

"Nurse Kate has already arrived and is waiting for you." Davis meets her eyes in the rearview mirror for a moment.

"That's cool." Arabella nods and then turns to me. "You'll be there, too, right?"

I squeeze her hand. "Of course. We're a team," I remind her.

When we arrive at the condo building, I can see Arabella's eyes getting bigger. Then Davis pulls into the garage.

"This is my favorite part," he announces as he pulls in. "Watch this."

The gates close behind the car, and we're lowered into the ground.

"Oh my gosh! What is this?" she asks.

"It's a car elevator." Davis grins as he looks at her.

"They make elevators for cars?" Arabella marvels.

"Believe it or not, it gives us more room to park more cars."

"How many cars do you have?" Arabella asks.

"More than I should."

"You didn't answer the question," she insists.

I nudge her shoulder. "Bells, it's not polite to ask."

She purses her lips. "Why?"

"Because it's a form of asking about someone's finances. That's not your business."

She shrugs. "He's a doctor. Of course, he's rich."

I can't help but laugh. I suspect it's the Martin family money that's financing his car habit.

"You can help me count them when we get to my floor," he tells her.

The elevator stops, and when the gates open, he drives out and parks in a spot. I always thought the cars around his belonged to other building residents, but now I know that isn't the case. There are several very high-end cars here.

We climb out of the vehicle. "Which ones of these are yours?" she questions.

With a loud sigh, he opens his arms. "All of them. Well, the MG in the corner is my dad's, but it's here because my mom was tired of it being in her garage and my dad not working on it."

Arabella walks around the garage and counts nine cars. "Wow. That's a lot. We don't even have one."

"Okay, smarty-pants," I say. "Let's get you upstairs. How are you feeling?"

She shrugs. That means she's tired. Davis and I have talked about not pushing her too hard, so when we see she's getting tired, we need to slow down.

The elevator arrives and takes us directly to Davis' apartment. I escort Arabella through the kitchen to the connecting door. "He has two apartments?" she asks as we pass through.

"Where we're staying is a separate apartment, but they're connected. It would usually be for a nanny or housekeeper. But it has its own entrance, too, which is what we'll use when Dr. Martin isn't with us."

Arabella wanders around, examining everything carefully. "This is much nicer than our place."

"It is, and I'm grateful we get to be here for a little while, but just remember we're guests," I remind her. "We won't live here forever."

"You can stay as long as you need to," Davis says over my shoulder.

I walk Arabella back to the master bedroom. "This is where you'll sleep. You have your own bathroom and a television, but if I catch you watching it in the middle of the night, we're going to be having a different conversation."

"Are you staying with me?"

I shake my head. "You need some space while you're still healing, but I'll be right out on the couch, and Nurse Kate will take the second bedroom."

As if on cue, Kate, a large woman with flaming red hair, walks out in jeans and a T-shirt to introduce herself.

"Hi! I'm Nurse Kate." She extends her hand.

Arabella smiles widely and shakes it. She loves when adults treat her as an equal and not a sick little girl. "Hello."

"We're going to do lots of things together, and I'm going to be here to help you get better. Is that okay with you?"

"Yes. That's what my sister told me."

Davis gives me a puzzled look. He looks like he might have something to say about the sleeping arrangements, but he keeps his mouth closed. After a moment, he turns to Arabella. "Who wants pizza tonight?"

"Me!" she exclaims.

"What kind sounds good?" he asks.

"Hawaiian!"

Kate and I look at each other and shake our heads.

"I love Hawaiian pizza, too." Davis turns to me. "What about you?"

"I'm probably going to have a salad. I'm afraid some of the greens are going to go bad if I don't eat them up."

He purses his lips. "I'll order you the margherita." He turns to Kate. "What about you?"

"Can I have a mushroom and olive pizza?"

"If you insist. I think you'll be eating that alone," Davis warns.

She chuckles. "Works for me."

"I'm getting one with everything on it. But I'm going to steal a slice or two of your Hawaiian." He winks at Arabella as he reaches for his cell phone and places the order.

When he's finished, he turns to me. "If you have a lot of greens, would you mind making a big salad for all of us?"

I nod. "I'd be happy to."

"I don't want any salad," Arabella announces.

"That's fine. I have great cucumbers, carrots, and the grape tomatoes you like so much."

She looks at Davis. "Way to ruin a pizza dinner."

"Says the girl who's having fruit on her pizza," I barb.

"It's my favorite!"

I ruffle her hair. "I know it is. And it's very nice of Dr. Martin to treat us. It's a special welcome party just for you."

"I like him," she whispers.

I nod. "He's a very nice man."

When I look up, Kate winks at me.

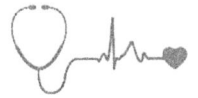

Arabella didn't last long after our pizza dinner. Kate got her settled in the room and let me know that she'll be listening for her through the night, so I can get a good night's sleep. Then she disappeared back down the hall.

"I think Kate is trying to tell you something," Davis says.

I look at him, puzzled. "Do you think she wants me to take over my sister at night? I've always done that, and I'm happy to be in charge."

He shakes his head. "I think she's trying to tell you that you can leave if you want to in the evenings. Or instead of sleeping on the couch, you can sleep in one of my beds."

"I would never do that."

"You have help. Why not enjoy it while you can?"

I roll my eyes.

"And it gives us the opportunity to go out on occasion. Dating, like we talked about."

Why does no one see this from my perspective? I need to protect myself. I'm already worried about Arabella becoming too accustomed to a lifestyle I can't afford. I can't let her see me and Dr. Martin as a couple, because we can't stay forever. There's nothing here that can last.

I take a deep breath. "The couch is just fine, and plus, if

Arabella needs me, I'm close."

He stands and picks up our dirty plates and the empty pizza boxes, taking them back over to his kitchen. "Of course, it's your decision. But always know, you can stay with me or in one of my guest rooms."

"I appreciate that, but it's too far away from Arabella." I stand in the doorway between my unit and his. The bedrooms in his condo are upstairs on the second floor.

"As she just told you, you have Kate to cover nights, and with a baby monitor set up, you could be there in seconds."

"I understand. But it might send the wrong message. And again, I worry it's too far away from her."

He crosses his arms. "Does that mean you don't plan on finding a job?"

"Of course, I'm finding a job. What would make you think that?"

"You don't want to leave her." Davis pours himself a glass of an amber liquid.

I groan. He's taking me too literally. "No, I'm looking for a new job, one with plenty of flexibility. I need to pay rent and feed us good meals."

"Not while you're here, you don't."

I smile, trying to be patient. "I know, but we can't live here forever. What will your girlfriends say if they find out we're next door?"

"I don't bring women home. I usually go to their place or a hotel, so I can come home and sleep in my own bed."

I have so many responses to that, but I hold myself back. Instead, I reach for his arm. "Really, I appreciate this. More than you'll ever know."

He gives me a single head bob, and I turn to leave. "Can you leave the door open?" he asks as I move through the kitchen. "If there's any problem, I want to be close."

My heart melts a bit. "Of course."

Two mornings later, I walk into the kitchen after my run and a shower with a purpose I haven't had in quite some time. Kate and Arabella are already huddled at the table working.

"I can't believe how quickly you found a job," Arabella says, putting her pencil down on her schoolwork. "Two days must be your record."

The temp agency called last night to offer me a three-week daily gig. It took me much longer than two days to find something that seems workable, but if Arabella wants to think I'm magic, that's fine with me. If I'm lucky, they'll like me enough to hire me full time. That really would be magic.

"I'm pretty excited about this one." I pour myself a to-go cup of coffee. "It's close enough for me to walk to. I'll be working with a production company that makes films targeting women viewers."

"There's a reason they say Vancouver is Hollywood North." Kate smiles. "Last week I had a Ryan Reynolds sighting. He was coming out of a trailer by Queen Elizabeth Park."

I nod. That happens a lot here. While we hate what they do to the traffic, we love seeing our city in films and television. Lucy has been in several background scenes of a murder mystery series because they film by her office. It's fun.

"I'll just be answering phones while they're filming in soundstages on the edge of town and on location out in the suburbs."

"Are you going to see anyone famous?" Arabella rocks from side to side in excitement.

"They're not filming in their offices, so I doubt it. And I was told to bring a book, which tells me the phones don't ring too often, but it's important that they're answered."

"All right, Arabella, let's shift gears and get ready to head out here in a little bit," Kate says. "Everyone has important things to do today."

Kate is going to take Arabella to a physical therapy appointment. They want to see her do more exercise and start getting her lungs conditioned. I'm already so grateful we have Kate on our team. The two of them head back down the hall to their bedrooms, and I busy myself getting my things together until my phone rings.

When I see it's my mother, I take a moment to decide what to do. I let it ring three times while I debate whether I'm up for the fight. I need to be in a good headspace for my job this morning.

But then I think about Arabella and what she needs, so I yell goodbye, wait for them to respond, and step out into the hallway before I finally answer. "Hello?"

"It's me," she says.

I feel like being a bitch. "Who?"

She sighs. "It's your mother."

"What can I do for you?"

"Where do you live now?" It's phrased as a question, but she's asking as if she deserves that information.

I step onto the elevator. "You need my bank details to make a deposit?"

"No. I'm standing outside your shithole apartment, and the landlord told me you moved. Something you failed to tell me."

What is she doing back here? "Ah, right. Like you didn't tell me you'd been living in Seattle and were no longer with Thomas. Maybe I didn't have time to tell you because I've only talked to you by phone for the last three years, and the one time I see you, you left your ten-year-old daughter, who just had major heart surgery, in the hospital."

"I don't need this. Where are you?"

"I don't need this either. Tell me what you want. I will not allow you to just traipse in and upset Arabella's routine.

She was crushed when you left, and I won't let you do that to her again."

"I'm here to stay. Because of you, Travis kicked me out."

"I don't see how that's possible. I've never spoken to the man."

"You called in the middle of a big dinner party. He asked all kinds of questions about what I was doing on the phone. You messed up my life—again."

That stings, though I know it isn't true. "I'm on my way to work. Maybe we can meet you downtown this evening for dinner."

"I'm not going downtown. The traffic is horrendous."

"You could take SkyTrain."

She snorts. "No. Gross. I wouldn't be caught dead on public transportation. Tell me where you live, and I'll meet you there."

"No, thank you. There is no room for you at our house. You're on your own. And if you aren't interested in meeting us for dinner tonight, let us know when you're available, and we'll happily meet you."

"You have ruined my life," she seethes. "So you're going to fix it."

"Fine. Text me Travis' number, and I'll let him know I'm to blame for your narcissistic personality."

"I will not let you ruin that relationship any more than you already have. Tell me where I can find you."

I sigh. "I have to go, or I'm going to be late."

I disconnect the call and walk the eight blocks to my new job. The weather is perfect, and I can definitely see why they would want to film today.

When I arrive at the building, there's an envelope with my name on it at the security desk, and inside is a key. I've just let myself into the offices when the phone rings.

"Good, you're on time," says the voice on the other end. "All we need you to do is to answer the phone and transfer the callers to the appropriate number. Do you see the list of names and extensions? If they're looking for Jerome Turner, you can text him. He's the boss."

"I see the list," I answer. I look over the directory of names, extensions, and cell phone numbers as I shrug out of my coat.

"The phone needs to be answered in two rings. But most people know we're here, so the phones should be quiet. You can read a book or something."

"Thanks," I say to a dead phone line.

I put the phone down and walk around the nice office to check out all the framed posters of television shows and movies. Some of them look familiar, but I can't be sure. I then sit down in the reception chair and open my book.

The phones are relatively quiet until Arabella's school calls. "Ms. Brooks, your mother is here looking for Arabella."

"Okay. Well, as you know, Arabella is not coming to school for the remainder of the year. She's just had heart surgery."

"Yes, we're aware of that," the secretary confirms. "But your mother seems concerned about Arabella's whereabouts. Is she with you?"

I close my eyes and imagine ways I could actually hurt my mother. "She's with her tutor right now, and I'm at work."

"Ah, okay. Of course. Sorry for even asking. We just thought we should follow up."

I roll my eyes. "Yes, I know how Arabella's wellbeing has always been your primary concern. I need to go now. Goodbye."

I hang up the phone, fuming. My mother is relentless, but involving the school is a low blow. I cannot let her back into our lives when she has nothing to offer us.

I draw in deep breath.

My cell phone pings.

Mother: Where are you?

I certainly have no desire to have her show up here.

Me: I'm downtown. The offer to meet for dinner tonight still stands.

She doesn't respond. I then realize I missed a text from Davis earlier.

Davis: Good luck today! Dinner tonight with Arabella is my treat to celebrate.

That makes me smile.

Me: Sounds fantastic. We can meet at the house and decide where to go.

I look back at my book but decide to check in with Lucy instead. I haven't talked to her since we left the hospital. That's been nearly three days now.

Me: Remember me? Your long-lost friend?

Lucy: Are you the short, plump redhead who does cartwheels on crowded streets for fun? Or maybe the anorexic brunette with a huge thigh gap that walks around like she's on a runway?

Me: Thigh gaps are gross.

Lucy: Ah, you're my beautiful BFF. I miss you. How are things going? How's Arabella? How's the apartment?

Me: We're good. I currently have a temp job with a production company answering phones. And Bells is doing therapy with Nurse Kate and settling in nicely.

Lucy: That all sounds fantastic, but you know those aren't the only details I want. I need to run, but are you free for dinner later this week? I'd love to see Bells too.

Me: Let me see what this job is going to be like, and I'll let you know.

Lucy: Sounds good, but don't make me wait too long. We have so much to catch up on!

Me: Miss you.

The production company receives a flurry of calls around ten and then again around two, but that's about it. I'm reading lots of naughty romance, and I love that I'm getting paid for it.

The afternoon's main excitement occurs when a delivery driver drops off a small box. I text Jerome Turner, the director on the project, to let him know about the package, and he informs me he'll be sending over a runner named Mark to pick it up.

Mark finally arrives just minutes before I'm scheduled to leave. "Hi, I'm Mark Chow," he says as he enters. "Sorry, traffic is a bear."

I nod. "I'll bet. Anything after two is a nightmare." I hand him the box. "But you made it just in time."

He nods. "I don't suppose you're headed out to the suburbs, are you? If I drive you home, we could use the carpool lane."

I shake my head. "I'm sorry. I'm walking home."

He nods. "It was worth a try. At least I got to see your smile."

I laugh. "Real smooth, Romeo."

We walk downstairs together, and he gets into a luxury sedan and waves before pulling into traffic. I turn the other direction and walk the eight blocks back to the condo building. When I arrive, Davis is playing cards with Arabella.

"Hey! How was your first day?" he asks as Arabella hops up to give me a hug.

"It was just fine, thank you." I smile at them. "How are things with you? Therapy go okay, Bells?"

"Yep," she says. "Let me show you what they taught me."

I nod, but Davis gives me a look and gestures toward his kitchen. "Give me just a minute," I tell her. "I'll come find you in your room."

She nods, and I step over to join him in his kitchen.

He pulls the door closed behind us. "Your mom called me today at the hospital. She wanted me to tell her where you live."

My eyes go wide. "Whatever you do, please don't do that. She called me this morning. She says her boyfriend broke up with her because I called to tell her about Arabella's surgery. She's back to make me pay for that."

He shakes his head. "That doesn't even make any sense. Why would he do that?"

"Her version is because I interrupted a dinner party. My feeling is that he saw how self-centered she was and dumped her."

"I agree." He reaches for my hand. "I didn't tell her anything, and I never would."

"Thank you."

"Listen, I know the little card shark over there is going to be looking for you, but while I have you here, I'd like to formally tell you that Arabella is no longer my patient, and I'd like to take you out on a date. Tonight doesn't count, as we'll be celebrating with Arabella. We can walk over to Stanley Park and go to the Cactus Club."

I nod, agreeing to that, but I'm still trying to formulate a response to this larger conversation when he speaks again.

"This also wouldn't be a date, but what would you think about you and Arabella joining me for dinner with my family at my parents' on Sunday? They live on the water, and they'd love to meet you both."

My heart squeezes in my chest. That seems complicated or like it might complicate my feelings. "I don't know. That seems like a lot. Meeting your family?"

"I know, but there's a private beach with lots of cool shells Arabella would like. We wouldn't have to worry about her getting jostled or injured, and I know she would have fun."

He looks at me with sad, puppy-dog eyes, and I find I can't say no. Or maybe I just don't want to. *It will be good for Arabella, after all.*

When I nod, his eyes twinkle with excitement. "Great! It's all settled then. Now, let's get ready for dinner."

Chapter 13

Davis

The drive from downtown Vancouver south to the University of British Columbia is bumper-to-bumper traffic. We're headed to my parents' for dinner, and they live on the bluffs over the water close to UBC. It's a Sunday afternoon, and it should be easy, but the weather is clear and people want to explore.

"Maybe this is a mistake," Paisley says, twisting her hands together.

Paisley is nervous. She shouldn't be. Despite what people read in those stupid supermarket tabloids, my family is pretty easy going, and we get along well. "We're fine. They won't start dinner without us. My brothers are likely in the same traffic."

"Why don't you let us off here at the corner and Arabella and I will take a rideshare back to the condo? You can go on to meet your family, and I can get a few things done. I need to clean the bathroom," she adds after a moment. "It's a disaster."

I laugh out loud at that. "No, I will not drop you off so

you can go back and clean your bathroom. Who does that?"

"Only my sister." Arabella snorts. "When she's nervous, she cleans. Everyone else eats."

"I bake when I'm nervous," Paisley retorts.

"Yes, I've noticed that as well," I tell her. "Your baking is getting to my waistline. Let's take a break on cookies. Well, except for those soft oatmeal raisins. Those are to die for."

Paisley cracks a smile and sits back for a minute. But just when I think she might be relaxing, she speaks again. "I should be bringing something. You never arrive anywhere without something for the hostess. They're going to think we're trash."

"My mother would never think that. You're my guests. You'll be fine."

Arabella leans forward from the backseat. "Do you think I could go down to the beach and put my feet in the water? I haven't been to a beach in forever."

I look at her in the rearview mirror. "Absolutely. I think that would be a lot of fun."

We finally navigate away from the traffic and pull up in front of my parents' home. The gate opens, and I wave to Felix Pérez, my parents' and Martin Communications' chief of security.

The house comes into view, and like always, it makes me smile. Its contemporary style is mostly windows. I've always loved that you can see through the house to the ocean beyond.

"Is this the house you grew up in?" Arabella asks.

I park and hop out to open the back of the Range Rover. There I pull out the things I brought for Mom. "Not totally. We moved here when I was in high school."

"It must have been super cool to live so close to the water," she says.

"It was, but I probably took it for granted."

"Where did you live before you moved here?" Arabella quizzes.

"We weren't far from here, but not right on the water. My dad worked downtown."

Arabella's eyes grow big. "He had to drive in that traffic every day?"

"I don't think it was as bad as it is today. Plus, Felix, the man who opened the gate for us, drove him so he could return calls and work while he was in the car."

"That's a lot of work."

I nod. "I think that's why I wanted to be a doctor. When I was growing up, I thought my dad worked too much."

I gather everything together, and when we turn to look, my parents are standing at the threshold of the door with giant grins on their faces. My mom is so excited to meet Paisley. I've never brought anyone home before.

Paisley stands at my side as she takes it all in. "Lord, please help me not make an ass of myself," she mutters.

I bump her shoulder. "You're going to be fine. They are not the king and queen. They're really very kind people."

"I'm sure they are — to normal people."

I laugh. "You're more normal than we are."

Arabella is already over talking to my parents.

"We better go save her before they eat her," I tease.

"What?"

"I'm kidding."

"Davis said I could go to the beach," Arabella is telling them as we walk up.

"I've been dying to put my toes in the water all day. I'll go with you," my dad says.

"Mom, Dad, this is Paisley Brooks," I tell them. "And it seems you've met her younger sister, Arabella."

My mom steps forward and embraces Paisley. "Please call me Julia, and this is Chip." She gestures to my dad. "It's so wonderful to meet you. Thank you for making the trek out here."

Paisley fidgets. "Thank you so much for inviting us. I

wish I'd thought to bring something. I know it's rude to show up empty-handed."

My mother smiles and waves it off. "We don't need a thing. Just you being here is all we want."

My dad and Arabella head down the path to the beach, and Paisley and I follow Mom into the house. "I have a wonderful champagne cocktail, if you'd like one. It's quite refreshing. I also have water, soft drinks, wine, and a full bar if there's something else you prefer."

"Your champagne cocktail sounds perfect," Paisley says.

"Your usual, Davis?" Mom asks as she walks over to the bar cart in the sitting room.

"Of course. Thank you." I take a seat on the couch. "Henry called me earlier and said he had a soccer game on the pitch in Kits and wouldn't be here until close to dinner, but where are Phillip and Griffin?"

"They're out by the pool," Mom says. "I thought I wouldn't overwhelm Paisley with them yet."

Paisley looks at me, alarmed.

"I didn't warn her," I say, giving her a smile.

Mom sighs. "I'm grateful to have a few women at the table today. Paisley, I apologize in advance. When my boys are at home, regardless of their age, they act like they're ten."

"Then Arabella will fit right in," Paisley says. And with that perfect comment, I know tonight is going to be okay.

Mom hands her the champagne cocktail and me a glass of bourbon, and she sits down with us. "I understand you two met when Davis did Arabella's heart surgery."

Paisley's eyes flash to mine briefly before she nods. "He saved her life. I'm so grateful."

"And I understand you're staying in the extra apartment?"

Paisley sits up in her chair, ready for a fight, as if my mother has accused her of something. "Uh, yes. For a little while we are. Our apartment is a ways away, and being close to the hospital has really helped me support Arabella. Davis also helped connect us with a nurse, and she can stay with us in that apartment, which is allowing me to go back to work."

Mom nods, not fazed by any of this. "I love that apartment. Those natural light boxes are fantastic. It feels like you're getting daylight and not in a black hole of an interior apartment with no real sunlight."

"The apartment is fantastic. I love the way it's decorated. Did you do that?"

Mom preens at the compliment. "I did, thank you. I'm very good at spending my children's money. They were good for many years spending my money, so I enjoy it the other way around when I get a chance."

Paisley laughs.

"I understand you are an artist," Mom says after a moment.

"Well, these days I do whatever work I can find so I can take care of Arabella. Art is my first love, but getting Arabella healthy is my priority."

Mom nods. "I am a collector of art. Would you like to see some of what we have?"

"I'd love to!"

Mom stands, and I already know what she's going to do. I follow with interest.

Paisley stops as she enters the formal living room. "Is that a Tara Donovan?" She walks over to the wall that looks like it has a giant, bumpy, white piece of handmade paper attached to it. It's lit from behind.

My mother grins. "I'm so impressed you recognized it."

We continue through my mother's house, looking at pieces she's collected. "This room is a favorite," she says as we enter the sunroom, where natural light filters through all colors of twisting and turning shapes. "It's all art glass."

Paisley nods. "I noticed the Dale Chihuly chandelier when we walked in."

"Isn't it beautiful?" Mom sighs. "They come once a year

to clean all the glass, and I love the way it sparkles when they've finished."

We continue into a formal living room, and Paisley stops abruptly. "*You* bought the piece?" She turns to look at my mom. "*Adrift in Silver?*"

Mom nods, her smile bright. "Paisley is such a unique name, and when Davis mentioned he'd met you, I knew this had to be yours."

We're standing in front of an ordinary piece of driftwood, but the belly and bottom have been dipped in metal. It looks as if it's floating in a bath of quicksilver.

"How?" Paisley shakes her head. "That was such a small show at a gallery on Granville Island."

Mom laughs. "I got a call from an art buyer I work with. She sent me a picture—which, by the way, didn't do it any justice. And I told her to buy it on the spot. It's a gorgeous piece. She's been on the lookout for more of your work ever since."

Paisley blushes, but she also looks prouder than I've ever seen. "That's very kind. I'm honored to be in such esteemed company here in your home. I haven't done much work since that show. Right now, I'm focused on getting Arabella healthy and getting us back on our feet and out of Davis' hair."

"You're not in the way," I pipe in. "The offer to stay as long as you need to still stands."

Paisley continues wandering through my parents' collection, and my mother excuses herself to return to the kitchen. I follow Paisley over to a Jackson Pollock.

"I'm in a house with a Jackson Pollock and a Tara Donovan, and I'm prominently displayed," she says, her eyes shining. "I never would have dreamed it."

"It's exactly where you belong." I kiss her forehead. I wish I could show her what the rest of us see. Paisley should never feel intimidated by anything or anyone. I wish I could convince her to take a chance on herself.

"Let's join my brothers by the pool," I suggest after we've hit most of the highlights in the collection. "I don't think they'll throw you in. Me, I'm not so sure about."

"You think your brothers would throw you in the pool?"

I nod. "Yes. To embarrass me in front of you."

She shakes her head. "We could fix that."

"How would you suggest we do that?"

"Push them in first."

I link my arm with hers. "I love the way you think."

"I'll lure them to the edge of the pool, and you can do your magic," she says with a wink.

"I save all my magic for you."

She blushes, and my heart swells. I can't believe this fantastic person is currently in my life.

We go back downstairs, but we end up on the patio, rather than going all the way over to the pool. The sun won't set until well after eight this evening, so we're going to eat out here, listening to the waves below on the beach. Paisley and I sit, enjoying our drinks, as Hilary, our long-time housekeeper, helps my mom set the table.

After a few minutes, Arabella and my dad return, covered in sand. "Look at what we found!" she announces.

She opens a cloth bag and inside are more shells than I've seen in a while. She pours them out on a side table and sorts through them. "Chip told me these are whelks, conches, winkles, top shells, cowries, and limpets. And look at these sand dollars!"

Paisley goes to sit next to her and listens to the stories Arabella has from spending time on the beach with Dad.

Mom comes to sit next to me. "They're delightful."

I nod. "I know. I hope I can talk them into staying a while longer. It's good for Arabella to have a stable situation."

She pats my hand. "She's not out for your money."

"No, she isn't. Though I suspect her mom will be. They have a strained relationship, and she's recently resurfaced here in town. She hasn't asked yet, but she will."

Mom nods. "Felix thought she'd be your challenge."

I sigh. "But Paisley is nothing like that."

"I know. Look at her with her sister. She puts everyone before herself. After her sister is doing better, she will need to find more balance in her life."

I nod. "She has a long road ahead of her."

"When she's ready," Mom says, "I'll help her with her art. She's incredibly talented."

"She doesn't like owing people. You'll have to be careful about it."

"I can be a silent benefactor. I don't mind." She smiles, and I know with a snap of her fingers, my mother can and will make Paisley a household name.

Henry arrives in a whirlwind. He kisses Mom on the cheek and meets Paisley before bumping shoulders with me.

"This is refreshing," he says. "You don't typically bring women home. Must be serious."

"Henry," Mom says firmly. "I wanted to meet her. She's the artist who did the driftwood dipped in silver."

Henry opens his mouth, but then Dad interrupts.

"Dinner is ready!" Dad calls as he sets a giant plate of various grilled meats and two large portobello mushrooms on the table. Thankfully that distracts from further conversation about Paisley and me.

As we all gather at the table, my brothers Phillip and Griffin finally materialize as well, pushing at one another until they come to stand on either side of Paisley. They're doing that to goad me.

"I don't think so," I say, taking her hand.

We find our seats around the table on a beautiful Vancouver evening. Arabella sits next to my dad, and they talk about space. For a ten-year-old, she seems to have a lot of knowledge about the universe.

"Did you know there are more stars in the universe than there is sand on all the beaches on Earth?" she asks.

Dad shakes his head. "Is that true?"

Arabella nods enthusiastically. "It is!"

"I'm a bit of a fan of the universe myself," he tells her. "I have satellites for my company circling Earth. I also know the universe has no center and is constantly getting bigger every second. That means you could never travel to the edge."

"Do you think there's alien life out there?" she asks.

My dad shrugs. "What do you all think?" he asks, looking to my brothers.

"It would make sense," Griffin says. "I mean, if you think about it, they're finding other life-type forms on Mars, and math tells us there are other suns, so it seems logical."

"I think so, too," I say. "But I hope Stephen Hawking is wrong and they would be friendly and not like in the movies, which is what he published before he died."

"I read his paper," Arabella says. "It was scary."

"You read his paper?" Mom asks.

"I didn't understand all the math in it, but he was very interesting," she says. "He was a theoretical physicist so he's all about the odds. In his mind, the human race would not do well with other alien life. But he had some interesting things to say."

"How did you learn all of that?" Henry asks.

"When you have a lot of doctor appointments, you either read or watch YouTube."

"You don't play video games?" Phillips asks.

"Not really. Paisley says they kill your brain."

The table cracks up.

Davis leans over. "Besides working for the family business, Phillip is an investor. He owns The Lion's Den, a few gaming companies, and he's also part of a consortium that's trying to bring a professional lacrosse team to Vancouver. He's got some connections in the movie industry as well."

"Leave it to a child to step in it for me," Paisley mumbles as she looks down at her plate.

Phillip grins. "I'll tell you what. I have this great game

you should try."

"I can only play it on Paisley's phone."

He looks at her and smiles. "I've got you covered."

Paisley looks at Phillip. "We do not need a tablet loaded with games."

Phillip shrugs. "I was thinking Arabella could be one of our beta testers."

"That sounds awesome!" Arabella says.

"Slow your roll." Paisley looks at Arabella, who sits back and crosses her arms. "She doesn't need a job," she tells Phillip. "She needs to get stronger and go back to school and hang out with kids her own age."

Phillip holds his hands up. "I agree. But that doesn't mean she can't help me out now and again."

Dad clears his throat. "Let's table that thought for now, shall we?" He turns to Paisley. "Have you considered Point Grey Academy when she's ready to return to school?"

"Well, chances are we'll return to Richmond, where we live, and that commute on a bus is too far."

Dad nods. "She'd really bloom with kids that share her level of intellect."

"I agree," Paisley says. "I talked to them a while back, but they don't have any full scholarships, and the ones they give wouldn't be enough to make it for me. One year's tuition is more than a year of university."

I hold up my hand, and my dad nods.

"I'm on their board of trustees," Mom says. "I'm sure we can figure something out. Maybe a donation of your artwork toward the annual fundraiser would help."

I suppress a smile. Leave it to my mom to work an angle to get Paisley back to her art.

"We have a lot to do before we can even consider where Arabella will be going to school in the fall," I say, giving Paisley's leg a comforting squeeze.

The sun sets as we finish the meal, and we remain on the patio as my parents' staff moves heat lamps into place and lights them. I look over at Paisley and smile. Having her here makes everything more enjoyable. I hope she feels the same way. She's fit into my family so effortlessly this evening.

For dessert, we enjoy homemade strawberry ice cream sundaes. Arabella makes the biggest one I've ever seen, and Griffin and I gossip about what's going on at the hospital while Phillip and Henry talk shop about what's going on with the family business. They're trying to fight competitors from other countries who want to come into Canada.

"We need a stronger lobby in Ottawa," Henry says.

After finishing maybe half her sundae, Arabella crawls into Paisley's lap.

I look over at my mom. "I think we've worn her out."

She nods. "Yes, the conversation around here is suddenly very dry."

Catching my eye, Paisley stands, with Arabella wrapped around her. "Thank you so much for having us. Dinner was amazing. And I truly loved seeing my artwork among so many prominent artists."

Mom stands to hug them both. "You are just as talented, if not more so. I can't wait until you're able to produce more work."

I hug my brothers goodbye, and my parents walk us out to my car.

"It was so wonderful to meet you both," Dad says. "We hope to see you again soon."

Paisley nods. "We had a wonderful time. The food was fantastic, and the company was exactly what we needed. Thank you so much for having us."

"You're welcome any time, with or without any of my children," Mom says as Paisley gets Arabella settled in the car. "In fact, I have tickets to the Monet exhibit coming through town next month. Would you be interested in joining me?"

"Please go with her," Dad begs. "It would save me."

Paisley grins as she closes the car door. "I'd love to go with you."

Mom clasps her hands together. "Wonderful. It's a date. I'll be in touch."

With one last wave, we get in the Range Rover and begin the trek back downtown. Arabella snores quietly in the backseat.

"Your parents were wonderful," Paisley says.

"Thank you for saying so," I tell her. "They're good people, and they really liked you both. I think if we were ever interested in heading out of town for a weekend, we could leave Arabella with them."

Even in the darkness, I can sense Paisley tensing immediately. "I don't know that I'm in a place where I can go away for the weekend."

"Okay, okay," I say. "It was just a suggestion. No pressure. You know what you need to do."

I suppress a sigh. I want to spoil her and enjoy some time with her alone. That's the only way she's going to realize what her life is missing. I need to figure out how to make that happen.

Chapter 14

Paisley

"Have you talked to Mom?" Arabella asks out of nowhere at the breakfast table on Monday.

I shake my head and try to keep my face neutral. "I haven't, but would you like to call her sometime?"

Arabella's face lights up. "Can we? I want to tell her all about the shells I found at the beach with Chip."

"I'm sure she'd love that." It comes out more sarcastic than I would have liked, but Arabella doesn't seem to notice. "Right now, I have to go to work, but we can try to reach her tonight after dinner."

She nods. "Sounds great."

After gathering my things and saying goodbye, I leave Arabella in Kate's very capable hands. They have a physical therapy appointment and an EKG today, and then she's going to take her to Stanley Park to look at mushroom formations and talk about how math exists around us, even in nature. I'm so glad Kate is a math person. The thought of doing math gives me hot flashes.

I emerge on the sidewalk and begin my walk to the

studio offices. They're working on soundstages not too far from downtown this week, and I'm hoping I might find a way to stop by. They're filming a holiday romance that will run at Christmas time, and I'd love to see how it all works.

When I walk into the office, Mark, the runner I met last week when he came to pick up a delivery, is waiting for me. "Great! You're here. Mr. Turner said if you were here before I left, I could bring you to the lot. So I waited as long as I could. Do you want to come?"

My eyes grow wide. "Yes!"

"Cool. He said you could forward the phone to your cell, so you can still grab it if anyone calls."

It takes a minute, but I eventually figure out how to do that, and Mark helps me test to be sure the system is working. Then we load up in a big Mercedes.

"It must be nice to run errands in this car."

He shakes his head. "Believe it or not, it's too big."

I look around and snort. "Maybe for you, but I could manage it."

"It's a bitch to park. All the parallel parking spots are made for a Mini."

"Okay, you've got me there. Do you get to take it home?"

"No. It's Mr. Turner's personal car, so I have to be careful with it. I got lunch at a drive-thru the first week I worked for him, and even though I cleaned out all the trash, I left a wayward fry, and he was pissed. I almost got fired."

I shake my head. *Good grief.* "Too bad you can't take this bad boy home. You could impress a date or two with this car."

"I know! One day, when I'm directing my own shows, I'm going to buy a huge, ostentatious car like this."

"As you should."

"So, are you dating anyone?" he asks, making a sort of awkward segue.

"I am seeing someone," I tell him. "But I'm keeping

things light. My focus is on my little sister and saving some money so we can be more secure."

He nods. "I get that. It's so expensive to live here."

"I sometimes dream of moving to one of the outer islands and just hiding, but my sister's only ten."

"Is she a half-sister?"

I shake my head. "My parents tried for years to have a baby after I was born, but it wasn't happening. Then they gave up, and my mom got pregnant with Arabella. I'm thirteen years older than she is."

"And you're looking after her?"

I nod. "My dad passed away a few years ago, and he was the glue of our family. It was too hard for our mom, so she found a rich guy to latch on to, and she left us on our own." Even telling him that much of the story is embarrassing.

"That's cool." As we approach the soundstages, Mark fidgets in his seat. He looks over at me but doesn't say anything.

"What's going on?"

"Mr. Turner has been known to be a little handsy. My advice is to watch yourself and make sure you're not alone with him at any time."

My eyes widen. "Oh. That's good advice. Thank you."

I text Kate and Davis.

Me: I'm out at RedBox Soundstages for the day. I'll let you know if I'm going to be late.

Davis: Who is the director on the film?

Me: Jerome Turner—not of the Turner 5 fame, but of Hall Brothers Christmas movie fame.

Mark drives the car up to a gate. "Hey, Charlie."

"Mr. Chow. Welcome back. You can go right in. You

know the drill."

Mark pulls through and heads to a giant hangar. Outside, there's a flashing red light. "We have to wait until the light stops flashing before we can go in," he explains as he parks.

I nod. "I'll follow your lead."

When it stops blinking, we quickly open the outside door and walk into the darkened soundstage.

Mark navigates through and around wires, ropes, can lights, scaffolding, and all sorts of odds and ends on the floor until he arrives at a large man sitting in a director's chair. Very cliché.

"You made it." Mr. Turner looks me up and down like I'm a piece of meat.

I'm suddenly uncomfortable. "Thank you for inviting me," I say, trying to be polite.

He pulls a chair up close to his and positions it so I'd be practically facing him. He pats the cushion. "Have a seat, and I'll tell you all about what we're doing today."

Out of the corner of my eye, I see Mark's face morph into horror. I need to be cautious. "Oh, I'm good here. I was going to run to the restroom right quick. I drank a big cup of coffee before we got on the road. Can you point the way?"

He grumbles.

"I've got you covered," Mark says. "Follow me."

I follow Mark to the restroom. "I'm not sure I want to stick around to watch the filming if I have to sit facing him," I say before going in.

"We can stand in the back, and I can drop you at the SkyTrain station once he forgets we're here."

I nod. "Perfect."

When I return from the restroom, I stand with Mark in a dark section of the studio and watch a couple walking along a fake snow path. We're deadly silent, but I lean over Mark during a break. "I can't believe how fake the snow looks here, but once it's on television, it looks so real, and they'll be outside."

Mark nods. "The miracle of television."

"Where's Paisley?" Jerome suddenly yells.

My stomach drops. "Right here."

"You're supposed to be here with me."

"I'm good from here. I don't want to be in your way."

"Come. Now." Mr. Turner yells.

Mark gives me a look that says either I do it or head home. Putting one foot in front of the other, I walk toward Mr. Turner. As I get to the brighter part of the studio, I look around and am shocked to see Davis.

What. The. Hell? He's off today, but I didn't expect he'd be following me around.

I turn my attention back to Mr. Turner, and this time he's turned another director's chair toward him. He pats the seat. "Sit." He adjusts himself, and if I had to swear in court, he has an erection.

No. This is not going to happen. I don't need this job that much. "I'm sorry," I tell him. "My little sister is post-op from open heart surgery, and my ride just arrived to take me back. There's something she needs, so I can't stay. But I super appreciate the chance to see how the magic is made."

Everyone stops and stares at me. Mr. Turner is apparently used to getting his way. He looks me up and down again. "You're here to work."

I nod. "I understand that, but the reason I work temp jobs is that sometimes I need to care for my sister. Would you like me to call the agency and get a replacement?"

He breathes through his nose. "No, we'll do that."

I turn and wave goodbye to Mark, knowing I'll probably never see him again, and I silently send him my thanks. As I approach him, Davis turns, and we walk out of the soundstage together. I follow him to the car and put my seatbelt on. Without looking at him, I ask, "How did you know?"

"I just had a strange feeling," he says. "I called Phillip

and asked about Jerome Turner, and then he got me on the lot. Did you know he's been sued three times for sexual harassment?"

I shake my head. "I didn't know, but Mark, his PA, warned me he could be a bit handsy. I was staying clear."

Davis shakes his head as he starts the car. "That man could have hurt you. That's not right."

"I'm grateful you came. Mark couldn't take me to the SkyTrain station quite yet, and so I was stalling until he could."

"You always have the rideshare app. I'll connect you to my account so you don't have to worry about it."

I shake my head. "You don't have to do that." I look out the window as we drive, trying to sort through all my feelings. A few minutes later, my phone rings. "Well, here goes getting fired again." I push the call button. "Paisley Brooks."

"We understand that you've walked off the job?" The woman from the agency doesn't greet me and just jumps in.

"Mr. Turner was making me uncomfortable." I'm determined to hold my ground.

She's silent a beat. "Did he touch you in any way?"

"No."

"What did he say?" she pushes.

"He invited me to the soundstage today, and when I arrived, he pulled a chair to face him and kept patting the seat, asking me to sit in it. He said he was going to show me what they did, but I would've been facing him, not the stage. He kept adjusting himself, and I'm pretty sure he had an erection. I wasn't comfortable with what he was asking."

"I see." She sighs. "He doesn't want you to come back."

"That's fine. If you have other work for me downtown, that'd be great. If you don't, I understand."

"Call and check in the morning," she says. "We always get calls for help when people are out sick. I'm sorry about how this turned out, but I'm grateful nothing happened."

"Me too."

I set the phone in my lap. I don't know if that counts as getting fired or not. But I think it means I should start looking again.

"Are you okay?" Davis asks.

"Yes, thank you. I'm fine," I tell him, and he's quiet after that.

I'm not sure where we're going, but after a while, I can tell Davis is headed toward Granville Island. It's one of my favorite places in Vancouver. It used to house the school I went to, Emily Carr University of Art and Design, but they've moved to a new campus now. It always had galleries, but these days the university buildings have been renovated into work/live condos and artist lofts. But they're pricey. You have to be a successful artist already to afford them. There's also an incredible market there with everything from handmade jewelry to fresh fruit to premade gourmet meals.

"Where are we going?" I finally ask.

"I thought we'd grab some lunch and talk about what you want to do. I probably know someone who'd give you a job that won't include sexual harassment."

"You don't have to fix everything for me," I murmur.

"I don't mind." His hand covers mine.

I want to pull away, to do this on my own, but more and more, that doesn't seem possible. And more than that, it doesn't seem like what I want. I don't know what to do with my feelings for Davis Martin. I just can't quite convince myself this is real, that it would be okay to let this happen.

We park and walk over to a beautiful waterfront café. I order a BLT, and Davis orders a roasted chicken sandwich. Then we sit for a while and enjoy the beautiful day. The rain didn't want to give up this year, and it almost seemed like it was going to last forever. "I love Vancouver when the weather is like this."

"So does everyone else." He smirks.

"I know. It's why so many people move here, but they

don't stay. At least most of my friends didn't. It's too expensive."

"Okay, let's get to the matter at hand," he says. "What kind of work are you looking for?"

I shrug. "I'm not picky at this point. Mostly, I just need to be able to leave when my sister gets sick. Once she goes back to school, I'll need to be where I can get to her relatively quickly, within an hour by bus."

"I have a few cars. You could always borrow one."

I give him a tight smile. "I won't always be living with you."

"You can stay as long as you want. I promise."

"I really appreciate that. But it doesn't seem responsible. I can't make my whole life plan be: depend on Davis. That would be taking advantage of you. It's everything you hate about women." I reach across the table for his hand. He shakes his head, but I continue before he can speak. "I think you're a wonderful person. I don't know how you happened to me, but I'm also at a loss. I've been doing the best I can for Arabella for a long time, and that's all I know how to do. I'm not good at making time for things just for myself, and I've learned not to count on anyone. My mother reminds me that's not safe over and over again. So please don't think I'm not grateful, and I'm sorry if I try your patience, but I really am trying to let you in a little. I just have to go slow."

He nods, but it still doesn't seem like he understands, so I try another approach. "If you're footing the bill for us all the time, we're no different than Renee."

He sits up straight. "That's not true. Renee wants to spend my money and live off of my name. I'm using my money to help you because I can. I want to support your efforts so I can keep you close."

I sigh. "Well, right now you're super close to unemployed with minimal prospects."

"Are you sure you don't want to do more art? Seems like you have lots of prospects there."

"I always want to do art, but that doesn't feel like a viable career for me at this point. Selling that piece your mom bought was a fluke. It takes a lot of time and energy and financing to get started, and those aren't the things I have."

Our food arrives, and as we eat our lunches, we turn to lighter conversation. I learn that Davis typically spends his days off in the winter skiing up at Whistler and mountain biking or sailing in the summer.

"Aren't you worried about getting hurt and ruining your hands or something?" I ask.

"No. I'm careful. I pay attention to the other skiers, and I don't do anything stupid when I'm on a bike. What do you do in your free time?"

"I haven't had a ton of free time these last few years. Besides work, I hang out with Arabella. She likes to play cards, as you know, but she's a card shark. Don't play poker with her. She counts cards."

Davis laughs, and I can tell he doesn't believe me. He'll learn.

"What do you do for you?" he probes.

I shrug. "As I told you earlier, I struggle in that area. But I run when I can, and I do read. It's a wonderful way to transplant myself into a new world and meet men who don't break my heart or lie to me."

He shakes his head. "I've always been honest with you, and if anyone's heart is going to be broken, I suspect it's going to be mine."

I sit back in my chair and laugh. "I don't worry about you, though. There will be plenty of ladies lining up to help pick up the pieces."

He rolls his eyes. "There's no convincing you."

I smile sweetly.

"Ready for a walk?" he asks.

"Sure."

He stands and throws some money on the table, and then we wander through the buildings over to the gallery that once sold my work. I see it's a set up when Davis's mother, Julia, is there with another woman.

She lights up when we enter. "Paisley, it's so good to see you. I wanted to introduce you to my art buyer, Isla Farrow."

I hug her and then offer my hand to Ms. Farrow. "It's wonderful to meet you."

She squeezes my hand with both of hers. "Do you know how long I've been looking for you?"

I shake my head, feeling a little overwhelmed.

"When I saw your piece here in Gwen's gallery all those years ago, I emailed it to several of my clients. The only reason Julia got it was because she replied first. But every person I sent the photo of your piece to wanted it. I'm here to ask if they can commission you to do a few more pieces."

I feel like I can't quite breathe. "I don't know." I'm intimidated by all the eager eyes looking at me.

"Part of the commission would be for them to pay you half upfront," she adds.

"What does that mean?" Davis asks.

"Depends on the size of the piece, but for something similar to the one Julia has, I would start pricing at fifty."

My mind is whirring. Fifty what? It wouldn't cover my costs at twenty-five dollars. That would be hard. Julia paid five thousand dollars. I would hope they'd pay at least that.

"That's fifty thousand," Julia points out.

My brows shoot to my hairline. This can't be real. I mean, I know the art market is crazy, but wow. I never dreamed someone would value my work that way. *Be practical,* says the voice inside me. *Don't get too excited about this.* I can't get in over my head. I clear my throat. "Before I commit, I'd like some time to see what materials I can find. I need to have decent driftwood to make the project worthwhile."

"I think that is more than fair," Isla says.

"And I think that means we're going out to Martin

Island," Davis suggests.

Julia gasps. "Yes!" She clasps her hands in front of her. "That place is perfect for collecting. Right on the north shore there's wonderful driftwood…and shells Arabella would love to add to her collection."

I've never heard of Martin Island, but Julia's enthusiasm is contagious, and I can't stop myself from smiling. "Okay, that sounds like it would be worth a look."

"We can go on Wednesday, if you'd like. I don't have any surgeries, and I'm not scheduled," Davis says.

I nod, feeling slightly overwhelmed.

"Excellent. Now there's one other thing," Isla says. "Please follow me."

She leaves the gallery, and we walk around the corner where she pulls a key out of her pocket and opens a glass door. She walks up the stairs into the space over the gallery. "This unit doesn't have a renter right now, and I understand you haven't been working on a project for a while. I'm guessing you might need some workspace?"

I feel like I've forgotten how to nod. I suppose I do need space, if I'm actually going to do this. But I can't get my mind around that yet.

"If you're open to it, for the ten percent I'm going to take from the sale of these commissioned pieces, you can use this space for free," Isla continues.

I look around the open room. It has a bit of a warehouse feel, but it's totally a workable, and even a livable space. *Could I really support myself this way?*

"It has an unimpressive bathroom, and the kitchen has an old fridge, but it works. You could set up a microwave, and we can help you find some tables for your smelter and other supplies."

I nod. Suddenly, I really want to give this a try. "Well, it seems like you've thought of everything," I say, giving Julia and Isla a look that lets them know I can see what they're up to. But I can't help but smile. "Let's see what I can find on

Martin Island."

Chapter 15

Paisley

I've checked with the temp agency each day this week, but so far there's nothing for me. I'm not sure if it's because I walked off the job or they don't have work. But either way, I'm back to square one there. Part of me thinks I should embrace this possibility of working as an artist again, but there's a nagging voice that says that's too good to be true. Either way, at least it means I have today free to go on this excursion.

Arabella and I follow Davis along a path to the marina, and we approach a large speedboat that sits in a prominent slip. "Is this your boat?" Arabella asks.

"It's actually my parents'. We're going to borrow it. It's called *Here Fishy Fishy*. My dad has a sense of humor."

I laugh. "Does he even fish?"

"He owns fishing poles, but I'm not sure about bait." Davis loads up the boat with our picnic lunch and his medical bag. "Actually, he does enjoy fishing. We usually have a freezer full of salmon from a river that runs through our property up north."

Having their own property makes sense. I saw how much security his parents had around them when we were at their house. It was discreet, but it was definitely there. It must be hard to get away and be a tourist somewhere. And I can't imagine the number of people it takes for them to do that.

"I packed a nice picnic lunch, and we'll stay out at the island as long as we'd like to," Davis explains as he helps us in. "And the speedboat is big enough that you can bring back all the driftwood and shells you want."

We slowly leave the marina, towing a smaller float. The views are spectacular. I sit on the back bench while Davis and Arabella navigate us around Stanley Park and under the Lions Gate Bridge into the Georgia Strait, which is the large body of water between the mainland and the hundreds of islands.

"Look over there!" Davis points to our left.

It takes a moment, but then an orca comes up and sprays out its blowhole. Quickly, we see three more sprays. We're in the middle of a pod. They're not paying a lick of attention to us, just making their way through the water to a destination unknown. They're so graceful and beautiful. Davis cuts the engine, and we float. The stunning black and white animals glide through the water and slowly move beyond us. It's really cool to watch them. This is the closest I've ever been.

"That totally made the trip," Arabella announces.

I think it made mine too, and we haven't even reached our destination.

We continue on, and Arabella stares over the side of the boat at the deep blue water. "The water here is dark," she notices.

Davis nods. "It's very deep here. There's a US nuclear submarine base just over the border in Washington state, and they run drills in the area."

"How do you know?" she asks.

He shrugs. "I've seen them."

"Were you swimming?"

"No. They cruised right by us."

She looks at him, confused.

"They weren't fully submerged."

I shake my head, shut my eyes, and turn my face to the warmth of the sun. "This is perfect."

After driving around for about an hour, Davis cuts the engine again as we approach a small island. "Welcome to Martin Island."

"You own this entire island?" Arabella asks.

"I don't personally own the island. My family does."

"Why don't you live here?" Arabella wonders aloud.

"My father bought this decades ago, and he thought about building a private getaway on it, but it was expensive to bring over electricity and clean water. We used to come out here and go camping, and these days we visit sometimes to enjoy the nature. When we were young, my brothers and I found some nests."

"What kind of nests? Eagle?" Arabella asks.

He nods. "We do have three eagle nests around the island. But we also found black swift nests. They're medium-sized black birds that nest in the rocks, and they're almost extinct."

"Are you saving them?" Arabella questions.

"We're trying. And at the beach where we'll land, you're going to see some northern abalone shells. We have such a large colony here that marine biologists come out to study them. They're also on the endangered list."

Davis pushes a button, and there's a rattle that startles me. "What was that?"

"That would be me dropping the anchor. I'm not in the mood to chase the boat today."

Arabella giggles. "Have you done that before?"

Davis nods. "It got caught in the current and was far away by the time I realized it. I had to race to the boat to save it, and it almost beached itself on the rocks in that inlet. It would have been toast."

We leave the boat and climb into the small, attached

float. Davis disengages it, and an engine propels us to the rocky beach. It's perfect for driftwood. The rocks here are large but smooth and round. As we approach, I can see several pieces of driftwood that are a beautiful shade of gray with rounded edges. When I searched for the perfect pieces before, it wasn't this easy. I didn't have access to a beach that gets almost no foot traffic and where the tide delivers driftwood.

My heart leaps as we reach the shore and get out. Maybe I can do these commissions after all. It would definitely give us some financial stability to get even twenty-five thousand dollars in the bank. We've lived on less than that. Maybe we could even find a better apartment next to a better school for Arabella.

"You look lost in thought," Davis says softly as Arabella explores. "Care to share?"

"I was just marveling at how great the driftwood is here." I turn to look at him. "You've saved the day yet again."

"I'm happy to be able to share all of this with you. And I know Isla and my mom will be thrilled if you take on these commissions."

I walk over and pick up yet another piece that will work wonderfully. "It's hard for me to believe that's real. But I'm excited about this in a way I haven't been in a long time."

"You've got enormous talent." He steps in closer. "We need to work on ways to make you understand what the rest of us see."

"Thank you for believing in me, even when I don't always believe in myself."

"We can come back anytime, but you should load up with as much as you want. I can make multiple trips to the boat if we need to."

"I feel like a kid in a candy shop," I say, rubbing my hands together.

Arabella comes trotting over. "Look at this sand dollar."

Davis bends down. "This is a living sand dollar."

"How can you tell?"

"See these little hairs on the bottom? Those tell us it's alive. Let's put it here in the water and let it do its thing."

Davis searches the beach a moment and finds a white sand dollar. "This is no longer alive. Let's take this one instead. It will look great with your shell collection."

I hold up a shell. "So would this one."

We all hunt for items to collect, and it makes me think about other things that would be amazing to work with. I could do a multifaceted sculpture with rocks, shells, and driftwood. "I have an idea. It may not work, so I don't want to take too much. But this is a wonderful place."

"What are you thinking?"

"I'm going to play with a few ideas I have in my head, but I'll start small," I assure him.

He puts his arm around me and kisses my forehead. "It's all up to you."

I find several more pieces of driftwood. They need some polishing, which I'll do with a quick sandpaper rub, and then after dipping it in silver, I'll oil the wood. I stand and look around. The rocks here are interesting—flat and smooth. These would be popular with people who stack rocks, and that gets my creative juices going, too. I add a few rocks to my pile of materials.

"Would you like to take a walk around the island?" Davis offers.

Arabella nods enthusiastically, and I feel the same way. "I'd love it as long as we won't disrupt the animals."

"We'll be careful," Davis assures me.

The island is small compared to some of the others in the area, but it will still be a good walk around the perimeter. Davis grabs our lunch, and we follow him as he heads up a trail. The island is almost entirely covered in tall pine trees. We come to a spot, and Davis pulls out a pair of binoculars. "There is the first nest."

We look up into the trees, and there are two bald eagles, each the size of a small child. They have us in their sights, but they're not paying any attention. Thank goodness.

"They're beautiful," Arabella marvels.

We walk farther into the island to a rustic cabin. "My dad, my brothers, and I built this when we were young," Davis explains as he pulls a set of keys and unlocks it. "I have to warn you, it's pretty barren. This is really only a shelter from the weather."

We walk into the dark space, and there are a few canned goods left behind, but it really is just a giant room with some wooden bunk beds without mattresses. I follow Davis, and a cobweb hits my face. I yelp and do the yucky dance as I wipe the web away and hope there isn't a spider in my hair.

"You're very cute when you do that," Davis says with a chuckle.

"She hates spiders," Arabella informs him.

"What do you hate?" he asks her.

"Mean people."

She answers so simply, but I know there's a lot of meaning in those two words. Because of the ASD, Arabella has always been the smallest in her class. She's been picked on constantly. Then there are the people we've run into who haven't treated us well because we weren't dressed in name brands and had old, ragged shoes. It all breaks my heart.

Davis ruffles her hair. "I agree. Mean people suck."

"What are you afraid of?" she asks.

"I'm afraid of bears."

Arabella jumps. "Are there bears on the island?"

Davis shakes his head. "We're safe. Vancouver Island has one of the largest populations of brown bears, but they follow the salmon. Since we're just off the Georgia Strait, it's too far to swim. There aren't a lot of brown bears here."

Arabella nods and seems satisfied with his answer.

Davis picks up a folding picnic bench in the cabin. "I

thought we might eat on this."

He steps outside and unfolds the table just beyond the shelter. It's perfect for the three of us.

As he unpacks, Arabella and I are amazed at what he produces from his bag. "I have a black forest ham with Swiss cheese and spicy mustard, a peanut butter with homemade strawberry jam—"

"I want that one," Arabella announces as she snatches it from his hand.

"And I have a turkey with cheddar cheese and bacon."

I sit back. "I'll take half the ham and half the turkey."

Davis grins. "That's what I was thinking."

He pulls out some small bags of chips, and Arabella dives for the ketchup ones. Those things are nasty, but she loves them. And he has a beautiful fruit salad and shortbread cookies, plus sparkling water for all of us.

"We're eating well today." Davis rubs his hands up and down his thighs.

Indeed, we are. After we finish our meal, we spend more time wandering the island. I pick up some interesting pinecones, bark, rocks, and a few other things I can't totally identify. Then we climb back into the raft and make our way to the speedboat. All the activity has Arabella exhausted, so she lies down in the boat's cabin, and I stand with Davis as he navigates us back to the marina.

"Thank you for being so wonderful today." I just have to shake my head at this person who has endless time and energy for us. I feel a bit anxious thinking about how much we owe him.

"My pleasure," he says. "This was a lot of fun. I'll get the driftwood, shells, rocks, and the rest of it over to your studio as soon as I can."

I totally forgot about that part. I guess I thought they'd magically appear at the studio. "No rush. I'll need to get the commissions before I can buy the silver and the oil."

"Have you considered gold and platinum?" he asks.

"I did when I was doing the one your mom bought—and also rose gold. But that takes money."

"With a commission, you'll have money upfront. That should help."

I don't want to admit how far over my head I feel. "But I can't spend it all. What if they change their mind and don't like it? I wouldn't be able to return anything I've used."

"That's what Isla handles," he says in a way that manages not to make me feel stupid. "Part of her ten-percent fee is to make sure you're covered. She'd either find another buyer or they'd lose their money."

I nod. That makes me feel a lot better.

When we finally get back to the marina, Felix is there with two men.

"We'll take all this to the studio on Granville Island," he assures me.

I want to resist this help, but I know there's no point. I'm just making things difficult for myself for no reason. "Thank you," I say instead. Then I hustle and pick up Arabella's stash of things she found today.

Davis carries her back to his condo, and she curls into his chest, her eyes closed.

"Is she okay?" I ask.

"She's fine," he replies. "It was just a lot today. She can rest now, but we should wake her for dinner, so she can eat something before she goes back to bed."

I nod. He sets her down on the couch in our living room, and I get her things to her room. While Davis orders ramen for dinner, I fire up my computer in his kitchen and look at what it's going to cost me to order silver, silver polish, tea tree oil, and a smelting pot and hot plate. It's several thousand dollars, and that's without gold, platinum, or other metals that might be fun to experiment with.

"What did you find?" Davis asks as he comes up behind me and rubs my shoulders.

"Mmmmmm. That feels so good." I refocus on the

screen. "It will cost a few thousand dollars to get it all set up."

"Okay. Would you like my credit card?"

"God, no," I quickly reply. "No. I would never."

"I know you'll have it soon."

"There's no rush. There's planning I can do without this. No need to spend money before I have it." I feel a little panicky, just thinking about it.

"Whatever you think is best," he says.

We set the dining room table in Davis' condo. He lights candles, and Arabella is still napping, so we leave the door open between the units, rather than wake her just yet.

When the food arrives, we sit down next to each other.

"I like that you're wearing my shirt," Davis tells me.

I look down at his Harvard Medical School T-shirt. "It's my favorite. I warn you. I may never give it back."

"I don't mind." He smiles at me over a twirl of ramen.

"Why did you go down to the States for medical school?" I ask.

"It's very similar medicine to here, and I wanted to get away from Canada and go where people didn't know who I was. I wanted to experience life without constant attention."

"And what did you find out?"

He sighs. "I met an exceptional woman and dated her through all of medical school. I introduced her to my family, and we spent hours talking about our plans for the future. I was sure we were going to marry."

My eyes are wide. "What happened?"

He shrugs. "We had different schedules, and she couldn't get a residency in Boston, so she decided to go home to Indiana for hers in obstetrics. It was close to graduation, and I got out of my rotation early and went home to surprise her. I had an engagement ring in my pocket and a dozen roses. I was ready to propose and figured we could work out the details."

I had no idea he'd been in this kind of relationship. *Interesting.*

"I heard her talking to someone, and I figured out she was on the phone," he continues. "She mentioned my name, and my ears perked up. I was expecting her to say something complimentary. Instead, she talked about being in love with the person she was talking to, and she told him he just needed to be patient while she married me and got everything set up."

"Wait, so she was marrying you for your money?"

He nods.

"Did you find out who she was talking to?"

He nods again, and pain flashes through his eyes. "It was my closest friend from med school. He was the one who'd introduced us, and I realized they'd set me up."

I sit back hard in my chair. "I'm so sorry. No wonder you don't trust anyone."

He takes my hand. "I trusted you from the moment I met you at The Lion's Den. I don't normally do things like what happened between us that night, because I never want to take the chance that I might be photographed — or worse. But there's always been something that tells me I'm safe with you."

I smile. "You're very dangerous, Davis."

"I am?"

"You make it easy for me to lose focus, to forget all the things I'm responsible for." I look down at the table. "You make me want to be selfish."

He closes the distance between us. "You could never be selfish," he says. "But I must confess, it is my plan to wear you down until you can't say no. I want you to let me in, to make me a real part of your life. Is it working?"

He reaches for my hand, and we stand, our bodies almost touching. I put my hand on his chest, trying for one last moment to fight this. But why? Our eyes lock, and he looks at me intently. "Yes," I tell him.

His lips touch mine, and my knees go weak. If his arm hadn't snaked around me, I would be a puddle on the floor. I

reach around his neck and lace my fingers in his hair.
When we break apart, I'm breathless.
"Please stay with me tonight," he begs. "I need you."

Chapter 16

Davis

Arabella finally stirs on the couch, so I put my plans for Paisley on hold while she comes into my kitchen to eat. She's pretty tired from all the walking and excitement today, but the beef broth is good for her, and I'm glad to see her out and experiencing things.

Still, she doesn't last long, and Paisley soon whisks her off to her bedroom. When she reappears, Paisley lets Kate know she'll be sleeping upstairs in my condo this evening, but she'll have the intercom with her, and she'd prefer Arabella not know.

Kate nods. "We'll be fine. I have a feeling she's not going to wake up in the night, but if she does, I've got her. Get a decent night's sleep."

Paisley thanks her and returns to me. I wait for her in the doorway. She's biting her lower lip. I want to bite that lip. I need Paisley like a man in the desert needs water. She's captured my heart without even trying.

"I need you," I tell her again. "Please stay the night and let me worship you." My hands wander as I trail kisses along her collarbone up to her ear. Her breathing hitches.

I pick up the sound box so if her sister calls, she can go to her, and I move her into the bathroom. We're both covered in ocean spray from our day on the water.

As she begins to unbutton her shirt, I stop her. "Tonight is all about you." I undo each button, kissing her as I go. Reaching behind her, I unhook her bra, and she wraps her arms around herself.

I gently ease them aside. "You don't ever have to hide yourself from me." I suckle her breasts, trying not to leave any marks. But I'd love to mark her as mine.

I slide her shorts over her hips, taking her panties with them. I love beautiful lingerie, but there is something so sexy about a woman in a basic bra and panty. I pull her close, pressing my hardness against her. I kiss her deeply then pull away. "I've been waiting so long for this."

I urge her into the shower, and she turns to face me, her tongue touching, feeling, and tasting my mouth as the water cascades over us. My cock hardens further against the softness of her belly. She picks up the soap and rubs it up and down my back, her hands sliding easily over my skin as she moves them downward and over the curve of my ass, kneading the soft flesh.

Then her soapy hands glide over my hardness, and I groan my appreciation. If I don't stop her, she's going to get me to my grand finale before we start. I part her legs and sink my fingers into her silkiness. Her breath catches as I circle her bundle of nerves and dip inside her wet channel. I need to taste her. I pull out my fingers and suck them greedily. She's still stroking my cock, bringing me to the brink of orgasm.

I drop to the floor, the hard tiles digging into my knees. I lean her back against the wall and lift her leg over my shoulder, positioning her dripping pussy inches from my face. Her fingers lace through my hair as I pull her to my mouth and lick and suck, drinking all her juices.

The pressure of her fingers on my head tells me she's

close. I want her to come for me before I take her. I give her three fingers and pivot them in and out, reaching in far enough to find that special spot. "Come now!" I demand.

"Daaaaavvvviiiissssss!" she groans.

I feel ten feet tall, and I can't take it any longer. I stand and bend her over. She pushes her ass toward me, teasing and beckoning. I push in, and she's so tight from her climax. It takes a few tries to get in deep. Once I'm settled, I lean over and find her bundle of nerves. I strum her like a guitar while I pound into her.

Then I realize I'm not wearing a condom—something I've always done—so before I finish, I pull out and let the ropes of my satisfaction coat the wall of the shower.

"That was fantastic," Paisley says as we rinse off.

I reluctantly turn off the shower, and we drip water on the floor as I find a large fluffy towel and dry every inch of her. She shivers, and goose bumps appear on her arms. I wrap the heated towel around her shoulders and rub briskly. Kneeling in front of her, I nuzzle my face against her pussy again. I lick and kiss her clit as my cock hardens again. But I'm not sure my knees can take more tile floor.

"You're ready again," she murmurs. "We must do something about that." She reaches for another towel and dries me, slowly and teasingly patting and rubbing me all over, avoiding my hardness until the end.

"That sounds like an excellent idea," I confirm as my cock bobs for more attention. I pull her close and take her face in my hands, looking deep into her eyes. Her eyes close as I part my lips and lean forward to kiss her with increasing intensity.

I break away to pull out two condoms and place them on the bedside table. I can't believe what this woman does to me.

She crawls into the bed, and something falls into place inside me. There's no place I'd rather be.

The next morning, my phone is ringing when I get to my office.

I drop my bag on the floor and reach for the receiver. "Dr. Martin," I say in greeting.

"Hello, Dr. Martin. This is Vanessa Brooks."

Here we go. That didn't take long at all. I almost feel a sense of relief. Let's just get our cards on the table, and I can figure out how to deal with this. "What can I do for you, Ms. Brooks?"

"Please, Davis. We don't need to be so formal. Not when we're virtually in-laws."

I clear my throat. No way I'm taking that bait. "What can I help you with?" I ask, trying hard not to sound annoyed.

"I need you to know that I'm aware you're screwing my oldest daughter." She pauses a moment, perhaps for dramatic effect. "If the press were to be made aware that you've taken advantage of both of my girls for your own perverse pleasure, I'm sure the hospital would be forced to make several changes. I mean, a crying mother on the evening news would be a disaster for you."

I could play her game for a while. Anything she leaks will be based on lies, but it will still be humiliating and messy, particularly for Paisley and Arabella. I could never stand by knowing that kind of pain was coming for them. So instead, I decide to cut to the chase. "How much money do you need to go away?" I ask. "And I don't mean away from me, but to leave your daughters alone permanently."

She cackles. "I'm sure you won't miss a few million."

"I would need a non-disclosure statement signed that also would prevent you from ever discussing this with your daughters."

"That's fine. I don't need them."

My stomach sours. How did Paisley and Arabella come from someone like this? "Give me some time to pull together the details and the documents we'll need."

"Perfect. I'll send you the wire information."

She hangs up before I can say anything else, and I call Felix. "Vanessa Brooks just called and made a threat, which is actually a demand for money, as you predicted. She has no real case against me, but I can't let her torture Arabella and Paisley. So I'm just going to deal with it."

"What are you going to do?" he asks. "You know I would prefer that you go to the police. This sounds like attempted blackmail."

"I know. But that would also mean I need to let the hospital know about Paisley and Arabella staying in my extra apartment. Arabella's no longer my patient, but it's still a conversation I would prefer not to have, particularly in the press. I'd also hate for Paisley to hear this about her mother. I don't know that I'm ready for that."

"She must know her mother is a grifter."

I sigh. "I'm not sure she does. She knows her mother has a habit of relying on men for money, but hearing the details about it? Hearing what her mother is willing to trade for money? That would be awful. She doesn't deserve that, especially if I have the power to prevent it."

"Well, I do understand your perspective," he concedes. "So what do you want to do?"

I tell him my thoughts and the legal documents that will be needed, and he promises to get the wheels in motion. "Thanks," I tell him.

Just as we end the call, my cell phone pings, calling me to the emergency room. A seventeen-year-old needs a triple bypass, and the surgery consumes my afternoon. This boy had undetected ASD, and it makes me think of Arabella and Paisley all over again. I'm so grateful I'm able to help them, and thankfully, this boy also seems strong enough to survive.

Chapter 17

Paisley

"Here's your check for four commissions," Isla says with a big smile.

I've spent the morning and early afternoon organizing the studio and all the things I collected on Martin Island, and Isla has just popped in to say hello. She hands me a check, and when I look down at it, I have to count all the zeroes twice. It's for ninety thousand dollars. Any moment, Ashton Kutcher is going to jump out and tell me I'm being punked. I called her after my trip to the island and told her I'd found enough natural materials to produce quite a few pieces, but somehow, I still didn't realize this was actually going to happen.

"If you can manage a few more, I think Gwen would love to put them on display downstairs in her gallery," she tells me. "I know they'll go quickly."

I stare at the check. This is so much money, and it's just the beginning. Isla and I have a deal that gives her ten percent of my sales and me this studio above the gallery for the next year. It all sounds perfect, but fear coils in my stomach. What if I can't recreate what I did the first time? What if these clients don't like what I make for them? I could be the sculptor equivalent of a one-hit wonder.

I force myself to look up and take a breath. The sun shines through the studio windows. This is what I've always wanted, and I need to stay with that thought. This will allow me to provide for Arabella too. I turn to Isla. "I have to ask. What happens if they change their mind?"

"The buyers who've commissioned you?" Her brow furrows in confusion.

I nod and look away.

"When I told them I'd found you and you were open to making a piece for them, they were thrilled. I highly doubt they will change their minds, but even if they do, they've committed to the payment. They'll have to sell the piece themselves if that's what they decide." She comes closer and stands in front of me, reaching out to touch my arm. "They know these are limited, numbered pieces. Trust me, they're going to love whatever you design. You've picked the most beautiful and knotted driftwood. I can't wait to see what you transform them into."

I look down at the check, still trying to make sense of all this. "I've never seen this much money with my name on it."

Isla puts her arm around me. "You're going to see a lot more. Remember, this is just the first half."

I manage a nod. "Okay, then. Once this check clears, I'll order my supplies."

"You can have as much time as you need, but let me know if you come up with a timeframe after you've had a chance to think it over."

When I say nothing, she busies herself looking at the materials I brought back from Martin Island. She points down at a box with rocks and shells and other non-driftwood items. "What are you thinking about doing with these?"

I smile. "I'm not completely sure, but I have some ideas. I promise I'll show them to you as soon as they're ready. But first I need to work on the commissioned pieces."

She nods. "I can't wait to see them. Oh—next month there's an artist's studio tour here on Granville Island. If you have some pieces ready by then, we could include your studio to build some hype for you. Not only would that benefit those who have already bought your work, it would also increase the value of your future work."

"That sounds amazing. I'm so grateful for all these opportunities. I hope I can meet your expectations."

Isla embraces me again. "You have so much talent. Don't doubt yourself."

I feel better knowing I have her support, and it does make my heart sing to think about creating with all these wonderful raw materials. After giving me a hug, Isla heads out, leaving me with my heart racing. *Ninety thousand dollars.* Holy crap. I take a picture of the check for posterity and then look at the time on my phone. Davis should be finishing up surgery shortly. I have to share this with him.

Me: Isla just left and I'm $90K richer. Dinner is on me tonight. I'm off to the bank to deposit it before someone changes their mind.

He immediately replies. Guess his surgery is finished already.

Davis: No one will change their mind. You're too talented. We'll go out to celebrate with Arabella. I know just the place. See you about 7.

I look around the studio one more time, slowly realizing that this is happening. In my heart, I know I have Davis to thank. He makes everything better, and he makes me stronger in the process. I just wish my brain didn't feel so scrambled.

I practically skip my way back to the Audi Davis let me

borrow to get to the island, and I drive straight to the bank. They deposit the money with no fanfare or celebration. It's almost disappointing that they don't understand how monumental this moment is.

When I return to the apartment, Arabella hops up from where she's working with Kate at the table to meet me at the door. "We both got packages." She turns and shows me gray boxes with gold edges.

"Who sent us gifts?" I wonder aloud.

"Dr. Martin!" Arabella claps her hands. "He sent us fancy clothes."

"He did?" My eyes grow wide.

"There's a card. Mine told me to be ready to wear this tonight." She shows me a beautiful pink silk, sleeveless dress with a tea-length full skirt. It's perfect for a ten-year-old girl.

"It's beautiful!" I tell her.

"Why are we going out?" she asks. "I've never been anywhere this fancy."

"Well..." I pause. Once I tell Arabella, there's no turning back. I can't disappoint her. I have to make this work. I *want* to make this work. I take a deep breath and explain that I'm going to be working as an artist again, using the driftwood and items from nature we found on Martin Island to create sculptures people will buy.

"That sounds like the most fun job ever," Arabella says.

"I agree," I tell her. "And we're going out, because I've already sold some pieces, even before I have them made. It's amazing!"

She squeals, and we hug, and we bounce around the room like crazy little girls. Arabella can't stop jumping up and down. Nurse Kate shakes her head.

"Open your box," Arabella says when she stops for a breather. "I want to see what he got you."

I nod. The box is from Nordstrom. I pull off the top, and when I clear the tissue paper away, my jaw drops. I lift out a shimmery black silk slip dress with spaghetti straps, a deep V neck, and a mini skirt. It's Gucci. Underneath it are a box of silicone petals and a black lacy thong, along with a pair of nude Gucci heels. I shake my head. It's an entire outfit.

I recognize Davis' writing on the envelope. He actually wrote this himself. *When did he have time?*

Congratulations on the first of many commissions. We'll celebrate tonight and always.
Davis

My heart is in my throat, and I'm not sure how much more excitement I can take today. Arabella runs off to her room, and Nurse Kate walks over to look at all the riches.

"Davis has Felix picking up the three of you here at seven," she tells me. "You're having dinner at the Blue Water Café. I'll be by to get Arabella at nine, so you can enjoy the rest of your evening."

"Kate, that's too much," I tell her.

"Nonsense," she says with a smile. "You deserve a break."

I hug her. "Thank you."

I head down the hall to find Arabella. "We've got two hours," I tell her, poking my head into her room. "I guess we should start getting ready. How about you take a bubble bath, and we'll curl your hair all fancy?"

"Can we?"

"Absolutely."

"What are you going to do with your hair?" she asks.

"I'm not sure. What do you think I should do?"

"I like when it's really straight and shiny."

"I think that's a great idea. I'll flat iron my hair. But first I'm going to take a good long shower and get all lotioned up."

"I'll get in the bath." Arabella runs to the bathroom and gets undressed before we've even started the tub. Her scar is still an angry red, but she's looking fantastic. She has a spark and energy she's never had before. No man who loves her will ever care about her scar. I wish I understood why my mother is so superficial. My father loved her, warts and all, and her warts are big, fat, hairy ones if you ask me.

We draw a bath for Arabella, and while she soaks, I step into the shower. What a luxury that this place has enough hot water for both of us.

Once I'm out, Arabella is still essentially swimming in the tub, so I decide to broach the subject I've been avoiding. I owe it to Davis and to myself. And I think I can let Arabella know what's happening without getting into too many details.

"Arabella, do you think you'd feel okay if I started sleeping in one of the beds in Dr. Martin's apartment, rather than on the couch in ours? I think it would be more comfortable."

She puts her face in the water and blows some bubbles before answering. "No. I don't mind."

That seemed way too easy. "I wouldn't be sleeping in the living room," I clarify again. "But I'd have the monitor, so if you needed me, I could come immediately."

"You're just going to be in a room upstairs, right?"

"Yes, but—"

"Okay. That has to be better than sleeping on the couch. And I kind of like having the bed all to myself."

I smile at her. "Okay, thank you. We'll give it a try then. And, maybe soon, we can find our own apartment close to an excellent school for you, and we can start over."

"Why would you want to leave here?" Arabella looks at me, confused.

My heart lurches, but I force a smile. "Sweetie, we're guests. We can't stay here forever. We need to let Dr. Martin have his condo back to himself."

She gives me a look, not seeming convinced.

"He's done so much to help us. He looked out for us when we needed him most, right?"

She nods, thoughtfully. "Maybe he'll want to marry

you."

I almost choke. Arabella's having the thoughts I can't allow myself to have. I pull my towel tighter and busy myself straightening the things on the counter in the bathroom. "You are silly," I tell her, forcing a laugh. "And you need to get out of that tub if we're going to get you ready on time."

Chapter 18

Paisley

By the time seven rolls around, we're dressed and ready to impress. Davis knocks on the door between our apartments.

When Arabella opens it, he hands her a bouquet of flowers. "These are for you. You look beautiful."

Arabella preens. "Thank you. I love the dress. Thank you for buying it for me."

"I thought we should all look our best to celebrate your sister this evening."

"I think that's a great idea. Where are we going?"

"It's a place called the Blue Water Café, in the Yaletown neighborhood. We'll have a private room all to ourselves. What do you think?"

She nods. "Do they serve chicken nuggets or strips?"

He laughs. "It's mostly seafood, but I think we'll find something you like on the menu."

She nods, and Davis looks up at me. I'm feeling a bit awkward and try not to fidget. This dress feels like little more than a slip, but that's okay. It'll be worth it.

"You look positively stunning."

"Thank you." I smile at him in his perfectly fitted suit and shirt without a tie. "You look very smart yourself."

He kisses me on the cheek. "Congratulations on your big day."

"Thank you. I have to still produce something, but I'm excited to get started. Tomorrow, I'll order some supplies, a smelter, and the silver."

"We'll come back to that," he says. "Don't you worry about it now." He steps back into his apartment for a moment. "The weather is a little cool, so I asked my mother what she might have that would keep you from freezing to death. She sent this over." He produces a silver pashmina, which glitters in the light.

"It's perfect," I breathe.

He steps back to his apartment yet again and then brings a bag to Nurse Kate. "I got your favorite meal from Luigi's. Thank you for coming to pick up Arabella so we can stay out a little later tonight."

Nurse Kate's eyes grow large. "Is that the everything vegetarian calzone?"

Davis shakes his head incredulously. "Would I get you anything else?"

"Thank you, and it's no bother to come pick up Arabella," Kate says. "If it wasn't such a special night, I'd insist she stay here with me."

Davis nods. "It is a special night, and if we don't hurry, we're going to lose our reservation. Felix is downstairs ready to drive us. Are you both all set?"

We nod. I wrap the beautiful silver pashmina around me, and we walk out to the elevator.

"You look positively beautiful," Davis whispers as I walk by.

Downstairs, we slide into a Bentley, and Arabella sits between us as we make our way through town. In the Yaletown neighborhood, all the streetlamps are natural gas, a relic of the old times. I've rarely had a reason to come here, but tonight, we're headed to the best seafood restaurant in all of Vancouver.

"Have you ever been to the Blue Water Café?" Davis asks.

I look at him over Arabella's head. "I don't believe so. But I've heard great things about it."

"They have great oysters—"

"Ick!" Arabella announces.

"They have all sorts of things on their menu, and if you don't find anything you like, they'll make you something you do," he assures her.

"You said it was a seafood restaurant. I do like fish and chips," she says.

"I would bet they have fish and chips." Davis smiles down at her.

Arabella looks up at him. "Paisley asked if it's okay if she spends the night at your house, and I told her it was. I also told her it was okay to marry you if she wanted to do that."

Davis' eyes go wide for a moment, and then a smile spreads over his face. "All this is fantastic news," he tells her. "Thanks for keeping me informed."

She settles into her seat, and Davis gives me a smoldering look over her head. That's not at all the way I'd planned to convey that information, and I'm a little embarrassed, but that's what happens with a ten-year-old in the mix.

I turn and look out the window, waiting for my cheeks to cool down, and in no time, we arrive at the restaurant. We walk in with Arabella holding Davis' hand. It melts my heart to see her so happy. Even if she does have a big mouth.

Heads turn in the restaurant as we enter, and from the looks of things, many people recognize Davis.

We're shown to the Wine Room, and the noise from the restaurant is suddenly very muted. "This is amazing," I say as I look around. The room has hundreds of bottles of wine lying in neat cubicles, ready to be served.

We take our seats, and our server joins us, with two people standing behind her. "Good evening. Welcome to the Blue Water Café. My name is Cory, and assisting me are Trina and John. I understand we're celebrating something tonight?"

Davis nods. "We are."

"Fantastic. The chef has pulled together an eight-course tasting menu for the two of you." She looks at Arabella. "What sounds good to you?"

"Do you have fish and chips?" she asks.

"I believe we can make that happen. What do you like with your fish and chips? Tartar sauce or ketchup?"

"Both, please."

I shake my head. Arabella seems so grown up. Boy, am I in trouble.

"How does shrimp tempura sound for an appetizer?"

"Very good," Arabella volunteers.

"As her cardiothoracic surgeon, could I ask you also include some raw veggies so she doesn't land herself back on my table before she's sixteen?"

Cory nods. "Of course."

"You don't have to be a buzzkill." Arabella stares him down, and I have to fight with all my might not to let the corners of my mouth turn up.

"I'm just looking out for you." He reaches for his water and takes a sip.

She looks between the two of us. "What kind of sleepover do adults have?"

I've just taken a sip of my water, and it comes right out my nose. Thankfully that distracts her from getting an answer to her question. I will have to have that conversation with her, but I want to be able to explain a few more things than are polite at dinner when I do. After my coughing stops, I clear my throat. "Let's talk about what you and Nurse Kate are learning."

"We went over to Stanley Park and walked in some of

the forest and the rose garden. We talk about math in nature."

"Math is in nature?" Davis asks.

"It's everywhere. I see it in even the shelves for the wine and the tiles on the floor."

Davis grins. "What did you learn?"

"There's the Fibonacci spiral. We saw it in a pinecone, but it's in pineapples, sunflowers, and even some of the shells I collected."

"That's pretty cool."

"There's also natural symmetry. Do you know what symmetry means?" Arabella looks at me.

"Umm, yes. Balance, right? Things being equal on both sides?"

She nods. "See? My sister is very smart."

"I know." Davis slides his hand over my thigh and gives it a gentle squeeze.

"Symmetry occurs naturally in flowers. But also, things happen in odd numbers."

Davis looks at her, seeming confused. "What is odd?"

She shakes her head at me as if we're the only two who understand this. "Like odd and even numbers. Can you divide it by two or not divide it by two. Flower petals are often found in odd numbers. It's about balance, and balance equals beauty."

Davis sits back, impressed. "You've really learned a lot with Nurse Kate."

She nods. "I like math and science."

"I think that's great," I say.

We have a wonderful appetizer, complete with veggies, and soon after that, our second course of miso soup and Arabella's fish and chips arrive. We've barely made a dent in it when the salad course arrives, a twisted take on an heirloom tomato and mozzarella salad. We continue chatting and laughing, and Arabella makes a modest dent in her meal before Nurse Kate arrives.

"You both enjoy your evening and try to sleep in a little

tomorrow." She winks and gathers Arabella's things. "We'll find plenty to keep ourselves busy."

I blush, knowing Nurse Kate knows what adults do during sleepovers. I should warn her about Arabella wondering, but I'll let it be a surprise instead.

Once they're gone, Davis turns to me. "Does a sleepover mean you're going to stay the entire night with me?"

I pick at the fork tines in front of me. "Let me check my Magic 8 Ball." I pull a pretend ball from my purse and shake it up. "It says, *All signs point to yes.*"

Davis leans in and kisses me softly. "That's excellent news." He kisses my shoulder, and his hand inches up my dress.

"I explained it to her as opting for a bed rather than the couch, but she seems to have made some additional assumptions." I cover my eyes with my hand.

The waiter enters to refill our glasses of wine, and then Davis raises his to me. "Congratulations on a spectacular first commission. You deserve it, and so much more."

We clink our glasses together as Davis inches his hand up even higher. The only thing shielding us is the tablecloth.

The door to the room opens again, and in comes our main course. Placed in front of us are four beautiful scallops with perfectly golden edges in a green sauce. When I take my first bite, the flavor bursts in my mouth.

"This is my favorite thing here," Davis says with a smile.

"I can definitely see why."

We enjoy a berry sorbet before they bring out dessert, which is a decadent chocolate souffle. I'm both overwhelmed and completely stuffed, but I can't resist the chocolate-dipped fortune cookie served with a port wine as our final course. Davis pushes a few buttons on his phone, and then Felix walks into the room. "Are you ready, Dr. Martin?"

"I think we are."

"I was going to pay for dinner," I remind him.

"I already took care of it," Davis says as he squeezes my leg.

"There seems to be a crowd waiting for you," Felix reports. "May I suggest we take a detour out the back door through the kitchen?"

"Excellent idea."

I look at Davis, confused. "Why would people be waiting for us?"

"It happens sometimes when it's a slow news night. Once a young celebrity does something stupid, they'll be more interested in that."

We walk through the kitchen, and Davis stops to talk to the chef. "Fredric, dinner was fantastic."

I nod enthusiastically. "Outstanding. Really."

He grins. "I'm so glad you enjoyed yourselves. Please come again. I'll have abalone next month, and of course, the mussels will be the best of the season."

"We'll be back," Davis promises.

We walk out the back door of the restaurant and into the waiting car. "Felix, can you drive around for a bit?" Davis asks. "Take the scenic route if you would."

Felix nods. "Of course."

Davis pushes a button, and a screen rises to separate us from the two men in front. "Come here," he urges me.

I unbuckle my seatbelt and lower myself to the floor between his legs. I can't come up with a good enough reason to fight this right now. So many good things are happening, and they're all because of Davis. If that doesn't call for indulgence, I don't know what does. I reach for his hardness and caress it through his pants.

Davis looks down. "You're so beautiful looking up at me right now."

"I'd like to show you my appreciation for dinner tonight."

He chuckles, and I feel so powerful as I unbuckle his

pants and pull his long, thick, veiny cock free. The tip is oozing, and I lick it away. "Mmmmmm…" I moan. "You taste so good."

"Are you sure you wouldn't want to sit on it instead?"

I look up at him as I take it deep in my mouth, swallowing and trying not to choke. I roll my wet mouth all over and fist it as I suck the purple head as deeply as I can.

I hear his breath hitch, and his hand laces through my hair as the head hits the back of my throat. The back of the car fills with sloppy sounds as I bob on his cock. Davis' groans and grunts tell me he's close to losing control, and I like that.

One of my hands finds its way to my hot button. I have to relieve the tension. The rhythmic sway of the car is getting me hotter and hotter.

"Give me your hand," Davis demands.

I give him my free hand.

"No, I want the one you're using to play with yourself."

I give it to him, and he puts it in his mouth, licking my fingers clean. This only serves to turn me on more.

"Baby," he warns. "I'm going to come."

"Fill my mouth," I tell him. "I want to swallow it all."

He rolls his head back and looks up at the ceiling of the car as the first salty spurts hit the back of my throat. I keep bobbing almost until the end. Then I lick my lips and swallow it down.

"Fuck! That is so hot." Davis tucks himself back into his pants and pulls me up onto the seat next to him, cuddling me close.

Shortly after that, we pull up at his building. One of Felix's men opens the door, and I know they know what we did. I try not to let that embarrass me. When we exit the car, my knees are red. There's now no question as to what we were doing. I feel myself blushing as Davis reaches for my hand.

"Thanks, guys," he tells them. "Have a good night."

Davis guides me to the elevator, swipes his fob over the pad, and pushes me against the wall. "If I wasn't sure the guard was watching us, I'd lick your pussy until you come all over my face right here in the elevator. Instead, I'll wait until we get upstairs."

Heat blooms in my chest. "I love it when you talk dirty to me."

"What else do you love?"

"The way you play my body like a fine instrument."

"That's because it is."

We arrive at the penthouse, and Davis quickly steps into the kitchen to close the door between the apartments. I take the opportunity to remove my panties and hook them over my finger.

He takes them from me and sniffs them. "Fuck, you smell so good."

He sits me up on the counter, and between his three fingers inside, pivoting in and out of me relentlessly, and his mouth vacuuming up my clit, I'm soon gripping his hair and calling his name.

"Take your dress off," he demands.

I stand and pull my dress over my head. I'm reaching to peel away the petals when he steps forward and does it for me.

He ravishes my breasts, and I may have a small orgasm just from that stimulation. "I love how sexual you are," he growls.

"I want you to fuck me hard, and I want it now."

Davis shucks his suit off and continues kissing me. He turns me over. "This alabaster ass would look better pink."

"I need to be spanked, I guess."

He pushes me down so my breasts are against the cold granite. He grabs my hair and wrenches me back as he pushes in deep. I cry out with a mix of pain and ecstasy. The first sting of a slap hits me, and pain and pleasure swirl again.

He lets go of my hair, and I rest my cheek on the

granite as he pushes in and out, hard and fast. He reaches around me to strum my clit, and all I can see is white as my body explodes. Just a few moments later, he follows.

Then we're still for a few moments as we catch our breath.

Davis nuzzles my neck. "You never cease to amaze me."

Chapter 19

Paisley

Some of my supplies are already being delivered after I ordered them this morning, so I'm busy putting together my studio. I found several tables and some storage shelves in place today when I got here, thanks to Davis making sure I have what I need.

My phone rings. It's my mother. I ignore the call, but she immediately calls back.

"Sorry, Mom, but I'm swamped. Can I call you later?"

"No!" she cries. "Please. I need some help."

"What's going on?"

She's crying. "I'm stuck at the border. Customs is requiring I pay twenty-five thousand dollars or they're sending me to jail."

I stop what I'm doing and look out at the gray sky. "What?"

"I was given a hand-blown glass bowl. I thought it was pretty, and I was going to sell it for a few hundred dollars to someone I know in Seattle. But Customs is saying it's a Rex Stanford and is worth over two hundred and fifty thousand dollars."

I roll my eyes. Like hell she didn't know that. Chances are she thought border patrol wouldn't know and she planned on selling it for much more than she's saying. She's always working an angle when it comes to money.

"If I don't pay the import taxes, they'll keep the bowl and try me for smuggling. I could be deported permanently from the U.S. Can you please call Davis and see if he'll lend you the money? I'll pay you back as soon as I'm back over. Travis will give it to me. I'm your mother. You know I'm good for it."

I roll my eyes. Once I send it to her, I'm pretty sure the money is gone. I sigh. "I don't know. Davis is in surgery today." He's actually doing something for Martin Communications, but I would never bother him about this. Plus, he doesn't need further evidence that my mother is a wreck. "If Travis will give you the money, why can't you just get it from him now?"

"He's with his friends fishing up in Alaska this weekend. I can't reach him. Please call Davis. I'm in a holding room until I can get the money. Please," she cries loudly.

To say I'm irritated would be an understatement.

"This is so little money to him," my mother continues. "He's a billionaire. This is like a coffee for you or me."

I snort. *A coffee?* I don't buy coffees. "*If* I can get the money—and I do mean *if*—where do I send it?" I ask.

She gives me her banking information.

"I'll see what I can do. If I can work it out, this is only a short-term loan, and you'll need to wire me back the money in a few days."

"Of course. Thank you, thank you, thank you," she repeats.

I disconnect the call. I'm not going to tell Davis. No way. But I could actually send it to her myself. I don't know that it's the right thing to do, though. I think through all the potential scenarios. If I give her the money, does it mean Arabella will have to go back to public school? I was hoping that after meeting Julia and Chip, an interview at Point Grey Academy would be an option, but I don't know when those payments would be due. If I wire her the money and after what I've spent on supplies, I'm down to twenty thousand dollars. That makes a new apartment difficult, and that's if I can find someone who'll rent to me. Then it hits me. This is a live/work loft. We could move in here.

I look around and try to picture how that would work. We have a mattress and box springs in storage for the corner. We could pull out our crappy television, too. It would give us a year, and maybe this will be the motivation I need to get my work done.

My mind whirls. I am going to see another ninety thousand eventually, and if I can maximize my work time, we won't be without money for too long. Maybe I can take another trip out to the island for more driftwood as well.

Isla mentioned being part of the Studio Tour. That may be of value, and I can do some more experimenting. I pull a sketch pad out and begin considering my plan. Can I do it?

But why am I going to all this trouble for my mother? What is it about her that makes me jump whenever she barks a command? I want to be stronger, to just ignore her, but she's the only family Arabella and I have. I sigh. I asked her to pay for Bella's tutoring, and she wouldn't. She left us barely hanging on. But that's not the kind of person I want to be.

I spend nearly an hour working out my plan for sending Mom what she's asked for. I finally call my banker and let her know I need to wire some money. She doesn't ask many questions, just taps on her computer.

"The money is on the way," she tells me. "She should have it within an hour. It'll be up to her bank to credit it."

I sigh and thank her. Once we've finished the call, I send Mom a text.

Me: The money is on the way. I expect the full amount back in forty-eight hours.

Mom: Thank you. I will get the money and send it to you right away.

My phone rings. "You sent me Canadian dollars. That's only nineteen thousand and change. They want twenty-five thousand U.S. dollars. When can you send me another eight thousand?"

My stomach drops. "You didn't specify that you needed U.S. dollars."

"Are you kidding me?" she screeches. "Get Davis to send you another eight K."

Fuck. "Well, you're certainly very welcome, Mother. I'm so glad to be able to be here for you." *Why did I send her any money at all?*

I return to setting up my smelter, trying to distract myself. When I was in school, I developed a stamp of my logo for my work. To test my smelter, I make a coin and stamp my logo on one side. My vision becomes blurry as I stare at the coin. I wish my father was here and could tell me how to handle all of this. He was the only one who knew how to manage Mom.

After a little while I set the coin aside, call the banker back, and send the rest of the money. I don't want to, but in for a penny, in for a pound.

Me: The money is sent.

I don't have any chairs, so I lean up against a wall and slide to the floor. The tears flow. I've done what I thought was right. Why don't I feel any better?

I hear a knock at the door. I try to ignore it, but the knocks persist.

"Open up, Paisley," I hear Davis call.

I'm shocked. He had plans today. I wipe the tears away with the palm of my hand and try to make sure my makeup isn't giving me racoon eyes.

Davis knocks again. "Open up now."

I swing the door wide. He takes one look and pulls me in. "What's going on?"

I've made his T-shirt all wet. "I'm just overwhelmed with all of this."

He steps back and looks at me. "Is that it?"

I nod and wipe my eyes again. His T-shirt has some mascara smudges.

He looks over how I've set up the loft and spots the coin. "What is this?"

"I was testing the smelter. My logo is stamped on all my art."

"Even my mom's piece?"

"Yes. It's on the foot of one of the branches."

"You could do something with this. It would be a great business card or coin in this case."

"A silver coin would be pretty expensive to give away."

"You could use a different metal that would be less expensive. Maybe something like pewter. And we can develop a stamp for the other side that has your website on it."

I sigh. *A website?* I've not even thought about something like that. That takes money, photos, and skills I don't have. My heart races, and I push the tears back.

"You don't have a website, do you?"

I shake my head. "It's too much."

"No, it's not. I'll help you get started." Davis steps away, and he must send out several emails, because I hear his phone ping several times. "Okay, Delilah Bennett is a professional photographer. She's going to meet you at my parents' home. She'll take some pictures of you with the piece my mother has, and she'll make plans to come over when you're working to take more photos. Delilah works for Adam Janssen. He's Griffin's best friend from school. He does public relations and websites, and they'll design everything for you."

My blood pressure rises. "How much is all of this going to cost?"

"Five or ten thousand dollars, but it's worth it."

I nod. There's more money flying out the window. I realize at least I still have that much. "I'm just nervous spending all of what I have in case it's a while before I get the rest."

Davis tilts his head to the side. "I know this is a lot of money for you. But this is just the beginning. This is all going to be good in the long run."

I chew at my thumbnail.

"Let's go get Arabella and head into Stanley Park. We can walk to the Brewpub, if you think she'd enjoy that."

"I think she'd love it."

He pockets the coin, and after I lock up the loft, we walk to his car. I'll need to figure out a few things, but I bet Arabella and I could move here by the beginning of next month and give Davis his space back.

As we drive back to the condo, Davis gets a phone call about a difficult case, and it allows me to scan my phone for new messages. So far, I don't have anything from my mom about the rest of the money. That must mean she got it and that's all she needs from me. I saw that coming and did it anyway. There's no one to blame but myself.

Chapter 20

Davis

When Felix called to tell me Paisley had transferred more than thirty-two thousand dollars to a U.S. account, my heart stopped. What is she up to? I really hope Vanessa hasn't gotten her claws into Paisley's commission money, but I don't dare ask. I don't want to upset Paisley while she's already having such a hard time managing all this. It just doesn't particularly make sense. According to the background check, Vanessa's bank balance in the Caymans is over a half-million dollars. And she's living a life well beyond what her daughters are.

I've ignored Vanessa's calls to follow up on the money she wants. I don't want to deal with her, and I think there are other ways to get her out of the girls' life. Felix and I are working on a few angles. We're more interested in how she grew that bank balance she has offshore.

"What's for dinner?" Arabella asks as the three of us walk down the sidewalk together from my condo.

"I thought we'd go to Stanley Park and hit the Brewpub. How does that sound?"

"They have my favorite grilled cheese sandwich. It even has cheese on the outside of the bread."

"Ohhh. That does sound very tasty," I tell her.

Now that she knows where we're going, Arabella runs ahead. I look over at Paisley. "I spoke with Dr. Cavanaugh today."

She turns to me, surprised. "What did she say?"

"Arabella has lost four pounds since her surgery."

"Four pounds isn't too much, is it?"

"It is when she only weighed fifty-three pounds to begin with."

Paisley lets out a breath of air. "What do we do?"

"I think she needs to have a protein shake for breakfast. And at lunch we're going to power load her meals for maximum calories. Dinner needs to be healthy but also full of protein and iron and lots of vegetables."

"She's not going to be too excited about steak and spinach tonight."

I smile. "It's okay. She can have the grilled cheese. I'm most interested in her gaining weight, but not becoming addicted to junk food."

Paisley nods. "I get it. Junk food is cheap, and we've eaten a lot of it because it's affordable."

"You know, I've told you this before, but you don't have to move out."

She gives me a strained look. "I can't tell you how much it means to me that you've been so generous, not only with your time and your house, but with checking on us and making sure we're going to be okay."

"You know I don't mind."

She places her hand on the center of my chest. I can feel her pulling away, and I don't know how to stop it. "I'm afraid we're becoming too attached to all the benefits of living with you. This is not our life. I can't just pretend it is forever. We struggle from check to check. We live in cheap apartments and try very hard to eat healthy. There's rarely fresh produce and most vegetables come from cans."

"But it doesn't have to be that way."

"I know you think my art is going to take the world by storm, and I've never had anyone be so supportive of me, but…" Her voice cracks.

"Just promise me you won't disappear," I beg.

She manages a smile. "Why would I do that? You promised me four orgasms in one night, and we've not gotten there yet."

I laugh loudly. "I think we should try chasing that one tonight."

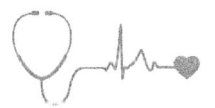

On Saturday evening, as I drive out to the Vancouver Country Club, I think about last night. We didn't even try chasing Paisley's goal. Instead, we came home, put Arabella to bed, and curled up on the couch. She still hasn't said anything about the money she moved, so I'm not sure what's going on. But I don't have a good feeling.

Today, I'm meeting Michael and a couple of my other buddies, Steve McCormick and Jack Drake, for a round of golf. We met while doing our residencies and fellowships, and outside of my three brothers, they're the only people I trust.

Standing at the tees on the first green, Michael keeps itching his jock.

"You know," I tell him, "I can prescribe you something for that itch."

"My dick is chapped," he retorts and drives a ball almost three hundred yards down the fairway.

The three of us laugh hard.

"You're just jealous," he counters. "I've got a young thing I've introduced to her sexual awakening."

I roll my eyes. "Please. Is this the young nurse from

labor and delivery?"

"It's her roommate. She can't get enough of my dick."

"Wait," Steve says as he prepares to tee off. "You fucked someone you worked with and then started with her roommate? Are you suicidal?"

"We're all good," he assures us.

I shake my head. That is going to blow up in his face.

"We missed you last night at The Lion's Den," Jack says. "You could have met Cinnamon and Savannah."

"Those are the girls' names?" He must be pulling something. No way those aren't stripper names.

"Those are their names. Where were you?"

"I reconnected with the woman I met at The Lion's Den a few months ago."

"Where?" Jack asks. Jack is a plastic surgeon and has a bevy of women himself.

"When?" Michael presses.

"She came into the emergency room a month or so ago with her little sister." I'm not straying from the truth. I'd like Paisley to meet them, and hopefully, they'll hit it off.

"How old is the little sister?" Steve asks.

"She just turned ten."

"Are you sure it's not her kid?" Michael asks.

I nod. "I'm sure. I met their mother. She's a train wreck."

"Wait, you met her family?" Jack asks, his eyes wide.

I nod. "And she's been out to the compound and Martin Island."

The guys all stop and look at me.

"What are you telling us?" Steve asks.

I tell them all about Paisley moving in with me while Arabella was in the hospital, and how I want something real with her.

We move down the fairway, and I chip onto the green.

"She wants to keep it light, and you don't?" Michael asks.

I line up my putt. "We're going slow...sort of anyway. But I think I want it all with Paisley."

"Why would you do that when you could have a different woman every night?" Jack asks.

I look at Jack. "Because she's not out for my name, my money, or any notoriety. She's authentic." *And it's making things complicated.*

"Are you sure having her so close all the time hasn't pushed you over the edge?" Steve raises an eyebrow.

"She's fucking amazing. She's a talented sculptor, and she put her life on hold when her psycho mother up and left her with her younger sister, who has complicated medical issues."

"Isn't it boring to have sex with the same woman over and over?" Jack asks.

I chuckle and shake my head. I don't have anything more to say about that.

"Whoa," Michael says. "You haven't offered any good gossip. Does that mean you're officially off the market?"

I sink my putt. "Men, I think that just may be the case."

"No way!" Steve insists. "You? Of all of us, I thought you'd be the one who'd go last. You've never wanted a woman long-term."

"That's not true," I counter.

"Elaine Getty." He raises his brows at me and dares me to argue.

During my pediatric cardiology fellowship, I met Elaine, but she knew I was too raw to commit to more than fun. After my girlfriend, Joyce, and my best friend from medical school screwed me over, I wasn't open to anything real. "She knew my fellowship was my priority. I wanted to be a top pediatric cardiothoracic surgeon, and I needed to focus on that. After a while, she got ready for more and moved on."

Steve glares at me. "Bullshit. If you'd wanted more with her, you could have done it. Most of our friends got married during our medical training. You chose not to."

I roll my eyes. "And how many of those who married during the most stressful times in our lives are still married to the same person?" I pull my putter from my bag. "Look, I've not been the best at committing. I've always made it clear that if someone wanted more than fun, they could move on. Most women who seek me out are looking to increase their social profile. I do want to marry. I want a family. But I want to do those things once, not multiple times."

Steve holds up his hands and surrenders. "I'm happy for you if this woman is it."

"I think she may be."

"Then why are we here?" Michael asks. "Let's get ourselves off the golf course so we can get you home and in bed with her."

"We want to meet her—and soon," Jack adds.

"How was your game today?" Paisley asks that evening as I sit down with her and Arabella on the couch. "Did you hit them long and straight?"

I look at her with my eyes wide. "Do you golf?"

"Oh, God no!" She cuddles into me. "I Googled how to ask about a golf game."

I throw my head back laughing. "That's funny!"

"Well?"

"I wasn't the best of our group, but I wasn't the worst. Steve is a natural athlete. He puts in minimal effort and kills us."

"Steve is an orthopedist, right?"

I nod. "He works with the hockey and football teams in town. Michael always has some new club he's trying out, and he's usually the worst of us. Today, he had a chipper-putter, a totally illegal club, but we don't care."

"Illegal? He could get arrested for having that club in his bag?"

I laugh again. "No. It's illegal in terms of what's allowed if the round is going to count toward his handicap. But he's so bad, if he thinks a chipper-putter is going to make his game better, we don't care. We're just out to have fun together. We're not trying for the PGA."

"So it was a good day?"

I take a drink of my water, trying to rehydrate myself after drinking too much beer on the golf course. "It was. They're anxious to meet you."

"Me? Why?"

"Because they know I'm crazy about you."

Arabella looks at her and grins.

"That seems like we're walking into relationship territory," Paisley says.

I look at Arabella, who is now pretending to avidly watch the movie.

I stand and offer Paisley my hand, and we walk into the kitchen. "Yes, it is relationship territory. We're free to date now, and that's what we've been doing. Plus, you sleep in my bed every night, you've met my family, we spend time together, and we support one another. Why can't we be in a relationship?"

"Because I've said from the beginning, I don't have room in my life for a relationship. Arabella has to be my focus. We're just dating casually."

"This is a real relationship," I tell her, frustrated that she can't see what's happening right in front of her.

She recoils.

"I'm sorry, but I think your insistence that things are casual undercuts what we are." I run my fingers through my hair. "Arabella is getting better. You're doing a great job caring for her, and you are worth taking time for as well. Think about what *you* want."

She sighs. "Right now, that's all I'm capable of giving you."

"So that means you won't meet my friends?"

"How are you planning on introducing me? As your girlfriend? Your friend? Your friend you fuck? Or maybe as the sister of a patient you're putting up in your nanny apartment?"

I rear back, not because of the crudeness of her comment, but at how different our perspective is. "I would introduce you as Paisley Brooks." I shake my head. "Never mind. You mean something to me, and I want to share my life with you. I thought I meant something to you."

She blows out a breath of air. "You do mean something to me. But my life is a dumpster fire. Why anyone would want to meet me is beyond my comprehension, particularly a group of guys you golf and hang out with. To them, I'm a one-night stand and not worthy of their time."

She turns, and I watch her back as she returns to the living room to be close to Arabella. My friends and I had fun today. I'm disappointed that she thinks so little of us. I'm more disappointed that she thinks so little of herself.

I follow her back to the living room. The two of them are curled up watching their movie. "I'm going to go take a shower. Arabella, have a good night. Paisley, will I see you later?"

Kate is working with us less now, and she has the weekend off, so I'm not sure if Paisley will go for it, even without our argument in the mix. But I just want something concrete from her.

She looks up at me, her eyes wide. "Sure. I mean, I guess so."

"Good. See you then."

I shower and dress for bed. I turn the television on and watch the local news while I wait for Paisley, but she never comes. After watching a repeat *of Saturday Night Live* and an episode of *Seinfeld*, I wander back toward her apartment, and she's still curled up with Arabella, both of them sleeping on the couch. I turn off the TV, and after covering them with a blanket, I head back to my room.

I lie on my back with my arms crossed behind my head and stare at the ceiling. I suppose I should tell Paisley how I feel. She must know, given all I've said, but I'm not sure how she'd take it if I said it outright. Actually, I know she won't take it very well. But that might also be the only way to get through to her.

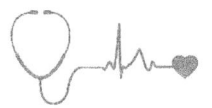

I'm not sure when I fell asleep last night, but the sun came up too early. I roll over, and there's a warm body in my bed.

"Good morning," she mumbles.

"Hey. When I checked on you last night, you were dead asleep on the couch. I didn't want to wake you, so I covered you with a blanket."

"Thank you. I woke up a few hours ago because my bladder was screaming at me. We fell asleep watching our movie. I don't want you to think I'm avoiding you."

"Are you sure? Because you were pretty honest with me last night."

"I'm positive. But…"

I look down at her, waiting.

"I'm sorry about last night. You want more than I know how to give you, and I don't know what to do."

"I do want more, but I'm also patient."

She looks at me with her left brow cocked.

"I'm *trying* to be patient."

"I have so much going on. Isla talked me into committing to take part in the Studio Tour, and she wants me to create nine pieces for that. And then she wants me to think about doing a show at the gallery downstairs."

My eyes grow big. "That's great, isn't it?"

She bobs her head from side to side. "Maybe. I don't know." She sighs. "It's so much pressure, and what if I commit to all of this and Arabella needs me? This isn't like a normal job where I can just quit. If I commit to this, I have to follow through."

"I'm here to help you. If you need me or any resources, you know I'm good for it."

"I'm coming to depend on you, and that makes me nervous."

I shake my head. "Why would that make you nervous?"

"Because you make it easy, and that makes me too comfortable."

"I know you've been without a support system for the past few years, but I'm not going anywhere. I want to be part of your life and Arabella's life. You don't have to do this all on your own." I pause, trying to find a way to make her smile. "Well, I'm not going to do your artwork. That's your thing, and I'll stick to heart surgery, which is my thing. But I can get more driftwood, order supplies, shuttle Arabella places when Nurse Kate's not working, or just help you relax."

"Relax, huh? I think I could do with some relaxing right now."

I roll her onto her back and press my hardness into her center. "I think this may work."

She giggles. "Aren't you going to your parents' this afternoon?"

"Yes, and they're counting on you and Arabella being with me." I hold my breath a moment, praying she won't resist on this as well. I can tell she wants to, but after a brief internal battle, she nods. "But we don't have to go until after lunch," I assure her, running my hand up the side of her leg. "We've got plenty of time."

"Arabella's asleep on the couch. I can't be too loud and

wake her."

I grin and quickly lock my bedroom door. I wouldn't want to have to explain what we're doing, but this is a perfect Sunday morning. I can't resist her.

I roll a condom on, part her legs, and enter her slowly. I'm not out to win any races or get my kink on. I want to make slow and gentle love. I move in and out of her while my hands and mouth play with the spots I know drive her wild. She moans.

"You're so beautiful when we're like this."

I suckle at her breast, flicking the hard tip with my tongue. She gasps.

"I love your breasts. One day I want to fuck them and give you a pearl necklace of my cum."

"Yes, please," she breathes.

My thumb strokes her hard nub, and her channel constricts.

"That's it, baby. Come for me." I bite down on her nipple while I increase pressure on her clit, all while pushing deep inside her.

Her body trembles, and she grasps the sheets for leverage as her back arches. She holds her breath as her climax overtakes her.

I follow her over the cliff and pull her close. Our hearts beat as one.

"That was incredible," she says. "I've never experienced anything like this with anyone else."

"Me neither. And it gets better each time we do it."

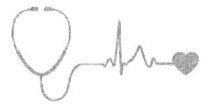

My dad is anxiously waiting when we arrive. "You made it!"

"I thought we would never get here," Arabella says.

"These two were all kissy-face this morning."

You gotta love the honesty of a child.

"Hey, Dad. What's the hurry?" I ask.

"We have a pod of porpoises swimming behind the house going after what we think is a school of squid."

"You mean a squad of squid," Arabella corrects.

I'm certain my dad knew they're called a squad.

"How did you get so smart?" we hear him ask as they walk down to the beach.

I open the front door, and Mom and Henry are waiting for us with drinks. "Well, if it isn't the happy couple," she says with a grin, and internally I groan. I need to get my mom on the right page before Paisley freaks out.

Paisley turns a beautiful shade of pink and gives Henry and Mom a quick embrace before sitting down.

"Isla tells me you've committed to the Studio Tour, and then you'll have eleven pieces that will move down to the gallery for your own show! That's so exciting!"

"Ah, well, she told me nine, but thank you. I'm nervous, and I know I wouldn't have gotten this without you. I'm eternally grateful."

Mom steps over to her and gives her a hug. "I'm so excited for you. Isla asked that we include my piece and mark it sold in the display."

"You don't have to do that."

"I'm not one to buy and sell, but let me just say, I paid five thousand dollars for your piece almost four years ago. You've sold the next four for fifty thousand dollars each. The remaining will easily go for more than that. That makes mine an investment that even my husband would tell me was worth it."

Paisley shakes her head. "I highly doubt people are going to pay that kind of money for something they can find on any beach here in British Columbia."

I'm going to let Mom work her magic here, so I just listen while I pour Paisley a drink and one for me. I lift the bottle of scotch to Henry, and he shakes his head.

"That's what people used to say about Jackson Pollock paintings," Mom counters. "Who would ever pay even five thousand dollars for paint splashed on a canvas?"

Paisley sighs. "I see where Davis learned the art of arguing."

"Mom taught us all well." Henry smiles as he walks over to the bar for a bottle of water.

I hand Paisley one of my mom's pink concoctions. She raises her brow at my mom in question.

"Pink lemonade with a splash of vodka and limoncello," Mom replies.

Paisley takes a tentative sip. "Mmmmmm." Then she takes a much larger one. "I can't drink too many of these. I might agree to one of Davis' crazy ideas."

"I'll get the pitcher," I tease.

We all sit down, and Henry tells me about an issue they're having with the federal regulating body in Alberta. I'm so grateful to be far away from the family business.

Phillip and Griffin arrive a little while later. They've been deep sea fishing and brought back two Chinook salmon, both weighing over a hundred pounds and about fifty inches long. They show us pictures as proof.

"What are you going to do with all that salmon?" Mom asks.

"Eat it," Griffin responds.

"I should have asked that differently. Given you don't cook and don't have a cook, what's your plan?"

"We left it at the marina, and the fishmonger will filet and prepare both fish for us. We'll share it with you. I'll save some for a special night and some for the barbecue."

"What's a special night?" Paisley asks.

Mom leans over. "He thinks I don't understand, but what he's trying to say is he'll cook for a woman he's trying to bed."

"Ohh..." My brothers and I all taunt him after Mom's

mic drop.

Paisley turns pink, and I put my arm around her. "We've not been able to get anything past Mom since we were ten years old."

She shrugs. "I grew up with two brothers, so I knew how your minds worked."

"Where's Dad?" Phillip asks.

"We've had a pod of porpoises off shore all afternoon. He took Arabella down to check them out."

"Oh cool." He rises and heads out with Griffin hot on his heels.

"You thought they had the fish in the back of their car and were planning on leaving it here," Henry scoffs.

"You bet I did," Mom replies. "It wouldn't surprise me. I also expect we'll see at least one of those fish in our freezer. Do you like salmon, Paisley?"

"I love it. But I'm not a cook. I can bake. My cooking skills include mostly putting a frozen pizza in the oven."

Mom laughs and shakes her head. "I'll be right back. I need to make sure your father pulls the right vegetables from the fridge."

"Why doesn't Griffin bring Teresa to Sunday night dinners?" Paisley asks in a low voice.

"She's been here before, but she doesn't enjoy them."

"Why not?"

"She and Griffin have been dating off and on since high school. She's done some things to him we're not crazy about, and I know she senses that." I don't want to go into all the details with Paisley. Teresa is a bitch, and Griffin for some reason still dates her.

She nods thoughtfully and doesn't press the issue.

When Dad returns, he goes out to start the grill and roast the vegetables to go with a prime rib he has in the smoker. Paisley volunteers to help Mom, and I'm left to fend for myself. I wander outside to find my brothers.

They're lounging on the deck, watching Dad work.

"Where's Arabella?"

"She found some new shells she wanted to show her sister." Griffin gestures back toward the house.

Dad is carefully watching his vegetables. "That girl is sharp as a whip. Mom and I got her into Point Grey Academy for the fall. Mom wants to tell them tonight. Do you think it will go over well?"

I nod. "I do think Arabella will be ready to return to school at that point. What does the scholarship situation look like for her?"

"Paisley just got ninety thousand dollars and is living rent free," Phillip pipes up.

I look at him, annoyed. "Yes, they're living in my nanny apartment, but she has bills and expenses. She's managing her sister's recovery and restarting her art career."

Henry puts his bottle of water down and looks out over the water. "Mom has a great eye and wouldn't have bought the first piece if she didn't think it was good. Other people will see the same."

"I agree, but she's never had much money," I tell them. "She doesn't even own a car. All this is overwhelming."

"It may seem that way, but if I were you," Henry says, "I wouldn't get too wrapped up in this girl. Seems like she could be a miner. She's in this for the secure lifestyle."

I shake my head. Henry is way off base.

"I think you need to consider Henry's perspective," Griffin says. "I know she didn't stalk you, but once she met you, she knew you were her ticket out of the ghetto. It's great that you're helping her care for her sister, but more than that gets risky."

"She has a lot of baggage, and this is a train wreck waiting to be splashed all over the tabloids," Phillip adds.

My dad hasn't looked up at me or told my brothers to back off, so there's part of him that must agree with what they're saying. But I think they're wrong, and that's all that matters. I don't feel like arguing because it's not even worth it.

I sigh. "Thanks for the advice."

Out of the corner of my eye, I see movement, and I turn to find Paisley coming out onto the deck. From the look on her face, she's heard their conversation. *Shit.*

Chapter 21

Paisley

His brothers think so little of me, and he says nothing? I feel like I can't draw a full breath.

After this morning, I thought we'd turned a corner. I was honest with him, and he didn't even flinch. He had me believing maybe we could be something more. But I should have known letting my walls down would be a mistake. If I could grab Arabella and leave without making a scene, I would run so far and so fast. I'm humiliated.

The look on Davis' face is pure surprise.

Yeah, I heard what they said and, more importantly, what you didn't say.

I struggle to paint on a smile. "Your mom wanted you to know that as soon as the vegetables are done, the table is set and ready to go."

Davis looks at me like a deer in the headlights.

"Sounds great." Chip says. "I should be pulling these in just a few minutes."

Davis crosses to me with concern in his eyes.

"Not here. Not now," I hiss softly.

He nods.

We eventually all sit down for dinner, and my stomach turns. I don't belong here. I don't want to be here anymore. Davis pats my leg. "Are you okay?"

I give him my plastic smile and don't answer.

"Look—"

I shake my head sharply. "As I said, not here."

I don't take part in any of the conversation, not that I could. The Martins talk over and push through each other, leaving little room for small voices. It's only when Julia asks me about the loft that I say anything.

"It's coming along. I have more supplies arriving each day, and I think I've figured out what I want to do for some of the next pieces."

She smiles. "I can't wait to see it. I'll be there for the Studio Tour. It's such a fun fundraiser. Patrons wander in and out to see how you create. It's a rare opportunity, and it opens you up for more possible buyers. Clarence Mills usually does an amazing display as he shows how he makes his totems."

I manage a nod. "I can see him from my window. Everyone has been so welcoming. The Granville Island Broom Company gave me one of their brooms for my space. I was so honored."

Julia nods. "I love how supportive the community is there. You're going to be very happy."

"I think so."

The conversation turns back to Martin Communications, and I can't listen. My mind is jumping from one thought to another. Davis knows I'm not out for his money. But when his brothers say something, he doesn't defend me. Why? I'm not sure I need to find out. I've known for weeks I needed to get out of his space. I guess now is the time. I'll prove they're wrong about me.

Once dinner concludes, we say our goodbyes and climb back into Davis' car. "Can we talk about it now?" he asks as we pull away.

I glance toward Arabella in the backseat and shake my head. "Maybe later."

"Thank you for coming tonight," he says. "It seemed a little hairier than usual."

"It was generous of your family to allow us to come." I stare out at the Vancouver streets, illuminated by the yellow-orange glow of the streetlights.

When Julia told me Arabella would be invited to attend Point Grey Academy in the fall, I was thrilled. I'll just need to move forward with that on my own. The Studio Tour will put a lot of buzz out there, and if people like my work, we can live frugally, and I can send her to school at Point Grey.

When we arrive back at the condo, I steer Arabella toward her bedroom and call over my shoulder to Davis. "Goodnight."

"We need to talk."

"I can't right now."

He comes after me and takes my arm as Arabella goes on ahead. "We still need to talk."

"It's been a long day, and I'm tired." As I pull away from him, I pat his chest.

"I don't like us going to sleep without this resolved."

"I don't think there's anything to resolve."

He looks at me for a long moment, but then turns and retreats to his own apartment. I shut the door between our units and crawl into bed with Arabella.

My mind is active as I work through everything I'll need to do in the morning. We're not scheduled with Kate tomorrow, as she's now working mostly with other clients, so nothing to worry about there. Arabella and I will need the bed and a few small items from storage, but we'll be able to make living at the loft work. I'm going to leave the clothes Davis bought us here. We haven't worn everything, and hopefully he can return them.

I should write all this down, but I don't want to disturb Arabella. The change will be hardest on her. Seems it always is.

Though it feels like I don't sleep at all, when the sun shines on my face, it wakes me. I leave Arabella sleeping and walk out to find a note from Davis.

> *I didn't wake you to go running. I'm in surgery all day. Let's grab dinner tonight. You can choose.*
> *Davis*

It makes me sad. I can't continue like this anymore. This life isn't real. Whether Davis feels the same as his brothers do or not, if they keep after him, eventually he probably will. I need to stand on my own and provide for Arabella, like I always have. That's my job; that's my life. I won't have anyone think I'm trying to do things the way my mother does.

I pack my bag, and when Arabella wakes, I ask her to do the same.

"Why?" she asks.

"We're going to live in our own place again. It's going to be so much fun living in the loft on Granville Island."

"But what about Davis?"

"He's going to live here. This is his house."

"But there isn't a bed at the loft."

"Our stuff will arrive from storage today. If it doesn't, we can camp out on the floor like we used to do."

"But I don't want to leave here," Arabella says, her eyes wide.

"Why not?"

"I want to stay and be part of Davis' family."

"Sweetheart, it doesn't work like that. We're not in their family. They were kind to us, but we have to live on our own, like we always have."

"Davis asked me if I would want to be part of his family, and I told him yes."

I shut my eyes because I'm seeing red. How could he

ask her that and get her hopes up?

"I'm not going!" Arabella walks back to her bedroom and slams the door.

"You can't stay here by yourself."

"Nurse Kate can stay with me."

"Sweetie, she has her own life apart from us. You know that. She's already cut back on her time with you so she can help other kids, and your tutoring is just about finished for the season, so soon she won't be around much at all. Now that I'm doing my art, I can take you to all your appointments. We'll see them again, but we need to move into our own place before Davis has to ask us to go. If we overstay our welcome, we won't be able to be friends after that."

That seems to put Arabella at ease. She's been very spoiled over the last two weeks, and I know this is going to be hard for her. I leave a note for Davis and a check to cover our expenses over the last month and a half.

She packs up her things, and I call a rideshare to take us over to Granville Island.

When the car arrives, Arabella clings to my side.

"We're going to be okay," I assure her.

"I like being rich better than being poor."

I snort. "That's usually the case, but we're not really poor. We have each other, and the rest is just window dressing."

"What do we tell Mom?"

Other than the money she owes me hasn't arrived? "She's always able to contact me. She'll find us if she needs to."

"My shells!" she shrieks. "They're in the cupboard in my room."

I roll my eyes. "I left my key behind. We'll see if Davis can send them to us."

"Maybe he can take us out to dinner tonight and bring them with him."

I shake my head. "We have dinner. I brought the leftover sandwiches. There's even a peanut butter with strawberry jelly."

Her shoulders hunch. "I'd rather have a fried chicken sandwich and french fries from the Cactus Club."

"Sorry. We'll be mostly back to eating at home. But the good news is that your new school is going to be so much fun."

"I don't know if I believe you." She crosses her arms and looks out at the people on the sidewalks as we inch out of town. We would have probably done better with a water taxi.

When we finally arrive, I open the door to the loft, and the air is stale. I take a deep breath and hope I can be strong and not let Arabella see me cry.

Just before lunch, the mattress and box springs arrive in giant cardboard boxes. We may not have a headboard or bed frame, but at least we won't be sleeping on the floor.

"I thought we could make this part our bedroom, and we have a little bit of money so we can buy some things to decorate the walls. The Studio Tour is coming up, and we'll want to make it pretty."

"What would you do if I wanted to become an artist?" Arabella runs her fingers over my colored pencils.

"You know that I'll love you with my whole heart, no matter what you decide to do. If you want to become a busker at a SkyTrain station and sing Pearl Jam songs, I'll put a dollar in your cup every day."

"Only a dollar?"

I shrug. "Being an artist means we're broke."

She giggles and powers up her tablet. I should have left that behind since Phillip bought her one that was entirely too expensive, but I let it slide. Her shells are important to her, so I'll need to get those back. Davis is probably going to come by tonight, and I need to mentally prepare for that.

Things have been so crazy that I haven't seen Lucy since Arabella was released from the hospital, and maybe we can go see her tonight.

Me: Are you free to get together tonight?

Lucy: Yes! I've missed you so much. How is the munchkin doing?

Me: She's doing great. We've just moved into a loft on Granville. We need a distraction tonight.

Lucy: I can come to you and see your place, and then we can go to The Perogy Place? I've read they make perogies to die for.

The Perogy Place is inexpensive. We can make that work.

Me: That sounds perfect. What time works for you?

Lucy: I'm out of here at 5 and will come right over.

Me: See you then.

"Bells, Lucy is going to come by, and she wants to go out for dinner tonight."
Arabella looks up from her tablet. "The Cactus Club?"
I shake my head. "We thought we'd walk over to a perogy place in the Market."
Arabella looks and bounces her head from side to side before going back to whatever she's watching.
I feed her some lunch, and then we spend the afternoon decorating and enjoying our new space. I'm not sure it's truly going to be comfortable as a live-work kind of place, but we're going to make it happen. "We can do this," I say aloud.
Arabella comes to stand next to me and slides her hand in mine as we survey our work. "I hope one day we'll have some good luck."
Her comment breaks my heart. "Sweetheart, we have

the best luck of all because we have each other."

When Lucy arrives, I hold her tight.

"You look good, at least," she says.

I chuckle. "He insisted on healthy food. That's a cardiologist for you."

"What happened?"

"I'll tell you in a bit," I say. "Fortunately, the tour here won't take long." I hit the highlights and fill her in on my plans to work as a sculptor again and the pieces I've already sold. Her eyes light up, and she hits me with question after question, but I'm starting to feel anxious as it gets later and later. "Let's get out of here," I suggest. "I have a feeling Davis is going to show up."

"Why would he show up?"

"I'll tell you over dinner. The Perogy Place here we come!"

I lock up and turn all the lights out, hoping it looks empty and he'll search for me elsewhere. I know what I did was pretty classless, but I'd rather rip the Band-Aid off than drag out the inevitable any longer.

I pull Arabella away from the book she's been reading, and the three of us walk over to the restaurant, which is a little café just a few blocks away. Inside, the walls are painted bright yellow, and the tables have white wicker chairs. The menu is huge. Who would have thought there were over a hundred different flavors of perogies? We order drinks and a giant sampler with over twenty-five different kinds of perogy. I'm looking forward to the caramelized onion garlic.

Arabella has her tablet and quickly becomes immersed in a show she's downloaded and watching with headphones.

"How are you doing?" Lucy asks with concern.

I sigh. "The tears are close, but so far I've been able to keep them away."

"Why would you do that? You've been through so much in recent years. You need to let it all out."

I shake my head. "I can't with her around." I nod

toward Arabella. "She needs to see me strong. But trust me, I'm going to find some time to cry."

"Why did you move out?"

I sigh. I don't even know how to explain this. "Well, it was always my plan. I can't take advantage of his kindness forever."

"Weren't you dating now? That had to change things, right?"

"I guess that's what we were doing, but I needed to keep it casual. I don't have room for a relationship, and a relationship with someone who's done so much for me is just too messy."

"Is that how he felt?"

I shake my head. "His family owns the largest telecommunications company in the country, and they're listed as one of the ten wealthiest families in the world — like Queen of England wealthy."

"And he wanted a relationship with you."

"That's not the point. It wasn't realistic. He had to be slumming it with me."

"Did he say that? Because if he did, I'm going to cut his balls off. You may not have a million dollars in the bank, but you're a class act."

I take a deep breath and squeeze Lucy's hand. This is why she's my best friend. I've ignored her for weeks because of my own personal drama, and we get back together like we've never been apart.

"What else?" she asks. "Why did you leave now?"

I take a deep breath. "I overheard a conversation."

"Between?" Lucy leads.

"Between him and his brothers and their father. His brothers seem certain I'm after Davis' money and last name."

"What did he say to them?"

"Not much of anything. He thanked them for their advice."

"What? He didn't defend you?"

I shake my head. "We were at his parents' house for dinner. I couldn't bear to hear any more, so I stepped out and let him know I was there. He wanted to talk about it later, but I knew what I had to do. Whether he believes them now or not, they're convincing him I'm after his money. My only choice is to prove that isn't true." I settle my head in my hands for a moment. "It just sucks because he nearly had me convinced we might be something. And he definitely had Arabella convinced."

"Oh, sweetie, I'm so sorry." Lucy leans over and gives me a tight embrace.

I try to wipe my eyes so Arabella doesn't see, but I think she does. There is nothing about me that's stealthy.

Our perogies arrive, and Arabella takes her headphones off to eat, so our conversation shifts gears. We talk about how she's feeling, and everything she's been learning and doing since she came home from the hospital. Hearing it all from her perspective reminds me what a huge difference all this has made for her. We may be back to living on our own, but I'm determined things will never be the same for her again. She deserves to reach her full potential, no matter what it takes.

When all the perogies are gone, Lucy talks me into ordering a coffee, and Arabella returns to her headphones and tablet screen. Lucy fills me in on what's been happening for her at work, but eventually her questions return to my life.

"Have you heard anything from your mom?" she asks.

I roll my eyes. "Nothing good. She did call a week or so ago when she was stuck in holding at the border. She needed money to pay the taxes on something she was trying to import." I tell her the whole sordid tale.

Lucy shakes her head. "That's bullshit. They would have held on to the item for several months."

My jaw drops. "She said they'd leave her in a holding cell until she had the money, and her boyfriend was out fishing. She was also looking at deportation if she didn't pay it."

"So you sent her money, didn't you?" Lucy closes her eyes. "You finally actually have some money, and she's right there to take it away."

"I know I shouldn't have sent it, but I didn't want to close the door on that relationship—for Arabella's sake."

"I understand," Lucy says, though she doesn't look happy about it. "You're not the one who did anything wrong here."

We talk for a while longer, and finally, Arabella and I head back to the loft. I hold my breath as we arrive, but fortunately, the hallway is empty.

Lucy sticks around while we wait for her rideshare. "Listen, let's plan on an outing this weekend," she says. "I'll rent a car, and we can drive up to Whistler for the night."

I shake my head. "I need to have new sculptures done for the studio open house. It's only three weeks away. I don't have time."

"Okay, how about we head to the beach in White Rock for the afternoon?"

White Rock is a community right on the border with the US, and it has white sandy beaches. "I love that idea."

After she leaves, I pull my phone out and turn it on.

While it powers up, I put Arabella to bed, drawing the fancy curtain we purchased around the mattress to give her some privacy, and prepare for what I expect to be a crapload of messages.

But there is only one.

Davis: Why?

Chapter 22

Davis

I'd be much more anxious about Paisley and Arabella if I didn't have Felix's team keeping an eye out. We don't advertise this, but my mom owns the building where Paisley's loft is. She thought Paisley would want a place for her art and a possible place to escape to if she needed a break from the Martin clan. How right she was.

I lean back in my office chair, look out over the hospital parking lot, and dial the phone.

"Davis?" Mom says. "Why are you calling so early on a Tuesday morning? I would have thought if you weren't in surgery, you'd be sleeping in."

I rarely have the chance to sleep in. She must be thinking of one of my brothers. "She left me yesterday," I say with more emotion that I expect to hear in my voice.

"What?" her voice softens.

I sigh. "Sunday night when you sent her out to get us for dinner, she overheard us talking about her."

"What do you mean?" Mom is suddenly very alert.

"Dad told me about you pulling strings to get Arabella

admitted to Point Grey Academy. I asked if there was any scholarship attached. Phillip piped in that Paisley lived rent free and had just gotten a giant commission, and then Griffin and Henry added their thoughts about her being out for our money and name. I disagree, but I didn't want an argument, so I just thanked them for their advice, somewhat sarcastically, but it seems Paisley didn't catch that bit. She just heard me not defending her."

"Hmm. I see." Mom sighs. "And how did you apologize?"

"I immediately went to her and wanted to explain, but she was firm in putting me off until we got back. And when we got home, she told me she didn't want to talk about it. That she already understood. And she stayed with her sister."

"And?"

"What else is there to say? Now she's gone to live with Arabella at the loft. I'm sure it's because we've made her feel unwelcome. She's been worried about taking advantage of my hospitality since the beginning, and this has convinced her she was right all along." I pause to take a breath. "I felt like I was finally making progress in getting her to trust me, to believe I have a real interest in her. We've been out on a few dates, and I know she's special. I want to be with her."

I hear a sharp intake of breath. "She's been hurt by everyone she loves. I can imagine her walls are firmly up. And she's used to doing everything for herself, so that probably just seems safer. Leave it to your brothers…"

I try to hold my emotions in check. "I don't know what to do. Felix has someone monitoring them, so I know they're safe, but…"

"Have you reached out to her?" Mom asks.

"I sent her a text asking why she left."

"I take it she didn't respond."

"Her phone was off. I kept calling, but I didn't leave a message."

"She's under a lot of pressure right now," Mom says

after a moment.

"I know she is. She's also full of self-doubt. But I've seen her drawings. They're fantastic. She has this plan for the rocks she picked up on the island. It's going to be incredible. But don't tell her you know about it. I stole a look when she wasn't paying attention."

Mom sighs. "Women were always so easy for you and your brothers when you were growing up."

"That's because they were interested in our bank account, not because they were interested in me."

"I'm so grateful I met your dad when I did. He was determined even then, but when he talked about his vision for our future, we had no idea how successful he'd become. I'm grateful he's never doubted my love for him was anything but genuine."

I snort. "Every woman you try to set me up with wants social status and an open credit card."

"I don't think all of them are out for those things, but sometimes you need to kiss a few frogs."

"I've kissed lots of frogs, but I knew the moment I saw Paisley in the emergency room taking care of her sister that she was it for me."

"Then you need to get her back."

We talk for another twenty minutes and eventually agree on a strategy that might work. As I prepare to disconnect the call, I realize I forgot something. "Mom, I want to pay for Arabella to attend Point Grey Academy."

"Sweetheart, your father and I already did. Arabella is so bright and capable, and we didn't want to put any pressure on Paisley. Your father and I just adore them, and I'm so glad you do, too. Now you need to fix this so you can get back together."

"Well, I'm not sure we were ever actually together. But that's what I'd like. And I know if anyone can help me get there, it's you. Thanks for your advice and all you've done for Paisley. I'm sure I don't say this often enough, but I love you.

Thank you for everything you do for me."

"You're welcome, and I'll expect a generous donation to many of my favorite charities."

"I give to them all the time," I point out.

"But I want you to give to them without complaining."

I sigh. "Okay, fine."

After I disconnect the call, I feel significantly better about my future. I'm going to get Paisley back. I can do this. I know I can.

Chapter 23

Paisley

Stretching my back, I look over at Arabella. We've been here for five days, and she's been watching too much television and hasn't gotten out. She's already finished what she needs to do for school, so she's bored.

"Bells, let's go for a walk and do some exploring."

"No thanks."

I turn my head and give her the I-don't-think-so look. "Come on. Maybe we'll hit the ice cream spot in the Market."

She eyes me speculatively. "I'm watching a show."

"You can watch it when we get back."

"It's raining," she rationalizes.

"It does that nine months a year here. You have rain boots. Come on. Stop with the excuses, and let's go get some fresh air."

She's been in a funk since we moved earlier this week, but her health is important—mentally and physically. We walk downstairs, and she slips her hand into mine. We walk out to the waterfront and down toward the end of the inlet. I'm not sure how far we'll make it. The rain is steady but not too heavy. Perhaps it will taper off.

"Do you miss him?" Arabella asks.

I shrug. "Probably. Do you?" I jump in a puddle and splash us both pretty good.

She giggles and nods. "I like him. He always did nice things for me." She jumps in a puddle and gets me soaking wet from the base of my raincoat to the tops of my boots.

"I'm sure we'll see him again."

"You said that about Mom, and we don't see her." Arabella gives a slide into the water, making a giant spray, and a lady who comes running from behind us takes some of the water and grunts.

I give Arabella a look. "Be careful."

"It's not like she wasn't soaking wet already." She shrugs.

"Let's not do that anymore," I say, since we're seeing more people on the path. "Bells, I don't know how to explain Mom. For some reason, right now, she needs space. It doesn't mean she doesn't love us; it just means something inside her is broken, and somehow, she needs to figure out how to fix it."

"What if she never fixes it?"

I pull Arabella in close. "We'll always have each other. I won't leave you or move on. I'll always be here for you, and you'll always be there for me."

"I'm cold. Can we go back and have grilled cheese and tomato soup for dinner?"

I nod. "I think that's a great idea. But let's see if we can walk all the way to the end."

"You can't. Did you know Granville Island isn't really an island?" she challenges me.

"Well, it's not like there's a bridge, so sure, I know that."

She shakes her head. "The road is a bridge, but they wanted more space, so they filled in part of False Creek on the back side over by the theater. It was really hard to do, and when the water rises it floods, so they stopped, but the connection means it's no longer an island."

"Who told you this?" I ask.

"I read about it on their website. I was curious. You can take a water taxi from downtown or drive around."

We keep walking until the trail ends at the hotel on the eastern tip of the island or whatever you call it since it's no longer an island. We stop and watch a giant sailboat with a team of at least fifteen people make their way out of the marina. Arabella waves to them with a bright smile and several wave back. I love that she's so pure of heart.

"I'm ready for some grilled cheese and tomato soup," I tell her after a moment. "I think we've earned it now." The chill and rain are making my fingers cold.

We turn around, and I catch a face that's familiar a few yards back. I march toward Felix, the Martins' head of security. He doesn't move, just waits for me in his spot. "What are you doing here?" I ask.

"The Martin family is concerned for your safety, so my team and I are keeping an eye on you." He doesn't flinch or even look apologetic.

"Why would anyone care about us?"

"You both are very important to the Martin family. I'm here to make sure you are well and safe."

This doesn't make any sense. "Have you been watching us all week?"

"We've had eyes on you since you moved into Davis' home."

"There are cameras?" I screech.

"No cameras in Davis' home or in your apartment," he assures me with a smile.

I relax, at least a little. "You can tell the Martins we appreciate their concern, but we'll be fine. No one knows of the connection between us. We've not said anything *and* despite what they may think, I'm not interested in their name or their money."

"I let them know, but until they tell me otherwise, my

team and I will be around. We'll try to be more invisible."

I roll my eyes. I want to grab him by the collar and shake him silly, but Felix scares me. I think he was once part of the Cuban Intelligence Directorate—the Cuban version of the CIA or KGB. Not someone to mess with, regardless.

I storm off, but I know Felix isn't too far behind.

When we get back to the loft, I make grilled cheese sandwiches—on wheat bread, at least—while heating some tomato soup. Once it's ready, I make up plates for us.

Arabella holds up the corner of her sandwich and looks at me. "You burned the grilled cheese."

I'm not up for this fight. "It isn't burned. It's just a little darker than normal. I'll trade, if you'd prefer."

"No!" she shrieks. "Yours is worse. Why can't we go out to dinner?"

"We don't have the money to eat out all the time, and it isn't healthy," I remind her. "This was your idea anyway." I take a big bite of my sandwich. "And it's perfect for a rainy day."

She huffs and takes a bite. "I want my shells. Have you asked Davis for them? Can we go get them?"

"I'll reach out about them," I assure her. "Don't worry. We'll get them back."

She gathers her food, returns to her spot on the bed, and goes back to her show. I decide to let that slide. I need to get everything ready anyway. Tomorrow, I will dip at least three pieces of driftwood. It takes a lot of preparation, and I have to have everything managed precisely so the heat of the liquid silver doesn't catch the driftwood on fire.

After I get everything set up, I wander over to Arabella and sit with her on the bed. She's not watching TV anymore, so we curl up together, and after a few minutes, she cries into my shoulder. Davis not only captured my heart, but hers as well. I hate that this is causing her pain.

As I'm drifting off to sleep, my cell phone vibrates.

It's after one in the morning. Who would reach out to

me? I look at my phone, and my heart races.

Davis: I miss you so much.

I reread the simple line at least a dozen of times. How do I respond to that? *Arabella's shells.*

Me: Arabella left her shells behind. Would you be willing to leave them some place I can pick them up?

Davis: No.

What? Then another message pops up.

Davis: I'd love to take you both to dinner, and I'll give them to her. We need to talk.

Me: You're going to hold her shells hostage? When your brothers shit all over me and you didn't defend me, that made everything clear. Arabella cried herself to sleep tonight because she misses you so much. I don't understand what you want from me.

Davis: I'm so sorry. I didn't respond to my brothers because I don't care what they think, and it wasn't worth arguing. They don't know us. I know you're nothing like what they said. But you wouldn't talk to me, and then you just left.

I suppose that makes sense, but I can't let go of my anger. I think it makes me feel safe. The only way I know how to do this is by myself.

My phone vibrates in my hand, and it's Davis, but I send it right to voicemail. I'm not ready to talk to him. His velvety voice will break me down, and I can't have that.

So now it's my turn to cry myself to sleep.

Chapter 24

Paisley

When I wake up the next morning, the rain pelting the loft's windows tells me the storm has increased. It's almost July. We're going to go from this intense, unending rain right into a hot summer. And a dark, gray morning like this makes it almost impossible to get moving. Arabella's still a lump on her side of the mattress. But today's the day I'm dipping at least three pieces of driftwood, and that gets me motivated.

I putter around the loft, making coffee and getting out supplies. Half an hour later, I'm dressed and have breakfast ready for Arabella, who is showing some signs of life. While she eats, I get three distilled water baths ready, which will set the silver and stop any burn after the items' quick dip in the almost two-thousand-degree molten metal.

Next, I line up the pieces I'll be dipping, inspecting them one last time for any loose pieces or dirt that could ruin the silver. Everything seems good. I put on my apron, goggles, face shield, and gloves—all able to withstand any splashes. The windows are open, and the fire extinguisher is at the ready.

"Are you ready?" I look over at Arabella, and I can tell she's anxious. She put an overnight bag next to the door, just in case we start a fire. That instills confidence.

I pick up a piece of wood with special tongs and, in one motion, lower it into the silver and pull it out, moving it immediately to the water bath. The apartment soon smells like a fireplace as the hot silver boils the water.

Arabella jumps up and down. "You did it."

I nod, following with the next two pieces of driftwood in rapid succession. "I think we might be able to do six pieces today."

Arabella's eyes grow big. "Yeah!"

I give the sculptures twenty minutes in their water baths and carefully take them out. I'll add feet later so each piece will sit flat. I refill the water baths and begin with a second set of wood, soon giving me six pieces.

But this is the easy part, really. Once they've cooled, the silver is covered in black dust and needs to be polished, and I'll need to fix the pock marks that always appear.

I work all day and also dip several of the rocks. The pinecones didn't work and almost ruined my silver, but it was a good experiment. I'm considering casting the pinecones and trying to create what I want to dip out of another material. I have to think on it.

"What do you think?" Arabella stands back, looking at the large pieces of dipped driftwood that now fill our living space.

"I love it," I tell her. "It feels great to be working as a sculptor, and you were a terrific assistant. What do you think?"

"This one is my favorite." She points to a particularly knotty piece of driftwood. Two nobs fell off during the process, and I may try to recreate them, but I haven't decided. Time will tell. I'll have to see how they look as I begin to polish.

There's a knock at the door. Arabella and I look at each

other, not sure what to do. I finally walk over and open it to find a neighbor. I've seen him around but haven't met him before. He's standing in a ratty old pair of Levi's that, before Davis, I would've thought looked absolutely delicious on him, and the Henley tight across his chest would've melted my panties. But not anymore. *Damn you, Davis Martin.*

He holds up Arabella's bag of shells. "I noticed this on your doorstep this morning and wasn't sure if you knew it was here."

"My shells!" Arabella scampers over to grab it from him in her excitement. "Thank you." She disappears toward our bed.

"Sorry, she's been looking for those."

He leans against the doorjamb and gives me a sexy smile. "I'm Jim Matthews."

I smile back and extend my hand. "Nice to meet you. I'm Paisley Brooks."

"It smells like a campfire in here. What are you up to today?"

"I'm sculpting with mixed media."

He looks into the loft but can't see much from the door, thankfully. I'm not ready to show what I'm working on. "What about you?" I ask. "What kind of art do you do?"

"I paint—oils," he says with a grin. "Also, would you be interested in getting a drink tonight?"

My eyes widen. If only I were interested. "I can't. My sister is too young for hanging out in a bar."

"Your sister?" His eyes pop. "She's not your daughter?"

"No, she's my sister." I look over at her fondly as she sorts through her shells.

"Davis had to drop them off," she says. She lines them up to make sure they're all there. "Why didn't he come in? He could have taken us to dinner, and we could have had a sleepover. I don't mind sleeping on the floor if he stays over."

I look at Jim. My face, I'm sure, is turning purple.

"Thank you for making sure we got those."

He nods and grins again. "No problem. Let me know if you ever want to get away for a drink or something."

I clear my throat. "I will." I begin to close the door.

"Do you know about the Studio Tour?" he asks.

I stop. "My agent has talked me into participating."

"Great. Mine too. I can't wait to see what you're creating."

I hold the door firmly, ready to shut it. "Likewise."

He leans in. "Don't be offended. My paintings are mostly nudes. I'm always looking for a model if you're interested."

I laugh. "You're a comedian."

He looks me up and down. "You're perfect."

"I have a boyfriend."

He nods. "Okay. Let me know if you change your mind."

My phone rings, and it's a perfect excuse to shut the door and leave Jim firmly on the other side.

When I look at the caller ID, I stop for a half second. It's Julia Martin. I can't ignore her; she's my benefactor. "Hello, Julia," I say in greeting. I try to sound upbeat, but to me, I sound totally fake, and I'm sure she can hear it.

"Hello! How is it going?" she asks.

I take a deep breath. "It's going well. I dipped six pieces today. They look great, and I think they're all going to work."

"That's wonderful," she gushes. "Are we still on for the Monet exhibit tonight?"

Oh shit. I close my eyes. "I'm so sorry. I forgot about that. I'm afraid I don't have a sitter for Arabella."

"That's no worries. Chip was thinking he'd come into town with me and take Arabella out for dinner and a movie. They're playing some old Disney films in Stanley Park. He would have Felix with him, so they'd be safe."

My pulse quickens. "Are you sure? I'd hate to put you

out."

"Paisley, Chip would walk through hot coals to get out of going to the exhibit with me. Plus, we adore Arabella."

"Did Davis tell you—"

"Yes, Davis told me you've moved out. He misses you terribly, and my children have all gotten an earful from me, but that is all I will say on the subject."

"Okay." I'm not sure what that means, exactly. "Well, if you're sure, I'd love to go to the exhibit. What time will you be here?"

"I'll pick you up at seven. The three of us can have dinner at Dockside restaurant. That will give Felix's team time to get Chip from the airport. He's up in St. John at a meeting with a local tribal council about putting a cell tower on their land."

"He shouldn't have to rush back for Arabella."

"Trust me, he's not. They want the tower on their land, but not where his team wants to put it, but he's going to enjoy the afternoon with them, regardless. The chief and Chip are old friends."

"Then Arabella and I will see you at seven, and dinner will be on me since you are so kind to take me to the exhibit this evening."

Julia chuckles. That's the sound of her not planning to allow me to pay for dinner, but I'll still try. "I'll pick you up at seven, and we'll walk over."

After I hang up, I look around and realize the loft looks like a train wreck. My apron, goggles, gloves, face shield and boots are scattered around the room. The distilled water baths are nasty on the floor, and there are water marks from the water boiling over. I pull Arabella's attention away from her shells and tell her the plan for tonight.

Her eyes shine with excitement. "I'm glad Chip and Julia are still our friends."

"Me too, Bells. We're very lucky."

We spend what's left of our afternoon cleaning up, and

I keep all the windows open, despite the cool air, hoping it gets the campfire smell out.

Then I take a quick shower, and at exactly seven, the front-door buzzer sounds. "We'll be right down," I say into the intercom. "Let's go." I extend my hand to Arabella, and we bound down the steps to Julia, who's elegant in a beautiful dress.

She hugs us tightly. "I've missed you both."

"Paisley made us move out of Davis' condo so we would remain friends," Arabella announces. "Guests are like fish. After a few days, they stink."

I look at the ground, wishing to disappear. "The honesty of a child," I murmur.

Julia smiles down at her as we begin to walk. "I'm glad we're still friends, too. Are you looking forward to *The Lion King* tonight?"

"It was my favorite when I was little. Plus, Chip and I can get ice cream afterward."

"Says who?" I ask.

"Me!" She giggles.

"Don't make Chip buy you a bunch of crap and then you're up all night with a tummy ache."

"Don't worry. I can take a lot."

"Then we should fill your tummy with lots of good food high in iron," Julia suggests. "How does steak frites sound with a spinach salad? Dockside makes an amazing, warmed spinach salad. And the frites have truffle oil, which makes them oh so good."

Arabella looks up at me for approval. She knows we've been watching our pennies, but I don't want Julia to know I sent money to Mom. "I think it sounds great," I tell her. "I may have that too."

The restaurant is inside a boutique hotel at the tip of the island, and we're seated as soon as we arrive. We're tucked into a beautiful table on the patio with a gas heat lamp on low, just to take the bite out of the evening air. Our view is the end of False Creek, and we face Science World and the geodesic dome built for the 1986 World's Fair. It looks like a giant mirrored ball.

Julia orders an expensive bottle of wine, but I don't even flinch. I did some research, and the tickets for tonight's exhibit were over five hundred dollars, and those were the cheap tickets, so I'm sure ours were much more than that. Arabella and I order the steak frites, Julia orders salmon, and we all order the spinach salad.

"How are you doing?" Julia asks while we wait for our food.

I nod. "We're both okay."

"Davis brought me my shells but didn't knock on the door. Is he mad at us?"

"Oh, Bells." I smooth her hair and cup her cheek. "He'd never be mad at you."

Julia shakes her head. "No, he's not mad at all. He made a big mistake and is working on fixing it. We just need to be patient."

To change the subject, I tell her a bit about my process today and what a good assistant Arabella was. Then the waiter returns and sets a beautiful plate in front of each of us.

Once we're all eating, Julia turns to Arabella. "Are you getting excited about your new school?"

My heart drops. "I wasn't able to make the tuition deposit, so I'm pretty sure we lost our spot."

"Nonsense. Did they tell you that?"

"No, I got one notice and never replied," I tell her. "They've still been sending information, but I haven't paid much attention to it because I couldn't make the payment."

She shakes her head. "I arranged for a full-ride scholarship. The whole boat—tuition, her computer, plus all the random fees that come up."

I sit back, stunned. "I...I don't know what to say. I didn't understand that." Tears pool in my eyes. "This is such a wonderful gift. I can't...I can't even begin to tell you how much it means that you believe in Arabella and me."

Julia reaches for my hand. "You're an amazing woman, and even if you and Davis don't find your way back to one another, I wish for us to remain friends."

I dab at the corners of my eyes to keep the tears from ruining my makeup. "Thank you." I nod. "I'd very much like that, too."

"Me too," Arabella pipes up. She reaches for my hand. "It's okay, Pais. We're going to be okay."

I smile at her and shake my head. I'm so grateful for the Martin family. First, Davis saves Arabella's life and provides us with resources I'd never have accessed otherwise, and now his parents have opened professional and educational doors that were previously closed to us.

"I should tell you that I promised the board at Point Grey you would donate a piece for their silent auction next May," Julia adds after a moment.

"Of course. That's the least I could do. I'm happy to put something together for them."

There is a bit of commotion around us, and when I look up, Chip is approaching. Arabella jumps up and runs into his arms.

"Hey, there, short stuff. Are you ready for a movie?" he asks.

"Can we get ice cream too?"

"Absolutely!"

I stand, and Chip gives me an embrace. "You look fantastic."

"Thank you. Are you sure you're okay with taking Arabella tonight?"

"You are the one saving me." He smiles and kisses Julia. "Have a wonderful time."

He and Arabella head out the door, and Julia and I stand to leave. I ask the server for our bill.

"Oh, it's already taken care of," he assures me.

I look at Julia, and she shrugs. "I never agreed. You

didn't need to buy tonight. It was Chip's treat since he doesn't have to go."

"What's he going to do to make it up to you?"

She chuckles. "You know me too well." She hooks her arm in mine, and we make our way out to the waiting car. "I want a gazebo in the backyard."

"Oh, that will be amazing."

"I know, won't it?"

We take a short ride over to the Vancouver Convention Centre where the Monet exhibit is located. It's open to the public during the day, but this evening it's reserved for a private event.

Flashbulbs pop as we exit the car, and one of the Martins' bodyguards walks up with us. We're ushered in to wander through the interactive exhibit, which is beautiful, but it seems many people are interested in getting time with Julia. She's always polite and introduces me as her friend. I'm grateful for that.

"How are you enjoying the loft?" Julia asks when we finally get some time to chat.

"It's a great place to work, and Arabella and I are adjusting to living there. It's been fun meeting my neighbors. I love how supportive the community is."

"I'm so glad to hear it. I love that area. It's its own little artist colony."

"I also love that everything is within walking distance."

She nods. "The ultimate convenience." We pause to look at a painting, and then she turns to me again. "Arabella said Davis stopped by and left her shells but didn't knock?"

I panic a little. I have Davis and his mother in very separate categories in my mind. I'm not sure how to have this conversation. So I try not to. "Isn't it amazing how many strokes are in each of Monet's paintings? He has more talent in his little finger than I have in my entire body."

Julia's not having it. "Why are you changing the subject?"

I sigh. "Davis and I... I needed to make a change. Arabella and I couldn't indulge in his kindness forever, and I worried it looked like I was taking advantage."

"Do you think that's how Davis felt?" Julia asks.

I can't tell what she thinks about any of this. I sigh. "He always said he didn't feel that way, but the last time I was at your house, I overheard his brothers warning him that I was after your name and your money. Nothing could be further from the truth, but I don't know how else to make that clear."

Julia shakes her head. "I didn't raise my boys to be competitive, but they are with one another. I tried to raise them to be respectful of women, to be grateful for how fortunate we are, and to work hard." She nods at a woman she spoke to earlier and keeps walking. "The world and their experiences have shaped them. Henry has probably had it the worst. He's always been the one Chip has expected to take over the business. It's a lot of pressure, and he never had a choice. The other boys have been able to follow their passion, but our family has always been in the limelight. We are fortunate in so many ways, but it is a challenge to know who is truly your friend and who wants something from you. They've all been burned by people they trusted, and because of that, I worry they've closed themselves off from love. I was so relieved when Davis brought you and Arabella out to meet us. I could tell you genuinely cared for each other."

I don't know what to say to her. I don't know what to think about any of this. It just seems so surreal.

We stop in front of a Monet self-portrait from when he was in his early thirties. Even by today's standards, he'd be considered handsome. "Being a member of our family is not easy," she says after a moment. "I'm glad you're taking the time to consider how it will affect you and what it will mean if you and Davis move forward."

I look over at her. Why does she not understand how absurd this is? "I could never do what you do," I whisper to her.

She turns and stares at me. "I wasn't raised to be some kind of socialite. Quite the opposite. My mother wanted me to be an accountant or lawyer. I had to learn to do this. It's work I enjoy and believe is important. I want you to have a career and a life you feel proud of, and I know Davis does too. You need to be your own person. You have no idea how many mistakes I've made—" She leans in. "—and still make. Don't think you need to emulate me in any way."

For a moment, all I can do is nod. "Thank you so much for inviting me this evening, and for everything you've done for me and Arabella. I don't know how I'll ever repay you, but I will try."

She hugs me. "I didn't do any of this so you'd have to repay me. I did it because you're important to my son, and because I like you and believe in your talent."

Chapter 25

Paisley

I wake with a start on Monday morning due to banging on our front door. It's barely six a.m.. *What the hell?*

I'm still dressed in my jeans and T-shirt from last night. Lucy came over yesterday, and since Mother Nature treated us to a beautiful day, we spent it at the beach, actually getting some sun. Then we crashed hard last night.

The banging doesn't stop. I look through the peephole, and my heart tells me not to open it, but nevertheless, my brain sends a message to my hand to unlock the door.

When I open it, my mother is standing there in a dark pair of designer pants, a pair of multicolored stilettos, a bright blue blouse, and a pair of large sunglasses.

"How did you find us?" I demand.

She shakes her head. "Arabella told me where you were."

"When did she do that?"

"She texted and said you'd moved out of Davis' condo, which I can't believe you didn't tell me you were living with him. What a disappointment. That man is worth billions, and you could have had it all. Anyway, I've missed you, so I drove up and came right over."

I haven't fully opened the door, and I put my hand on my hip. "Did you bring my money?"

She pushes past me. "It hasn't been deposited yet? I'll call the bank today and find out what's going on. You should have told me you hadn't received it."

I march over to my phone and count the messages she didn't respond to. "I did. Eighteen times. Why are you here?"

"Can't a mother come by and see her daughters?"

"Sure, but you're not a mother. You lost that right when you abandoned us for a boyfriend."

She flips her hair over her shoulder. "Don't be so ugly. I raised you better than that."

"You didn't raise me at all. Dad did."

She looks around the loft. "Where's Arabella?"

"She's sleeping. Why don't you come back later?"

"Arabella?" she singsongs.

"Mommy?" Arabella squeaks from behind the curtain that gives us privacy in bed.

"Yes, baby. I came," Mom says in baby talk.

My stomach turns. I'm disoriented, and I'm a mess. The loft is a mess. I've been working on dipping other things, and everything is disheveled and unorganized.

Arabella tears out of the bed and runs to Mom. I cringe. It's too early for this. I go over to the coffeemaker and start a super strong pot. I'm going to need it.

Mom starts poking through things and looking around at my art. None of it is done yet. Her face sours. "Why does it smell like a forest fire in here?"

I sigh. "I've been working on a few projects."

She walks over to one of my experimental pieces that isn't working. I need to salvage the silver.

"Why are you wasting your time and money on this garbage? No one will want to buy this." She picks up the destroyed pinecone and drops it like it's going to bite her.

I pick it up and throw it in the trash. "I was trying something."

"Right." Her eyes roam the mess the water made.

I haven't had the energy to clean it up, particularly when I just keep making the same mess over and over again. I've also spent quite a bit of time replaying my conversation with Julia in my head since I saw her Saturday night. And then I gave Lucy the update yesterday. She is definitely Team Julia…and Team Davis as well. She says it's ultimately because she's Team Paisley. I have yet to entirely get there.

"You really should work on your housekeeping skills," Mom notes, breaking me out of my haze. "No man wants to marry a slob." She picks up a polishing cloth that's streaked with black from the silver polish.

"Mommy, don't be silly," Arabella admonishes. "We were working on art. I watched. It was super cool. She—"

"How are you affording this? Is Davis Martin setting you up? Is he going to keep you on the side?" Her eyes are hopeful, and I can see her plotting how a relationship like that would be good for her. *No way.*

I look at her in horror. "Mom, I'd like you to leave. Go find the money you supposedly sent me and get it into my account. Arabella and I will meet you later today."

But Arabella is holding Mom's hand tightly. She doesn't want her to go. Mom looks down at her. "How about you and I go find some breakfast while your sister cleans up?"

Arabella nods. She runs to get her sweater and tugs it on, but before they can get out the door, I stop them. "Before you go, take your medicine."

Arabella goes over to the sink, gets a glass of water, and tips from her daily pill container a handful of pills that will increase her iron and ward off infection and rejection.

I'm frantically finger-combing the mess on my head and hoping my eyes aren't raccoon eyes. "If you give me a second to find my shoes, I'll join you," I offer.

"You don't have to," Mom says as she inches Arabella

closer to the door.

I look Arabella in the eyes so she knows I'm here for her. "You've got my number if you need me."

Arabella is now trying to pull her hand away from my mother's, but she won't let go. "You can come with us," she tells me.

"Mommy wants time with her baby girl," Mom coos with one hand on the doorknob.

The hair on the back of my neck stands on end. "I'll join you. Let me find my shoes and pull my hair into a ponytail."

Mom sighs. "You stay here and clean up this disaster. We'll grab some croissants from the French bakery in the Marketplace and be back in a while." She swings the door open and practically shoves Arabella out as I look frantically for my sneakers.

"I—"

The door shuts behind them, and I know something is up. I shove my feet into shoes and run down the stairs to catch up with them. I look left and right, but I don't see them. I wasn't that far behind. I race to the Marketplace and look around. I can't find them anywhere. The bakery is empty. I call Mom's phone, and it takes a minute to connect. It chimes, and then there's a recording, "I'm sorry, but this number has been disconnected. Please check your number and try again."

My heart thrums in my chest, and my stomach churns. I'm feeling lightheaded, and I grasp a display of greeting cards to keep from falling over.

Felix appears at my side. "What's wrong?"

"Did you see my sister and mother?" My eyes roam the open market again.

Felix's brow furrows. "Your mother was here?"

I nod. "She just showed up and took off with Arabella." I'm trying hard to keep the rising panic out of my voice.

"No. They didn't come out the front door."

"Are you sure?"

He nods.

"My mom talked Arabella into going out to breakfast. She promised her croissants from the French bakery. She wouldn't wait for me."

Felix speaks quietly into a radio as I frantically look around the food stalls, making sure they're not hiding anywhere. It's early, so there aren't many people here. I run back to the loft and take the stairs two at a time. They're not there.

Felix is behind me moments later. "We've got the perimeter staked out. We didn't see them go by, but there is a back door. It's typically locked, and you never use it, so we didn't have eyes on it at this time of day."

I cover my face and struggle to breathe. Felix puts a hand on my back. "You can do this. Breathe in and count to three, and then breathe out."

"Where could they have gone?"

"My team is going to canvas the area. I've got people converging here as we speak."

I close my eyes a moment. "She said they were going to go out for breakfast and they'd be back."

I lean over with my hands on my knees. Breathe in. *One...two...three...* Breathe out. *One...two...three...* I repeat this a few times until the dizziness fades.

I look out the window and hardly anyone is around. How could they have gotten by Felix's team? They're the best. My hands shake. I need to keep busy, so I start picking up the mess created by my work and move the pieces to a different spot. Then I move them again.

An hour passes and still nothing.

Then I remember something. Mom said Arabella had messaged her. I scramble to find Arabella's tablet next to our bed and search it to find the conversation in an encrypted chat app.

I cringe when I open it. She's been talking with Mom since she visited after the surgery.

Mom: My beautiful Arabella, make sure you don't tell Paisley about our talks. It would kill me if she took you away from me again.

Arabella: Paisley loves and misses you Mommy. Please come home.

I scan through. She's been pumping Arabella for information.

Mom: Dr. Martin seems to really like Paisley.

Arabella: He's very good to us. We even went to his parents' house. They have a house on the cliffs on the water. Today, I saw porpoises off shore. Chip tells me they were eating a squid squad.

Mom: Where do they live?

Arabella: I'm not sure. It's a nice house. They also have an island that Davis took us to.

I cringe when I read her directly asking about me and Davis.

Mom: Do you sleep over at Davis' house?

Arabella: No we live in an apartment next door, but with Nurse Kate. Paisley sleeps in his place because there's no room in our house.

It breaks my heart when I read about our move.

Arabella: When are you coming home? I miss you so much. We moved into the loft, and I don't like living here as much as I did with Davis. Paisley cries. She doesn't think I know, but I do. We need you Mommy.

Mom: Where did you move?

Arabella gave her our address.

Mom: I'll be there soon, sweetness. Be strong and be ready. We'll find a place where we can all live and be happy.

There are several unanswered texts too.

Arabella: I know Davis fixed my heart, but it's broken because you're not here. Where are you Mommy?

Arabella: I have a great shell collection. When can you come and see it?

Arabella: Mommy, I know you worry about my scar. I can have an operation that will make the scar invisible. I'll do that for you if you'll come home.

Arabella: I hurt so bad because you aren't here. Please come home, Mommy.

I wrench my eyes away and give Felix the tablet. The tears flow steadily down my face. I feel helpless.
"We're going to find her," he assures me. "Try not to worry too much."
Suddenly, the front door bangs open, and I look up, praying it's Arabella.
Turns out it's the second best thing, which I don't even realize until this moment. It's Davis.
He rushes to me and envelops me in his arms. "Are you okay?"
I can't even shake my head as I crumble. "She took my sister," I cry.

Chapter 26

Davis

God, I've missed holding her. Having her in my arms is like a missing piece clicking into place. "We're going to find Arabella. Don't worry."

"She doesn't have her medicine." Paisley pulls away and begins frantically searching for things. "She'll need more medicine this evening."

I do some calculations in my head. "It's important that she takes them, but if need be, she'll be okay for a few days."

"A few days?" Tears fill Paisley's eyes. "I gave Arabella's tablet to Felix. She's been talking to our mom on it. Maybe we can communicate with her that way."

Felix looks up and nods. "The chat is through an encrypted app, and Vanessa hasn't been on it since last night. We also don't think your mother came up from Seattle this morning. We're checking the camera footage at the border for her. The last two times she crossed as Veronica Brennan."

Paisley freezes in place. "What do you mean? Who is Veronica Brennan?"

"It's a false ID. She has at least four aliases that we

know of."

Paisley looks a little woozy. "What?"

I lead her to a chair and sit her down. "When Felix did the background check, Vanessa Brooks came back as a false name. When they located her in Seattle, they learned she'd been connected to several wealthy men as Victoria Babcock."

"How can that be? Are you sure?"

I shake my head. I don't have an answer for her.

Felix pulls a chair up next to her and takes one of her hands while I hold the other. "Your mother was born in a small town in Texas into a large family that was fairly wealthy. They have oil money. We think when she was nineteen years old, she was the getaway driver during a bank robbery in Dallas, Texas. A security guard was shot and killed, and as an accessory, she would have gone to jail for a very long time. Instead, she somehow got the identity of Vanessa Banning and crossed into Canada, and she's been on the run ever since."

Paisley pulls her hands away and crosses her arms around her middle. "Vanessa Brooks, Veronica Brennan, Victoria Babcock, and what's the other one?" She looks at Felix.

"Vera Browning," he supplies.

"Her aliases all have VB initials. Shouldn't that tell us something?" She chews on her thumbnail.

Felix nods. "That's a good point. She landed in Regina when she first came to Canada, and there's no record of her and your father getting married, but when they arrived in Vancouver five years later, they presented themselves as a married couple. Do you remember any wedding pictures or anything like that?"

She looks across the room. "No. I don't recall any wedding pictures. There were no pictures at all, really. We were never a family that took a lot of pictures. Was my father's identity fake, too?"

Felix shakes his head. "We don't think so. We were able

to find his birth certificate, and it checks out without any questions. But given how your mother continued to work below the radar, we believe he knew."

She looks at me and nods. "A few things have clicked into place."

"Like what?"

"Why my mom was so panicked when my dad got sick, and why she didn't want to deal with the hospital and Arabella's illness."

I nod. "That would make sense—and why she left you both behind."

"She worked a regular job, though," Paisley points out. "She worked as an office administrator for a builder before my dad was ill."

"She's never reported any income to the government," Felix says.

"She went to Dallas a few times, but it was always for her job," Paisley murmurs. "One time she was gone for almost six weeks. I know my dad had to talk her into coming back. I guess this answers some questions about why she'd want to stay."

"Do you know when that was?" Felix asks.

Paisley thinks for a moment. "It would have been about eight years ago."

Felix nods and looks down. "The man they convicted of the bank robbery murder was released about that time."

"Do you know who he is?" Paisley asks.

"His name is Ricky Monroe. He now lives in Seattle, and they're in regular touch."

Paisley looks like she's been hit by a bus. Unfortunately, that's not all the news. Now for the big reveal.

"We found she has half a million dollars in a Cayman account that she's used to leverage wealthy men who then put her up," Felix begins. "Her biggest whale was a Travis Anderson. She'd told him she was working on a startup, and he was poised to invest when you called. From what we can gather, he figured out you existed, which caused a rift, and he cut her loose."

Paisley's head whips up. "Wait. She has half a million dollars in a bank account, and she won't send me the money she owes me?"

"She has a slush fund offshore," Felix confirms. "We think her family may have set it up for her, or maybe it's money from the robbery."

I put my hand on hers. "Paisley, what money does she owe you?" I'd much rather her reveal what she's done than have to be interrogated about it.

Paisley sighs and looks at her hands in her lap. "She called me a few weeks ago wanting me to get you to send her twenty-five thousand dollars because she said she was in a holding cell at the border for a tax payment on a piece of art glass she got caught importing. I thought about it a lot, but in the end, I decided helping her was the right thing to do, so I sent her Canadian dollars, and she freaked out." She takes a deep breath. "Then I sent her more. She said her boyfriend was away for a few days, but he'd be good for the money, and she'd get it right back to me. But she hasn't."

"That's the thirty-three thousand dollars you wired to a U.S. account," Felix confirms.

Paisley looks up. "How did you know that?" She looks between me and Felix and sighs. "Never mind. Don't answer that. I already know. I wasn't going to ask Davis for money. And a part of me knew she would probably cheat me, but I wanted to do the right thing and help her if she actually needed it."

I put my hand on hers again, but I don't trust myself to say much of anything. Paisley has such a good heart, and I'm so angry with her mother. The girls were living practically in squalor while she had plenty of money to help them out but refused. Talk about a selfish bitch.

"You don't have to worry," Felix tells her. "I can get the money back. We followed the transaction, but I didn't know what it was for. Now that I do, I can reverse the funds. That should get her attention, and perhaps she'll contact you. This is actually quite helpful." He smiles at her, and I know he's hoping she'll smile in return.

We're all quiet a moment. I hope right now I'm watching a phoenix rise from the ashes as Paisley finds herself.

"Was she even at the border when she asked for the money?" Paisley asks.

Felix looks at something on his phone. "We don't have a record of her crossing the border into the U.S. on that date with any of the four identities we have. That doesn't mean she didn't cross under another we don't have yet. But it seems strange that she'd be in a holding cell for import taxes. Typically, they'd impound the item and store it for thirty days while they waited for her to pay."

"She lied to me," Paisley murmurs.

"Our software will claw the money back. Chances are she'll be in touch as soon as she figures it out it's gone."

"What if that's too late for Arabella?" she whispers.

I hold her tight and kiss the top of her head. I need to be strong for Paisley. But once we have Arabella returned, I'm going to make sure their mother is squished like a bug. She can't continue to treat her girls this way.

There's a commotion outside the door, and then my parents rush in.

"Oh my God!" my mother exclaims. "We came as soon as we heard. Are you okay?" she asks Paisley.

Paisley nods, even as her tears begin. "My mother took Arabella."

"She's the child's mother. What kind of recourse do we have?" Dad asks Felix.

"Paisley is Arabella's legal guardian, so we've notified the police," Felix explains calmly. "They've issued a missing child alert with a medical emergency."

There's no place here to sit, so my mother wanders over

to the shelves, which are now full of new sculptures. "Paisley, these look amazing," she practically shrieks. "Has Isla seen them?"

Paisley looks over, seeming confused. "Oh. They're not done yet. I've only dipped them. They need to be cleaned up and oiled."

"I wonder if I should get a second one," Mom muses.

"You're not paying for another one," Paisley declares. "Actually, I'm working on a thank you, which is a little different. If you end up not liking it, you can choose one of these."

She reaches for Paisley and wraps her in a hug. "There's no need to do that. I'm here to support you."

Felix and my dad are now huddled together. I suspect he's getting a full update on the situation.

Mom releases Paisley. "Other than this mess, how are you? I've been thinking of you. I had so much fun with you at the Monet event, and I've been thinking about what we could do next. Maybe a girls weekend."

Paisley nods. "That sounds like a lot of fun. Point Grey Academy called, and we're going out next week—" Her hand comes to her mouth. "What are we going to do? What if she's not back?" Her tears erupt again. "I'm sorry," Paisley says as she wipes her eyes with the heel of her hand.

"You have nothing to be sorry for." Mom looks around. "How about we go across the street to The Keg? We can get a drink and some food, and if Arabella and your mother return, we're very close. I think I need a strong Caesar." A Caesar is Canada's national drink—Clamato juice, Worcestershire sauce, horseradish, and vodka.

"I don't know if it's a good idea to leave," Paisley frets.

I feel like a change of scenery would do her good, but I'm also not going to push. She needs to be in charge here. If I have to stand in here for the rest of the day and all night, that's what I'm going to do.

"Tom Shaw from my team will remain here," Felix

assures her. "You can go get something to eat. If anything happens, we'll call you immediately. I've also cloned your phone, so if she calls, we can record it and, hopefully, get a successful trace."

Paisley still looks conflicted.

I lean down. "Sweetheart, if you want to stay, you can absolutely stay. I go where you go."

She looks at Mom and nods. "I could use a stiff drink myself."

"Outstanding!" Mom hooks her arm in hers, and they walk out ahead of us.

Dad hangs back with me. "She's in better shape than I thought she'd be."

I nod. "She's very strong."

"I'm really sorry I didn't say anything when your brothers were questioning her intentions the other night. Your mother told me she overheard, and I feel terrible. I want you to know I don't feel that way about her at all."

I shrug. "I didn't want to fight with them about it. Their opinion doesn't matter to me, and they're wrong. She isn't out for our money or name."

He nods. "Your mom and I agree."

"I love her, Dad. I haven't told her yet, but I do. I just hope I can get her to come back to me."

"I know you do, and I'm happy for you." He squeezes my shoulder as we head out the door, leaving Felix and Tom behind. "Now what's the plan for her mother?"

"That woman is poison. I want her out of her girls' lives."

"Then let's figure out what that's going to take."

When we get to the restaurant, we join Mom and Paisley in a large U-shaped booth overlooking the channel. We order lunch, and Mom keeps Paisley busy chatting.

We have a leisurely meal and a drink or two, but eventually, my parents have somewhere they need to be, so they walk us back to the loft. We go upstairs, and they return to their car.

There's been no change and no new information, so Paisley sits down on her bed, and we turn on the television. Somehow, she comes across old reruns of *Made in Canada*, a comedy about backstabbing television executives that was terrible when it came out and is even worse now. It's probably perfect, though, because neither of us can focus enough to pay attention.

Time passes like molasses in winter. Felix's team has found a table and chairs, and they've set up a computer on their makeshift desk. Paisley goes over to stand at the window, staring out at the crowds of people. Her breath is shaky. I hate seeing her like this.

We've texted her mother through the app, but the messages are not even showing they've been read. The money has been removed from her U.S. account and returned to Paisley, but so far, she hasn't checked the account to realize that.

Afternoon becomes evening, and the rain returns. Paisley watches out the window and waits. Felix and his team report that they've figured out a possible phone number for her mom, and they're waiting for the phone to be turned on so they can track it and, hopefully, find where they're hiding.

We order in dinner from the Greek place in the Market, but Paisley doesn't leave her spot by the window and isn't interested in food. When it's close to midnight, I pull her into my arms. "Let's lie down a bit. You need to rest, and if she calls, we'll be right here to answer your phone."

Reluctantly, Paisley lies down with me, and I fall asleep as soon as my head hits the pillow — a remnant of my days as a resident. When I wake in the middle of the night, I find Paisley back to standing at the window. I approach and wrap my arms around her from behind, and we look out the window together. I don't see Felix's men anywhere, but I know they're out there.

"Would you like a cup of coffee?" I ask her.

"What?"

"I asked if you'd like me to make you a cup of coffee."

She nods.

I busy myself in the kitchen, and together we drink our coffee and watch the sun rise in the west. Under normal circumstances, this would be romantic, but not now. There's nothing but anxiety in the air right now. Felix returns shortly after breakfast to wait with us.

Over twenty-four hours after her sister and mother disappeared, Paisley's phone rings. The number is blocked. We look at Felix, and he nods. Paisley answers on speakerphone.

"Hello?"

"Hello, darling," comes through the speaker.

"Mom? Where the hell are you? Arabella needs her medicine."

"I wouldn't worry about that," she says without a care in the world. "Your boyfriend stole some money from me yesterday."

"What? That's what you're calling about?" Paisley cries.

"I want my money back," Vanessa says calmly.

"That's *my* money. I lent it to you. You told me you were going to repay me. If you needed it so badly to pay taxes, why is it still in the account?"

There's a brief silence before her mother responds. "Where did you get that money? You told me you were broke."

"I am broke—well, I was. I sent you money from the commission I got from selling some of my art."

Her mother snorts. "You mean someone's buying that campfire crap? Damn, people really are stupid."

I'm glad Paisley can't see my face right now. It takes all I have to remain silent. How could Paisley have come from this woman?

"Mom, where are you, and where is Arabella?"

She sighs. "I don't know how you put up with her nonstop talking. All the questions and facts. It's just nauseating."

"Where is she now?" Paisley begs.

"She's in the other room." She's quiet a beat. "Where were we? Oh yes, you need to get me a million dollars. If I'd known you had some money, I would have asked for more in the first place."

"I don't have any more." Paisley starts to cry. "Mom, that was for Arabella, for the things she needs and a place to live near her school and those expenses."

"School is free. If public schools were good enough for you, they're good enough for Arabella. You've ruined any chance of her having a decent love life with that giant scar you put on her chest."

"Her heart is still beating, Mom. That's what we've given her. Please, Mom, bring Arabella back."

"I'll let you have some time to conference with the Martins," she says, as if she hasn't heard me. "I want a million dollars."

"You can have two million if you'll go away permanently," I interject, unable to keep myself quiet any longer. Felix shoots me a withering look. My comment was not part of his plan.

"Ahh, Prince Charming has come to save the day," she says with a laugh. "Let's say fifty million, and I'll go away permanently."

"I want her back tonight," Paisley insists.

"If you transfer the money, you can have her back. But if you try to take it back, you'll find I have a few friends you won't want to meet."

"Like Ricky Monroe?" I sneer. "I'm not scared. I just want Arabella back and you out of their lives. I'll send you half, and when Arabella returns, you can have the other half."

"No," she says flatly. "All up front or nothing."

"Tell me, how long are you going to be able to handle

Arabella?" Paisley interjects. "I mean, if a day is too hard, what about a week or two? She really likes to cuddle at night."

The line goes silent for a moment, and I wonder if she's hung up. "Tomorrow morning, Arabella will be standing across the street from your building," she finally says. "As soon as you see her, you'll deposit the second half. Once it hits my bank account—and I mean an additional twenty-five million dollars—Arabella will be released. If you don't send the money, you'll never see her again."

I look over at Felix, and he nods. There's no going back now, I suppose. "Fine," I grit through clenched teeth.

"You can't do this!" Paisley says, turning to me.

But her mother thinks she's speaking to her. "Honey, I hold all the cards here," she retorts. "I can do whatever I want."

Felix looks at his computer and gives us the thumbs up. It seems he's successfully traced the call.

"I don't ever want to see you or hear from you again." I can hear the anger in Paisley's voice.

Her mother just gives an evil cackle and disconnects.

"What if she doesn't return her?" Paisley cries. "What if she's hurt her?"

"It's all going to be okay," I assure her. "She's motivated by money, so this is going to work."

Paisley pulls away from me. "This makes what your brothers said about me true. I don't want it to be like this, but I don't know what to do."

I pull her close. "It does not make what they said true. They're trying to protect me, but they're wrong. This kind of thing just comes with our life, and in this case, I'm more than happy to solve a problem with money. It's my choice. If anything were ever to happen to Arabella, I'd never be able to live with myself."

Felix clears his throat. "We were able to track Vanessa's phone during that call. I'm sure it's a relay and she's not actually in that location, but it's another step closer to her. I've been in touch with the police, and they will follow the person who brings Arabella. We'll also track the money. If it's the same account she used when you sent her money, as soon as it hits her account, it's transferred to the Caymans. We've got that covered."

Paisley nods her thanks, and Felix directs his team to move a couch up from the gallery downstairs for more workspace.

"I know it's the middle of the day, but come lie down with me," I tell her. "You have to be exhausted."

She follows me to the mattress behind the curtain, but she seems unsettled. "I can't have sex with you," she whispers.

I shake my head. "I didn't ask you for sex. I just want you to rest. But if you want me to go down on you so you can sleep, I'm happy to do so."

Her eyes grow big. "No way!"

I kiss beneath her ear. "I can be quiet, and they'll never know." I rub the seam of her jeans between her legs. "I've missed you so much. I want to taste you and make you feel good."

She reaches for my hand, rolls me onto my back, and tucks herself against me. "Thank you for coming…and for all your help. I hate using your money, but I don't know how else we'd get her back, and I—"

"Stop. I regret not confronting my brothers. Going forward, I will make sure they understand our relationship. My parents know you aren't out for our money. We're going to get through this together. And Arabella will be home in twenty-four hours."

Chapter 27

Paisley

As much as it feels good to have Davis' warmth next to me, sleep is not my friend right now, and my attempt at napping is futile. The sun is shining today, and I'd rather be working on my art, but it seems ridiculous to do anything other than wonder if Arabella is safe. What will being without her medicine do to her? Does she miss me or would she prefer to live with Mom?

I make some coffee and offer it to Tom Shaw, our current bodyguard. I don't have cream or sugar, so he'll have to just muscle through, but I need to be alert. Felix and his team order in sandwiches for a late lunch, and I take two bites of mine, not even registering what it is.

Davis has been on the phone, confirming the assets he liquidated and moving things around in his accounts, preparing to send the money.

"I still think giving her what she wants is a mistake," I tell him. "Maybe I can reason with her." Surely, I could talk some sense into our mother, remind her of how things were before Dad died. I can't accept that the person she was is gone.

Davis looks up and pulls me into his lap. "Sweetheart, as much as I want to believe that your mother is a rational person, for some reason, she's not. Arabella is more important to me than the money, and I know she's more important to you than anything else. Felix is working to make sure the money won't be gone forever, and even if we don't get the money back, it doesn't matter as long as we have her."

"But I'll never be able to reimburse you."

"I don't care." Davis kisses my temple and holds me tight. "It's all going to be fine. Let me do this for you. Arabella is our priority."

Felix clears his throat as he approaches, and I jump up, ready to hear what he has to say.

"We know where they are," he says with a smile. "They're at the Fairmont at the airport."

"Are you sure?" Davis asks.

He nods. "They were able to fully trace her cell phone. The call ran two seconds longer than we needed to figure out the final location." He looks at me. "You did really well."

I sigh. "This isn't something I want to be good at."

Davis squeezes my shoulder. "That would make her just thirty or forty-five minutes away."

Felix gathers everyone around and continues his update. "Vanessa has a flight booked for Costa Rica using her Victoria Babcock alias. We have federal police ready to arrest her after she goes through customs and is preparing to board the plane."

"Arabella is her daughter," Davis points out. "Will that cause problems with the charges?"

Felix shakes his head. "They're not looking at her for the kidnapping yet. She'll be arrested for a whole host of other offenses—entering Canada on a false passport, working and living here illegally, an extortion plot against Canadian citizens, and also under an extradition request out of Dallas, Texas."

My eyes pop wide. I can't believe any of this. "She

really was a mother to us before my dad died."

Felix nods. "I'm sure she was. She might have put her past behind her for a while, but grief can make people do strange things."

"What about the person who's delivering Arabella?" I ask. "Will he be arrested?"

"Yes. We think he's going to meet your mother in South America, but we can't be sure where or what name he'll be traveling under. We'll keep you posted."

When the meeting breaks up, Davis insists that I take a shower and get dressed. "I made a reservation at The Sandbar. I know you like sushi, or you can have something else, but you need to eat. Standing at the window isn't doing you any good."

I know he's right, but I wish there was something I could do to push my mom to just return Arabella. "I hope Arabella doesn't hate me for this," I murmur.

"I won't let her," Davis assures me.

He picks out a cute summer dress and some wedge sandals, and after I'm ready he leads me a block away to the restaurant, which is below the bridge into downtown. We're seated at a table outside, and the weather is perfect tonight.

The hostess leaves us menus and asks, "Can I get you something to drink?"

"We'll take a bottle of the Henry Family Estate 2020 Fumé Sauvignon Blanc."

"Very well. I'll get that for you."

I look at him. "I'm not sure I can drink wine tonight." It will knock me right on my ass.

"I hope you'll at least try this. The Henry family are friends of my parents, and my mother loves this wine. It's a light white."

I nod. "I can try it." I look at the menu for a few moments before setting it aside. I'll ask the server for a recommendation on the sushi.

"What are you thinking?" Davis asks.

"Sushi."

He grins. I hate being so predictable. "They have a fantastic sushi tower. Would you want to share that?"

I shrug. That makes it simple. "Sure."

The server arrives and takes our order as the hostess returns with our wine. After a quick taste we're alone, and Davis holds up his glass. "To forgiveness — me for my egregious error and your mother for what she's putting you through."

We each take a sip of our wine.

I set my glass down and stare at it. "I've already forgiven you, but I'm not sure I'll ever be able to forgive my mother."

He nods. "I understand. I know this is a lot. Money can be a curse, whether you have it or you don't. I don't want you to forgive her because she deserves it, but because you deserve to live without anger in your heart."

I nod. "Honestly, I'm embarrassed that my mother has done this, that she's holding you hostage. I would completely understand if you wanted nothing to do with me after this."

He shakes his head. "You have nothing to be embarrassed about. This is exactly why my family has Felix's team with us at all times. All kinds of people think they can get a quick payday, and he knows how to handle it. I'm more worried that you're going to want nothing to do with me since you're learning the hard way what it can mean to be part of my life."

"I don't see that happening."

The server places a large tower of sushi between us.

We talk about lighter subjects for a while — things going on with the nurses at the hospital and my art and how it's progressing. For a short time, I don't worry about Arabella, but then I feel guilty that I'm out on a date with Davis and not focused on her.

After dinner, we return to the loft and Felix confirms that the police have positioned a camera in Mom's hotel room and are watching the hotel. He says Arabella has asked to talk to me, but Mom keeps putting her off. She is relatively safe, and Davis reviews the footage and agrees that her health seems fine, despite the lack of medication.

I sleep for a few hours. My body makes me, and the wine probably helps, but then I'm back up and back at my post, looking out the window. When it hits five thirty Wednesday morning, I take a quick shower. In thirty minutes, the first payment will hit Mom's bank account and the tracking will start.

As I finish getting dressed, I smell Davis' woodsy aroma even before he touches me. Wrapping his arms around me from behind, he kisses my neck. "How are you doing this morning?"

I shrug. "I'm anxious for this to be over."

When we walk out to the main room, Tom stands. "The money has hit her account, and it's been moved to the Cayman account. The police have eyes on your sister, mother, and a gentleman."

I'm suddenly wide awake. Who needs coffee now? Certainly not me. "Where are they? Have they moved out of the hotel room?"

"Not yet. Your mother is preparing for her flight."

"She's planning to get away with this and leave Ricky to take the fall again."

"What a sap," Tom mutters, and I agree.

Felix arrives with breakfast sandwiches, and he has two members of the RCMP with him—federal police. Tom walks him through what happened last night and how things have progressed this morning.

Tom's phone rings. He answers and listens for a moment. "They're picking up the rental car," he tells us. "They're going to be on the move."

"We've put a tracker on their rental car, and we'll keep them in sight via a helicopter once they're out of the airport no-fly zone," Felix says.

My stomach is flipping and flopping. Davis wraps his arm around me, and I lean into him. I check my watch and let out a breath of air.

"Boarding her flight starts in a little over an hour," Felix says. "She won't know things aren't going to plan until it's too late."

I munch on my egg-white with cheese and bacon on an English muffin and wait.

When Felix's phone pings, he looks at it. "They've just crossed King Edward Boulevard."

That means they're close. "Should I go downstairs to meet them?"

He shakes his head. "It's not smart to let them know we're on to them. He won't get away."

Then my phone pings. "It's my mother." I read her text aloud.

Mom: Arabella is close. You can look out your window and see her in a car approaching. Send the second half of the money.

"Tell her it's done," Felix says.

Me: Money is on the way.

Felix is listening to an earpiece. How did I not notice that before?

"Let's go downstairs and get Arabella," Davis says.

I fly out the door and take the steps so quickly it's like I'm floating. We emerge from the building just as the car pulls up. My eyes lock with Arabella's, and she runs to me. Her tear-stained face and red, swollen eyes tell me she's been upset for a while, but I hope that's all over now. I scoop her up and hold her tight.

"I'm so sorry," she keeps repeating.

"It wasn't you. I know that," I tell her. "As long as

you're okay." I pull back and look at her. She's a little sallow, but she's here with me.

The police are arresting the man who brought her. "Mom's not in the car," Arabella tells me. "She's at the airport."

I squeeze her again and debate telling her the truth. After a moment, I decide it's the right thing to do, even if it upsets her. "She's being arrested too. I'm sorry."

Arabella shakes her head. "It's all my fault. I missed her so much, but she didn't really miss us."

I kneel to look in her eyes. "I don't know, Bells. She's been broken since Daddy died. We can't fix her. She needs to fix herself."

I carry Arabella back upstairs with Davis just behind me. I sit her on a stool, and he looks her over while I get her medicine and water. We're all silent as he listens to her heart.

After a moment, he looks up at us and smiles. "I don't know who did that surgery, but the heart sounds fantastic." We all chuckle, and Arabella wraps her arms around his neck. In that moment, I realize I feel whole again, now that Arabella and Davis are with me.

The rest of the day is a blur. Arabella talks to several Canadian and U.S. police officers. Felix reports that the money wired to Mom has now been returned to Davis. He also reports that he's transferred the rest of what was in Mom's account into an account in my name at the same bank in the Caymans. "It's outside Canadian reach, and since she's your mother, it's yours to use as you wish."

I feel suddenly very flush, but before that can sink in, Julia and Chip return.

Arabella runs over and hugs them both. "I was so worried I wasn't going to see you again."

Chip gets down on one knee so he's eye to eye with her. "That will never happen. We will always find our way to you, and this won't ever happen again. Don't you worry about that."

"Was the adventure fun?" Julia asks.

I'm grateful she's calling it that. I like that approach.

Arabella shakes her head. "Not really. We walked downstairs to a car and drove to the airport. I wanted to get out of the car and come back, but she wouldn't let me." She tears up.

I reach for her. "You did absolutely nothing wrong. I'm so sorry this happened. You're safe now, and you don't have to worry about anything else."

Arabella buries her head in my neck. I set her up with her headphones and tablet on the bed, and she watches a show but wants to sit right next to me. I get it. She'll worry for a while that I'm going to leave or disappear. I feel the same way about her.

Davis comes and sits at the end of the mattress, and my heart swells. "This may not be the right time, but I want you to know that I'm completely and utterly in love with you," I tell him.

"Good, because I'm in love with you, too," he replies. "The both of you." His eyes shift to Arabella, who is oblivious. "Will you consider moving back into my place?"

I sigh. "You've done so much for us. I don't want to feel dependent on you." It's the same issue we've always had, but it's not going away.

"You're not dependent," he counters. "In fact, I believe you have quite a bit of money in the bank as of today." He gives me a look, and I have to laugh. "But I want to take care of you and Arabella, and my place is already all set up. If you move in, I want you to live on the residence side now, and I want Felix to assign us a driver and bodyguard. I don't want anything like this to happen again. Your mom had access a normal person wouldn't have, but it was too easy for her to walk your sister out and into a waiting car. I don't know what I'd do if someone tried that with you."

I look at him, completely dumbfounded. "I guess if I'm going to have you in my life, this is part of the package."

He smiles. "That's exactly right."

"I don't want to give up the loft, though. It's a fantastic place to do my artwork."

"I would never ask that. However, I am going to have a sofa sent so more people can sit and wait while you create. I'm not crazy about members of Felix's team sitting on the bed."

"That's fine."

"Can we move you over tonight?" he asks.

"If it's okay with Felix and his team."

Felix agrees and dispatches one of his men to drive us. After a dinner of pizza at the loft, we pack our things, and within the hour, we're back at Davis' place.

When we get inside, he gives Arabella a tour and shows her the bedroom that will be hers. "We can have someone come in and decorate it any way you like," he tells her.

"Can I paint the walls black?"

"Why would you want to do that?" I ask.

She shrugs. "I just want to know what I can do."

Davis laughs. "My mom has a designer, and I'll have her get in touch. If you want black, we'll figure it out, but I thought you'd prefer pink or—"

"Pink?" Arabella steps back with her hand on her heart. "What about me says pink? Gross!"

"She's on her way to becoming a teenager," I warn. "It's not too late to change your mind."

"Oh, yes, it is. You've both got me, and I'm not changing my mind." He pulls us in for a sappy group hug.

After Arabella is settled and falls asleep, Davis pulls me into his bedroom. I guess it's our bedroom now? I can barely process that thought as we mash into each other's arms, moaning. Our mouths grind together, and our tongues tangle, sucking and licking, lost in each other as we make up for the time we've missed together.

I gasp at the feel of his hard cock pressing into my sex through my jeans. He hikes one of my legs over his hip, his hand diving into my pants. Every nerve is on high alert. He wriggles his fingers as he digs into my soaked center. He does things to me no one else can. He pulls my thigh up to his waist, gripping my ass and rubbing my center harder. I breathe all my feelings into his ear—filthy, naughty, and erotic…no words, more like noises—frantic, hungry noises.

With an animal grunt, he slams me against the wall. He peels my jeans away, taking my panties with them. In an instant, his body slams into mine.

"How does this feel?" he growls.

"God, I've missed you." I can hardly think straight.

"Your pussy is so hot, so wet, so sweet and soft… Ready for me."

"Feel my pussy, baby…oh yeah." The room fills with wet slapping sounds as his fingers fill me and stretch me wide.

"Come for me!" he demands.

"I gonna come up against this fucking wall…ohhhhh that feels so fucking good," I rasp. "I need you inside me. Fuck me right fucking now!" I whisper hot and wet into his ear. "C'mon, baby, fuck me now. I want you deep inside me."

He lays me down on the bed and fumbles with his zipper. I pull my T-shirt over my head and drop my bra to the ground. He pulls his Henley off, and I marvel again at the beauty of his body.

"I missed you, too." He tugs on his cock a few times as he watches me. "Are you ready for this?"

I reach for my breasts and stroke them. "Yes," I breathe.

He urges me back, stretching and spreading me wide. His hands wander over my breasts, the tips hardening to his touch. Then they drift over my stomach, down over my hips and thighs to my knees. "You're so beautiful spread out like this for me." His lips press softly against my skin.

My fingers tremble as I grasp his cock, all thick and hard and leaking onto my fingers, while he suckles my breast. I moan. "Ohh yeah, yeah, that feels so good."

He snickers as he slides his tongue along my collarbone to below my ear, burying his face in my neck and nibbling at my throat.

His fingers trail a hard line up my slit, probing slightly, teasing me.

"Please…" I beg, my voice harsh and hungry in his ear. I give him a firm tug, stroking him as his finger pivots in and out of my channel.

"Come for me, and I promise to fuck you hard," he murmurs.

The wave is coming, and I couldn't hold it back if I tried.

"That's it. Surrender yourself to me. Give me what I want."

The room fills with the sound of flesh slapping, and I see white as my climax reaches its pinnacle. Grabbing the sheets for leverage, every bit of blood in my body pools in my center as I release the biggest orgasm I've ever had.

As promised, Davis pushes inside me, stretching me wide. His cock is like an iron pipe, and he nails me into the sheets, strumming my clit like he's doing a guitar solo. As he increases his pace, another orgasm spasms my body until finally he groans and fills me.

He kisses me deeply, holding me tight, his throbbing cock so deep inside me. We lay drenched in sweat, the last few spasms vibrating through my trembling thighs. After a moment, he drapes his leg over my thigh, my hand to his face and my breath coming in staccato bursts. Shaking, I kiss him again.

"That was exquisite," he says.

I smile. "I never realized how much I like dirty talk."

Suddenly, he pulls in a sharp breath. "I forgot to wear a condom, and I hope that doesn't upset you, because I'm having a hard time caring. I'm ready for anything that lies ahead for us."

I sigh, but I can't stop my smile. "I'm not sure I can take

much more excitement right now, but I've had the depo shot. We're good."

He gets up on one arm and looks at me. "You can't run away again if you're unhappy. If we're going to be together, I want us to be partners. We have to work things out."

I nod. "I was never unhappy. I just didn't want you to wonder about my intentions, so I was prepared to show you and your brothers that Arabella and I can do it on our own."

"I understand. I know that was hurtful, but know going forward that I don't care about my fucking brothers' opinions. I am amazed by your strength, and I know you can do it on your own. But I want to do it with you. Promise you'll talk to me."

This man is so amazing. All I can do is nod.

Chapter 28

Paisley

"You've got this," Davis assures me.

I run my hands down the front of my dress, which is more glam than I was looking for, but probably appropriate for the occasion. I feel much more vulnerable in a fancy dress than I do in jeans and a T-shirt. Tonight is the Studio Tour, and I need all the strength I can get. I still feel like I'm playing at being an artist instead of actually working as one. But every time I look around my loft, which is now full of works in progress and a few finished pieces, I know that's not true.

The last few weeks have been hectic, so I've hardly had time to process this. It looks like Mom will take a plea deal here, and after she's served her Canadian sentence, she'll be deported to the U.S. to answer her charges in Texas. I've been ignoring her calls. She has nothing to add to my life at this point. Arabella continues to get stronger every day, and she's become a very active almost eleven-year-old. She wants to take figure skating lessons. We'll see.

And Davis and I have found a nice routine and settled into a partnership of sorts. I feel solid and supported, and I'm getting past feeling dependent. So for the first time in a long time, I don't feel like I'm waiting for the floor to fall out from under me.

Well, except for my nerves this evening, I guess. Isla has helped me arrange my work for maximum impact, and she's arranged for some hors d'oeuvres to be passed. The event officially started twenty minutes ago, and no one has walked in yet. It's not like I expected to see them trampling over each other to come into my studio, but I hope someone will eventually wander in.

I watch as a young couple peek in the door but don't enter. This is going to be a long night.

"Stop fidgeting." Davis rubs my back as he stands next to me. "You look beautiful, and tonight is going to be an enormous success."

Suddenly, another face appears in the doorway, and this time it's one I recognize. Lucy runs in with her mom in tow. "Oh my God! Look at you!"

I open my arms and give her a hug. "Thank you so much for coming. Hello, Mrs. Yang. So far you're my only visitors tonight, so dig in, and you may be taking home a lot of appies."

Lucy munches a scallop wrapped in bacon. "If they're all as good as this, I'll take whatever you want."

I chuckle.

Angela, Lucy's mom, strolls over to where my work is on display. She spends quite a bit of time looking and seems to be making a face as she examines several of the pieces. I worry she doesn't like my work very much. Then she liberates two glasses of champagne from a passing server and hands me one. "You've taken something so mundane, that we often ignore, and made it elegant. These are beautiful. You have so much talent."

I blush.

"That's exactly what I thought the first time I saw her work." Julia has arrived and smiles widely as she joins us.

"Angela Yang, I'd like you to meet Julia Martin. Julia bought my first piece and has helped me do all of this. And Julia, this is Lucy, my best friend. Angela is her mother."

After they exchange greetings, Julia hugs me tightly. I look around and realize several other people have come in. I don't know if that makes my nerves better or worse. "This all looks fantastic," Julia says.

"Thank you. Isla suggested the light blue paint for the walls and the stands for the work. I just do as she asks."

"That's exactly what I like in a client," Isla says as she greets Julia and kisses her on the cheeks.

I turn back to Angela and Lucy. "Thank you so much for your kind words. If you're still here at ten, I'm unveiling a piece that's a thank you to Julia. If you like these, you may like that one as well. She has been so kind to me."

"We'll be here," Lucy assures me.

"For now, you should go check out the other artists," I tell them. "One of my neighbors paints nudes."

Davis materializes at my side. "And you know this how?"

"He introduced himself and told me," I say innocently. I'm not about to add any details.

"He offered to paint Paisley," Arabella says.

But it seems I have Arabella for that. I suppress an eye roll. "He wasn't serious."

"We'll check out his work and see if you have anything to worry about," Mrs. Yang jokes. She pats Davis on the arm.

I giggle. "Davis already knows he has nothing to worry about. He's mine, and I'm his."

Davis winks at me and stands a little straighter.

After that, things are rolling, and the night flies by. I meet several of my commission clients, who are eager for their art. One of them is the actress Alison Pate, who's currently starring in one of the top-rated shows on television, which happens to film here in Vancouver.

"I love these," she gushes. "My piece is going to be

fantastic in my house in North Van. I can't wait. Isla tells me you have five buyers and eleven pieces. I like several of them, so I won't be picky."

"You've made my day," I tell her.

"*Architectural Digest* is coming in to take pictures of my home in a few weeks, and I promise I will prominently display it."

"You're very generous. Thank you."

She leans in close. "Let's hang out sometime. We can go to lunch, and you can tell me how you snagged Vancouver's most eligible bachelor."

There's a commotion, and we turn to see Henry, Griffin, and Phillip arrive. A photographer is busily snapping pictures, but Isla politely shoos him out.

"She didn't snag me," Davis says, clearing his throat. "I snagged her."

She offers her hand and smiles at him. "Alison Pate. I'm secretly in love with your brother Henry. Would you feel comfortable introducing us?"

I'm stunned by her confidence. It's so not Canadian.

But Davis just smiles and motions for his brothers to come over. They do so a few minutes later after taking a look at all my work. Henry approaches first and kisses me on the cheek. "You look amazing, and your work is incredible. I had no idea you were so talented."

I give him a strained smile. I know what he thinks of me, and I'm not sure what to make of his presence here—any of Davis' brothers, actually. "Thank you."

Phillip pushes him out of the way. "Let me get a word in before you bore her with work or something." He smiles at me. "You do look incredible, and I always knew you were talented."

I manage a nod. "Thanks."

Griffin stands back a little ways, with Teresa on his arm this evening, talking to Davis. Neither of them looks my way, but I'm not going to let it get to me.

"Henry, this is Alison Pate," I say after a moment. "She's purchased one of my pieces, and evidently, she's a fan of yours."

He looks at her and offers his hand. "You look very familiar."

"I would hope so," I tell him. "She's the star of *Bombshells*."

His eyes grow wide. "Of course. You're wearing more clothes now than you do onscreen."

She giggles, and they wander away.

"That made my work easier," Davis says. "Thanks."

Griffin finally comes over.

"Nice to see you," I tell him. "Thank you for coming tonight."

"I wouldn't have missed it for the world."

I wonder if that's true. I look over and see Teresa chatting with Julia. Julia seems less than thrilled, and Teresa is overcompensating.

Then Lucy reappears with her mom behind her. Mrs. Yang is looking tired. She's been on her feet for the last three hours, at least. I lean over to Davis. "Can you pull out one of the chairs in the closet and offer it to Lucy's mom? She looks like she could use a seat."

While he pulls out all four chairs for the few who may be interested, Lucy walks over to me. "Have you actually seen your neighbor's nudes?"

I cringe. "No, are they bad?"

Her eyes widen as she shakes her head. "Holy cow, I'll be using my vibrator tonight for sure. They're very…sensual."

I snort.

"I bet Davis would love to have one of his paintings of you," Lucy teases.

I shake my head. "No way. I don't care to have anyone but him see me that way."

Lucy chuckles. "It would be memorable."

"Hey, Lucy." Davis walks over. "How were the other

studios you visited?"

"It's been great," she tells him. "Everyone has approached tonight differently. Some have exhibitions. Others aren't even there. They have a security guard, and it's like walking through a museum. I guess they're not looking for any additional work. Paisley's neighbor who does the nudes has some beautiful work. You should check it out. I bet you'd love one of Paisley, and I hear he'd love to do it."

With that, she grins and goes over to check on her mom, who is talking to Chip. Arabella is sitting with them, focused on her tablet. I can feel Davis tense next to me.

Henry comes over with Alison still perched to his arm. "What has you all riled up?"

"The artist next door offered to paint Paisley. Nude!" Davis says with a hint of malice.

Griffin and Phillip walk up.

"What's wrong with that?" Alison asks. "The female body is beautiful."

That has Griffin and Phillip on high alert.

"It's sleazy of him to ask her to model for him," Davis says through clenched teeth.

"What are you talking about?" Phillip asks.

I throw my hands in the air. "Go next door and see his paintings. Lucy says they're very sensual. And before you even say anything, I told him no thanks."

Most of them don't even question this and walk right out the door, leaving me standing with Griffin and Teresa. I have no idea what to say to them, and fortunately, a couple approaches to talk to me about my work.

"Where do the ideas for these come from?" the woman asks.

I smile at her. "I can't entirely explain it. I just see it. But sometimes it takes some trial and error too. I have an idea for a pinecone, but the liquid silver is almost two thousand degrees, and they burn up."

"Where do you find such beautiful wood pieces?"

"I just see them out in nature and pick them up." I would never share that I found them on the Martin's private island.

"We were told we could have one of your coins?" the man asks.

I smile. "Yes. They're my business card. They don't work as currency, but I hope they'll help you remember me."

"You are so clever."

"Thank you," I say as they move away.

Then Isla comes running up. "I have two interviews for you—one with the *Vancouver Sun*, which could also be picked up by the wires, and the other is the first of several interviews for an in-depth article in *Artistry*."

My eyes grow wide. *Artistry* is a publication that prints on expensive, heavy paper and has stunning photos, and they do deep dives into artists. Just being mentioned in the magazine is considered a golden ticket.

"That's...that's fantastic. Thanks." This is all becoming so overwhelming.

She nods. "I'm happy to do it. Watch for the *Sun* reporter to come by shortly."

I nod, feeling shellshocked as Isla walks away, but Davis puts his hand on my back, and the simple touch calms me. "Remember, you've got this. You've worked hard, and you deserve this."

I nod and take a deep breath, just as I see Kate arrive to take Arabella back to the apartment. She doesn't want to go, but it's almost ten and time for her to go to bed. Kate has a lot less trouble getting her out of here than I would alone, so I'm grateful yet again as I wave goodbye and they step out.

After they've gone, I turn back to Davis. "Are you upset about my neighbor?"

"He is very talented, but I'm not sure I want you modeling for him, even if it was for me."

"I don't think I'd feel comfortable doing it, but I'm glad you no longer want to kill him."

He shakes his head. "Of course, I do. You can totally tell he's slept with all his models."

I look at him indignantly. "How?"

"He captures women in the middle of their orgasm. One woman has a see-through scarf draped around her as she masturbates."

My hand covers my mouth. Just as I'm recovering, a petite redhead wearing wild cat-eye glasses approaches with her hand extended. "Ms. Brooks, my name is Ginny Thompson. I'm with the *Vancouver Sun*. You have quite a display here. It seems to showcase your reaction to the environmental collapse."

My brows reach my hairline as I shake her hand. "I think of it more as the ebb and flow of our water. British Columbia has its stunning mainland full of lush trees and rivers flowing freely. But it also has the multiple islands and inlets. They all work cohesively together, and that's what I feel my work is about."

Her face lights up, and we go on to have a conversation about the beauty of our province. She records it, which makes me a little nervous, but she seems genuinely interested in what I have to say.

Isla hovers nearby during the interview, and after a few minutes, she steps in. "It's time," she tells me.

"Thank you," I tell her. "Ginny, I'm so glad you could make it tonight. I have a piece I'm unveiling in a few minutes if you'd like to stick around. It's a gift for a friend who made sure I was here tonight."

She nods. "I'd love that. Thank you."

I excuse myself from Ginny and move to the front of the room. Isla taps her glass to get the remaining crowd's attention as she wheels a covered stand over to the center of the loft.

I step forward. "Thank you all so much for being here this evening. I've displayed once before in my lifetime, and it was in the gallery downstairs. I was honored to have my piece shown in such a prestigious gallery as a student at Emily Carr. So if you're looking for up and coming artists, be sure to follow their website. They also have an amazing newsletter where they highlight artists."

"Thank you," Gwen, the owner, says.

"I didn't know you were here." I blush.

That gets a chuckle from the crowd.

"I'd also like to thank my agent, Isla Farrow. She connected me with one of her clients who bought that very first piece."

"She beat me by seconds," an older gentleman says from the side of the room.

Again, the crowd chuckles.

"Through pure luck, I met Julia again years later," I continue. "She introduced me to Isla, and together they went about convincing me to find the time and energy to create more pieces. While six of these are already sold, there are five remaining, and they'll be available at my showing next month at the gallery downstairs."

There is polite applause.

"Julia, can you join me?" I ask.

She walks up, all smiles.

"Thank you for being my first buyer and for making me a real artist. Thank you for making sure that I'm here today celebrating. You've become a special friend to me and my little sister, and we'll always be grateful to you and your family."

The crowd claps, and I walk over to the stand. "You know nothing is more nerve-wracking than showing the world a new sculpture that has never been seen by anyone else." Taking a deep breath, I pull the sheet off the piece.

Isla gasps. Julia pulls her hands together, and her eyes light up.

I think they like it.

Suddenly, the room explodes with overwhelming applause.

The sculpture is a group of rocks that have been partially dipped in silver, then gold, and then rose gold, and it ends in pool of copper-coated rocks. "This is called *River Rocks*," I tell them. "It's one of a kind."

"It's so wonderful," Julia says. "Thank you."

Isla looks at me. "I hope it will be one of a series. I'd love at least one more."

"Make it two," the older gentleman says.

I'm stunned. "It's up to Julia," I tell them.

"We're going to talk about that," Isla assures me.

I thank everyone again, and the party starts to break up. Some of the other artists from the neighborhood have popped in. I even wave at Jim.

Isla comes rushing over. "Please promise me that won't be the only one. It's so flawless. And you can tell it was a hit."

"Truly, it's up to Julia." I lean in. "If she doesn't like it, you can sell it for her."

Isla shakes her head. "She loves it and is toying with my emotions. I swear, she's going to drive me crazy." She throws her hands in the air and races off to speak with the man who mentioned he was interested in some of my pieces.

I package up a box of the scallops wrapped in bacon for Lucy and her mom. Mrs. Yang pats me on the cheek. "I'm so proud of you," she tells me. "You deserve all of this and more."

"Thank you." I hug them both.

I notice Henry leaving with Alison. I nudge Davis. "Maybe it's a love connection."

He shrugs. "Maybe for tonight. She was also very interested in the artist next door."

I shake my head. "She may not have Martin money, but she has quite a bit. She's also used to the limelight. She wouldn't be a bad match for him."

"But the question is, can she give up her job for him?"

I stop and look at him. "Do you expect me to give up my job?"

He kisses the tip of my nose. "Nope, but I'm not the future CEO of Martin Communications."

We wave goodbye to Griffin, Teresa, and Phillip as Julia approaches. "You know it's fine to make more of the *River Rocks*. They only make my pieces more valuable."

I chuckle. "I owe this all to you. *River Rocks* doesn't even come close to repaying you."

She rolls her eyes. "I don't want repayment, but I will take grandchildren," she teases.

My pulse quickens.

"I'm on board, and I'm working on her," Davis assures her.

My head begins to spin.

"Davis tells me we won't be seeing you at dinner tomorrow night."

I look over at him, trying to school my surprised look.

"We're going to spend the day at the aquarium," he tells her. "I'm surprising Arabella with a tour of the otter and penguin habitats, and she'll get to feed them. After that, she'll likely be tired, so we'll spend the evening relaxing and ordering in pizza."

Julia smiles. "Hopefully, next week then."

I nod. "We'll plan on it. And Julia, I know I ambushed you with the rock sculpture, so if it's not your taste, please don't feel obligated."

She shakes her head. "Are you kidding? I love it. I know just where to put it, too. There's a spot in the backyard that leads to the pool that I think will be perfect. It's almost as if the water is running."

"That's what I was trying to achieve."

She kisses me on the cheek. "It's beautiful, and it was beyond anything you needed to do. I'm just glad you're settling in here."

"I love the loft." I smile. "And a little birdie told me you own the building we're in and the gallery downstairs."

She shrugs. "I'm a patron of the arts. It's one way I can

give back."

"I'm very lucky to have you in my corner."

We hug her goodbye, and she and Chip make their departure, the last of the crowd to go.

"I hope you didn't mind that I told my mom we couldn't make tomorrow evening," Davis says. "I needed a night with you and Arabella to myself."

I step in and kiss him softly. "It's your family. I'm fine with whatever you want to do."

"Good, because I promised Arabella the aquarium, and I don't like to break my promises. And tomorrow night, we can do as little as possible."

I sigh in his arms. "You read my mind. Arabella is going to love a day at the aquarium, and doing nothing tomorrow night sounds perfect."

I put a few things away and tidy a bit, and then Tom is waiting to take us home. We settle in the back of the car, and I snuggle in close, realizing how tired I am. I breathe in Davis' woodsy scent and feel so safe. I know we belong together. And whatever path that means for us, being together is all I care about. "Thank you for all your help and support tonight." I sigh.

His arm tightens around my shoulder. "Thank you for letting me."

Chapter 29

Paisley

Sitting behind thick plexiglass at the Alouette Correctional Centre for Women in Maple Ridge, I wait patiently for my mother. It was strange asking to see Violet Boyd, but turns out that's my mother's birth name, not Vanessa. She arrived here last week from the holding center, and she's been calling and messaging relentlessly. With the Studio Tour out of the way, my head felt clearer, so I discussed my options with Davis and Felix. I'd like to be rid of her once and for all, and maybe even have some closure in the process, so hopefully, this is a step in that direction. And anyway, Maple Ridge is only about an hour outside Vancouver, so it's not even a terrible inconvenience.

After a few minutes, she arrives wearing gray sweatpants and a T-shirt under a gray sweatshirt with the ACCW logo on the left chest. She still has her typical smile.

Once she's seated on the other side of the glass, she picks up a telephone receiver. "Darling, you look just awful. I've seen you in the gossip columns, and you're always in jeans and a T-shirt. Now that you and Davis are an item, you should dress for the photographers."

"It's good to see you too, Mom. You're looking good, all things considered." I'm trying to be kind because I don't want a fight. Once we start arguing, I'll get nowhere.

She pats her hair. The gray roots are showing and without product, her hair is a mass of frizz. "You're very sweet. Thank you."

I give her a strained smile. She asked for this meeting, and Felix strongly suggested I come, so I have. She also wanted to see Arabella, but that will happen when hell freezes over.

"Where is Arabella? You didn't bring her with you?" Mom searches behind me.

"No. She's not interested in seeing you. You kidnapped her for ransom, Mom. She doesn't feel safe ever being around you again."

Her eyes cloud for a millisecond, but then she's back to her typical self. "How are things with you and Davis?"

I look beyond her at the corrections officer in full body armor with a taser on her hip. "Nothing to report."

"Oh, come on. Tell me some good gossip about him."

"Really, there's nothing to tell." *That's not the kind of relationship we have*, I'd like to say. And even if it was, I know she's just fishing for stories she can use against me or sell to the tabloids or something. "How is your case progressing?" I ask.

She waves that away. "Can you believe all the silly charges? They don't understand why I did it. I was only looking out for you and your sister."

"I don't see how you could possibly think what you did was looking out for anyone but yourself." She looks away. "Mom, I know you've been on the run since you were a teenager."

"And then I met your father," she says. "He knew about my history and always protected me."

I nod. "He always protected you and Arabella and me.

It's a shame you didn't do the same for us after he died."

"You were efficient. You didn't need me," she scoffs.

"Arabella did," I counter. "And I had to drop out of school to help her."

"Why are you complaining about this?" she asks. "According to the *Vancouver Sun,* your ugly art is the talk of the town."

"I'm not complaining. I'm only pointing out facts you seem to want to ignore. What is your lawyer telling you?"

"They're working with the U.S. government on the extradition. I think my mother is coming up. I hope you'll get to meet her."

My stomach drops. *I have other family?* I carefully school my features. No good can come from letting my mother see my excitement about anything. "She's our grandmother. We'll be happy to meet her."

"I need some money," she says after a moment.

Her eyes meet mine, and there isn't an ounce of remorse. I shake my head. "I'm sorry, but I can't and won't help you."

"I'm your mother, and you have my money. You need to help me."

"I don't need to do anything but drink lots of water and go pee."

"Don't be so vulgar."

I begin to stand. "If this is why you insisted I come, I'm going to leave."

"Please wait," she says into the telephone receiver.

I look at her, waiting to hear what she has to say. "What do you want?"

"I need to pay my lawyer more money to keep fighting my case. Can you help me? You took my money."

"I didn't take your money."

Her eyes blaze in anger. "Fine, Davis took my money. I need it back to pay my attorney's fees."

"That's why you wanted to see me?"

"Give me back my money."

"You've done a lot of things that make it hard for me to trust you or want to help you, but you pushed me too far when you took my sister and used her to extort people for money. Any empathy I had for you is gone. You lied to me for years and left me to clean up the mess you abandoned. No. I don't have to do anything."

I turn and walk out of the jail. I feel pretty good about leaving her behind. I don't know if it's closure, exactly, but I don't feel guilty, and that's progress. I also feel lighter because Davis is waiting in the car in the parking lot.

I swing the car door open wide and sit down heavy. "We can go now."

"How did it go?" Davis asks.

I bob my head back and forth and pull the seatbelt across me. "I think it went okay."

He turns to me. "What was so urgent that she needed to see you?"

"Money, of course. There wasn't much to the meeting, really. She asked about Arabella, told me I needed to dress better for the cameras. But what she really wanted was money. Money for her legal bills to fight what she's done. She says I've taken her money."

"That takes some serious balls. But we were expecting her to ask since Felix moved the money she's been relying on for years."

"Once things settle down, I'm going to find out who the security guard was that was killed in her bank heist. I'd like to give that money to his family."

Davis nods. "You're very generous."

"She got that money through conning and grifting. I don't want it."

Davis nods. "I'll support whatever you want to do."

"She said her mother was coming for a visit, and she'd like me to meet my grandmother, something I never knew I had."

"Do you know when she's coming?"

I shake my head. "I'm sure she'll let us know, as long as that continues to be something she wants."

"When the time comes, I'll go with you if you want. You don't have to do this on your own."

I squeeze his hand. "Thank you."

"Dinner with my family still work for you this evening?"

I nod. We're having dinner at the Beach House, a beautiful restaurant in West Vancouver that overlooks the city and the water. "I just need time to get ready first."

He chuckles. "This is the West Coast. You can wear jeans and a T-shirt everywhere."

I look down at the Devo concert T-shirt I picked up at a secondhand store years ago. "Davis," I warn. "I need to go home and shower the antiseptic smell of the prison off of me and put on something nice."

"You know I think you're beautiful no matter what you wear."

"That's because you want to get lucky," I say. "But I'm sure the rest of your family would prefer not to see me dressed like this."

We inch our way back to the condo through the traffic, and I still have enough time to take a leisurely shower and prepare myself mentally for time with his brothers. I'm still uncomfortable being around them, knowing what they suspect about me, but I've been told they're bringing dates tonight, which I hope will provide a distraction for all of us.

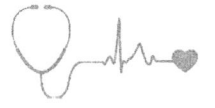

When we arrive at the Martins' house, Arabella is waiting for me outside. "I asked Felix to let me know when you were close so I could come meet you," she says.

I give her a big hug. "I missed you today. How were the pool and ocean?"

She smiles brightly. "It was great. I want to go on a sailboat back to Martin Island, but Chip says you have to approve that first."

"Let's figure it out," I tell her. "I wouldn't mind going with you."

"How did it go with Mom?" she asks very discreetly.

I know some of this is beyond what her ten years of age can understand, but I don't want to hide anything from her.

"It was fine. She asked how you were doing."

"I hope you told her I'm still mad at her."

"I did."

"Is that what she wanted from you?"

"No, she wants us to pay for her lawyer, so she doesn't have to be in jail."

Arabella's eyes grow wide. "Are you going to do that?"

I shake my head. "Nope. When she took you away from me, she went too far. She's going to need to figure out how to get herself out of the mess she created."

Arabella slips her hand in mine, and we walk back to the restaurant's private dining room, which has a large table with eleven chairs around it.

"Paisley!" Julia gushes. "You look amazing in peach."

"Thank you. Davis picked it out. He knows I can choose jeans and concert T-shirts, but I'm not so good at nice clothes."

"He has quite the eye," she says, looking at him.

He shrugs. "The personal shopper at Nordstrom has the eye. I just have the money."

Julia laughs. "That makes much more sense."

Alison Pate walks in with Henry, and I look over at Julia to gauge her reaction. She smiles, but it doesn't meet her eyes. Alison hasn't won Julia over yet, but it looks like she's getting close to winning Henry.

A tall, thin blonde who Phillip introduces as Molly

Jennings is his date for the evening, and Teresa stands stiffly with Griffin. They're not even smiling at each other. I truly do not understand what makes that relationship work.

Arabella and I make polite small talk with everyone while the waitstaff gets us drinks and sets out appies.

"How are your pieces coming?" Julia asks.

The room quiets down, and everyone seems to be listening. "I'm getting closer," I assure her with a nod. "The gallery opening is next weekend, and I should be ready." I look around the room. "You all are welcome to come, but don't let Julia put any pressure on you."

"It seems everything you create is worth money these days," Phillip notes.

I know he probably meant it as a dig, but I just shake my head and laugh. "Burning pinecones is my new hobby," I tell him. "Not sure there's much profit in that."

That gets a snicker out of the group, and I shrug. "I've tried molds, but I'm never happy with the results."

The table devolves back into various conversations, and once Henry is busy chatting with someone else, Alison leans in. "You might see me in your building soon." Her eyes twinkle.

"Really? Why? Anything special?" I smile at her.

"I commissioned your neighbor to do one of his paintings of me."

My eyes pop. "Really?"

She nods and leans over to whisper all the details in my ear.

"I love it," I tell her with a nod. *Better you than me.*

"We definitely need to meet for lunch," she adds after a moment. "Filming wraps up and moves to post production in a few weeks, so my schedule will be more flexible."

"I'd love that," I tell her.

"Maybe your friend Lucy could come too?" Alison actually seems shy as she asks.

Lucy will be over-the-moon excited. "I'm sure she'd

love to."

Alison smiles. "She was very funny, and I liked how the two of you treated me when we met."

My brow furrows.

"Most women don't like me. They think I want to steal their boyfriend or it's a competition thing."

"Well, you're a gorgeous lady, and I suppose when you're paid to wear a bathing suit and skin-tight club clothes, that can be intimidating to some women."

"Well, they can have my crazy workout schedule and the green smoothies I drink twice a day."

I make a face. "You're a brave woman. Let me know what works with your schedule, and we'll make it happen."

Shortly after that, dinner is served, and over the next two hours, we enjoy a delicious meal while the Davis brothers bicker like children. I watch as Arabella becomes clearly tired. Once we've finished dessert, I give Davis the look.

"Well, it's been fun hanging out with you all, but Arabella needs to get some rest," he announces. "It's doctor's orders. We're going to head home."

"Before you go," Phillip says, and I brace myself. Who knows what he's going to have to say this time. "I understand you overheard a conversation my brothers and I were having at our parents' last time you were at dinner, and you know we suggested you were only interested in Davis for our name and money. We have since come to understand that isn't the case, and it was wrong of us to assume what your motives were." He looks around the table, and Henry and Griffin nod their agreement. "I'm very happy you are a part of this family. I'm truly sorry for what I said. It was out of line."

"Thank you." I look at him. "Was that hard to say?"

The room is silent. He seems unsure how to answer.

"I mean, did someone write that and make you say it?"

His eyes widen. "No, I—"

"Gotcha!" I just couldn't resist putting him on the hot seat.

Fortunately, when he looks back up from holding his head in his hands a moment, he has a giant grin.

"Thank you for saying that," I tell him. "I love Davis with all my heart, and I actually wish your last name was Rogers or something and then no one would care."

"Being involved with this family is not for the faint of heart," Henry agrees. "And we're glad you and Arabella are here."

Julia's eyes shine with tears. I know she told them they needed to pull their heads out of their asses, but I'm amazed that they actually did. I'm very touched.

We hug everyone goodbye, and I agree again to meet Alison for lunch when she's done with her filming.

As we pull into the traffic to cross the Lions Gate Bridge back into downtown, Arabella has fallen asleep in the back. Davis looks over at me. "What were you and Alison talking about?" he asks softly.

"If I tell you, you can't repeat it to Henry."

Davis shifts in his seat. "If it's something that will embarrass him, I can't promise that."

"I don't think it will embarrass him." I think about it for a moment, and I hope it wouldn't. "At least that's not her intention."

"Then tell me."

"She's commissioned Jim, my neighbor at the loft, to do a painting of her. They're working out confidentiality agreements so he won't share the work or make other sketches he could sell."

Davis shakes his head. "I get the feeling that guy sleeps with all his models."

"I mentioned that to her, and she was quick to tell me that won't be the case with her, and that it won't be a complete nude. They're going to work on a pose, but it sounded like we see more of her on TV than we'll see in the painting."

Davis nods. "Okay, then. Pretty sure that will be a first

for Henry."

That makes me laugh. "She seems like a nice person, and I really think she's lonely. She wants to go to lunch with Lucy and me."

"That sounds like trouble," Davis says, raising an eyebrow.

"You never know…"

Chapter 30

Davis

After weeks of warming Paisley up to the idea of getting away for four days, she has finally agreed to go somewhere with me for Labor Day weekend. We can fly anywhere, but even if Arabella is going to be staying with my parents, I know Paisley won't want to be far from her. We have our cabin in the mountains or a weekend out on Vancouver Island as options. I just want something memorable. This will be our first extended time alone together. Thoughts about these various possibilities fill my mind any moment I have downtime, including right now as I try to relax a moment after a surgery on a teenaged boy who needed three stents went long this morning.

I roll my neck as I walk back to my office and feel almost giddy between the success of the surgery and the tantalizing possibility of being away with Paisley in a few weeks. It really feels like we're moving forward.

My friends haven't really met her, though, and I should introduce them. That's another important part of moving forward. And it is Friday… I slide in behind my desk, and before I even check my other messages, I fire off a text to Steve, Michael, and Jack.

Me: Hey, anyone up for meeting for dinner and drinks tonight at my place? I thought you could officially meet Paisley and Arabella.

Michael: Sure. I can meet the woman who stole you from us.

Me: She didn't steal me. I was out with you guys last week.

Steve: Michael is an idiot. I'll be there.

Jack: Michael spends his life working with women, so of course he's becoming one. I can be there. I'm on call beginning at nine, so no plying me with liquor.

Me: Great. We can put some meat on the grill and kick back. See you about 7.

Then I realize I didn't run my impromptu gathering past Paisley. She's offered to meet the guys, but she's not a fan of surprises, so I'd better cover my bases.

Me: I've invited the guys over tonight. I haven't seen them for a bit, and you haven't met them. It will just be low key...

Paisley: It's your house—you can do what you want. But it sounds fun. Do you need me to do anything?

Me: It's our place, not just mine. You live here with me. If you would like to find a place that's for both of us, let me know. I'll move for you.

She sends back a kiss and a heart emoji as I type my next response.

Me: I'll call the cook and she can marinate meat for us and set up some sides, so she may be in and out of the condo today.

Paisley: I'm at the studio. Arabella and I are having lunch at the Market today, and I'm bribing her with ice cream.

Me: You can bribe me with other things. [Eggplant, peace sign, peach, and three droplet emojis]

Paisley: If you're expecting three orgasms, you better get your friends out early.

Me: I [heart emoji] **you.**

Paisley: XOXO

I read back through our messages and think about how well Paisley is settling into a life that looks totally different than it did just a few months ago. Something has shifted, and she has a confidence she was lacking for so long. I'm so grateful she's coming into her own.

My pager sounds, and it's back to work. Seems I have a twenty-three-month-old with an irregular heartbeat. It could take just a few minutes, but with a patient of that age, it's likely to be the rest of my day.

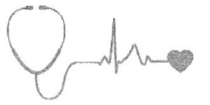

Sure enough, it's nearly five by the time I return to my office, but I'm happy to say we diagnosed that little guy's

ASD before it was catastrophic. I settle in behind my desk and check my messages. There are several missed calls from my attorney. Glancing at the clock, it's five now. I don't know if he's gone home for the day, but I'm going to try anyway.

"Ken Olston," he answers.

"Hi, Ken. This is Davis Martin. I'm returning your message. I wasn't sure I was going to find you still at the office on a Friday."

He chuckles. "I'll be here for a while. Your dad has me working on a few things."

"He usually does."

"I've been receiving calls from Violet Boyd's attorney," he tells me. "Violet's mother, Laura Boyd, is coming to Vancouver and would like to meet with her granddaughters."

My stomach drops. Paisley mentioned this after she saw her mother in jail. "I can check with her. I don't know if she'll be interested in doing that or not. Does she have a specific time frame?"

"Yes." He rattles off the dates of her visit.

I jot them down and note that Paisley's gallery opening next weekend is the day this woman plans to arrive. *Hmmmmm...* "I'll talk to Paisley," I tell him. "If she agrees, how would you suggest we meet her? Your offices? A restaurant? Our home? My parents' home? I want to make sure Paisley won't feel ambushed or uncomfortable."

"It's up to you," Ken says. "Since the prison is over an hour's drive away, it's hard to say where she'll be staying."

"Please find out the next time the attorney calls. But I should note that Paisley and Arabella have no desire to meet with their mother."

"Understood. She's not leaving jail at this point, anyway."

"Okay. We're having company for dinner tonight." I look at the time. "In less than two hours, so need to go, but I'll try to talk to her soon."

"Sounds good."

I sigh. I don't know if this is going to be good news for Paisley or not.

I head toward the men's locker room to change into street clothes when I'm stopped by Jeannine Bartlett.

"How dare you!" she shrieks, and my face stings from her slap.

My guess is that she got the notice from the College of Physicians and Surgeons of BC. "It's nice to see you, Jeannine. What's going on?" I back away from her carefully.

Her hair is windblown, and she's dressed in workout clothes. Her hands are fists at her sides. "I knew you were a jealous prick, but I never guessed you would stoop so low as to get my license revoked."

It's good to see my letter of complaint was taken seriously. "Look, that wasn't my goal. It was the CPS of BC's decision. I only reported what I saw as malpractice from the condition of the patient and the family."

"I can have the mother testify," she threatens.

I nod. "Sure. She's out in the all-women's prison in Maple Ridge for a whole slew of offenses here in Canada, and then they want to extradite her to Texas on accessory to murder charges. I'm sure she'd be a fantastic witness for you."

Her face is almost purple with rage. "You're messing with my life." She raises her hand to strike me again, but I grab her wrist and lean in close.

"You mess with your patients' lives every day. You had no reason to do what you did to Arabella Brooks."

Spittle sprays from her mouth as she spews obscenities at me. Fortunately, her scene is attracting some attention, so several members of the staff and hospital security come running. Nothing she's saying makes any sense.

They treat her like a patient who is mentally unstable and give her a shot of sedative before they wheel her away. I pick up the paper she was waving at me and scan it quickly. A hearing has been scheduled where she'll need to defend her decision-making process on Arabella Brooks and three other patients who have died in the last three years.

Eric Silver, the head of cardiology, rushes over. "What the hell was that?"

"She got this." I hand him the letter. "She's blaming me for messing with her life, but there are four kids on the list. I only flagged one. Looks like they dug deeper, and this might have been a pattern with her."

Eric glances through the letter and rubs his hand over his two-day growth. "We're so fucked if they choose to litigate this."

I nod as I move past him. "She's our liability."

I walk into the locker room and quickly pull on my jeans and a Henley. I slide my feet into a pair of loafers and head out to my car. I'm not surprised to see Felix talking to the police. It seems when Jeannine arrived, she took it upon herself to smash her BMW into my Range Rover, pushing it into the concrete wall, most likely totaling both cars.

"That's some serious rage," I say as I approach.

Felix introduces me to Officer Peterson.

"Do you know who might be this upset with you?" the officer asks.

I chuckle. "Yes. I was just confronted by Dr. Jeannine Bartlett. Seems her medical license is on the verge of being pulled, and she's blaming that on me."

Officer Peterson takes notes. "Why would you have anything to do with that?"

I explain what happened with Arabella, trying to break down the medical jargon into easy-to-understand language.

"The sister wanted the surgery but not the mother?" he asks, seeming confused.

"The older sister is thirteen years older, and she's the legal guardian because the mother was living in Seattle, conning men out of money."

"How can you be sure?" he asks.

"Well, her mother is currently in the women's correctional facility in Maple Ridge for a long list of offenses."

He looks up from his notepad. "And how do you know this?"

I explain my relationship with Paisley to the officer. It doesn't seem to faze him in the least.

As I answer his never-ending questions, I realize my friends are likely arriving at my condo. "Can I at least tell my girlfriend I'm on my way?"

"Just a few more questions." The officer steps away a moment, leaving me to watch the tow trucks pull Jeannine's car off of mine. Yep. The Range Rover is totaled. I liked that car.

The officer comes back, asks for my driver's license, and speaks into his radio. "Yes, ma'am, it's him."

"You can let him go before his lawyers jump all over us."

He looks up at me. "Sorry to keep you, Dr. Martin. We'll be in touch if we need anything."

I smile. Despite the many aggravations, I do enjoy the perks of being a Martin at a time like this. I give him my contact information and agree to reach out if I think of anything else that might be helpful.

Felix calls a car to drive me home, and once I'm on the way, I call and text Paisley, but she doesn't answer. Of course, today will be the day that all my friends arrive on time and I'm already almost an hour late. And this is the day we're stopped by every light between the hospital and my condo. My frustration builds as the clock ticks past eight. I could have walked home faster.

I think about my friends. They're great guys, but they can be overwhelming. I can't be sure I'm not going to walk into World War Three at my house. But when the elevator doors finally open on my floor, I hear laughter from the rooftop patio. When I walk out, everyone is sitting with drinks in hand, and Michael is working the grill.

"Hey!" Jack says. "You made it to your own party."

I snort. "I did. You'll never guess what happened." I

tell them about my run-in with Jeannine and the mess in the parking garage.

"Did they admit her under a psychiatric hold?" Steve asks.

"I'm assuming they did, but I don't know for sure. If they knew about the car, there would be no doubt."

"Did you ever sleep with her?" Michael questions.

I shake my head. "No way, man. She went to school with Griffin, and he may have, but we've always just clashed about professional style."

"Wait until the press gets a hold of this." Paisley groans as she comes to give me a hug.

"What did I miss?" I ask as I pull her to me. "You all met Paisley and Arabella?" I ask the group.

They nod. "Paisley was a gracious host and smartly put your most expensive scotch out for us to enjoy," Michael reports.

The fifteen-thousand-dollar bottle of Scotch I imported from Scotland is on the table. I save it for special occasions, and it was nearly full this morning. Now it's practically empty.

"That seems perfect," I tell them. "I wanted you all to know each other, since outside of my family, you are the most important people in the world to me."

I look out at Arabella, who is happily entertaining herself on the rocks in the rooftop park with Kate, who's here for the evening to help out. Jack wanders out to the path, and Arabella comes over and seems to engage him in her game. She's jumping from rock to rock, as if the ground is lava. I have a feeling both Paisley and I are paying more attention to their conversation than the one going on around us.

"I like to watch *Rin Tin Tin* on YouTube," Arabella says as she hops around him.

"Is that now in English?" he asks. "It used to be only in French."

"I watch it in French. It's good for my language skills."

Arabella says.

Jack pauses a second. "I'm impressed," he says.

She looks at him. "Did I hear you say you're a plastic surgeon?"

He nods.

"Do you fix scars?"

I feel Paisley tense.

He nods. "Sometimes I can make them disappear, or at least be smaller."

"I have a big scar. My mom says men won't like it when I get older, so I need to probably get it fixed."

My heart breaks for her.

"Do you feel comfortable sharing it with me?" Jack asks.

I've never seen him in his medical element. I know he dates women who are beautiful, but he always tells us what he could do to improve their looks. This could go south quickly.

"You're a doctor. You've probably seen worse." Arabella pulls her outer shirt over her head and stands in just a camisole.

Michael and Steve are in deep conversation, not paying attention, but Paisley and I are.

"Who gave you this scar?" Jack asks.

"Davis did. He saved me." She says that with such pride that my heart swells.

Jack looks it over for a moment. "He did a great job. It's a pretty small scar, but as you get older, it may seem like it's bigger. Once you stop growing, we'll be able to make it more invisible, but doing anything now won't help." Arabella nods and looks down at her chest. "But you know what?" Jack adds after a moment. "If a man doesn't love you despite all your scars—on the inside and outside—you should move on."

She looks at him and tilts her head. "You're pretty old. Will you still be working then?"

Paisley shuts her eyes, shakes her head, and grins.

"Hmm, that's a good point. I very well may have retired by the time you're all grown up, but I'll probably be able to recommend someone, so I've got you covered."

Her face lights up. "Thanks."

Jack watches her go back to jumping and walks back to the patio. Paisley goes out to meet him. "Thank you for that," she says.

"Absolutely," he says. "I do know how to speak about things besides tits and ass. I do a month-long trip each year to work with several surgical non-governmental organizations that go into developing countries to do plastic surgeries — things like repairing cleft palates, doing minor reconstruction, non-cancerous tumor removal, treating burn injuries, and cleaning out diseased tissue. I'm not all about lifts and tucks; that's just what pays the bills."

"It sure does." I chuckle. He drives a Ferrari in the summer months and a Range Rover in the winter months, not to mention his stunning home in Whistler and a penthouse apartment downtown.

I wander into the kitchen to see what's left to prepare for dinner tonight. Paisley is shortly behind me. I pull her into my arms and kiss her deeply. Right now, I'm wishing my friends weren't here. I wonder if they'd notice if we just escaped for an hour or two to our bedroom. "I'm sorry I was late," I tell her.

"Don't worry about it. The guys told me many stories about you and your lecherous ways."

I shake my head. "I was never a lech."

"The first time we met, we had sex in the dark corner of a bar. I know better."

"That was a one-off. I knew then you were the girl for me."

She laughs, but I really did.

We pull out the sides that have been warming in the oven, and soon we're ready to enjoy dinner. As we eat, I look around the table and smile. They're a good group of friends.

We deal with a lot of the same crap given that our parents have a lot of money, but they're all outstanding doctors who care about their patients and the care they get.

It's late when the guys finally head out. Throughout the night, they showed Paisley courtesy and respect, and she seemed to like them. She stands with me to say goodbye as each one leaves.

"Thank you for putting up with my friends," I say as I close the door for the last time.

"They were great. I didn't mind at all."

"I'm sorry I was late. Aside from the thing with Dr. Barnett, Ken Olston called me today."

Paisley's brow furrows.

"He's our family lawyer."

"Ahh." She walks into the master bath, and I hear her turn the water on to wash her face.

"As you suspected might happen, your grandmother, Laura Boyd, is coming to town sometime maybe next week and would like to meet you and Arabella."

I don't hear anything so I'm not even sure she heard me. Then she comes out, drying her face with a towel. "My grandmother wants to meet us?"

I nod. "You don't have to see her if you don't want to."

"I am curious about her. Next week will be busy with my gallery show coming up, but I'll talk to Arabella, and she can help me decide."

"That sounds like a solid plan. And I'm happy to talk it through with you, if that would be helpful. I'm on call this weekend, but I'm hoping when I'm not at the hospital, I can be here in bed with you."

Paisley gets on her hands and knees and crawls across the bed to me. "I can think of several ways we could entertain ourselves."

"I love the way you think."

Chapter 31

Paisley

The week has been a flurry of activity—it was a comedy of errors just getting all the pieces moved downstairs—but tonight is the night, and the gallery is all set up. Food and wine are ready to be served, and I'm nervous all over again that no one is going to show up. I don't have the draw of other artists this time.

But whether anyone comes or not, it looks beautiful in here. Gwen's space is so amazing. I'm displaying fifteen pieces—Julia allowed me to include her *Adrift in Silver* and *River Rocks*, as well as the five pieces that were sold through commissioning, so there are eight pieces left for sale. They may not sell tonight, and I'm telling myself that's just fine. I don't want to be disappointed, and no matter what happens, I know Isla will help me figure out the best path forward.

I do know Lucy and her mom are coming. That makes me smile every time I think about it. I have a small gift for them this evening. I feel so fortunate and want to share my gratitude for them being so good to me and Arabella for so many years.

Isla approaches, touching up final details in the space as she comes. Her eyes are sparkling, and her smile is wide. She squeezes my arm when she reaches me. "I'm so excited. There is so much buzz about your work. This is going to be a big night."

I look over to see a woman with a camera and a fancy extended flash taking pictures of the various pieces.

"She's with *Artistry*," Isla whispers. "They're going to highlight tonight's gathering in their article on you. And they've asked if we can set up a time for a private interview. Doesn't have to be tonight though." Isla gives me another squeeze. "Tonight, you are going to shine! I have no doubt. I've sent photos of your work out to all sorts of people, and there's a Saudi prince interested in a *River Rock* collection that spreads over two hundred feet."

"What?"

"He just gave me the dimensions. He'll send his yacht to pick it up. You'll be welcome to join the display as it works its way back to Saudi Arabia on the yacht, or you can fly in and meet the vessel for installation."

I can't even imagine working at that scale. "Do I have to answer now?"

Isla shakes her head. "It's a two-million-dollar commission, five million total."

For a moment, I can't breathe.

Davis comes up and puts his hand on my back, and I feel tremendously better. "Are you almost ready?"

"I think so."

"We'll talk more about that later," Isla assures me. "For now, just focus on this evening."

Gwen gives me a thumbs up to make sure the time is right, and when I nod, she unlocks the front door of the gallery and swings it open. Davis hands me a flute of champagne. "To a successful evening."

I smile as we toast, and then Lucy and Mrs. Yang are the first through the door. They beeline it over to me. "This looks amazing!" Lucy marvels as she looks around.

"Thank you."

Mrs. Yang pulls me in. "I'm so proud. We were at dinner across the way, and we heard people talking about you — a big table of people. They were coming over to see your work."

"That's great to hear," I say in a shaky voice. Now, I'm not sure what I'm more nervous about — people not coming or a big crowd of people overwhelming me.

People begin to enter in small groups. I watch Gwen place two red stickers on cards that accompany the pieces, indicating that the work has sold. One of them is *Stowed Away*, my most expensive piece, in the high six figures. My heart beats faster.

"Are you Paisley Brooks?" an older woman asks as she approaches.

I look at her, smile, and extend my hand. "Yes, I'm Paisley Brooks."

"I just purchased *Stowed Away*."

I smile. "Thank you so much. That's one of my favorite pieces of driftwood. I love that piece. I hope you enjoy it."

"I have the perfect place in my foyer. It will be front and center when anyone comes to our home. I'll display it proudly." She pauses a moment. "I don't mean to ambush you, but I'm Laura Boyd."

The name is familiar and her face is a little familiar, but it takes me a moment to search my addled brain. Then it hits me. This is my grandmother.

I take a deep breath. I want to run, but instead, I paste a plastic smile on my face and prepare for whatever is coming next. Is this woman just like my mother? "I was told you were coming to town."

She nods. "I flew in this morning, and I met with Violet today. I hadn't seen her in so many years."

"I knew her as Vanessa, or Mom."

The woman smiles sadly and searches my face a

moment. "I'm angry with her, too," she says softly.

That's not what I expected. "You are?"

"Yes! I've spent countless hours wondering how it all went so wrong when she was younger, and I've never figured it out." She touches my arm. "I don't mean to bother you on an evening you should be celebrating, but maybe if you have time tomorrow, we could meet for breakfast or lunch?"

I nod. "I would be happy to talk with you. I have to warn you, Arabella is worried you're going to do what our mom did and try to take her away." As if speaking her name might bring her over, I look around quickly, making sure Arabella is nowhere near. I don't want to navigate this with her right now.

"Oh goodness, the poor dear. From what I understand, you've both been through so much. I have no plans to disrupt anything. I just want to know you. I wasn't aware you existed until Violet resurfaced after she was arrested."

"That makes me feel better, and I think it will do the same for Arabella." I manage a smile. "We didn't know you existed, either."

"Your mother made a colossal mistake when she was very young. But it seems like finding your father was the best thing that could have happened to her."

"He took care of all of us," I say, fighting back tears. I wish he were here tonight to see this. He would have been so proud, probably out front pushing people in the doors.

"I can tell he did. And he must have taught you a thing or two. You've managed your sister's illness on your own, and today you have a stunning gallery opening."

"That's very kind of you."

"Well, I know you have lots of people to speak with this evening, so I won't monopolize your time." She hands me an elegant card. "This is my contact information. I'm staying at the Pacific Rim Fairmont. I can't believe there are three Fairmont Hotels all within a few blocks."

I smile. I've always thought the same thing. "The

cruises load up for Alaska and places all around the world right across the street from your hotel."

"Ah, that explains a lot. I've noticed many people walking around in shorts and knee socks, with cameras hanging around their necks."

I nod. I don't know what else to say, not here in front of so many people.

She clasps her hands in front of her. "I hope to hear from you."

"Thank you. I'll talk to Arabella and be in touch."

"You're very talented. My mother was an artist. I bet you got that from her." With one last smile, she turns to go.

My interest is definitely piqued, and she seems nice enough. But who knows? I need to be smart about this for sure. I watch her disappear into the crowd, and then a couple approaches me to talk about my process.

The night becomes a blur. The crowd ebbs and flows, and I meet so many people whose names I will never keep straight. Davis' family members all make appearances as well. I shake hands and answer questions and generally feel more appreciated and important than I have in a very long time.

Three hours later, when Gwen pushes out the last of the guests and closes the doors, she turns to Isla and me with a smile. "Everything sold."

"Really?" My heart stops. I can't even believe it.

"You also have commission requests from at least a dozen people."

"No way!"

Davis picks me up and spins me around. I think he's more excited than I am. "You did it!"

Julia and Chip remain with us. Chip has been entertaining Arabella most of the night, but after all the shouting and cheering, they come over to hear the good news. After I repeat this astounding information, Arabella hugs me tightly and then goes to find a spot to sit with her tablet across the room.

"I sent out fifty invitations to some of my better clients and a few that I want as clients, and I was surprised at how many of them came," Isla says. "You're the hottest ticket in town."

"What a wonderful evening. Thank you all so much. Honestly, this is a little overwhelming," I share.

Gwen smiles. "The team here at the gallery will have funds for you in less than a week, and they'll make sure everything gets delivered. And then Isla will begin working on the commissioning contracts, which will be another influx of capital for you."

I turn to Davis. "Some Saudi prince wants a super-sized version of what I did for your mother and is willing to pay five million dollars for it."

"Wow." He nods appreciatively. "Do you want to do it?"

"I'm not sure. I need to think about it, but I think I'm leaning toward yes. It would be an interesting challenge, and if I'm a flash in the pan, I should get as much work as I can now."

"You won't be a flash in the pan," Julia assures me.

"I agree," Isla chimes in. "Your most expensive piece, *Stowed Away*, was the first to sell."

"Well, hold that thought. My grandmother bought it," I tell them.

Everyone stares at me.

"She flew into town to visit my mother. She hadn't seen her in years and didn't know anything about her current life until the Dallas case reopened when she was apprehended here. Her name is Laura Boyd. She came to the show and is hoping we'll meet her tomorrow."

"Are you going to have Arabella come?" Julia asks.

I shrug. "Only if she wants to, but I suppose I'll go. I'd like to learn a little more about her." I turn to Davis. "Are you okay if I go? We can meet in a public place or wherever you think is best."

He nods. "As long as Tom is with you, I'm fine. And I'm happy to join you, too."

"It might be nice to have a buffer, and that might make Arabella feel better. We can talk to her about it in the morning."

"Yes!" Julia clasps her hands. "Because right now we're here to celebrate your debut and how well it went."

I shake my head. "I can hardly believe it. I guess I'm going to be busy for a while."

"I'd say so," Isla agrees.

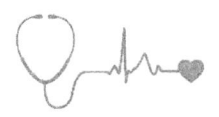

Arabella comes rushing in first thing in the morning. I really need to get better curtains for her room. There is just too much daylight getting in, and that means she's up too early and not getting enough sleep.

She crawls into the bed next to me, nudging me awake. "I had so much fun last night. I just knew you would be a success."

"Thank you," I tell her, struggling to wake up. "You're my number-one fan, and I love that. What was your favorite part about last night?"

"Chip and I did some math things, trying to figure out some of the math in the nature in your sculptures. My favorite was the first one to sell."

"Did you see the lady who bought it?" I ask.

She nods. "She was beautiful. She asked me my opinion, and I told her it was our favorite."

"Did she tell you her name?"

"No. Why? Was she supposed to?"

I shake my head. "No, but she introduced herself to me, and she's our grandmother."

Arabella tenses.

"It's okay. I didn't talk to her for very long, but she seems like a nice person. The only way we'll know for sure is if we spend some time with her. She'd like to meet us this morning. What if Tom and Davis went with us to meet her for brunch at her hotel?"

"You'll be there?"

"Of course. She's my grandmother too."

"I guess so."

"I'll tell you what," Davis says from behind me. I feel a little badly that we woke him up. "If you get nervous or feel worried about your safety, we'll have a signal and we can leave."

She nods. "Okay."

"You know what else she said that makes me want to meet her?" I ask.

Arabella shakes her head.

"She's upset with Mom, too."

"She is?"

"Sure. But just like when I get upset with you, it doesn't mean I don't love you. I'm sure she loves Mommy very much, but she's upset about the choices Mom has made and that she never knew about us."

Arabella thinks about that for a moment. "Okay, I'll go. I'll go get ready."

"Great. I'll be glad to have you with me," I tell her. "Can you please take a shower?" She nods and rushes out of the room, leaving Davis and me alone.

His hand snakes around my torso and underneath the T-shirt I wore to bed. He massages my nipples to very hard points. Liquid heat pools in my panties.

"I love you so much," Davis says. "I'm so fucking proud of how well you did last night, but even more of how you've managed Arabella and everything that's happened since your dad died. You deserve to have your dreams come true, Paisley. Thank you for being with me."

His fingers slip down to circle my bundle of nerves,

and I have to try hard to concentrate on what he's saying. "I love you too." I moan.

"I'm going to want you to say that to me again — and often."

His finger slides in and out of my soaked channel. He bites down on my nipple, and all the sensations burst at once, sending me over the edge. As my climax hits, Davis covers my mouth with his.

"You're so fucking sexy when you come."

I blush. "It's all because of you. Now, lock the door, get that dick inside me, and make me come again."

He smiles. "Your wish is my command."

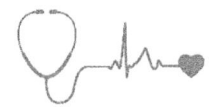

I spoke to Laura Boyd earlier this morning, and we agreed to meet for brunch at her hotel. I explained that Arabella was still feeling nervous, and she seems to understand. I just hope this goes well, and I'm not walking us into another mess.

When we arrive at the restaurant, we're shown to a large table in the corner where Laura is already seated. She stands to give me a hug, and I introduce her to Arabella.

"We met last night," Laura says with a smile. "Arabella is the person who picked *Stowed Away* for me. I'm very excited to get it home. The gallery is working with a customs broker to get it back to Texas."

"It's still my favorite," Arabella says shyly. If she could hide behind my skirt, she would.

Next, I introduce her to Davis. Tom takes a seat nearby, so he's close if we need him.

"Thank you all for coming today," Laura says once we've settled in. "I'm sure this is overwhelming. It was for me." She looks at Arabella. "I'm so sorry you've both had to endure so much on your own. But I'm grateful you've found Davis."

"You won't take us away from Davis?" Arabella asks.

Laura shakes her head. "Never. But if you ever need anything, I will be here immediately, even if I have to charter a plane and deliver it myself."

Arabella still looks wary. Heck, I'm not sure about this woman either. "Why did you want to meet us?" I ask her.

"I spent a long time wondering why my little girl did what she did and where she was. She broke her father's heart. There hasn't been a day since she left that I didn't think of her first thing in the morning and last thing at night—"

"And she never called you or emailed you?" Arabella asks.

Laura shakes her head. "She vanished, and we were left with nothing but a police investigation. We hired an attorney and private investigator to make sure they were correct in pressing charges against our daughter, and it turned out they were. It broke our hearts. But even knowing she'd likely go to jail, we always wanted to see her again."

"You sound like you were surprised by what happened when she disappeared," I say, trying to avoid too many details for Arabella.

"I was surprised," Laura says. "I never thought she was capable of something like that. Ricky was a nightmare boyfriend." She shakes her head. "I tried to keep my mouth shut, but she knew I didn't like him. I wear my heart on my sleeve."

"So do I," I tell her.

She smiles and pats my hand. "I wished Violet had found someone to quell whatever demons were inside her rather than make them worse, but I never knew what happened to her. The best thing about her being captured in Canada is that it's reopened her case and allowed me to reconnect with her and learn about her life since she's been gone. I always hoped she would find a worthy partner and start a family, and it seems that wish came true — at least for a time. You two are beautiful, smart, and so talented."

"Are you going to give her money to fight extradition to Texas?" I ask.

"No. She's made many poor decisions that led to that. Her brothers and I will be there to support her because she's part of our family, but she's on her own financially."

Davis smiles at her. "I'm glad to hear you say that. She put quite a scare into all of us when she walked off with Arabella."

"I bet she did." She looks at Davis. "Thank you for saving my granddaughters."

He dips his head. "I couldn't help myself."

We spend the rest of the morning and into the early afternoon talking. Davis finally looks at his watch. "We usually have dinner at my parents' on Sunday afternoon. Would you care to join us? I know my mother would love to meet you."

Laura smiles. "I would love to, but between all the travel and being out last night, I'm exhausted. If you're available, I'd love to meet you all again tomorrow. Maybe lunch or dinner?"

"Okay. I'm sure we can do that," I tell her.

Chapter 32

Paisley

It's been a little over a week now since my grandmother returned to Texas. She stayed for two weeks and met us every day. She seems truly kind, and Arabella and I were much more comfortable with her by the end of it. We're looking forward to heading down to Texas at some point to meet more of the family.

Arabella is starting to talk more and more about her return to school, and we've been making a list of all the things she'll need. I'm taking some time before I start the next batch of sculptures so I can give her my full attention before life gets busy again. I've collected a little additional driftwood and other objects, so I'll be ready, but I'm not in a rush, even though Isla has already finalized the latest round of commission contracts. Everyone has been very gracious.

I still haven't decided on the Saudi project, though I keep it in the back of my mind. I have mixed feelings about going over to install it. But it's an interesting challenge to consider. Things have been busy, and somehow, its finally Labor Day weekend. I can hardly believe I'm going away with

Davis. So much of my life has changed in the last few months. It's nearly unrecognizable.

The elevator pings in the condo, and I know that means Julia and a young friend she said she was bringing with her have arrived. Arabella seems nervous when I look her way. When they walk in, the girl is tall with jet black hair in braided pigtails and big brown eyes. She's wearing shorts and a designer top.

I smile as I go over to greet them. "You must be Jenny."

She nods, seeming a little shy.

I step aside and gesture to my sister, who is standing behind me. "I'm Paisley, and this is my younger sister, Arabella."

"Nice to meet you both," she says, just above a whisper.

We hug Julia hello, and then everyone stands a bit awkwardly.

"Arabella, why don't you show Jenny your room?" I suggest.

"Okay," she murmurs. And Jenny follows her upstairs.

Julia shakes her head. "Don't worry. They're going to have a great time tonight. Chip has plans to take them down to the beach to collect shells, and they'll spend time in the pool, I'm sure. Then we have movies and all sorts of activities for the sleepover tonight."

"It was so thoughtful of you to think of Jenny and invite her to meet Arabella."

Julia smiles. "Her father is president of the Point Grey Academy board of trustees. I'm kicking myself that I didn't think of introducing them sooner. Knowing someone in her class will make Arabella's first day a lot easier."

We move over to stand at the base of the stairs and listen. I hear giggling, which makes me feel better.

We sit down, and I offer Julia a drink, but she declines. "Are you excited about the cabin this weekend?" she asks.

A cabin? It's a giant house. "I think so," I tell her. "I

know Davis was hoping we'd go somewhere more exotic, but I appreciate him accommodating my nerves. It seems like a lot of trouble to get out of town for a weekend."

She nods. "It's been that way for us for a long time. But that doesn't mean it's not worth it. You'll get used to it. When are you meeting your friends tonight?"

I look at my watch. "In about an hour. We're just getting drinks and appies a few blocks from here. I don't want to eat too much since Davis and I leave before nine tomorrow morning. Nothing would be more embarrassing than hurling all over the back of the helicopter."

Julia rolls her eyes. "I hate that thing. I know it's the easiest way to travel, but I still hate it."

I nod. "Glad I'm not the only one. Maybe I should just ride with the staff," I joke. "Davis told me two guys left earlier today to drive up before dark. They had our food, along with the cook and a masseuse. This is so strange for me."

"Having so many people go with you on your escape weekend will be an adjustment. But the house is large, and you'll hardly even see them if you don't want to."

"I appreciate that you understand."

"There are upsides to the notoriety if you think positively, and I know you well enough to know that you will. You've seen how I support artists and musicians. But I'm also on dozens of boards and other volunteer positions because not only is my money important to people but so is my influence. You can change people's lives." I must look a little stressed out, because she squeezes my hand before she continues. "Enjoy your time together, start a family if you'd like, and do the things that excite you. When you're ready, I'll work with you to ease in to the other parts."

I snort. "I think Davis and I are thrilled just to be dating for now."

She smiles at me. "The best thing about the cabin is that you really will feel alone. I hope you'll enjoy the time to just be together. There's no light pollution there, so the stars are incredible. We usually bring the kids and friends up in November to see the northern lights dance over the lake. I can't wait to take you this year." Julia stands and walks back over to the bottom of the stairs.

"Girls?" She listens a moment. "We need to go if we're going to make our dinner reservations at Chez Fondue."

I shake my head. "You're spoiling my sister."

"She's the closest thing I have to a granddaughter. Don't hate me."

I chuckle. "Never."

The girls come bounding down the stairs, giggling like they've been friends forever.

"Paisley!" Arabella gives me a hug. "Jenny is a huge fan of B.T.S. too. She saw them in Korea when her dad had business there."

"She is so lucky, isn't she?"

Arabella nods. "Totally. And she has a scar on her tummy where she had her appendix removed."

"I think this means you'll be friends forever."

Arabella lights up. "You'll always be my bestest friend."

I squeeze her tight. "I love you, Bells. You have fun, and if you need me, we'll be home as fast as we can. We'll just be up at Davis' family's cabin."

"Okay. I think I'll be fine. If you change your mind and want to stay longer, that's good too."

My heart sinks a little at that. My sister is growing up so fast. But she's strong and happy and independent, and those are all good things. I can do this.

Julia herds them back to the elevator, and I wave goodbye, trying not to let tears form in my eyes.

I text Davis, who's out with his friends this evening, to let him know Arabella is off to his mom's.

Davis: That's great news. We're going to have a great four days. Enjoy tonight with your friends because it's going

to be just us this weekend. I love you.

Me: Love you more.

I grin and think again of how much my life has changed in such a short time. Six months ago, Arabella was desperate for surgery and sick nonstop, causing me to lose my fifth job as a customer service rep in a little over a year.

Now, Arabella is thriving, and we live at one of Vancouver's most exclusive addresses with the man of my dreams. People are paying serious money for things I create with my own hands. I'm humbled and amazed by every bit of this.

I put on a cute navy blue dress with a skirt full of pleats and cap sleeves with a high neck. It's a little old fashioned, but the buyer at Nordstrom knew this was perfect for me. I step into strappy silver sandals and touch up my lipstick. Just as I'm finishing, my phone pings.

Lucy: I'm here, sitting in the back corner booth. Alison is on her way.

I'm so excited to see them. After six weeks of ducking the press, Alison and Henry have recently come out as a couple, and it's been mixed reviews. But I think most of the haters are just jealous. I think she's lovely, so I'm hopeful she and Henry can make a go of it.

Me: Leaving now.

I send a message to Tom to let him know I'm ready to go. In seconds he's exiting the housekeeper apartment and ready to escort me downstairs.

We get in the car, and on the short drive over I look at pictures Arabella is sending me from Julia's phone. She seems to be having a fantastic time with Jenny. They're making faces and using filters so they look like cats.

I return a picture of me with a panda filter.

I then take a quick pic of just me in the car, no filter, and send it to Davis:

Me: I can't wait to have you all to myself for four days.

When we arrive, I tuck my phone in my purse, exit the car, and walk into the Rosewood Hotel's 1927 Lobby Lounge. It's a little trendy, but they can offer us some privacy, and it's not a place known to tourists for spotting celebrities. With Alison joining us, we have to be extra discreet.

As my eyes adjust to the dark bar, I see Lucy waving at me from the back. I practically skip to her. Alison arrives while we're hugging and is enveloped in our hug.

She has a brown package under her arm.

"What did you buy?" Lucy asks as we sit down.

Alison grins. "I have the sketches from Jim Matthews, and I thought I'd get your opinion."

I look around. "Are we going to be okay here?" I would hate for nude sketches of her to be plastered all over the tabloids.

She smiles. "Yes, they're tasteful. He knows about your family, so he didn't get too carried away."

I shake my head. "They're not my family. You and I are in the same boat. We're enjoying spending time with a Martin man."

She gives me a look. "You two are practically married. Henry and I are the ones trying to navigate this."

She unrolls the package, and there are four sketches. They're erotic, but not overly graphic. They're tasteful and beautiful.

"Do you just love these?" I breathe. "They're gorgeous."

"You think so?" she asks, seeming unsure.

"Which do you prefer?" I ask.

"I think this one." She puts a sketch with a strategically placed scarf on top.

"You could frame it for your house," I suggest.

She looks up and blushes. "I was thinking I might do that. They're beautiful, but I don't want my house to seem all 'I love me.'"

That sends us into fits of giggles.

Alison rolls up the pictures, and the server delivers three martini glasses with the bar's signature drink, the Hotel Georgia 19. It's a magical mixture with gin and flavors of lemon and orange and spice. The bar says it's been around since 1951, and I can see why. The taste is pure perfection.

We raise our glasses to toast as live jazz begins in the background.

"Can you believe we're here?" I ask Lucy.

"I always knew you'd get here," she tells me. "I'm just glad you brought me along."

"And I'm glad you let me push my way in," Alison adds.

Chapter 33

Davis

On Friday morning, Paisley and I settle into the back of the car for the trip to the helipad. She seems a bit jumpy.

"Arabella's going to be fine," I assure her. "We already know she had a lot of fun with Jenny last night, and she loves my parents."

"I know. I'm excited to get away." She smiles at me and reaches for my hand. "I think I'm a little nervous about being away with just the two of us."

"Why?"

"What if we run out of things to talk about?"

I stifle a laugh. "When has that ever happened?"

"I don't know. But if you decide you need time alone or something, just tell me. I brought my tablet and can read a book."

I turn to face her as much as the harness seatbelt allows. "We're going to have fun. We have a couple's massage this afternoon and then we're going to rest and relax and leave all our work drama back in Vancouver." I lean in close. "We can even walk around naked. Before I met you, I often walked around my house naked."

Her eyes grow big. "You did?"

"Sure! It was easy. I wasn't worried about a ten-year-old being scarred for life after seeing me."

Paisley laughs. "I don't know about scarred, but it would set her up for a lot of disappointment with men in the future."

We both laugh.

"Yes, I think it's best that you're the only one to see my goods." I kiss her softly. "I'm in love with you, Paisley, and this weekend I'm going to show you that every way I know how."

We arrive at the helipad, and Tom moves our luggage over to the helicopter. He sits in the front seat next to the pilot, and two of his men sit behind us in the third row. We're connected through headsets, and the pilot gives us a tour of the landscape as we fly north.

"My parents built this cabin as a getaway, but also a place where they could cut loose and enjoy themselves with friends," I tell her when the pilot takes a break from his commentary. "My mom was an avid water skier, and we all learned when we were growing up."

"There is water close by?"

"The home is off a natural lake and can sleep more than a hundred people. My parents have hosted heads of state, including once they had the Queen of England and her entourage."

I'm using trivia to distract Paisley, since I know she's nervous about the flight. Fortunately, the scenery is breathtaking, and we're back on the ground in less than an hour.

When we land, I take Paisley inside and immediately show her to my room at the cabin. She steps in and looks around at the king-sized bed, fireplace, projection television, and seating for at least a dozen people. There's a fully stocked bar with snacks, and a bathroom with a jacuzzi that overlooks the lake and seats six. "This room is bigger than the loft and any apartment I've ever lived in." She shakes her head. "You had this room when you were a kid?"

"No, my parents built this when I was in high school, and I was too cool to come up here with them. The doors in the hallway lead to four other bedrooms that my buddies stay in when they come up. It turns out my mother decided each of us would have our own suite with eventual room for kids."

She laughs. "She wanted grandkids when you were in high school?"

"Uh, no way. I know this will surprise you, but she's a planner. However, she does want them now."

"I know. She treats Arabella as if she's a grandchild."

"The pressure is on. I'm hoping we get in a lot of practice this weekend."

"I like the way you think." She kisses me softly.

"But first, we have our massages. They're set up out overlooking the lake. Come on."

I lead her down a path toward the lake to a shelter by the water. We usually use it to store canoes and other equipment. I'm not sure what they did with the snowmobiles, but now, it has beautiful curtains and two massage tables set up facing the water.

"Where are your neighbors?" Paisley asks.

"This is all our land. Felix didn't want someone to boat across the lake to us. Or for the paparazzi to have access on the other side of the lake."

"Wow."

The two masseuses introduce themselves and step out while we undress and lie down on the tables for a luxurious massage. We don't talk once they begin, and at one point, I think I hear Paisley snoring. But I don't sleep. My mind is reeling. I have big plans for this weekend.

After the massage, we retire to my room and the hot tub. As we soak, we watch the helicopter take off. It will be back Monday morning.

"I love all of this," Paisley says with a sigh. "I don't understand why your parents don't live up here year round."

"Well, in the winter they get enough snow that it can reach the eaves of the house."

"Ah," she says. "Okay, I totally get it. But does *someone* live here year round?"

I nod. "We have a house manager who lives in a small house tucked on the side of the main house. He makes sure everything is working, plows the snow, and keeps bears from hibernating in the garage."

"The garage?"

"One year a bear family took up residence in the garage. It stunk for months after they woke up and moved on."

"Well, I could certainly see myself sitting down by the water's edge to sketch and paint. And I'm sure there's fantastic driftwood here."

"You can do that any time you want."

Before we turn into prunes, we get out and pull on fluffy bathrobes to watch the sun set. That's happening earlier in the evening now, which means summer is officially over.

"The cook made a nice grilled Pacific snapper dinner whenever you're ready," I tell her.

"Oh, that sounds fantastic."

We eat in the dining room, lit only by candles, and we swap stories about our friends.

After dinner, we dress in warmer clothes — once the sun sets, it gets cool quickly — and head back outside. I take a wool blanket and Felix's team has set up a nice bonfire.

We snuggle up close and roast marshmallows to make s'mores. "I've never had these before," Paisley marvels as she licks melted marshmallow and chocolate from her fingers.

"I discovered them when I was going to school in the States."

"They're so good." Her eyes twinkle.

"We'd head out to the Cape and make them on the

beach at night."

We enjoy snuggling, and after a little while, there's an impressive meteor shower. "My mom wants to do a big trip up here in November to see the Northern Lights before they close the house up for the winter."

"She mentioned that," Paisley says. "Sounds like it would be fun."

"Do you remember when Arabella told us there were more stars than grains of sand on all the beaches on Earth?"

She drops her head on my shoulder. "Yes."

I pull the ring out of my pocket. "You are my star. I looked through a lot of sand to find you. After the first night we were together at The Lion's Den, somehow, I knew you were it for me. I spent every weekend looking for you. And when you came into my emergency room, I was certain someone was making sure we got together. These past few months have been crazy and glorious. I've asked your grandmother and Arabella, and they've consented. Now, I'm hoping you'll agree. Will you marry me?"

Paisley throws her arms around me and kisses the air right out of my lungs.

"Is that a yes?"

She giggles. "That's a yes."

I slip the cushion-cut, four-carat diamond on her finger.

The firelight and the dozens of meteors flying above are our only illumination. Our kiss grows more intense. My hand glides over her body, the body that will be mine forever. I lean her back on the blanket and push my hardness against her.

"Let me help," I murmur. With a flick I spring open her bra, leaving her nipples hard and wanting my touch. Licking from her ear to her shoulder, I stop just long enough to bite her favorite place while I unbutton her jeans and help her out of her pants and panties.

She shivers in anticipation.

"You're so beautiful like this." My hands squeeze and

pull.

Her body opens to me, and I slide my hand down to her mound, spread her wide, and stroke her most sensitive area. Her hips move and chase my fingers as she craves more friction. "I love how wet you are."

I can't stop touching her soft, silky skin. I bend my head and suckle at her breast, my hands roaming and exploring as I move to my knees, my open mouth pressing against her. My tongue darts between her folds, teasing and tantalizing. She clutches my hair as I push her toward climax, and I haven't even undressed.

She squirms, twisting under my diabolical touch, and I chase her orgasm, wanting it almost more than she does. My fingers push inside her, and I latch onto her clit and draw it deep into my mouth.

Her breathing is staccato as she clenches and then finally releases. I sit back on my heels, a big smile on my face, and lick my fingers clean.

"I want you inside me," she breathes. She reaches for me, but I slowly shake my head and stand. I unbutton my pants and remove them in a single motion, my dick standing straight from my body. I want her. I want everything she wants.

Paisley is still breathing hard and deep in her foggy bliss. "Are you okay?" I ask as I return to lie next to her, my finger slowly stroking her sex.

"I'm ready when you are." She looks down at me, daring me to enter. I'm up for the challenge.

I position myself against her and press against her channel, the head partially sheathed. "Hard and fast or slow and easy?" I ask.

"H-h-ard," she stammers, well past ready for me to take her.

"I was hoping you'd say that." I laugh as I ease in gently, rocking slowly to get deep inside. Once I'm fully seated, I stop.

With a smile on my face, I wait for her to beg. But she doesn't.

She flexes her hips and tightens her channel, holding me firm, but I don't move.

"Relax," I say. "Now, it's time for some fun."

I pull back, almost popping out of her, and then push back in, this time hard and fast as she requested. That draws a bit of a yelp from her. My hands move to her breasts while my cock nails her hard against the ground. I wouldn't be surprised if we're digging a hole. Her breathing changes, and I know the head of my cock is rubbing against that special spot. I can feel the nerves inside me gather as I climb the hill. Hard and fast, I pivot in and out of her, perspiration beading on my forehead, her body pushing to meet mine with every stroke.

"Come for me," I demand.

As she holds on to my shoulders, I go over the cliff, her channel gripping my cock so tightly as she follows me. When the last of our bliss has ebbed, I slowly pull out of her. Lying together, we watch the meteors stream across the sky. "What are you thinking about?"

She sighs. "I was just thinking how amazing tonight has been, how lucky I am that we found each other, and how well you use that monster dick in your pants."

I pull her close and grab the second blanket to wrap us as I spoon her tight. "I love you, Paisley." My heart races every time I tell her that.

"I love you, too."

"You are my everything. I've known it since the beginning."

"Thank you." She squeezes me tight. "For so long, it was always Arabella and me. I couldn't see a way it would ever be any different, and I was afraid to try. But the support I've received from you and your parents shows me what's possible. My heart is full, and I know we have a future more wonderful than I could ever imagine."

Dear Reader,

You are cordially invited to the wedding of Paisley Anne Brooks and Davis Carter Martin in Fiji. To accept the invitation, go to: https://dl.bookfunnel.com/dbq8qnk9p2

Unedited Preview: *Doctor of Women*

Nadine

"Excuse me!" says a woman with wild, crayon-red hair as we wait at the bus stop.

I hate mornings like this. The bus is late, so we've got two busloads of people waiting to be picked up. I've got to get downtown for a job interview, and it's not looking good for getting there on time.

"You're in the way," she says as I take my place in line to board the bus. Something jabs me in the kidney.

I shoot her a look. "I can't move any faster than the person in front of me."

"I need to get to work," she says through clenched teeth, still pushing forward.

"I imagine we all do. Relax, and we'll get there."

I look down at my phone. I think I connected to someone. *Oops.* I'll check it out later and apologize for pocket-dialing them. I end the call.

I board the bus, and an older gentleman smiles at me, stands, and offers me his seat. Red jumps past me into it and doesn't even thank him. I turn toward the man, and we share a look of mutual understanding. *She's a bitch.*

My phone rings, and I answer it in case it's my morning appointment. I'd hate to show up and they've canceled. "Nadine Fitzgerald speaking." The bus is loud, and I can't hear anything. "Hello?" I repeat.

"Can you tell me your home address?" the woman on the phone says.

"I'm not telling you my home address. You called me." I hang up. Damn scam artists.

My phone rings again. It's going to be one of those days. I don't recognize the number, so I ignore it. If it's important, they'll leave a message.

We're making our way down Seymour Street when the air fills with police sirens echoing off the tall buildings.

The older gentleman leans in. "Sounds like someone is in trouble."

I nod. "Glad it's not me."

The bus is overloaded, with standing room only, and every eye is looking out to the street, watching as at least six police cars appear and a helicopter circles ahead. The bus slows down to pull over, and my heart picks up. Today of all days? I don't have time for this if I want this job. What is going on?

The police rap on the door to the bus and ask the driver to step off. He holds up his hands and exits. Now everyone on the busy sidewalk has stopped to watch what is unfolding. Police in full tactical gear surround the bus and one boards.

"Nadine Fitzgerald?" he calls from the front of the aisle?

My stomach drops. I raise my hand. "That's me."

People jump away from me like I have a grenade.

"Come with me, please."

I sidestep through the crowd, confused at what I could have done to warrant so much police attention. I follow the rules. Okay, I speed occasionally, and I sometimes don't pay the parking meter, but what did I do? "How can I help you?" I ask when I reach the sidewalk.

"You called 9-1-1 and connected with the operator. Then there was a scuffle," the officer explains. "Is everything okay?"

"I didn't call 9-1-1."

He pursues his lips together and calls dispatch. "Dispatch, can you please replay the call?"

Suddenly, I hear, "...get to work." Then a grunt.

"I imagine we all do," my voice responds. "Relax, and we'll get there."

The recording disconnects, and he looks at me. "Was that you?"

"Yes, I was talking to a woman who was aggressive while we were in line to board the bus, but I didn't call 9-1-1." I look around. "Well, not on purpose."

"Why didn't you cooperate when the dispatcher called back?"

"I didn't know what was happening. I didn't recognize the number, and she was asking personal questions."

"She identified herself," he says.

"I couldn't hear her. The bus was loud."

I can hear the passengers still on the bus getting restless. "Come on, what's taking so long?" someone calls. "Arrest her and let the rest of us go to work."

Arrest me? "I'm very sorry."

"Can we go now?" the woman with red hair calls.

"Are you safe?" the officer asks, ignoring her.

"Yes, very. This was all a mistake."

He releases the bus driver and asks me to identify the other woman on the recording.

I roll my eyes. "Really? We can't chalk this up to a misdial?"

He shakes his head.

"It's the woman with bright red hair."

An officer returns to the bus and asks her to step off. She's a scrappy thing, yelling, kicking, and screaming as they finally have to remove her from the bus.

"You called the police on me? On me?" she screams.

I shake my head. "It was an accident."

The older gentleman joins us on the sidewalk and talks to the officer. Some of the police presence dissipates. Red Hair is being interviewed by the police and begging to be let go so she can get to work.

A news crew arrives and begins filming. The officer standing with me asks if the woman hit me or if there was some sort of altercation.

I shake my head. "The bus was very late, and there were more passengers than room. It can get like this during rush hour. It's nothing new."

"She started it," the woman yells, looking over at me. "She was walking slow, and I need to get to work. Now, I'm going to be even later than I was before this mess."

I'm so embarrassed.

"She hit me first!" Red adds after a moment.

I whip my head around. I didn't hit her. I shake my head at the officer in front of me. "I didn't touch her."

"Look at this bruise." She flexes her arm, and it's covered in bruises.

I think I'm going to vomit on the sidewalk. "I didn't touch her."

"Those bruises are older than twenty minutes," the officer replies.

"She hurt me."

The older gentleman steps back, and the officer he was talking to steps over and conferences with my officer.

This cannot get any worse. Well, it can actually get a lot worse. How the hell did a butt-dial develop into a major issue?

After a moment, one of the officers turns to me. "Ms. Fitzgerald, no more emergency phone calls unless there is an actual emergency."

I nod. "I promise."

They are arresting Red, and I step away. Today was Angry Monday for her. The older gentleman smiles at me.

"Thank you for sticking around." I'm grateful he was kind enough to put his morning on hold for me.

He shrugs. "I can walk the last few blocks." He hands me his card. "If you end up needing a witness for today's events, please call me. She seems like the type."

I nod, even as I pray that will never be an issue. "Thank you. That is extremely kind of you. And thank you for stepping off the bus to help me."

I slip the card in the side pocket of my purse and walk the rest of the way to my job interview. When I arrive, I'm an hour late. Human Resources meets with me, but they tell me they feel I should have called. It's hard to explain that when you're being interviewed by the police, you can't exactly phone someone to say you're running late.

When I'm finally done, I head back to my office. It's like walking into a tomb. I need a new job so badly. I want to work with people my age who like to go out after work and let their hair down and have fun. At the rate I'm going, I'm probably a virgin again.

No one even seems to have noticed I was late.

I check my emails and begin dealing with my day when my cell phone pings. I smile because it's my best friend, and she's wonderful to check on me.

Gina: How did the interview go?

I quickly search the internet and pull up the CTV broadcast of the bus incident to send to her.

Gina: What. The. Fuck? Is that you?

Me: Yes. I was an hour late for the interview, and I'm pretty sure they've hired someone else. No one here even cared that I was late today.

Gina: I need the entire story, but your dad owns the business. What are they going to say?

Me: I need an adult beverage. Are you up for drinks tonight?

Gina: Yes! There's a cute place not too far from Mercy Hospital. We can go pick up some doctors.

Me: I was thinking of Joe Fortes on Robson. Cute guys hang out there.

Gina: I'll need to go home and get my Louboutins and leather skirt.

Me: Or we could have fun in our work clothes and not care if they want to pick up a lawyer and an accountant.

Gina: Way to sell it.

Me: Shall we go at 5? They may have a happy hour?

Gina: I'll be there. I worked all weekend anyway.

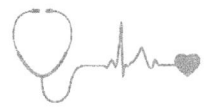

The second the clock strikes five, I turn my computer off and walk out the door. I didn't talk to anyone in the office today. And they didn't talk to one another. I hate it here.

I take a rideshare across downtown to get to Joe Fortes—a place to see and be seen. Whenever there's someone in town working on a movie, they end up here, along with the Who's Who of Vancouver crowd. It's fun for a moment.

An older woman smiles and puts a coaster in front of me when I arrive. "What would you like?"

I'm feeling adventurous. "Make me what you would make yourself."

Her brows go to her hairline. "Is there anything you don't like?"

"I'm not a fan of Jägermeister shots, but I'm looking to expand my palate."

She smiles. "Do you drink scotch?"

"I do."

She walks away and returns with a crystal lowball glass holding an almost clear round cube the size of a golf ball. She pours an amber liquid over it. "Try this."

I take a sip, and it burns as it slides down my throat. It tastes like butter with a pepper finish—very smooth. "Wow, that's good."

"Should be for two hundred dollars a glass."

My eyes pop wide. "That may be more than my budget allows."

"It's on me. You look like you've had quite the day."

"Thank you," I tell her, just as I hear a voice from behind me.

"Fitzy?"

Only one person on the planet calls me that, and my heart stops.

I can't face him today. My high school tormenter. The boy who pointed out to the entire class that I had boobs. The boy who told all his friends I was the last girl he'd ever want to be alone with. At least I wiped the floor with him with my grades, but he made me miserable, and I just can't today.

Michael Khalili sits down next to me and grins. "Hey! Long time no see."

"It's not been long enough," I reply.

He waves down to the bartender. "Nancy, can you get me—"

She places a pink carbonated drink in front of him with a cherry. "Your usual Shirley Temple."

I giggle. I can't help it. Nancy is going to get the biggest tip.

He rolls his eyes. "I'd prefer what she's having."

"Leave her alone. She's here to relax, and not with the likes of you."

I give Nancy a grateful look and mouth, "Thank you."

He picks up the Shirley Temple and drains it. "A Johnny Walker Blue on the rocks, please." He turns to me. "You get drunk here once, maybe throw up on the floor, and after that, you always get a Shirley Temple."

I smile. I want to celebrate how excited I am that someone dislikes Michael Khalili as much as I do. "Why are you here tonight?" I ask. "I mean, shouldn't you be off killing the environment with your dad's uber successful oil and gas company?"

"Put your claws away, Fitzy. I'm a doctor."

"They gave you a license to practice medicine, or did you buy that, too?" I'm not usually this sharp, and I wince at my delivery.

He raises an eyebrow. "Not only did they give me a license, but I'm one of Vancouver's best OB/GYNs. I specialize in high-risk pregnancy."

I shake my head. "I can't believe any woman would let you near her vagina, let alone allow you to help her bring new life into the world."

He laughs. "I have babies named after me."

"Why would anyone name their child Asshole?"

He bumps my shoulder with his. "I've missed this. We should have dinner sometime."

"No thanks. Those must be your friends over there. You should go measure your dicks to see whose is bigger."

He smiles at me. God, I hate him. "Nancy, can you put her drinks on my tab?"

"I already did."

He saunters away. Nancy comes over and pours me another glass. "It's on him."

I sigh. "And here I thought I was the only one who hated him."

She shrugs. "I like him just fine. He can take a lot of ribbing and always rolls with the punches. It's probably why he's such a good doctor."

Just as Nancy disappears again, Gina pulls up a stool next to me. She eyes my scotch. "I see we're going for the big stuff."

"See that guy over there?" I point to Michael, who is surrounded by what appear to be GQ male models.

"Which one? They're all hot."

"The one with the dark hair and five o'clock shadow,

dressed in designer clothes."

"He's sizzling and can't take his eyes off of you."

"He made my life miserable throughout middle school and high school. But he's buying, so would you like a two-hundred-dollar glass of scotch?"

"Bring it on."

"Nancy?" I call. "Can we put one more on his tab?"

She smiles. "Of course."

When it arrives, Gina takes a sip. "Damn, that is smooth like butter." She turns and holds up the glass, and he grins.

Narcissistic asshole.

"Was he really that bad?" she asks.

"No. He was worse."

To Pre-Order on Amazon:
https://www.amazon.com/dp/B0B9PC6B3Q